Cover Me

UNDER FIRE

CATHERINE MANN

sourcebooks
casablanca

Published by Sourcebooks Casablanca, an imprint of Sourcebooks, Inc.
P.O. Box 4410, Naperville, Illinois 60567-4410
(630) 961-3900
FAX: (630) 961-2168
www.sourcebooks.com

Printed and bound in Canada.
WC 10 9 8 7 6 5 4 3 2 1

To Rob, a man of honor, the man who holds my heart.

The true test of a man's character is what he does when no one is watching.

—*John Wooden*

Chapter 1

"KILL ONE. SCREW ONE. MARRY ONE."

Major Liam McCabe almost choked on a gulp of the Atlantic as his pararescue teammate's words floated across the waves. Today's two-mile swim was pushing toward an hour long. A light rain pocked the surface faster by the second. Still, there was no reason to think one of his guys had gone batty.

Liam sliced an arm through the choppy ocean, looking to the side. "Wanna run that by me again, Cuervo?"

Jose "Cuervo" James swam next to him, phrases coming in bursts as his face cleared the water. "It's a word game. Kill one. Screw one. Marry one. Somebody names three women…" *Swim. Breathe.* "And you have to pick." *Swim. Breathe.* "One to marry. One to kill. One to—"

"Right," Liam interrupted. "Got it."

He would have sighed and shaken his head except for the whole drowning thing. At moments such as these, he felt like a stodgy old guy more than ever.

"So, Major?" Cuervo stroked along and over the rippling waves. Storm clouds brewed overhead. "Are you in?"

On monotonous swims or runs, they'd shot the breeze plenty of times to take their minds off screaming muscles. The distraction was particularly welcome during intense physical training.

This word game, however, was a first.

A quick glance reassured him the other six team members were keeping pace with him and Cuervo. Each held strong, powering toward the beach still a quarter of a mile away.

Feet pumping his fins, Liam shifted his attention back to the "game." His body burned from the effort, but he had plenty of steam left inside to finish up. He was their team leader. Their commanding officer. He would not fall behind.

"How about I just listen first?" Water flowed over his body, briny, chilly. Familiar. "Let one of the others start off."

"Sure, old man," huffed Cuervo, spewing a mouthful to the side. "If you need to save your breath to keep pace. Okay, Fang, you're up."

Fang, the youngest of the group and the one most eager to fit in, arced his arms faster to pull up alongside. "Bring it on."

"Topic for first three. Brad Pitt's women," Cuervo barked. "Gwyneth Paltrow. Jennifer Aniston. Angelina Jolie."

"Jennifer's hot." Fang spewed water with his speedy answer. "I would do her in a heartbeat."

Liam found an answer falling from his mouth after all. "I'd marry Angie."

"Too easy." Cuervo snorted. "You've been married three times, Major, so that's not saying much for Angie."

Which just left... poor Gwyneth.

But then he'd always had a thing for brunettes. And

redheads. And blondes. Hell, he loved women. But he really loved brunettes. One brunette in particular, the one he *hadn't* married or slept with or even made it past first base with, for God's sake.

Focus on the swim. The team.

The damn game. "Cuervo, are we playing this or not?"

"Next trio up… topic is singers," Cuervo announced. "Britney Spears. Christina Aguilera. And Kesha."

Huh? "Who the hell is Kesha?"

"Are you sure you're not too old for this job?"

"Still young enough to outswim you, baby boy." Liam surged ahead of Cuervo. Swims were a lot easier on his abused knees than parachute landings or runs. But a pararescueman needed to be ready for anything, anywhere. Any weather.

Thunder rolled like a bowling ball gaining speed, and his teammates were the pins.

All games aside, this little dip in the rain was about more than a simple training exercise. More than team building. He needed his pararescuemen in top form for a mission they usually didn't handle—the external security for an upcoming international summit being held at NASA. Not normal business for pararescuemen, but well within their skill set to act as a quick-reaction force if anything went down. After all, isn't that what a rescue was? A quick reaction to something going down? Trained and prepared to fight back enemy-combatant forces if necessary to protect their rescue target.

This made for a tough last assignment. His final *hoo-uh*, *ooh-rah* before he said good-bye to military life. Since he was eleven years old watching vintage war movies on a VCR with his cancer-stricken mama, all he'd wanted was to be that man who took the hill and won the woman. His mother had lost her battle. But Liam had been determined to carry on the fight by putting on that uniform.

Damned if he would go out with a whimper.

Fang slapped the water. "Can we get back to the fuck-me game?"

"Hey," Wade Rocha's voice rumbled as deeply as the thunder, "no need to make this crude."

"Oh, excuse me," Fang gasped. "Now that you're married, you're all Sergeant Sensitivity." *Gasp. Stroke.* "I guess we'll call this… kill one, marry one…" *Gasp. Stroke.* "Make sweet, flowery love to one."

Rocha muttered, "You're just jealous, smart-ass."

Fang chuckled and spluttered. "Not hardly. Monogamy until I'm in the grave?" He shuddered. "No thanks. Not into that."

But Liam was.

He'd tried his ass off to make the happily-ever-after thing work. Tried three times, in fact. Problem was, he had a defective cog when it came to choosing a woman to spend his life with. Didn't help that he'd always put the mission first, something that hadn't sat well with any of his wives. A small fortune spent on marital counseling hadn't been able to fix the relationships or him.

And still, he couldn't get that one woman—that one brunette—out of his mind, no matter how many times he chanted, *"Old patterns, not real, get over her."*

He was a romantic sap who fell in love too easily. He kept looking for that classic silver-screen ending. Guy gets girl. Roll credits.

If only he could have persuaded Rachel Flores to go

out with him once they'd returned to the States. They'd worked together rescuing earthquake victims in the Bahamas six months ago. Had become good friends, or so he'd thought. After they got back, she never returned his calls.

Sure, if they had dated, the relationship would have self-destructed like all the rest. Then he could have walked away free and clear, no regrets, no lengthy explicit dreams that woke him up hard and unsatisfied. Now he was stuck with images of Rachel rattling around in his noggin until he wouldn't even notice another woman if she were waiting on the beach ahead wearing nothing but body glitter and a do-me smile.

Except there wasn't anyone on the beach. Just a stretch of sand and trees and a five-mile hike waiting to set his knees on fire after he hit the shore.

His life had been about training and service since he'd joined the army at eighteen. Became a ranger. Then got his degree while serving, became an officer, and swapped to the air force and pararescue missions.

Training. Honing. Brotherhood.

He'd sacrificed three marriages and any social life for this and would have kept right on doing so. Except now his thirty-eight-year-old body was becoming a liability to those around him.

One week. He had one week and a big-ass demonstration left. Until then he would do his damnedest to keep his team focused and invincible. He wasn't going to spend another second fantasizing about a particular sexy spitfire brunette with as much grit as his elite force team.

Liam narrowed his eyes against the sting of salt and

the pounding rain pushing through the surface like bullets. "I've got a new game, gentlemen. It's called Pick Your Poison." *Stroke. Breathe.* "If you've gotta die in the water..." *Stroke. Breathe.* "Would you choose a water moccasin? An alligator? Or a shark?"

⸺⁓⸺

Rachel Flores learned to break into cars when her mom rescued animals from locked automobiles. But she'd never expected to use that skill to lock herself and her dog *inside* a vehicle.

Checking over her shoulder, Rachel searched for military cops or a suspicious passerby around the tan concrete buildings on Patrick Air Force Base. The dozen or so camo-wearing personnel all seemed preoccupied with getting out of the Florida storm and into their cars at the end of the workday. Everyone was in too much of a hurry to spare a glance at her. Or maybe she was just that good at pretending she and her dog belonged here. Even though they totally didn't.

Death threats offered up a hefty motivator for her to circumvent a few rules.

Raindrops slid down her face, her hair and clothes slicked to her skin. She'd wasted valuable minutes trying to pick the lock, but the car was darn near pickproof. Which was actually a waste of technology, when combined with a vulnerable ragtop.

One way or another, she would get inside Liam McCabe's vehicle.

How ironic that after six months of fighting the damn-near-crippling urge to return his calls, now she was literally throwing herself in his path. Was that fair to him? No, but God, she was scared to death and Liam was a rock. If it were only her life at risk, she could have fought her own battles. But with other lives at stake, and given the explosive mess she'd landed in… she had nowhere else to turn.

Stifling her conscience and vowing to repay him for the damage, she shielded her hands from view with her body as she slid a penknife along the Jeep's canvas roof. Not a long slice. Just enough to slip her fingers inside and reach… for…

The lock popped. She secured her hold on her Labrador retriever's leash and pulled open the door. If all went according to schedule, Liam would finish work within a half hour, according to Wade Rocha's wife, when Rachel had risked calling to ask.

At least she'd been able to get on base easily, thanks to her work supplying therapy dogs to PTSD patients at military hospitals throughout Southern Florida. She'd wanted to drive straight to Liam's house off base and wait for him there. But once she'd realized she was being followed, her plans had changed. Going on base got rid of the car trailing her.

Temporarily.

She could have kept strolling around outside, nonchalantly waiting, except for the rain. She'd already ditched her SUV in another lot on base before walking with Disco over here. She didn't want to leave her vehicle too near Liam's workplace. No need to make it easy for people to figure out who she'd gone to for help.

She shifted the front seat forward and gestured inside. "Ride, Disco. Let's ride."

Her dog sprung forward like a streak of ebony

lightning into the surprisingly clean car. She'd expected to rake aside bachelor chaos. Just two neatly lined-up green canvas bags rested in back alongside her Lab. Still, a tight fit. God, hiding in here would be tougher than she'd expected. Rain drizzled down her neck.

Or was that icy perspiration?

She followed Disco inside. First order of business, cracking open a window for air. Hopefully Liam wouldn't notice, if she opened the passenger side just a little.

Next she pulled out a water bottle and small bowl from her backpack and filled it for Disco. She set it on the floor, the side closest to the open window. Once her dog started lapping away, she hunched back into the seat at an angle where she could monitor the temperature gauge on the rearview mirror, the number dropping, thanks to the rain and the setting sun.

With luck, the dark would offer a shield, along with her brown clothes and her dog's black coat, if they held still. Fear nearly immobilized her anyway as she thought of the silver sedan that had been following her for over an hour. The threatening phone calls yesterday. The mind-blowing secret she'd uncovered that made even the secured fortress of a military base unsafe for her.

She rested her cheek against her wet dog's neck. God, this was reckless and insane, but she was out of options. Liam was her last choice, last chance. Her last hope.

He was also the one man she'd been determined to avoid. The only man to truly tempt her since her soldier fiancé died during a deployment ten years ago.

Hell yes, she'd ignored Liam's voice mail messages once they'd returned from the Bahamas earthquake rescue six months ago. Her feelings for him scared her clear down to her toenails. Not just lust—although there was plenty of that oozing from her pores around him. But if it had been only sexual attraction, she could have resisted or just slept with him and moved on.

Liam made her want… more.

And if she felt herself weakening around Liam now? All she had to do was look at those three frilly garters dangling from his rearview mirror. Three reminders that the man had been married and divorced three frickin' times. The man might be a rock of support for her crisis, but when it came to relationships…?

He was a hot-as-hell train wreck.

———

Liam settled in behind the wheel of his Jeep, every muscle screaming for a soak in his hot tub. At least he'd made it through the swim and run, staying in front, leading the pack. He *would* lead his men to the end, but damn, his body paid the price.

He pitched his time-worn duffel onto the passenger seat and cranked the engine. His camos clung to his body from rain and perspiration even as the sun set. Heat still steamed along the asphalt. His shower in the locker room had been rushed, a quick rinse off. He preferred to haul his ass home and wash at his leisure there, the sooner the better if he expected to rustle up some supper before ten.

He checked his rearview mirror—complete with three lacy garters dangling a reminder of past mistakes—and waited for a dude on a motorcycle to pass. He backed out, then forward, steering onto the main roadway and into the flow of traffic. Cars spewed through the base front gate and into the civilian world as the workday ended. Rain hammered his windshield, but he slid the window open anyhow and just rolled up his sleeves. His musty clothes carried a special kind of funk. Right now, he needed that hot tub, a longneck, and solitude to nurse his aching body.

Alone.

Yeah, that one word summed up his social life these days, but better that than wrecking another woman's life. Elbow hanging out the window, he cleared the front gate. Palm trees lined the road, ocean just beyond. Salty wind spiraled through, whipping around his ripe musty scent mixed with something else.

His nose twitched. He breathed deeper and smelled…

A wet dog?

What the hell?

His ears tuned in tighter and he picked up the whisper of shallow breathing. Human sounding. Not his own.

His brain shouted an alert.

He had an extra passenger.

Instincts ramped into overdrive. He was trained in rescue, medical aid…

And *combat*.

He tucked one hand into his duffel, closing around the cool comfort of his Desert Eagle semiautomatic handgun as he worked to smoothly swerve the Jeep around traffic, over into the far lane. Close to the shoulder, without giving away his intent. Just three seconds. He only needed three… two… one.

Liam whipped the Jeep off the road and turned around in a flash. Gun level, he pointed it directly at—

What the fuck?

Rachel Flores?

The woman he'd half fallen in love with six months ago, *the* bombshell brunette he still thought about nearly every day, was huddled in the back of the Jeep with one arm around her black Lab. Her brown eyes stared back at him, dark as undiluted coffee and just as potent. Except they held terror, which was so unlike the fearless firecracker he'd met who'd climbed on piles of shifting rubble with her search and rescue canine. She was so tenacious in her work he'd often lost perspective on how short—hell, how *delicate*—she really was. Every cell in his body screamed to haul her over the seat and into his arms, to soak in the feel of her. The draw to her now was every bit as much of a slam in the gut as it had been when he first saw her.

Not that she'd felt the same, which still stung more than it should for someone he'd known for all of three weeks, six months ago. So why was she here? Hiding? Her damp hair was a tangled mess, trailing down her shoulders and onto her dog until they almost seemed connected. Disco growled low in his throat.

Liam pulled the handgun back slowly, pointing it toward the canvas roof. And still the fear didn't leave her eyes.

"Rachel?" He tucked his Desert Eagle semiautomatic back into his gear. "Holy crap, woman. I could have killed you."

"But you didn't." She exhaled slowly before leaning to whisper something in her dog's ear. Disco quieted, even if his muscles flexed with tension under his sleek coat.

Liam shoved the bag to the floor and extended a hand

to her. "Come up front and tell me why the hell you're holed up inside my Jeep."

"I would rather stay back here while you drive."

This was getting weirder by the second. An SUV sped past, sluicing a wall of water against the side of his Jeep. She flinched at the sound and away from his hand. Again, so unlike the charge-ahead Rachel he'd known before.

Something was wrong. Seriously wrong. The fear in her eyes intensified, reaching out to him and pushing back his own frustrations over being ignored, which was worse than being dumped.

"Are you in trouble with the law?" Not that he could fathom her doing anything illegal. His mind sifted through other possibilities as he resisted the impulse to smooth back her hair, comfort her somehow. "Is there a guy harassing you? An ex-boyfriend? A stalker?"

Now that sent his protective instincts pumping into an overdrive that rivaled anything her growling dog had going on. His hand gravitated toward his duffel.

She shook her head. "I'll explain everything while you drive. Please. Let's get back on the road and to your house."

A VW whined past, honking. Rachel huddled lower, her face paling under her honey tan complexion. He'd seen that look before on soldiers in the field—shell shock. She was right about needing to get to his house. He stood a better chance at being able to take care of her there.

"Fine, then. I'll drive and you can talk." He accelerated, wedging back into beach traffic. "How about you fill me in on what's going on here? You've gotta know you're worrying the hell out of me."

Windshield wipers slapped away sheeting rain again

and again until he wondered if she was going to stay silent the whole way back. He glanced up into the rearview mirror. Her eyes met his, and damned if the air didn't crackle as if lightning had zapped his Jeep. The tug he felt to this woman hadn't dimmed one bit.

Too bad her freaked-out vibes and those three wedding garters framing the rearview mirror in satin and lace had to wreck the mood. "Rachel?"

She blinked fast, her hand curving over her dog's head repeatedly. "I'm sorry about your roof. I'll pay for the repair."

"Repair?" Just that fast he heard the whistling air and felt a hint of rain coming from the passenger side. He looked right fast and... "Shit! You cut a hole in my car."

He loved his car. Hell, the Jeep had hung on longer than any of his marriages.

"A small slice," she rushed to say. "Just big enough to reach in and unlock the door."

He dialed back his shock—and yeah, some pissed-off emotions in there too—and let reason take charge. She had to have been desperate to accomplish all of that, undetected on base. Security had some explaining to do. "Why didn't you wait at my house or in the lobby at my squadron?"

"Don't you think I would have preferred that to cutting up your car and wedging myself back here?" Her voice rose with building hysteria. "Believe me, this is— you are—absolutely my last resort."

Now wasn't that a bite in the ego? "Glad to know you exhausted all your more palatable options first."

"That didn't come out how I meant." She sagged back, her damp clothes clinging to her gentle curves.

"I'm really hanging on by a thread here, Liam. Yes, I'm being threatened, but not by a boyfriend or stalker. It's complicated and scary as hell."

Her husky voice trembled. Whatever the cause, there was no denying the woman was frightened to death, the way his mom had been scared when the doctors told her she wasn't going to beat the cancer. The fight was over. His dad may have been around, but he hadn't been much on comfort. So she'd been pretty much alone, with just an eleven-year-old son trying to figure out how to make her stop crying.

"Why didn't you just call me? Rachel, you've got to know I would have been there for you in a heartbeat." Because yeah, he could kick ass in the field, play the whole master-of-his-universe role, but when it came to women, *this* woman? He had zip in the way of defenses. "Breaking into my car wasn't exactly safe."

"I'm desperate."

Or unstable? Possible. But it seemed unlikely. While they'd worked the earthquake rescue, he could have sworn she had nerves of steel. Which only lent all the more credence to her fear now. He nailed the gas until his Jeep ate up the miles.

His house came into view, a one-story green stucco with a couple of squat sago palms and a small yard he paid the neighbor kid to mow, since he was on the road most of the time. Who would Rachel have reached out to if he'd moved?

A week from now, he would have been past the multinational summit, and his team would have completed their high-profile security assignment. After that, he would be shuffled aside to finish out his remaining months of active duty in a job where they vowed his experience was more valuable than brawn—which meant his body was shit.

But he *was* here, and she needed him. He could do the comfort gig, the way he'd done for his mom. He turned into his driveway, thumbing the garage-door remote on his visor. Once inside, he shut off the Jeep, the door rolling closed behind him. Sealing them together in his house. Alone.

For the first time in six months, he had Rachel with him in the flesh, and when he looked at her, the last thing he thought about was his mother.

Chapter 2

FINALLY, SHE WAS SAFE. FOR NOW. ALONE WITH LIAM at his house.

Thank God, he wasn't going to kick her out. Relief rocked through her so hard, she wasn't sure her legs would hold her.

Rachel scooped up her backpack from the floor and wished her thoughts were as easy to gather. Liam lifted the seat and extended his hand for her. It would have been silly to refuse. She closed her fingers around his. The warm clasp, the strength, seeped up her arm with a comfort she felt greedy in accepting. She'd been right to come here. Selfish. But right.

As she hopped from the car, he watched her with a hint of suspicion and something else, something that drew her to him now just as it had before. She landed toe-to-toe with him. So close she could easily lean into his chest as he towered over her, a full twelve inches taller and ripped with whipcord strength.

His sandy blond hair was damp. The water darkened his thick short hair to more of a light brown. His tanned skin smelled of sun and soap. His rawboned features were angular and good looking in a rugged way, more than mere poster-boy handsome. Lines fanned from the corners of sea green eyes, lines that spoke of wisdom, experience, and a sense of humor. His camouflage uniform promised training to back up all that seasoned strength.

He was a man who'd lived a hard life and survived. While he was lean, his body wasn't some gangly twenty-five-year-old's that couldn't be trusted not to bust out an impulsive move. His muscled power was honed, thoughtful, even immovable.

Liam McCabe was a rare kind of man. He was a man to count on. And exactly the man she needed right now.

"Thank you." And she didn't just mean for helping her out of the car.

"I'm here to serve."

He half grinned, stroking back her hair in a way that was far more comforting than if he'd hugged her, patted her back, and mumbled soothing nonsense that wouldn't fix a thing. She could see the restraint in his eyes, the unanswered questions, but he was giving her what *she* needed most now. The space to hold herself together.

God, he was so appealing in a way that went beyond just the camo uniform.

How strange was it to be so attracted to him at a time she was scared to death. Must be adrenaline, like when they'd been in the Bahamas and she'd been so very, very tempted to jump into bed with him, even though they'd only kissed—a wowsa, knock-your-socks-off lip-lock that stayed with her even when they weren't touching at all.

At times like this, it was tough to remember he was a guy who effortlessly charmed women. He even married them just as easily.

He stroked her hair behind her ear a final time, calluses snagging her skin as he cupped the back of her neck. "Are you ready to go inside and talk?"

"Yes, please." She looked over her shoulder at her

dog. The black Lab tipped his head to the side, confusion stamped in his big chocolate eyes.

She understood the feeling well.

"Come, Disco." She snapped her fingers. Her Lab bounded effortlessly out to join her in the most organized garage she'd ever seen.

Tools dangled on a Peg-Board in perfect lines over a workbench, only a light hint of oil clinging to the air. Double-timing to keep up with Liam's long-legged stride, she charged toward the door leading into the house, walking under a mountain bike and a beach cruiser hanging upside down from hooks in the ceiling. She waited by a pristine riding lawn mower as Liam disarmed a security system and unlocked the dead bolt.

"Your garage is tidier than my living room." She hitched her knapsack over one shoulder, thinking of her rustic home full of well-worn leather furniture and dog toys.

"It's a temporary rental, since this is a short-term assignment. I'm rarely home anyway," he shot over his shoulder before pushing inside. "Not much time to mess anything up before I head off to the next base."

With that kind of moving history, she would have expected stacks of unpacked boxes rather than the topnotch organization. For all his intensity on the job, Liam had a laid-back humor that had made her wonder about what he was like outside of the work world. Still, she needed that analytical perfection now to untangle the mess she'd somehow landed in the middle of.

She walked through the laundry room that had only one basket of clothes on the dryer—presumably already washed, given the superneat state of everything else—and entered the eat-in kitchen. Disco's nails clicked against the terra-cotta tile floors. She took her time studying the eating area, curious about the man and soaking up clues for how best to share what she knew with him. To win him over, when so many others didn't believe her.

And yeah, she knew she was stalling, terrified he wouldn't believe her either. Having the cops disregard her had been frustrating. Having Liam look at her as if she were a loon? Just the possibility shredded her already-ragged nerves, especially with the weight of his curious gaze following her every step. She needed to sound credible, logical.

Sane.

While spit-shine clean, the place still shouted *bachelor*. Basic white walls, and tile floors with no real rugs to speak of, just a plain brown doormat for wiping off feet on the way in. An archway separated the kitchen from the living area with a black leather couch and a huge recliner.

And a *foosball* table?

Now that fit her more lighthearted image of him. Only Liam McCabe could have lightened her spirits in the middle of the hellish earthquake rubble.

What would it have been like if she'd scrounged up the gumption to call or see him during the past six months, before this crisis? She'd been only a short drive away since she'd moved from Virginia to Southern Florida, just far enough outside of Miami to avoid their pit bull banning laws. So close to him, without making contact. Like holding her hand just shy of the flame. Her skin heating, even blistering, but never daring to plunge right in and accept the fire.

Pretty much the story of her adult social life.

Her nerves kicked up a storm again to match the one pounding away outside. Pivoting toward him, she found Liam leaning against the laminate counter, his concerned eyes stroking over her frazzled nerves.

"Nice kitchen." She trailed her hand along the counter beside a surprising lineup of top-of-the-line cooking aids—a food processor, blender, and coffee grinder. "Do you actually use these as often as the foosball table?"

"My mom always said a man should know how to feed himself, not to expect a woman will always do the cooking. Although restocking a kitchen after every divorce is pricey. Chicks always get the kitchen stuff in the breakup. Guys get the foosball table. Not fair, but hey, that's life." His gemstone eyes went from lighthearted to intense in a flash. "Are we done with the small talk now? Because honestly, I'm worried about you."

And he had good reason.

"Can we sit down? It's... complicated." Understatement of the year.

He gestured to the simple oak table and pulled out a ladder-back chair for her.

Suddenly exhaustion rolled over her, heavier even than when she'd worked a round-the-clock SAR mission. She dropped into the seat, letting her backpack fall to the floor. Her dog stretched out on the scarred tile beside her.

Pulling up a chair, Liam rested a foot on his other knee, so very close to her without touching. More of that restraint showed on his face while he just waited for her to find the right words, figure out exactly where to start.

"Things have changed for me since the earthquake in

the Bahamas. The three weeks there really burned me out." Her emotions had been tougher to handle around Liam, another reason she'd been scared to contact him until life forced her hand. "I needed a new direction and found it with this group up in the D.C. area. They train therapy dogs for PTSD patients. About three months ago, I accepted the challenge to assist in starting a Southern Florida branch."

"Three months ago? And you finally decided to stop by and see me." He clapped a hand to his chest. "I'm touched."

A blush burned her face and down her neck. "I'm sorry."

And she meant it. She wished things could be different between them, but she couldn't change her past and how it had marked her.

He nodded tightly. As if she really had hurt him? But he was the man who fell in and out of love as often as he changed military bases.

"Rachel? Your new job? Your reason for being here?"

"Oh, right." She toyed with a cardboard salt shaker, fidgeting, edgy. She was running on fumes. "The new branch has been busy, but productive. We train and work with both emotional support animals and psychiatric service dogs."

"What's the difference?" he interrupted.

"Huh?" His question, his genuine interest, caught her off guard. "An ESA—emotional support animal—provides companionship, the presence offering a calming effect. But a PSD—psychiatric service dog—performs acts. It's about more than emotional support. A service dog may remind a person to take medications.

Retrieve a medication bag. Nudge the handler during a fear-paralysis stage. Provide deep pressure therapy during a panic attack."

She rolled the salt shaker between her palms. "But that's beside the point."

"And your point is?"

Her gut clenched. The *point* wiped away the possibility of flirting or attraction or what ifs. "I got a call from a caretaker that one of the veterans I'd been working with was having a breakdown that freaked out even the dog. So I went, helped calm the dog, and before I knew it, the combat vet, Brandon…" Her hands rolled the shaker faster and faster. "He told me things. Scary stuff about someone in his chain of command selling secrets from a satellite defense program. Brandon said no one would listen to him because of his PTSD."

Liam's foot slid from his knee, both boots on the floor. "And you believe him? This Brandon—?"

"Brandon Harris."

"You trust this Brandon Harris dude?" Skepticism and concern warred in his eyes. "In spite of the trauma he must have experienced recently?"

"I do." She nodded, the shock, the scope of it all, stinging through her veins again. "I encouraged him to speak with the base authorities, and they totally blew him off just as he'd predicted. They think he's whacked out and delusional even though he's actually a military cop himself."

His eyebrows rose at that. "Really?"

"It didn't seem to make them any more likely to listen to him. If anything, I think Brandon feared losing face in front of them."

Liam grabbed her wrist and plucked the salt shaker from her hands. He set it beside the pepper while still holding on to her. "What makes you think the security police are wrong? Brandon could be seriously unbalanced. It can happen all too easily after the kind of things soldiers face."

Clearly, Liam had shifted into protector mode, but at least he was questioning rather than simply dismissing her outright. Hope pawed around inside her, then curled up, solid, real—and scary, as she actually embraced the idea that someone might believe her.

And the warmth of his hand holding hers felt so good after the bone-deep chill of fear that had gripped her for the past two weeks. "At first it was just an instinct thing. So I offered to go with him to speak with someone higher up the chain, out in the civilian world, like the FBI or CIA."

"What happened then?" His thumb stroked her wrist, right over her racing pulse.

"A representative from the local branch of both offices took notes and said their people would look into it. We thought maybe things would get moving. They hadn't called Brandon unbalanced. They seemed to take him seriously. We waited to hear more… and nothing."

"Maybe they're investigating still."

"I would like to think so. Except then I got a threatening phone call that came from a 'caller unknown' number telling me to back off and keep my mouth shut or there would be consequences."

His thumb stopped moving, his eyes narrowing.

Panic bubbled low again as she remembered the disguised voice, the death threats. She gripped Liam's hand. "I reported it to everyone we'd spoken to. Base security said there was nothing they could do, since I'm a civilian. Local police said they didn't have enough to investigate, even if they did have enough manpower, which they don't, thanks to chasing drug lords and human traffickers twenty-four/seven. I went to the CIA again. They were polite, brief, and obviously completely unconcerned. I figured they wouldn't believe me if I told them I thought I heard clicking sounds on the phone line, like it was being bugged." She winced. "Are you ready to have me committed yet?"

"I'm still listening, aren't I?" He squeezed her hand.

She sucked in a bracing breath, the scent of ammonia cleaner hanging in the air. "Two days ago, someone tried to poison my dog."

"You think the CIA is after your dog?" he asked in a voice too calm, as if he thought she'd gone over the edge.

So much for help and comfort.

"No, I don't think the CIA went after Disco, but someone did. Someone who didn't like the questions Brandon and I stirred up." She tugged her hand free. "You *do* think I've gone bonkers."

He spread his hands wide. "Come on, Rachel. You have to admit, all of this sounds improbable."

"I know." God, did she ever know. And she hadn't realized until now how very solitary her life had become, completely focused on work, until she'd realized how few people she could turn to for help. She leaned in urgently, grabbing *his* hand this time. "Still, Liam, I heard what I heard on the phone. Then my dog was suddenly ill in a way that could only be poison. Even the vet said so. The timing couldn't be coincidental."

"Have you considered the man who told you that wild conspiracy story could have had a psychotic break? He was unstable to begin with. Could he could be the one threatening you?"

"Yes, I thought of that initially." Although it hurt her heart to the core to think of his pain-filled eyes, to think he might actually try to harm her. "But one of the threatening calls came while I was with Brandon, so unless he's got a partner, it isn't him. A partner for him seems unlikely, since he's cut himself off from everyone except me and his dog."

"Okay, then." While his eyes didn't declare outright belief, he wasn't walking away. "Does he know you're here?"

"No. I didn't tell anyone. I just dropped off my other dogs at the doggy day care and paid for a week before I left to drive up here. Why do you ask?"

"Do you think he would talk to me?"

"At this point, I can't answer that. He was really freaked out by that phone call I got when we were together working with his dog." She gnawed her lip before telling him the rest, risking what little faith he still seemed to have in her rationality. "I actually was going to come to your house, but halfway here, I realized someone was tailing me, someone in a silver sedan."

"Holy crap, Rachel!" He sat up straight in his seat, muscles bunching with tension under his uniform, long legs tensed for action. "You should have called the cops again."

"That hasn't gone so well for me lately, in case you haven't noticed." Her joke fell flat. But then, she wasn't feeling all that lighthearted. "Regardless, I was scared to lead the person straight to your house, so I went to the base instead, which worked, since the silver sedan peeled away once I got to the front gate. Hopefully, they'll think I just went to the military authorities again."

"Why hide in my car? Why not just wait for me to come out of work?"

The way he said it made her plan seem ridiculous now. Should she have just waited for him in the lobby at work? But she hadn't wanted to announce to the world she was with him. She'd been thinking of his safety.

Sort of.

Yet just being here, she'd put him at risk. "I thought I was protecting you. Maybe it wasn't the smartest plan." She thrust her fingers through her still-damp hair and wanted to just tug, she was so frustrated. "But I'm not some freakin' agent or cop or trained military professional. I'm a dog trainer. Give me someone to find or a canine to teach, and I'm good. But something like this mess? I'm in way over my head…"

The enormity of what had happened to her life kinked the tension so tight inside her, she shot to her feet, ready to bolt but feeling like a cornered rabbit with nowhere to go. Liam stood, clasping her shoulders and pulling her against him so fast she didn't have time to tense up. She tucked her head under his chin and simply deflated against him, her hands fisting in his camo jacket. His arms banded around her, as muscled and hard as she remembered from their one kiss. Not that he made a move on her now.

He didn't offer bullshit platitudes either or pat her back. He just held her while she breathed in the musky scent of him and absorbed some of his strength. She'd come to the right place after all. To Liam. A clock shaped like Texas hanging on the wall tick-tick-ticked away the seconds in time with Liam's heartbeat against her ear. One breath at a time, she willed down the panic to a manageable level. She tuned in to the world beyond her fears, taking in details like the feel of Liam's fingers in her hair as he cupped her head.

"Christ, Rachel," his voice rumbled hoarsely through his chest, "I'm so damn glad you're okay."

She squeezed her eyes shut as if to somehow hold on to the sound of him longer. She was a strong woman, damn it. She'd only lost control twice in her life: when her mother passed away and when Caden...

She froze in Liam's arms. Her hands fell from his chest.

And then he was gone. His arms, his warmth, his voice.

Eyes snapping open, she found him a few steps away, holding on to the counter, his back to her, broad shoulders moving with each ragged breath.

"Liam?" she said softly. Why had he pulled away? Had he felt her withdrawal? Were they already that in tune with each other? And God help her if they were.

He half glanced back at her. "I think we need to check in on your friend Brandon. We'll take him to base and we'll talk with some... uh, people I know there."

People? Realization trickled ice down her spine.

"You want to take Brandon to a shrink, don't you?" She didn't expect an answer and didn't get one. "You still think he's imagining everything? Or that he's the one harassing me, even if he was there when one of the calls came?"

He turned around, his shoulders braced, his jaw

determined. He might as well have put on a suit of armor, he was so visibly prepped for battle. For her. "We'll bring in officials along with a health-care professional. My presence will lend credence to your concerns. My number-one priority is making sure you're safe."

Just as she'd known he would, Liam was committed to helping her. She could only hope that help led to answers and not a straitjacket. "You're doing more than I could have asked for. I appreciate it."

"We'll go back to base first thing in the morning."

In the morning? "Why not leave now?"

"You're tired and wet. And while I know you're a kick-ass woman capable of taking care of herself, you're a drowned mess." He held up a hand; his half grin returned but didn't reach his eyes. "Sexy and gorgeous, of course. But a mess. Get a shower, something to eat, a good night's sleep, and you'll appear more rational."

What he said made sense. Except she wanted his arms back, even though that was selfish when she knew it couldn't lead anywhere. She was lucky he even spoke to her after the way she'd ignored his calls. "Where do I go to make the transformation into a regular-looking citizen?"

"Bathroom is first door on the right. I'll dig through my stuff and find some shorts with a drawstring and a T-shirt that's shrunk."

To keep from reaching for him again, she scooped up her backpack, yanking the zipper open with shaky hands. "No need to share your clothes. Aside from the fact they would be too big, I brought a spare outfit and some toiletries." She fished inside, pitched her wallet and a candy bar on the table before she held up a thin, folded stack of clothes. "I wanted to be prepared for anything."

She backed down the hall, her mind full of how panicked she'd been when she tossed things into her backpack willy-nilly. How scared she'd been. How much calmer she felt with Liam's arms around her.

"Then get to it." He pushed to his feet in a tall lanky glide. "I'll scrounge up something for us to eat."

She hesitated half in, half out of the bathroom doorway. "Liam?"

He looked up, his glance slamming into hers. "Yeah, Rachel?"

There were so many things she wanted to say to him.

About how she'd missed him.

About why she'd never called in six months.

About how that silence actually said more about how much he'd affected her than if she'd called him up to shoot the breeze. But she wouldn't.

She settled for "Thanks for believing me."

—∿—

Liam wanted Rachel to be right.

And damn, but that made *him* bat-shit crazy. He shouldn't be standing here in front of the stove, throwing together stir-fry for supper, actually hoping she was being chased by a military traitor. The possibility that anyone he served with could actually be involved in something as unthinkable as betraying their country churned acid in his gut.

Olive oil popped in the pan and splattered the front of his uniform. Draping a black apron over his neck, he wrapped the ties around and yanked the strings into a knot in front. He chopped the last of the red pepper and pitched it into the wok with onions, carrots, and broccoli. The routine of cooking helped him channel his thoughts. Here, he could do something. He could take care of Rachel, even if it was just by making sure she ate. The way he'd cooked a kazillion meals for his mother during her cancer treatments. If she ate right, maybe she would heal faster. And if there was food on the table, his father would actually show up, which made Mom happy, even though the whole "happy family" picture was a joke.

Shit.

Just cook and quit ruminating... except he knew damn well why he was thinking of his mom right now. Because having Rachel here made him start thinking about having someone at *his* table, in his house, in his life. Holding her for thirty-five fucking seconds had just about killed him. He'd pulled away to keep from taking advantage. She was vulnerable, for Christ's sake. He was supposed to be helping her.

Leaning into the fridge, he pulled out a leftover grilled steak from last night to cut up. After less than an hour with Rachel again, he felt himself tumbling head over ass in love with this woman who'd ignored him for six months. Now wouldn't his team have a field day laughing at that? While they played marry one, kill one, screw one, he played marry one, marry one, marry one. Liam *whack, whack, whacked* the steak on the cutting board, raised the knife again, and—

He felt eyes on him. Felt? Hell, was he becoming paranoid?

No. He trusted his sixth sense when it came to personal safety. He looked behind him and found...

Disco sat at the head of the hall, between him and the bathroom, staring him down. Making it very clear he was protecting Rachel.

"Good boy." Liam flicked a strip of sizzling steak into the air toward the dog. Disco caught it before it hit the ground. "Yeah, she probably has some rules about not feeding you table food. But technically it hasn't hit the table yet."

He settled back into preparing the meal, a ritual to make him feel more a part of family life and routine. Yeah, he missed having a woman around. He hadn't entered any of his marriages lightly. There'd been no shotgun weddings. He'd planned to spend his life with each one. So while he trusted his instincts in the professional field, his team had a point. His relationship radar was unreliable. He was out of the marriage market, and Rachel was too special to risk having a quickie affair with.

The sound of the shower spray hitting tiles drifted down the hallway to torment him, only to be made worse by the interruption as a body slid underneath. Rachel's body.

He grabbed the remote control and turned on the television, filling the room with the seven o'clock news. The lead story was kicking into gear about the upcoming international summit on satellite technology. Diplomats and military generals were traveling in from around the world. As he listened to the broadcaster detail the ramp-up, he couldn't help but wonder if somehow Rachel's airman might be losing touch with reality, blending the upcoming national summit with traumatic delusions. Regardless, they needed to talk with base security and make sure the young man wasn't a risk to himself or others.

And plug whatever security holes that had allowed Rachel to break into his car undetected.

"Breaking news…"

The announcement interrupted the regular report and his thoughts. Liam glanced up at the flat-screen mounted on the wall behind the oak table. A map of Southern Florida filled the image, with a star flashing over a street map of a neighborhood.

"City block explodes into flames… One resident is believed dead… more unaccounted for… Fire marshals are unsure of the cause, but terrorism isn't being ruled out…"

His sixth sense tingled with that bad, bad feeling to check his back… or Rachel's.

He looked up at the newscast again just as Disco whimpered, pawing at the cabinets. Florida was a big state. The odds of that blast having anything to do with her were a million to one. The same odds he would have given on her showing up in his Jeep.

Her wallet lay on the dining-room table, where she'd tossed it when she'd fished out her clothes from her backpack. Without thinking twice, he left the sizzling stir-fry and strode straight over to flip open the well-worn tan leather. He pulled out cards stuffed inside until he found her driver's license, checking her address.

Shit.

She lived on the same street as the one noted on the television screen. Right on the Miami-Dade/Broward

County border. No way in hell was that a coincidence. To hell with objectivity and keeping his distance. Someone was gunning for Rachel. *His* Rachel.

He slapped down the wallet and charged toward the bathroom door.

———

Rachel tipped her face into the stinging spray, needing to melt away the hellish tension from carrying around the burden of what she knew. Finally, she had someone who was willing to listen to her, to help her. And not just anyone.

Liam.

Her skin tingled with a heat beyond anything coming out of the showerhead. The bathroom steam was so thick it almost muted the avocado green tile of the outdated bathroom. Rivulets streaked down the brown striped shower curtain. Everywhere around her, she confronted reminders of Liam, packing her brain with images of him standing in this shower.

The scent of his aftershave clung to the air. Reminders of Liam greeted her eyes no matter which way she turned— his shaving gel, razor, shampoo, and sport body wash. The space was as clean as the rest of the neatly kept house.

A crack of thunder split the air, startling her. Maybe she should have just stood out in the rain and let it wash her clean. She'd certainly done so in the past on SAR missions—rain, storms, waterfalls.

Thunder pounded again. Louder. So close it sounded nearly on top of her. She shrieked in surprise before she could finish registering it was only someone knocking.

Knocking mighty hard.

"Liam?" she called out as the door exploded open.

His broad shoulders filled the door, his dark blond hair backlit by illumination from the hall. "Are you okay? You screamed."

She yanked the shower curtain to her body and said again, "Liam!"

Disco head-butted the back of Liam's leg, whining. He moved deeper into the bathroom.

Her hands fisted around the brown vinyl curtain. "I screamed because you scared the crap out of me."

"Sorry. Here." He yanked an oversized towel from the rack and tossed it to her. "You need to get dressed."

She snagged the towel with one hand while her other still clutched tightly to the shower curtain. "I'm almost through. I'll be out soon."

"We don't have any more time—" He stopped in his tracks. His eyes went wide, the sea green tint going stormy deep. His throat moved in a slow swallow before his gaze shot back up to her face.

She'd been attracted to him before, more than any man since her fiancé. But Liam had mentioned that *love* word back in the Bahamas. Such a beautiful, pain-filled word. Although he could have only been half serious about the whole love thing, she couldn't go there again, not even partially. She'd resisted the sensual draw during the three weeks they'd worked together on the earthquake relief. Although right now, with her defenses stripped even barer than her body at the moment, she found it almost impossible to resist stepping into his arms again.

"Liam?" Clutching the towel to her breasts, she swayed.

He scrubbed a hand over his square jaw, his eyes locked on her face. "Someone blew up your town house."

Chapter 3

SHOCK, THEN HORROR, CHASED ACROSS RACHEL'S FACE as she stood clutching the shower curtain and towel to her body. Droplets clung to her skin and her face. Were those tears on her cheeks? Ah shit, he was a sucker for a woman's tears. Always had been. Seeing *this* woman cry multiplied his weakness exponentially.

"Rachel." He stepped forward. "Are you all right?"

Her hand shot out. "Stop."

What had he been thinking? That he would scoop her up naked in his arms and check out if her honey-toned skin was an allover thing or a tan? Yeah, there was a time he would have been all about that if she gave him a thumbs-up. But she'd cold-shouldered him for six months. She'd come to him now for protection. Not sex.

"Hurry, we need to talk."

She blinked fast until the moisture cleared. "Believe me. I get that," she said, her voice carefully modulated. "Please step outside while I put on some clothes."

Her wet hair streaked down her back, the hot shower steaming a roll of mist around her legs until Liam could have sworn she was a mermaid rising from the mist.

A mermaid in a crap ton of trouble.

"Fair enough, Rachel, but talk to me while you're doing it."

He ducked into the hall and pulled the door closed

after him. The image of her wet naked flesh stayed imprinted in his brain. The scent of her hung in the moist air. And while part of him wondered how he could be this damn hard for her in the middle of a crisis, another part of him, the primal part, pounded a deeper truth in his core being that went beyond logic.

The part that acted on instinct.

She was in danger. And the heightened awareness was all about imprinting her deeper inside himself, keeping her close. Safe.

The water shut off on the other side of the door and he heard the rustle of her dressing. His mind filled in the blanks, given the small stack of folded clothes on the corner of the sink. Navy blue panties and a matching sports bra, jeans, and a tank top. She was a no-frills woman. But that just increased her appeal, since there was nothing to distract from her natural beauty. Her curves. Her soft, full lips—no makeup, just her mentholated lip balm.

And how screwed up was it that when he'd had a cold two months ago, a whiff of Vicks VapoRub on his chest had made him go hard.

He cleared his throat and almost managed to clear his mind. Almost. Not quite. "Hey, lady, I thought we were going to talk while you put your clothes on."

The bathroom door slammed against the wall as Rachel burst into the hall and charged past him, hips twitching as she fast-tracked away. "I'm a quick dresser. We can talk on the way."

He jolted, then pivoted on his heels to follow her. "Slow down." He cupped her shoulders. "Take a deep breath. Where do you think you're going?"

She gripped his elbows, the top of her head barely reaching his chin. "I need to get to my dogs."

"You can't go to your house. The whole block's on fire. And didn't you say your other animals are at doggy day care?"

Rachel went pliant under his hands. "Right. I forgot for a moment. How do you know for certain it was my place that blew?"

"I looked in your wallet and checked your address on your driver's license." He wanted to stroke away the worry from her eyes, but the scent of burning stir-fry stung his nose. He steered her into the kitchen again and turned off the stove before he burned down his own house. "Where exactly are your other dogs?"

She pulled a hair tie out of the pile of mess scattered from her backpack and scraped her hair into a pony-tail. The sounds of a car insurance commercial drifted from the kitchen. "The two dogs I'm working with right now... I took them to an in-home doggy day care, since I didn't know how long I would be gone. I should call her... Or should I?" Swaying, she gripped the back of a chair. "God, you're right. My mind's a jumbled mess right now."

His arm went around her before he could think. "Um, what exactly is a doggy day care?"

For a second, she rested against his chest. Her hair left a moist spot on his uniform, the dampness cool against his overheating flesh.

"It's called Wags and Whiskers, and it's located in a home environment. My dogs get run of a house without being kenneled..." Her voice trailed off. "I'm babbling, which is not wise when I'm trying to prove to you I'm rational. What does it matter where they are, as long as they're not in my house? Which according to you is burning to the ground."

"You said you'd told her you would be gone for a week." He stroked her head as she leaned into him. "But did you say where you would be going?"

"I didn't tell her where. Thank God. Only that I needed some time away and could be gone as long as a week." She looked up at him. "If they told someone, then why blow up my house?"

"I don't think they did. I'm more concerned with someone finding out you're not in your house."

"Oh, right. But if someone was following me here, they already know, which doesn't make sense." Her hands drifted up to clasp the front of his uniform. "Maybe it wasn't meant for my home after all."

Her touch heated through his uniform. He wanted her now every bit as much as he had six months ago, all of her, her body and her smile. And he could swear he saw awareness in her eyes. Could she be as frustrated and distracted as he was? She might not return his deeper feelings, but there was no denying the chemistry between them.

The reality of her being right about a threat sunk in deeper. In spite of her discussion of burnout, she'd been levelheaded when he knew her in the Bahamas. If someone was actually trying to pass along secrets, the timing and possibilities couldn't be worse, with a worldwide military confab only a week away, right here in his own professional backyard.

Was that coincidental? Or could it actually all be tangled up together?

No more time to think. Time to *move*.

"The house—hell, damn near a city block—was blown up hours ago. We need to get back to base and talk to authorities. Higher up this time."

"But what about Brandon?"

Brandon Harris. The veteran she'd been helping. Helping, right? Nothing more… Something that felt too much like jealousy kicked around in his gut.

Rachel was reaching down inside of him and taking hold just as firmly now as she had before.

Not. Wise. "I'll see what we can do about having someone pick him up and bring him in and I'll have someone check on the doggy day care place."

"Staking out a doggy day care? Oh my God, Liam." She pressed the heels of her hands to her eyes. "This is crazy."

"Damn straight, it is." He tossed the burned stir-fry down the disposal and yanked open the pantry. "You need to eat something on the way over. It could be hours before you get a chance."

He pitched a protein bar her way, snagging another for himself along with two cans of juice. Taking charge. What he did best. What she needed most from him now. And if what he feared was actually true, a lot more people needed him to get to the root of this mess before the unthinkable happened.

"You're a health-food nut." She eyed her candy bar beside her wallet on the table.

"And I'm guessing that comment means you aren't." He'd checked out books from the library on cooking healthy for his mom. "You can critique my food choice later. Come, Disco."

Her dog plunked onto his butt. Liam ground his teeth. Apparently no one had told the dog who was in charge. "No more steak for you."

"He only listens to me." She patted her leg and the dog walked up beside her. "Let's go. We can talk in the Jeep. And I can call Brandon while you're driving."

—⁓—

Brandon Harris had been told he possessed nerves of steel—on the football field. But he didn't play college football anymore and his nerves sucked, courtesy of his last deployment to the Middle East.

He threw his truck into park and turned off the headlights, past ready to pick up his dog Harley from the sitter and kick back with a beer at home. In fact, his whole life sucked these days, tough to swallow when he'd had the world by the tail for most of his life. But he wasn't at The Citadel military college these days or even in his job as a security cop in the air force. Since his return from Afghanistan, he was… in limbo.

And he was late picking up his dog, Harley.

He jumped out of the truck, his gym shoes hitting the sandy driveway outside the doggy day care.

Doggy frickin' day care, for Christ's sake.

Shaking his head, he scrubbed a hand over his shaggy hair, longer than normal these days. But then, he was on extended medical leave until they decided if he was a permanent or temporary basket case. Which meant he had to keep his appointments with the base shrink if he wanted to stand any chance at getting his life back.

Brandon slammed his door, triggering a distant ripple of barks. He flinched. His pulse ramped. He tipped back his head and stared at the crescent moon, dragging in calming breaths to ease the tightness in his chest. Sharp noises still did that to him. But at least he wasn't face down in the dirt anymore.

Thanks to his dog. And speaking of his dog...

He'd never have expected to be the kind to pay for a pooch-sitter. But since Rachel's pooch had been poisoned, he wasn't taking any risks leaving Harley alone, and oddly enough his mutt enjoyed the pack day.

Therapy dogs weren't allowed into all the places a service dog could go. And as much as he hated to be away from his new pet, he'd known he would need the workout in the gym after his therapy session. So he'd dropped off his Australian shepherd–beagle mix for the day at Catriona Whittier's business. Catriona, not what he'd expected from a doggy day care... person? Caretaker?

Not that he was sure what a canine-sitter was supposed to look like. A big burly guy who herded the pack? Or a prim, stern schoolmarm type who kept the pooches in line?

Catriona was neither of those. She was... quiet. Peaceful.

There'd been a time he lived for conflict on an adrenaline-soaked field. Football or battle. He was all-in, gung ho, and kicking ass. He'd had no idea how valuable peace could be until he lost it altogether.

He needed to quit staring at the moon and get his dog.

Brandon jogged up the driveway and around the pink stucco one-story on the beach to the fenced waterside area around back. A pricey piece of prime real estate she'd inherited from her parents. Or so Catriona had told him once.

Nearly mile-high palm trees swayed and rustled,

roots holding firm against ocean winds that were mere puffs compared to hurricanes of the past. Trees only got that tall over time. Their height testified to her long line of privilege.

Yet she chose to spend her days with dogs rather than the social set.

Barking their heads off at him from inside the house, a dachshund and beagle hooked their paws on the half-open windows, the fans cranked on high.

"Yeah, guys, I know you're there and I'm on your turf," he said.

It was easier to talk to the dogs than to people now. He cleared the house and came to the gate, a brightly painted sign illuminated with a spotlight: *Wags and Whiskers Doggy Daycare.*

He walked under the honeysuckle arbor just before the gate leading to a fenced backyard with privacy wood along the sides and chain link on the end that faced the ocean. The enclosed lawn sported baby pools, tires to jump through, and buckets of drinking water. Oversized doghouses were painted to resemble the main house. Little froufrou pampered fluff balls with bows on their furry ears mingled with the larger Labs and bulldogs.

So different from his boyhood farm where the animals had roamed free... although the scent of honeysuckle was the same. Except in that wide-open childhood, he'd lost more than one family pet to a roadside accident or a neighbor's buckshot.

The thought of something happening to Harley gripped him. And then, *bam.* There came that cold sweat again. His feet stumbled on... nothing. They just tangled up.

"Harley?" he shouted, grabbing the fence for

balance, searching the yard as motion sensors clicked floodlights on.

Catriona stepped from behind one of the doghouses. "Hey, Brandon, Harley's inside, zonked out from playing all afternoon. Come with me and I'll show you her favorite napping spot."

Catriona trailed her fingers down a wire fence around a dry baby pool with a Dalmatian curled up with her litter of puppies. She wound her way through the pack of dogs, lightly touching each on the head as she passed, fearless, at peace. This calm, collected woman didn't know the meaning of a cold sweat.

As always, his eyes were drawn to her, holding.

She had ginger hair, whispery fine and swept back with a headband. She always wore jean capris with a loose T-shirt, dark colored. Most likely so the dog fur and muddy pawprints didn't show. Not that she ever appeared anything other than serene, natural. She never put on makeup but always wore a hint of sunburn on her cheeks and a light sheen of perspiration that glistened better than the high-priced face creams Stella—his last girlfriend— had kept lined up on her side of the bathroom vanity.

Before she'd dumped his ass a month after he returned all loco in the head. Not that he could blame her.

Still, he couldn't help but think how Catriona was nothing like Stella or any type he'd hooked up with in the past. But he wasn't the same man now that he'd been before leaving for Afghanistan. A moot point, really, since he wouldn't be hooking up with Catriona or any woman. He had nothing to offer—in or out of bed. These days, he felt next to nothing, like someone had short-circuited his mainframe.

Given how raw he was today after the therapy session from hell, it would be best for all if he just hauled out of here. "No need to stop what you're doing. I'll get Harley and leave a check on the kitchen counter."

He was a fucking coward.

"Really, it's okay. I actually took some photos of the dogs, and there are some great shots of Harley."

Shots.

Crap.

The word *shot* alone turned his cold sweat downright icy. "Pictures?"

He forced himself to act normal. To pretend.

"A video, too." A smile lit her pretty hazel eyes. "That dog of yours is a real ham."

"Thanks. But I should go. Long day"—with the shrink, then pounding a punching bag, trying like hell to get back to work again. To get his military career back on track.

He'd gone to The Citadel military college on a football scholarship, played quarterback. Was pretty much a rock star in his hometown, the golden boy with a bright future in the air force as a security cop.

He'd understood a Middle East deployment would come his way. He'd expected and embraced the opportunity. He'd realized it would be tough—he wasn't delusional. Not then, anyway. He'd been prepped for the *possibility* of PTSD.

He'd just never really expected it to happen to him.

This fear that gripped his chest like a heart attack without warning. First time he'd heard fireworks after coming home, he'd damn near pissed himself.

Warrior strong?

Fuck.

She touched his arm lightly. "Are you okay?"

"Yeah, sure." He shook off the fog. How long had he been standing here, staring off into space? "We were talking about videos, right?"

"Exactly. Harley played in the pool to cool off, splashing like crazy. She's dry now, though." Her eyes narrowed too perceptively. "Would you like a cup of coffee before you head back out?"

"I just need to pick up my girl." Something cold nailed the back of his calf just below his shorts. He jolted around hard and fast. Only a dog. A familiar blue pit bull. "Isn't this one of Rachel's?"

"Ruby Two. Right. Which is funny, since she's blue. Both of Rachel's new trainees are here." She started toward the house, and he moved in step with her. "She took Disco with her when she stopped by early this morning."

"Where did she go?" He scratched the tightness in his chest. He'd been planning to call Rachel, to talk about... his dog. The whole pet-therapy gig. Not that he totally bought into it. He just liked having a dog. Nothing more.

"Rachel didn't say." Catriona swung open a reinforced screen door leading onto an oversized porch. "Just that she needed some time away and paid for a week's worth of sitting in advance, not that I ever worry about her settling up. I would give her the time for free in exchange for all the work she does."

He looked fast, searching for signs she was digging at his problem. He found nothing in her eyes but more of the peace. What would she think of him if he spilled all his whacked-out conspiracy theories? But he kept his mouth shut. Dumping that on her wasn't fair—hadn't been fair to Rachel either, she'd just caught him in a weak moment. Once he had his feet on solid ground again, he would get to the root of what he'd heard, find those responsible, and nail their asses to the wall.

For now, he had to bide his time and get his head on straight.

Catriona scratched Tabitha's head between ears that had been cropped with scissors before the Argentine Dogo been rescued from a Miami street gang. The gentle glide of her fingers against the sleek white fur seemed so damn soothing. "Thank goodness Rachel decided to get away, though, or she could have been hurt in that explosion."

He looked up fast to her face. "What did you just say?"

"The explosion, it was on Rachel's block. I thought I mentioned that earlier. Sorry, I'm so used to hanging out with the pooches, I lose some of my people skills."

She communicated just fine. More likely she'd told him while he was in his fog state. "There's a fire in Rachel's neighborhood?"

His mind started racing. This couldn't be coincidental.

In a moment of weakness he'd told Rachel Flores things he should have kept to himself. Going to the authorities had been every bit as useless as he'd expected. The golden boy was now seriously tarnished. No one took him seriously, and if anything, he'd just put himself and Rachel at risk by telling what he knew. He wouldn't have said anything at all, except he'd been hanging out with her and with Harley, and the next thing he'd known, he was spilling his guts.

Damn it, where was Harley?

In the house. Right. And once he had his shepherd he could call Rachel. He patted his pocket and realized he must have left his cell phone in the truck.

"I need to get my dog." He charged past her abruptly, the roaring in his ears almost as loud as the crashing waves hammering the shore. He'd become so dependent on the mutt, he couldn't face traffic without her for fear a car would backfire and he might...

He didn't want to consider what he might do.

Her feet sounded lightly behind him. "Are you sure you don't want some coffee? Or you could even stay for supper."

He turned to her, stunned. "Huh?"

"Supper. Food. To go with that coffee." She twirled a bit of honeysuckle vine between two fingers. "Nothing fancy, but I promise there aren't any dog hairs in it."

"Because you feel sorry for me?"

"Because I don't want to eat alone." She waved him along, walking sure-footedly even as a golden retriever and cocker spaniel played chase in circles around her feet. "Come on, you can help me make the hamburger patties. Gotta warn you, though, we'll be eating off paper plates. I hate to do dishes, since I already wash so many dog bowls every day. Like I said, nothing fancy."

Just completely normal. And tempting. But his life wasn't normal anymore. "Thanks. Maybe another time. I really need to track down Rachel."

Rachel disconnected Liam's phone with a frustrated jab. "He's not home, and he's not answering his cell. I don't know where he is. And Catriona's not picking up either."

She dropped Liam's phone back into a cup holder between them and hooked her elbow out the open window as they drove along the oceanside road. Streetlamps curved inward overhead, marking the roadway. The moonlight glinted off the murky water alongside, tiny ripples crawling across the surface. The air turned muggy as the after-storm humidity hung in the air and steamed up from the road.

Hot. But not nearly as hot as her town house currently burning to the ground. She tipped her head back on the seat, her chest tight at how close she and Disco had come to being caught in that blaze. How many other people hadn't been nearly as lucky? She couldn't bear the thought that anyone was even injured because of her.

Even if everyone walked away, how awful to lose everything. It was only a rental and she didn't own much, but the mementos she'd collected over the years were irreplaceable.

A thank-you note from a family after she'd located their toddler son in the woods.

Photos of her with her mom that she'd been meaning to scan into the computer and somehow never found the time.

A shoe box of memories from when she'd dated Caden, so little to commemorate a love that had filled every corner of her heart.

Her eyes slid to Liam. Tears clogged her throat. Her hand drifted to the top of her sleeping dog's head, resting between the two seats. Liam covered her hand with his. A sprinkling of blond hair on his arms glinted, lighter than the dark blond hair on his head, cut short to military regulations. For some reason she'd remembered it longer before, but then she'd heard rules differed for

special-operations warriors. And how funny to be thinking of his hair right now, but it was as if she needed to
soak up every detail, reassuring herself again and again
she'd chosen right.

"It'll be all right. We'll find Brandon Harris," he
said, sounding totally undaunted by everything that
had happened.

"How can you be so sure? Someone burned my
town house to the ground. I don't give a crap about
the contents, but the people who were hurt, what could
have happened… That's eating me up inside. I should
have been more persistent. I should have made someone listen sooner."

He squeezed her fingers before holding on to the
steering wheel again. "All we can do is focus on the now.
While you were loading the dog up, I went ahead and
called my friend in the OSI. I passed along Brandon's
name. Someone's driving over to pick him up now. That
may be why he didn't answer."

He'd placed his call when she wouldn't hear? Why?
What had he said that he didn't want her to know? Liam
was so charming and he'd told her how much he cared
about her. She'd trusted that, even if she wasn't a big
believer in the longevity of his "love." She'd tried to be
up front with him in return, because she honest to God
didn't want to hurt this incredible man.

What if she was wrong and Liam had been feeding
her a line?

God, she hoped she'd done right by Brandon. He was
already so suspicious of anyone military. Her stomach
roiled just thinking of how freaked-out he might be.
"And you trust this guy, your friend in the Office of

Special Investigations? You trust he'll be careful with Brandon and keep his traumatized state in mind?"

She'd come to Liam because of his air force special-operations connections, but now she wondered if those same ties would work against her. Not that she thought he would betray his country for even a second. But if he gave the wrong people the benefit of the doubt, she could be in even more danger. *Brandon* could be in danger.

Liam adjusted the rearview mirror, the three garters swaying. "I trust her completely."

Her? "But you still didn't tell her everything about what Brandon said, I hope."

"Not over a cell phone, no. I can't be sure of privacy until we're in a secure room. Even talking out here could be risky, so why don't we save the rest for when we get there."

She looked sharply from the water to the man, head-lights from oncoming cars streaking across his face, just as quickly gone, leaving him in shadows. The light and dark flashes reminded her of the two sides of Liam. At one moment he was the charmer who wowed her with his smile and wit. And in a flash he became the honed professional, a military man in charge of his universe.

She'd sought him out because of that professional side of him... not because she hadn't been able to forget him for even one day over the past six months. Right? She fingered the tear in the Jeep's ragtop. "Tell me more about your friend in OSI."

Where had that question come from?

From the part of her that liked his smile and that al-most quaint way he had of squeezing her hand.

"Not much to tell," he said. "We've been stationed together a couple of times, deployed together once. She's helped with intel on a few missions, always sharp, always right." He shot a quick glance her way. "I answered your question, and now I have one of my own. Why did you choose Florida for your big move?"

Her heart flipped. Because she'd heard *Florida* and thought of him? "The rescue group in D.C. that works with pairing shelter pets with vets identified this area for expanding the concept. The timing was right for me to move. I accepted the challenge for a change."

"That's a pretty radical change just because you're burned out on work. Most folks would opt for a vacation rather than another emotionally draining career field."

"I'm following dreams I'm passionate about." She shrugged, the wind lifting her damp hair and reminding her of the moment Liam burst into the bathroom. "I have no family entanglements. There's nothing to stop me from picking up and relocating if I wish. I guess I'm a lot like a female version of you—without the trail of ex-spouses."

"Fair enough. But why? You were damn good at your job." His praise reached across as tangibly as any touch. "More than that, you seemed intense about your search and rescue work."

"Too intense. I told you I burned out in the Bahamas and I meant it." Her emotions had felt all the more close to the surface with Liam around. She'd hoped returning to D.C., staying away from him, would bring balance back to her life.

No such luck.

"So you decided to work with PTSD patients? Sounds like a real party." He snorted.

"Okay," she said, half smiling along with him. God, he was so wonderfully irreverent. "I can see why it wouldn't seem the logical choice, but after so many failures in the Bahamas, so many dead people... dead children... I needed to do some saving."

His smile faded. "I get that."

Of course he would. She sometimes forgot how he'd once told her that he'd been an Army Ranger before shifting to the air force. Even now, there had to be unbelievable stress in his job, and somehow he'd managed to continue the grind for over a decade. "How do you hold tough through the ones you can't rescue?"

"I can't quit. There's always another one who needs me," he said simply, steering the Jeep steady on. "It's the only way I know to be."

Palm trees whipped past one after the other in perfectly spaced rhythm, leading toward a distant bridge like going from one rescue to another, week after week, month after month, until years passed. Lives were saved and still no life had been built.

How did a person go about building a life that wasn't wrapped up in the calling to rescue people? A calling that consumed a person until there wasn't time left for anything else. "What about retirement?"

"Are you calling me old?" He cocked an eyebrow.

A laugh burst free and even managed to deflate at least an ounce of tension with it. "Hardly. You're so honed and in shape, you could take down anyone I know."

And just that fast her admission of how very much she'd noticed his body was out there. Hanging in the air heavier than any salt-water-laden humidity. The attraction she'd felt for Liam hadn't lessened one bit.

As his bottle green eyes held hers, she could see an answering call in his gaze. He'd made it clear before how much he wanted her, and apparently time hadn't changed a thing between them.

If anything, the need had just increased. She'd been fooling herself that she could come here and keep it in check. Her whole body hummed with an awareness and fire that grew with each minute together, gathering force until she pressed her knees tightly together against the ache.

"Liam?" she whispered, and wondered at the husky, hungry sound that crawled from deep inside her.

He hauled his attention front toward a bridge only fifty yards ahead. "God, woman, you tear me up inside from wanting you. And you also have the strangest timing. Right now, we have somewhere to be. But let me be clear. Once we finish there, we're not pretending we're just work acquaintances anymore. You're not going to just fall off the planet without warning again. Got it?"

Wow, he was really laying it all out there. No dancing around the subject or giving them time to sort through feelings. And on top if it all, she still had to deal with an exploded town house and a possible treasonous threat. "I hear you."

Just these few hours together made her accept that the move to Florida hadn't been coincidental. The attraction to Liam was magnetic, to say the least. His eyes locked with her only for a second, but this man packed more in an instant than most put into a lifetime.

Then his gaze slid away, his attention back on driving, checking the rearview mirror—

"Shit!" he hissed.

Frowning, she glanced at him as they drove onto the mile-long bridge. "What's wrong?"

"Someone's following us and gaining fast... damn it." His arm shot out across her. "Brace yourself! We're about to be hit."

Rachel jerked around, expecting to find the silver sedan tailing her again. She looked and found...

Her navy blue SUV. With the customized license plate she'd chosen in honor of her dog. There was no mistaking the word *Disco1* as the Ford accelerated closer. Her Ford, which she'd left on base and now someone else was driving...

Her car rammed the Jeep.

Chapter 4

JOLTING FORWARD AND BACK IN HER SEAT, RACHEL braced against the dash with one hand and reached behind with her other to grab Disco's collar. If they'd been in her SUV, she would have had him in a crate, secured. Hell, if she'd been in her own vehicle, none of this would be happening at all.

"Liam?" she shouted against the roar of insanity. "Are you okay?"

"Fine," he said quickly, his voice calm, controlled, his toned body seemingly impervious.

Except she knew too well how even the strongest of soldiers could be brought down in a flash.

They slammed the concrete railing. Her body jerked and her thoughts fractured. She bit her tongue. The tinny taste of blood filled her mouth as the vehicle skidded. The echo of grinding metal shrieked along with honking horns. She looked out the passenger window as the Jeep scraped along the railing. The ocean churned below, dark and murky, waiting to swallow them if the barrier gave way. She looked up fast at the rearview mirror just as her SUV rammed them again.

The barrier had looked plenty sturdy when she'd driven over it earlier today. And now? It looked flimsier than a couple of two-by-fours holding out against a bulldozer.

Her heart lurched, then raced faster than the Jeep accelerating back into traffic. Squealing brakes sounded from behind them. She searched for ways to help, to alert Liam to anything that might help. In the rearview mirror, she saw a VW bug spinning out along the bridge, her blue SUV whipping fast. Oh God, what if this chase accidentally caused someone else to go over the side, into the ocean? Her dog jockeyed for balance with the same sure-footedness that had saved him when they worked disaster sites.

Liam steered on a dime and whipped around the other evening commuters. But so did the SUV, until it roared right up on their tail again. Whipping to the side, the vehicle—her car, which someone had stolen—accelerated beside them.

"Down!" Liam shouted, palming the back of her head.

She ducked just as a shot rang out. Both side windows shattered—driver's, then passenger's. Her heart in her throat, she reached to touch Liam's chest right over the steady thump of his heart. A sigh of relief cascaded through her. With her other hand, she reached back. Her dog nuzzled her, crouching low without flinching. He was trained well.

Liam covered her hand with his briefly, firmly, then took the wheel again.

"I'm fine," he said, the Jeep surging ahead. "But I need your help."

"Anything," she answered without hesitation.

"Sit up carefully and hold on to the steering wheel."

Um, what? She inched upward warily. "Are you nuts?"

"Hold. On." He grabbed her hand and placed it on the wheel.

He let go.

Sitting up fast, she held on tight, her shoulder pressed

to his. "This really isn't the time for you to find your sense of humor."

"No games. I'm calling for help." He arched off his seat to pull his cell phone out of his pocket.

A quick glance in the rearview mirror showed her the SUV was three cars back. "I would have been happy to do that, you know." She gripped the steering wheel, easier said than done with the Jeep barreling along the bridge. Humor seemed like a good idea after all, anything to steady her freaking-out nerves. "Nine. One. One. Try it. I learned it back in preschool."

"My help is a bit more intense than that, and they'll want to talk to me. You need code words and crap like that to get through."

"You have connections?" She narrowly avoided a slow-moving truck with stacks of orange crates.

"You could say that."

"Of course you do. That's why I'm here. I just didn't expect... Forget it." She didn't dare look at him, just held the vehicle steady as—thank God—they cleared the bridge. "Tell your connections those goons back there are driving my car, which means somehow they got on base."

The highway was marginally wider, at least. Except for the oncoming traffic on one side and a steep drop-off into the water on the other. Risking a look in the rearview mirror, she bit back a scream as the image filled with the car still hot on their tail. *Her* car. With two men in front, blurry shapes at such a high speed. Liam's curse hissed low and long, riding the wind whipping through the shot-out windows.

Bluetooth headset in place, he took the wheel back. "I've got it now."

He whipped past a Mack truck, then... nothing. No one followed them except the truck. For now. The hammering of her heart grew stronger in the aftermath. Her heartbeat?

No. His.

She still had her hand over Liam's chest, taking reassurance from the steady beat. *Betraying a little too much about herself.* She wasn't the clinging-vine type, damn it. She snatched her arm away and twisted her fingers in her lap.

People told her she had nerves of steel. She'd worked earthquake-ravaged regions, walking in rubble shifting with aftershocks. She'd trekked up a rugged mountain trail, searching for a missing child, with wolves howling in the wind. There had even been times she'd helped the police track an escaped convict. But sitting here while Liam's life was at risk because of her? That was threatening to send her over the edge faster than any jolt from a car. She shouldn't have come here. She should have gone from cop to cop to cop until somebody listened to her...

Listened to her say what? Bottom line, she knew so little. How could this bring down such a firestorm onto her life?

Dimly, she registered Liam speaking cryptically into the phone, lots of alphas and bravos and other code-sounding talk. And then an end to the conversation, roger and out.

He tossed the phone back into the cup holder between them and checked the rearview mirror again. "Looks like we've lost them. You did great, keeping your cool."

"Thanks, but I really don't deserve any praise. It wasn't like you left me any choice."

"Plenty of people still would have panicked. You're a good wingman." His eyes held hers in the rearview mirror.

Her stomach did a tumble that had nothing to do with fear. She looked down and away. Her gaze landed on his cell. "Your phone? May I use it, please?"

"Sure." His hand fell to rest on it. Nicks and scars shone along his knuckles. "But first I need to know, who are you contacting? You have to be careful who you speak to."

"Brandon deserves to know what's going on, even if I just leave a message. Maybe I shouldn't tie up your phone after all. I'll just fish my bag from the back." She started to twist around, the seat belt cutting into her neck. She reached to unbuckle—

Liam's hand shot out and stopped her with a light touch on the shoulder. Just a simple brush, but electric and immobilizing.

His hand slid away. "Stay put. Use my phone, since we're certain it's secure. If you reach your friend before we can get one of our people to pick him up, tell him to come straight to base, to the OSI. Once we get there, you won't be able to use your cell phone in the building." His brow furrowed. "On second thought, I think you should get your phone after all and pass it to me."

"Why?" But she was already reaching into the back even as she questioned him, careful not to ditch her seat belt even though it pinched like a son of a gun. She wrenched and yanked the backpack from beside her panting dog.

"If what you say is true about tapped phones, they could have been tracking you through your cell."

"Oh God." She unzipped her bag fast and tunneled inside. She handled her iPhone like it was a snake.

He snatched it from her hand and pitched it out the window, into the ocean. She felt the *plop* in the pit of her stomach. Had she lured these people directly to Liam? To Brandon too?

Damn it, she refused to let fear take over. She had to find her old calm under pressure. She may have brought this trouble to Liam's doorstep, but she would do her best to hold up her end of things. "Your phone, please? I need to call him and warn him now more than ever."

He scooped it up. "Here. Even though my phone's secure, keep it brief, just in case."

"Thank you…" For the phone and so much more. She really hated herself right now for all she was asking of Liam.

As she dialed, police sirens whined faintly in the background along with the ringing phone, ringing, ringing, until finally Brandon's voice mail picked up again. *Hell.* Her hand fisted around Liam's phone.

Leaving a message felt like a pitifully inadequate option, with buildings blowing up and a high-speed chase on a bridge. She couldn't even bring herself to entertain the notion that he wasn't picking up because whoever had been threatening her and Liam may have already gotten to Brandon.

Twirling a sprig of honeysuckle vine between her fingers, Catriona leaned a hip against the chain-link gate and watched Brandon, in his truck. He'd been sitting there for at least twenty minutes. But then he did that sometimes. Zoned out, thinking.

Except she wasn't doing much else either. Just standing here. A little pathetic actually, watching and drooling over him.

Although, who was going to rat her out? Her staff was made up of a couple of college students, neither of whom was here now. Her only real buddies weren't particularly verbal, sticking to barking or howling. While she understood every nuance of their sounds, the rest of the world wasn't going to pick up on any hint from them that their caregiver had a serious crush on a guy who barely knew she was alive.

A guy who sometimes seemed to doubt he was still alive himself.

Across the yard in the parking area, Brandon slumped in the front seat of his truck. She could see his fists clench tighter as if he was resisting the urge to pound the steering wheel. Instead, he gently—carefully—reached for his dog. He buried his fingers in the dense fur.

She couldn't pry her eyes away from how the sea breeze played with his dark hair, thicker than usual, since he'd let it grow while on leave. His face was bristly, just unshaven enough to be scruffy. Manly.

She knew he was on leave from the military after a rough deployment overseas and he had one of Rachel's therapy dogs, so he must be suffering from some kind of trauma. But beyond that? He was a mystery to her.

One she really wanted to solve. She tucked the honeysuckle into her pocket.

Unlatching the fence, she angled through sideways, careful not to let any dogs out. She secured the lock after her and walked gingerly toward his vehicle, slowly, crunching gravel to give him an advance warning that she approached. He had one elbow crooked out of the open window, country music drifting from the radio.

Still, he jolted when she cleared her throat. "Hey, uh, didn't see you coming." He stepped out of the truck, the engine still idling, radio humming. "Is there some kind of a problem?"

"I was going to ask you the same thing." She cocked her head to the side, late-night breeze caressing her cheek. "You look angry, and you haven't left."

"Rachel isn't answering. And so far, she hasn't left a message." He waved his cell phone, green LED panel glowing in the dark. He tapped the roof of his truck, music from the radio drifting softly through the open door. "I was just searching my iPhone and listening to the news for more details on that explosion. Shit, it sounds like it was really bad—Uh, sorry for cursing, Cat."

Cat? No one had called her that before. Except him. Now. "I've heard worse, but thanks for the apology anyhow."

"From what I can tell, the explosion wasn't just on Rachel's block. It was her building."

Her heart leaped up to her throat. "Oh, God. When did you last speak to Rachel?"

"This morning. And you?"

"When she dropped off the dogs, nothing more after that." She reached for her cell clipped to her belt, dialed… listened. Darn it. "Straight to voice mail. Her phone must be off." Or worse. "I'm sure she wasn't there. Who pays a dog-sitter and goes home?"

Still, something was very wrong here. Rachel never, never disappeared without leaving concrete contact info. She was too devoted to her animals.

He scratched his head. "I have a couple other numbers I can call, people who train the dogs with her. Maybe they'll know something."

Nodding, she pressed her cell phone to her chest. "You go ahead and call them then. I'll just take deep breaths so I don't hyperventilate."

She used to do that all the time as a kid, before she'd gotten her asthma under control. Inhalers. Not sexy.

Not that Brandon would find her sexy when they were worried about Rachel. Or even if they weren't neck deep in worry, why would he notice her in her baggy dog-lady clothes, covered in canine slobber? But she couldn't change who she was. She hadn't been able to do it to please her parents. She wasn't going to do it to win over some guy.

Even a guy as muscular, smart, intriguing—and strangely vulnerable—as Brandon.

His rumbling voice rode the breeze. Each time he spoke, her hopes rose, only to fall as he left yet another message or thanked someone for their time, even though nobody seemed to know a thing about where Rachel had gone today.

Cursing, Brandon stuffed his cell in his pocket. "Sorry, Cat—uh, Catriona, I mean. Sorry. Just distracted. Nothing from anyone on Rachel."

"No need to apologize. You can call me Cat. It's easier. My full name's unusual, to say the least."

Her name even made her laugh sometimes. Her parents had chosen it months before she was born, obviously expecting great things from her, with a flamboyant name to go with a grandiose future. But she hadn't been outgoing or particularly pretty no matter how much they paid to dazzle her up. Hair highlights and lowlights. Manicures and spray-on tans.

Underneath it all, she was still just herself.

She wanted to sit on the beach and read. She forgot her hat and wrecked the latest hair color her mother chose for her. She got sunburned and peeled.

The boys she had liked—the ones who'd liked her back—usually freaked out when they saw her million-dollar home and met her unmistakably pretentious parents. No one had been able to accept her for herself... until she'd stumbled on two stray puppies in a Dumpster when she was sixteen. They were starving, and the female bit her.

But then she'd seen the other three—dead—puppies. The biter had been protecting her siblings.

Catriona had picked up the scruffy puppy and tucked the fierce protector into her backpack—just to be safe. She didn't blame the little one for the bite, but she wasn't going to offer up her arm as a chew toy. She scooped up the other and held it close enough to see the fleas crawling around in its patchy fur. The little boy pup had trembled so hard, it peed on her. She'd taken them both home, names picked out before she hit the front stoop.

Freckles and Frisbee.

She'd expected her parents to argue about taking them to the veterinarian, but her mother had been strangely cooperative. It wasn't until they reached the vet's office that she realized her mom intended to have the puppies put to sleep.

For the first time in her life, Catriona stood up to her mother. She'd threatened to pitch a very embarrassing fit in the lobby full of people who would undoubtedly gossip. She would make sure everyone knew her mom, Vivian Whittier, was a puppy killer.

Her mom had ground her teeth but relented. Vivian had valued nothing more than her reputation as a philanthropist. So Vivian—Vivie—had changed tactics quickly, set up treatment for the puppies with instructions to arrange for them to go to a rescue, for a hefty donation. Her mom promised to go shopping for a pedigreed pooch that afternoon.

But Catriona wasn't budging.

The thought of giving up the two pups snapped a switch inside her she'd never expected. She was willing to bargain with the devil for those babies.

Worse. She was willing to bargain with Vivian.

Catriona had promised to attend the blasted cotillion classes. She would even try to fit in there and date boys her mom picked out.

If she could just keep the puppies.

Frisbee, the fighter, the spunky little protector, didn't make it. Parvovirus had sapped the life from her already parasite-riddled body. But the little guy, Freckles, the shy pup that peed when you looked at him?

He made it.

And with him, Catriona had found her mission.

Her fingers worked automatically over Tabitha's head, soothing, until her heart rate slowed and her mind cleared enough to tune in again to Brandon's voice.

"Hey, Rachel, when you get this message, give me a call or Catriona, either of us. We just need to know you're okay." He disconnected.

"Still no answer?"

He shook his head. "Afraid not."

A vein throbbed in his temple. Faster and faster still. The strain on his face, in his eyes, was worse than anything requiring an inhaler.

"She's okay." She touched his arm again. Thick corded muscles twitched and bunched under her fingertips, but she didn't pull away. "I'm sure of it."

"You can relax." He half smiled. "I'm not going to fall apart in the middle of your yard. I'm just honest to God concerned."

She didn't know what to say to that. How should she answer a person who joked about... what? PTSD, maybe? That would be the main reason a military guy would seek out a therapy dog, if they didn't have a visible physical injury. But Brandon didn't look how she would have expected a person suffering from combat stress to appear.

He was buff and tan. He cracked jokes. She would have expected him to be antisocial. Gruff.

But not open this way. Vulnerable, even. There were most definitely shadows in his expression and dark smudges under his eyes that made her want to pull his head to rest in her lap and stroke his thick, dark hair.

"I know, but still, you're worried and so am I. I know I said it before, but I keep reminding myself, paid for a week in advance."

He hitched his hands on his narrow hips. "Chances are slim she's hanging out at her place, knitting dog booties. And she does deserve to get away after the hours she's put in lately. Maybe she's tucked away with some guy having the time of her life."

God, he was hot. "But you're still worried." Which

made him ever hotter. But was he worried about Rachel being on a date? "Uh, why are you looking for her?"

"Why do you ask?"

Because… she was jealous? And how pathetic was that? Still she pushed, "From where I'm standing, you're more than concerned. You look really worried. Not that I'm diminishing how upset she'll be over losing her stuff, but her dogs are safe here, and thank God she decided to step away for the day. Right? So all's chill in the big scheme of things, as long as no one got hurt."

He seemed to weigh his words carefully. "There's a little more going on here than that. Rachel thought she had some kind of stalker. She reported it to the cops, but there wasn't anything they could do."

Catriona gasped. "You think someone actually set that fire on purpose?"

"It's a distinct possibility."

"Then we should call the police. Now." She lifted her cell phone, ready to report… what? She wasn't sure exactly, but someone should at least tip them off.

"I'll handle it." He gripped her hand.

Stopping her.

Searing her with his callused heat.

She swallowed hard and eased her hand away. "That's right. You're a cop, aren't you?"

"Military. Yes…" The corner of one blue eye twitched. "But I'm on medical leave right now."

"That doesn't make you any less of a police officer. All the skills you learned are still there and they'll listen to your suspicions."

"You would think so." He smiled.

Sorta.

"I can see how a cop could get cynical, but you do such an altruistic job. The honor in that just blows me away." And she hated that he didn't seem at all proud of what he'd accomplished. "You followed your dream. That's really cool."

"What about you? Is this"—he spread his hand to encompass her yard—"is it your dream?"

So they weren't calling the police.

She knew a subject change when she saw one. But if he felt everything possible was being done to investigate the fire, then she trusted him. Clearly there was nothing they could do for Rachel right now.

Why not answer his question? She could actually take a moment to talk to him in the muggy night, the most she would get out of a man who refused to have dinner with her. Catriona leaned back against his truck, letting the ocean and night sounds seduce her.

"I wanted to study veterinary medicine, but my grades weren't good enough." And for once her parents refused to buy her way into something she wanted— even if she promised to marry another vet. Not that she would have been so calculating. But her mother had always been on her to marry a doctor, so she'd thought maybe...

She shook off her thoughts, not that he was rushing her. He had a way of listening and waiting that was rare. "I decided to be a vet tech instead. I left home with my dog Freckles and worked my way through. I held down a job at a shelter for about five years, then my parents passed away."

There hadn't been much money left—Vivian had been a conspicuous consumer. But there had been a mortgage-free house. A gorgeous beach home that wouldn't sell for nearly what it was worth, in the current economy.

So she'd thumbed her nose at her mother and the entire neighborhood and started a doggy day care.

"I have the title free and clear to my parents' house and decided to open Wags and Whiskers. I'm able to take in fosters and rescues. I've never been happier."

She looked over the yard and the business she'd built. She offered obedience and agility classes. And she'd recently had a whole new world opened to her with some of her pets achieving certification to be therapy dogs. Not service dogs, but emotional support therapy dogs. She made trips to nursing homes and children's cancer wards.

A dark grin welled inside her. Her mom would have approved of the visits to hospitals, since there were eligible doctors around.

But Catriona wasn't there to snag some rich eye candy the way her mom would have wanted. She was there to make a difference. With her dogs, she had all the confidence in the world. For the first time, she wasn't beige.

She *existed*.

And right at this time when she was feeling like anything was possible, into her life walked Brandon Harris. Big, quiet, and hunky, he showed up on her doorstep to discuss dog-sitting for his Australian shepherd, since his gym didn't allow therapy dogs.

For nearly a month since then, she'd been waiting for a chance to get closer to him, and that opportunity had come tonight. She wasn't letting it slide through her fingers.

Catriona shoved away from the warm metal of the truck. "I'll leave you to finish up calls to whomever you need to speak with to do whatever it is you're going to do to handle Rachel's problem with the stalker." She rested a hand on his arm briefly, but it was enough. "Take your time. I have plenty to keep me busy securing all the dogs so we can go."

"Go?" He looked up sharply. "Where?"

"To Rachel's condo, of course. At least a drive-by to check on things." She looked back over her shoulder, a lock of hair catching in the wind. "We can be there for support if she's heard about the explosion and shows up. Make sure she's not alone, if some creep is there waiting for her."

His eyes held on her hair. On her mouth.

She lost her footing on… nothing really. The ground was flat. Her balance was just wonky.

God, she hated her lack of experience with men. Oh, she'd had sex plenty of times. Starting with blow jobs on guys at those horrid cotillion classes and moving on from there. She'd kept trying until she'd figured out she just wasn't good at relationships. After a while, it just wasn't worth the effort.

Until now.

Brandon placed his hand on her waist. The air snapped like lightning chasing across the ocean, looking for land.

Confusion shifted through his eyes. Then was gone.

"You okay?" he asked.

"Fine"—sorta, not really, damn it—"just tripped over a, uh, dog toy."

"Good thing I was here to catch you." His hand fell away. "But what about the burgers you wanted to grill? And if you're coming along with me, who'll watch the dogs?"

If she came along?

He wasn't rejecting the idea outright.

"The hamburgers will keep just fine in the fridge and we can hit a drive-through on our way." Did sharing a Big Mac in his truck count as a date? "And I have a list of college students who're willing to sub at a moment's notice for extra money."

"We could get back late."

"They're college students. Late night is their specialty."

"Right, all-night study sessions." When he smiled, the cleft in his chin called to her finger to tap it. "I should make those calls before we go."

Her skin tingled. They were really going to work together on this, hang out with each other beyond passing the time over dogs. She had exactly what she'd wanted since first meeting him.

Her gut twisted as she realized he was also everything her mother would have wanted for her. Handsome. Smart. He wasn't a doctor, but he was a war hero, and her mom would have been thrilled at the notion of him in uniform on Catriona's arm.

Except, ugh, her mother's approval should be the kiss of death. Better to think about all the times she and Brandon had talked while their dogs played in the surf. He wasn't just a guy who wore a uniform.

He was a man. An interesting, attractive man.

She refused to be like her mother, only looking at the surface. Brandon was more than a uniform. More than a "catch."

And he was completely too David Beckham–hot to ever look at her that way.

Her chest went tight. She was far from Posh Spice. More like a mustard seed.

Her confidence evaporated as she neared the house and considered locking herself inside as she'd done for the past seven years. Considered. And resisted.

Even if this was only about tonight, she wouldn't miss out on the chance to be alone with Brandon.

—*m*—

Liam pulled over onto the shoulder of the road, behind a row of palm trees, and killed the headlights. Finally, he was certain they were not being followed. They were safe, for now at least. Late-night traffic whipped past, headlamps streaking through the night as if there hadn't been a freaking life-and-death car chase on a bridge less than five minutes ago. At least none of the cars was her blue SUV with a dented front fender.

Until…

There it went. Her SUV with the vanity license plate on the front and scrapes down the side. Then it was gone. Past them and down the highway, police cars on its tail.

She relaxed back in her seat. "Liam, I am sorry to have dragged you into this mess."

His fists gripped the steering wheel as tightly as he clenched his jaw. He forced himself to relax enough to speak. "I'm glad you did, because now it ends."

"You can tell them it's not my imagination." Her joke fell flat.

But then, he wouldn't have laughed if she'd been a Grade A stand-up comic right now. Damn straight, she wasn't imagining anything. While he admired her grit, he couldn't find anything inside him except a deep rage and intense need to haul her close, safe. To hell with the past six months.

His arms closed around her and this damn well wasn't about comfort. She didn't pull back. She stared up at him, her pupils widening before her gaze fell to his mouth. They'd kissed before, briefly, and he remembered the taste and feel of her. Although no memory compared to the reality of having her in his arms again.

Just like before, he dipped his head toward hers, waiting for her to object, but she still looked back at him steadily. Her fingers curled around the back of his neck, then up into his hair, urging him toward her. *Yes.* The bands snapped on his restraint. He slanted his mouth over hers, taking in the softness slicked with mentholated lip balm. They were both hyped-up and sweaty and there was no way this kiss could go further out here. They couldn't afford to just hide forever. But for one crazy-ass moment here, touching her made the roar in his mind recede.

She was so wiry and strong, sometimes he lost sight of how soft she was, how curvy in all the right places. How much of a firecracker turn-on she became when she focused that attention on him. Her hands slid from his hair to his shoulders, farther down and under his uniform, under his T-shirt, nails digging into his back.

His senses went on overload, taking it all in. The press of her breasts against his chest. The scent of *his* shampoo in *her* hair…

And oh, God, her hair. The sleek glide of her ponytail through his fingers sent electric shocks bolting straight through him, making him hard and hungry for more of her. He would give his left nut to be somewhere truly alone with her where he could explore every inch of her body with his eyes, his hands, his tongue, until she was turned inside out from wanting him as much as he wanted her.

But they weren't somewhere else by themselves. And they were barely alone here.

The sound of cars, a honking horn, a crack of thunder, and finally he remembered where they were. Thought about what they were doing now and what they'd almost done right here on the side of the road in front of God and the late-night traffic. He gripped her elbows and eased her arms from him, her close-cut nails scoring a long, arousing path down his back before her hands slid free from his shirt.

She moaned and pressed herself closer. To hell with the garters on his mirror. "Don't stop…"

He folded their hands together between them. "We have to get back to base. To safety."

"Oh, my God, you're right." She pressed her palms to her face. "This is insane. I'm sorry for losing control like that."

And he'd put her at risk right now by indulging a need for her that hadn't dimmed one bit in six months.

She'd been smart to stay away from him all this time. There was a chemistry here that blew his mind, *dulled* his mind. He'd been half in love with her before, all the more reason for them to keep their distance, given his three-time-loser track record. Except distance was the one thing he couldn't give her now.

Because he was the only person who stood a chance of keeping her safe.

Chapter 5

RACHEL WONDERED IF SHE WOULD EVER FEEL SAFE AGAIN.

Sitting in the passenger side of Liam's Jeep, she entered Patrick Air Force Base for the second time today. She'd been scared out of her mind earlier and the feeling hadn't changed much. If anything, she was more rattled now that the enormity of the car chase and how she'd let that fear strip away all reason really hit her.

She gnawed her bottom lip, still tingling from the explosiveness of how they'd made out on the roadside. She'd known the chemistry between them had a life of its own. Over the past months she'd been tormented just thinking of their brief kiss in the Bahamas.

Somehow though, her memory had fuzzed over details. The crispness of his beard against her sensitive cheek. How broad his hands were, palming her back. How he'd skimmed them up and down her spine as he brought her closer, until her breasts pressed to the solid wall of muscles. Taking in all the sensation until hot desire flooded her, she wanted, needed, the outlet from all the pent-up fears and emotions.

Her heart was already pumping overtime, adrenaline searing her veins, and yet her body revved even more just thinking about how fast they'd lost control. If the sound of the traffic hadn't brought her back to reality, she would have had sex with Liam right then and there, and to hell with the consequences. She glanced at him

behind the wheel, his jaw tight in the glow of the dashboard lights. Pretty much the way he'd looked since he
pulled away from her. Restraint was costing him too.

A shiver of want rippled through her.

God, but she needed to rein in her feelings. She had to
focus on analytical details so she had her facts together
when she talked to Liam's friend in the OSI.

Rachel looked away from Liam fast, out over the
ocean. A low-flying cargo plane swooped over the bay
with the back ramp open. The big fat moon illuminated
people leaping out toward the open water.

"Training," Liam said simply, as if it was no big thing
to see people hurtling out of the back of airplanes into
the ocean.

And actually, not so long ago, that would have been
normal for her too.

Wind blowing through the missing windows stirred
memories of her experiences of being lowered out of
helicopters with her dog. Back in the days when she
had nerves of steel and didn't cower on the floorboards
of cars. Back before she'd worked an earthquake-
relief mission with a man who made her feel too much.
She'd lost her ability to distance herself and she'd
crumpled inside.

God, how she wanted to be herself again, fearless
and in control as she'd been before her job and some
criminal stalker sucked the strength of will from her.
She wanted to be the woman Liam had been attracted to
six months ago.

What a time to realize he hadn't even really been
kissing *her* on the roadside. He'd been drawn to the
woman she once was.

He spun the steering wheel, guiding the vehicle into a parking lot. "We're here."

Relief shuddered through her until she realized. "What about Disco?"

"Bring him."

She wouldn't have left him anyway. Rachel hooked Disco's leash and hopped from the Jeep. Liam was already at her side, his hand on a handgun strapped to his waist. When had he put that on, and why hadn't she noticed?

A series of entrances, passageways, and security codes later, Liam opened a final door into... not at all what she'd expected. She'd imagined being escorted into some kind of cold, sterile inquisition room. Instead she looked around what appeared to be more of a comfy lounge area. Granted it was all industrial, military-issue furniture. But the space contained a sofa, a couple of chairs, a table in the corner with a laptop computer and LCD projector. A television monitor hung from the ceiling.

Disco plastered himself to her leg. She sat uneasily on the sofa while Liam paced.

She toyed with her dog's leash, weaving the rough hemp length between her fingers. "What happens next?"

"We wait for my friend." He pivoted to face her just as the door opened again.

Rachel shot to her feet, her dog's ears radaring forward.

A man and woman stepped in—one in uniform, the other in civilian clothes. Not surprising, since the OSI was a mix of military and civilian employees. Still, Rachel was caught off guard. She'd expected older grim secret service–looking sorts, given that this building was full of grizzled men in camo and nondescript suits. The man—probably in his early thirties, despite a surplus of gray in his salt-and-pepper hair—wore a blue air force uniform and a huge grin. The woman—Liam's "friend"—sported sleek designer slacks and sky-high heels and brought with her an air of crisp efficiency and subtle perfume.

"Sylvia." Liam stepped forward, his hand falling to rest familiarly on the woman's shoulder. "Thanks for meeting us so quickly."

Sylvia patted his wrist quickly before he pulled away. "Absolutely. We'll do our best to sort this out." She gestured to the man beside her. "This is my associate, Captain Bernard. And I assume this is Ms. Flores? I'm Special Agent Cramer."

Standing, Rachel thrust out her hand and shook hands with both of them. "Yes, and thank you. I know you're here because of Liam, but still, I'm grateful."

Sylvia tucked her iPad under her arm. "That's what friends are for—and it also happens to be my job."

Friends, or more? If it had been more, then it was in the past. That much she was sure of. Liam had always been straight with her. While he may have had three wives—God, that freaked her out—he had a code about being faithful. He wouldn't have kissed one woman in the car while dating another woman.

But if Sylvia Cramer was in his past, was this his type? Sylvia, who wore sleek black designer pants and a white silk shirt, crisp pleats and her lanyard precisely aligned? Her pearl earrings matched her pearly white perfect teeth, which were a little large in a way that made her smile seem... off. But then, all that might be jealousy, since this woman could have leaped out of an airplane without a hair sliding out of place.

Sylvia gestured to the door. "Liam, if you wouldn't mind stepping out, please? Captain Bernard will accompany you."

As if there were really a question in there anywhere. And she'd used his first name, just as he'd used hers.

Rachel chewed her kissed-tender bottom lip.

"Of course." Liam turned to Rachel, squeezing her shoulder, and yes, she wanted to believe there was something more when he touched her. Especially with his kiss still imprinted on her lips and brain. "I'll be just a few feet away if you need me."

The door clicked closed behind Liam and Captain Bernard. Was it her imagination that it hissed like a portal, trapping her in a vacuum-sealed chamber with someone who'd shifted from ally to jailer?

Her inquisitor pulled a Coke from her purse and popped the top. Offering the soda can, she nodded back to the sofa, green with an iron framework. "Make yourself comfortable. I wish I had something to offer your dog, too. Would you like me to call for a bowl of water?"

"Thank you. If we stay here too long, then yes, he will need that and a trip outside." Rachel wasn't fooled for a second by the show of niceties. The woman was trying to work an angle, get closer with the drink and the concern for Disco.

Which should have been fine.

Special Agent Cramer actually was here to help, right? She'd come in late at night just because Liam called. Except Rachel felt the investigator's suspicion all the way to her toes. This agent was a person who didn't trust anyone.

"Relax," Sylvia said, settling into the chair by the sofa, resting her iPad on her knees.

"Easy for you to say." Rachel clasped the soda can between her palms. "No one tried to blow up your home today or run you off the road."

Poison one of her dogs.

Threaten her on the phone.

But hey, one thing at a time. No need to sound like a paranoid lunatic straight out of the gate.

"You're right. My day was quite mundane until now." She smiled again, pearly teeth flashing as the chilly gust of the air conditioner wafted around more of her subtle signature scent.

Sylvia smelled like expensive perfume and Rachel smelled of Liam's soap. And Liam had appreciated her just fine when she'd been covered in grime, working an earthquake rescue. He didn't need glam. She grinned inside.

Then remembered why she was here in the first place. "What happened to my condo?"

"The police are still investigating. But from what my people hear, it appears to be a kitchen fire that spread... quickly." She assessed her with icy-sharp blue eyes. "Now let's talk about what's been going on for the past few weeks."

"Talk?" Like chitchat over tea and finger sandwiches? While she trusted Liam, she didn't know this person, and clearly things on this base weren't as secure as they should be. "I'm not sure where to begin."

"Wherever you wish. I'm here to listen and do what I

can to sort through everything. I can also provide protection if need be. This is a win-win situation... as long as you tell me the truth."

"This just seems so informal." Rachel lifted the Coke, shifting on the sofa.

"I can assure you, I'm taking this very seriously." Sylvia tapped her iPad. "Our session is being taped, if that makes you feel any better."

"Ah, so you just officially informed me."

"That I did."

Rachel cocked her head to the side, starting to feel more than a little claustrophobic. "Should I have a lawyer?"

"This isn't a civilian police setting." Sylvia placed her iPad on the side table. "I have no jurisdiction over you. And nobody's read you your rights. I understood from Liam—Major McCabe—that you *want* my help."

"Of course I do. I'm sorry for acting paranoid. This has just been an insane couple of weeks where I've been let down by law enforcement. So forgive me if I'm overly cautious." She rested a hand on her dog's head, grateful they'd let her keep Disco with her. "Have you been able to track Brandon down yet? I'm worried about him."

"As well you should be, and we've got people searching now." She scooped up her iPad and, glancing down, tapped along the touch screen. "Let's just review everything again, in your own words rather than via Major McCabe. It's surprising what different people will pick up on or things that will come to mind for you because I ask a certain question."

"Ask away, then."

Sylvia tipped up her iPad, shifting her full attention back to Rachel. Not that she'd ever actually taken it off her. "Let's start with this surveillance video of you breaking into Major McCabe's Jeep."

———⁓———

Liam leaned against the wall across from the observation glass, wishing he could listen in as well, but Captain Bernard had already gone above and beyond in letting him stay to watch. The guy was a butt-kisser to anyone who outranked him. Usually that grated on Liam's every last nerve, but right now? He wasn't sure he could have let Rachel out of his sight completely. While he trusted Sylvia, the rest of the world was still suspect. Until they had some answers, he preferred to keep Rachel front and center.

Although she seemed to be holding her own—staying alert and apparently not fooled one bit by Sylvia Cramer's attempt to put her at ease and catch her off guard. Liam had watched his old friend often enough to know she was just giving Rachel a chance to calm down, to feel secure, and then she would attempt to rattle her story.

Or at the very least, shake new information free.

So he kept his eyes glued to the two women, unable to stop himself from comparing them. Sylvia—a sleek, sexy redhead he'd dated who should have been perfect for him. She was totally married to her job as a civilian employee with the OSI. She understood his lifestyle, the secrets, the long separations. She had the same in her job. They'd been a perfect—cool, chilly—match.

Zip for chemistry.

And then there was Rachel, with her uncontrollably

wavy hair as wild as the way she attacked life. Even when it zapped her to the core, as the earthquake SAR in the Bahamas had. Rachel threw herself right into the fire all over again here, helping veterans wounded in such a deep way, it couldn't possibly help but slice into her as well.

She was anything but calm. Anything but cool. And completely, sensually *alive*.

A hiss from behind him snapped him around quickly. Captain Bernard tensed, his hand slipping to his weapon strapped in an arm holster. A cipher-locked door opened—and two of his teammates stepped through.

Wade Rocha and Jose James filled the small observation room, both in uniform, but Rocha barely had the sleep wiped from his eyes, a mug of coffee in one hand and a candy bar in the other. The captain relaxed, his ever-ready smile sliding back into place.

Damn, but this long day was stretching into a long night.

Wade shot a quick assessing look at Bernard.

Liam smiled. "He's my baby-sitter, guard, handler." Also known to be a suck-up, but that was probably best left unsaid. "Take your pick."

Bernard just grinned.

Wade pressed deeper into the room. "Good evening, Captain Bernard. I saw the base commander out in the hall, and I could have sworn she was looking for you."

Bernard stood taller. "Really?"

"Yeah, Colonel Zogby's just out there. If you hurry you can catch her. We'll be right here while you speak with her. Can't leave without going past you."

"Right," Bernard said. "Thanks."

The captain rushed out the door, obviously eager for face time with a colonel.

Laughing softly, Wade pressed deeper into the room and clapped Liam on the shoulder. "What happened out there on the road tonight?"

"How did you know to find me here?" So much for security.

"We were called in by someone from the OSI. They didn't say why, other than that you'd been in an accident."

Jose stepped alongside them, an unregulation marathon T-shirt just visible through the open neck of his camos. "Major, saw your Jeep in the parking lot and it looks like shit."

Liam winced. "I know."

"I mean really shitty," Jose said, whistling softly. "Totaled-and-headed-to-the-junkyard shitty."

"Thanks. Wanna pour salt in the wound while you're at it?"

Jose pulled his hand out of his pocket. "I thought you might want these before they tow it away."

His fist opened to reveal the three garters that had hung from Liam's rearview mirror.

"Not funny today." Liam smiled tightly. "But thanks anyway."

"Just worried about you, old man." Jose stuffed the garters back in his pocket.

"Sorry for snapping at you. Having someone try to run you off the road has left me a little on edge." He backed toward the one-way mirror, grateful they'd both walked away unharmed.

Wade stepped closer. "Are you okay?"

His swim buddy looked straight into his eyes, no doubt checking pupils to make sure they were equal, which is exactly what Liam would have done. That medic training came in handy.

"I'm good." Liam brushed aside the concern. "Really. The Jeep did its job keeping us safe."

"Us?" Jose's eyebrows shot up. His eyes went to the one-way mirror framing Rachel seated across from Sylvia. "Hey now, wasn't she with one of the search and rescue canine units back in the Bahamas?"

Liam nodded, the heat, the dust, the intensity of that time rolling over him again. "Great memory you've got there, Cuervo."

"Memorable mission." Rocha nodded. "You kept in touch with her all this time and didn't mention it? I do believe my feelings are hurt."

Before Liam could answer, Jose continued, "But your Jeep. How did you even drive it the rest of the way here after you got hit?"

As they tag-teamed him with questions, he just let it keep rolling. It was easier than answering, and it left him free to study Rachel and try to figure out why his teammates had been called in as well. "Guess it's time to buy a new car."

Rocha dipped his head closer. "Really, dude, what's going on here?"

Was it even possible to whisper softly enough not to be heard in this place? Not really. And not that it should matter. Why was he suddenly second-guessing his decision to contact the OSI?

Since he'd found out the car chasing them was Rachel's. Something he hadn't discovered until after he placed the call to Sylvia. Whoever had accessed that vehicle had an in on base. Security was tight at the gates and a pass was needed to get through. It wasn't as if just anybody could have picked up her SUV.

Although he still would have ended up here, even if they hadn't been attacked. He just needed to be even more on guard since somehow, someone on base had been involved in the attack.

Monitoring the two women through the glass, he chose his words for his friends carefully. "Rachel's had some trouble with a stalker." Even thinking about those threats to her had his hands fisting at his sides. "She contacted me today for help, and the next thing we knew, someone tried to run us off the road."

Wade nodded slowly. "Okay, fine, so why come here instead of going to the police?"

"There's a military friend of hers involved, and the civilian cops haven't been much help to Rachel so far."

Jose scratched his buzz cut. "And why bring her to one of your ex-girlfriends for questioning? An especially hot ex-girlfriend, I might add."

"Sylvia and I had an amicable parting of the ways. It was never serious." And by now he was a frickin' pro at how to handle a breakup.

Time to change the subject until he had a better handle on what the hell was going on.

His attention shifted back to Rachel. Her back stiff, her hand resting on her dog's head, she looked strong and wary.

But alive. And he intended to do whatever it took to keep her that way.

~~~

If he had his way, they would all be dead before sunrise.

But that wasn't a wise strategy. And above all, he was a man who planned his next battle move very carefully.

Pitching a paperweight from hand to hand without so much as a glance, he studied the row of computer screens hooked to surveillance in the OSI building. This wasn't his office, but no one would question his being here. He had access anywhere he wanted on this base.

Headphones in place, he listened to the interrogation in progress between Special Agent Sylvia Cramer and Rachel Flores. While on another screen he watched the video footage of the Flores chick breaking into McCabe's Jeep earlier. When that tape had come to his attention, he'd backtracked through video feed until he saw her ditch her car. His people were supposed to have handled the whole situation, damn it.

How had such a well-planned operation become a cluster fuck so quickly because of one little lieutenant who barely had his head on straight?

Discrediting Brandon Harris's claims had been easy enough at first. Although who could have predicted Harris would find such a persistent champion in a lady dog trainer? A lady dog trainer who apparently had some connections. But he refused to let them or anyone else stop him.

His own connections were far more extensive, and he wouldn't hesitate to use them. He just needed to find more competent resources than the idiots he'd sent to torch Rachel's apartment. They'd gone rogue in trying to run McCabe's Jeep off the road and into the ocean. A staged accident was one thing. But gunfire in the middle of traffic, for God's sake? All mistakes they would pay for. People only acted under his orders. Going rogue was not acceptable.

He just needed a little more time to find Brandon Harris. The lieutenant hadn't gone home as he was supposed to—where he would have died in what the coroner would have written off as suicide. In one afternoon, two seemingly separate incidents would have taken care of Harris and the Flores woman.

Except now things were more complicated. Complicated, but not unsalvageable. It wasn't difficult to arrange accidents, better planned this time. He'd done it before for the greater good, to protect the weak, just as he'd done for his mother and younger brother.

His father had been a falling-down drunk. It had started with after-work mixed drinks to ease the tension of his corporate job, and his mom didn't say anything because his old man was nicer drunk. Or at least he was in the beginning. But then cocktails turned into shots, and it wasn't just after supper. Through the whole weekend. During lunch. Until his old man lost his job, which gave him an excuse to start drinking earlier, once he rolled his hungover ass out bed.

And he wasn't so nice anymore.

Once they were the same size, he'd pushed his father down the stairs hard enough to break his neck. Cops hadn't questioned it. Even if they were suspicious, they'd been called over a dozen times by the neighbors reporting domestic disputes. The police had likely looked the other way when it came to an abusive husband who happened to have stumbled down the steps.

Family secured, he'd left his mother and brother behind to join the military. No boot-camp sergeant could dish up anything even half as tough as what his drunken father had doled out with his fists, belt, electrical cords, whatever was in reach.

Nothing scared him anymore—except the prospect of losing power over his life again.

He'd survived wars, put himself through college, risen through the ranks by grit rather than pedigree. He wouldn't give up all he'd achieved. This country *needed* what he had to offer.

So he had to keep this contained and low-key, ensuring his plans for the international satellite summit went smoothly this week. Too much was at stake. Too many lives.

A handful of people—Harris, McCabe, Flores—were dispensable for the greater good. And he had two of them here under this roof right now, which didn't mean jack until he shut up Harris. And Rachel Flores was the connection to figuring out where the guy had disappeared to after his counseling session today. In a way, it was a damn lucky thing his people hadn't succeeded in their ill-conceived plan to run the Jeep into the ocean.

Shoving away from the console, he tossed aside the headset. He couldn't just sit here, cowering behind the techno equipment. He needed to be in the field, evaluating the enemies who could ruin his whole battle plan when he was so close to the goal. He needed to see everyone close-up, to read their eyes. He wouldn't interfere in the process by stepping into Sylvia Cramer's interview.

That actually could draw undue attention, not to mention piss her off. She could handle that end.

He strode down the hall, sparsely populated this late, which made the duo at the corner all the more conspicuous. Captain Bernard stood with the base commander, Colonel Mary Zogby. They exchanged salutes, as expected, and he kept right on walking. He and Mary avoided the hell out of each other, so it wouldn't look at all strange for him to make tracks past her.

As long as he kept his cool, nobody would think twice about him watching the interview in progress. His assignment here might only be temporary until the new satellite project was successfully launched. But there was only one other person on the base as high ranking as himself, and then Mary Zogby one rank below him.

His combat boots pounded carpet all the way to the observation room. McCabe, Rocha, James—they all snapped to attention, standing chin up, shoulders back, chest out, eyes forward.

And hell yeah, the rush of power that brought never faded. He was in control, respected. Obeyed.

"At ease, gentlemen," he said, stepping deeper into the room, Special Agent Cramer and that annoying Flores woman only a window away.

McCabe made eye contact first. "Good evening, General. What can I do for you, sir?"

Chapter 6

LIAM RELAXED—SOMEWHAT—AS MUCH AS ANYONE could in front of General Ted Sullivan. The gray-haired veteran was a by-the-book workaholic with a reputation for running a tight ship. And he was clearly in control of whatever was going on here tonight. He'd already sent Wade Rocha and Jose James to another area to speak with Captain Bernard. Although why they had been called eluded him.

Now he stood in the small observation room with the general, waiting for Rachel's interview to end. Liam respected the senior ranking official in some ways—for the most part, the general knew his shit, and no question, the guy could keep up on a training swim and run.

Except after a while working with him, it became apparent the guy didn't get nuances. And there was no humor, no fun, and definitely no "marry one, screw one, kill one" games.

While crossing paths with Sullivan made this temporary stint at Patrick Air Force Base stressful, there was also a certain level of peace in knowing there wasn't a chance of anything going wrong with the summit on this guy's watch.

The micromanaging general wouldn't allow it.

Which explained why he was here. The man almost never slept. And that could bode well for Rachel, which was all that mattered now.

Captain Bernard rejoined them quietly—no surprise, since a renowned butt-kisser would never be far from the highest-ranking person on the premises. Colonel Zogby stepped into the doorway and swept the room with an assessing glance before she stepped back out.

Sullivan leaned forward and punched in a code on the panel by the door. Sound flooded the observation room—Sylvia Cramer interrogating Rachel.

"Let's go over what Brandon Harris told you one more time to make sure I have this right," Sylvia said, even though it was clear the smooth agent wasn't missing a thing. "Where were you when he first shared his suspicions? At his place?"

"At a dog park," Rachel answered without hesitation, although her espresso-dark eyes turned flinty at the implication her meeting might have been more than professional or even casual friendship.

Something he hadn't considered. But he should have. Damn it, she clouded his thinking.

On the other side of the window, Rachel held her ground. "And Brandon wasn't in the car—my car—that tried to run us off the bridge."

"How can you be sure?" Sylvia pressed. "It was dark. You were busy ducking bullets, even steering the Jeep."

A few feet away, General Sullivan pressed a palm to the wall by the one-way mirror and leaned closer, intent on Rachel's answer. His eyes all but bored through the glass into both women.

There was intense. And then there was *in-tense*.

"I've worked in stressful situations before with search and rescue missions." A hint of irritation flashed in her eyes, but she held her cool, stroking Disco's head.

"Shifting rubble in the aftermath of an earthquake. Pitch-black woods in a storm, looking for a missing toddler. Tracking escaped convicts. I could go on and on. But the point is, I'm as sure as I can possibly be. Brandon Harris was not in the car that rammed us."

"Fair enough." Sylvia swept a hand along her immaculate auburn hair. "If we go with the assumption he wasn't in the vehicle, then who else could be gunning for you?"

"Who else?" Rachel's ability to hide her frustration with the extended questioning seemed to be wearing thin—which was no doubt Sylvia's intention. "Who else besides the person in the military that I'm accusing of espionage? Individuals who could be in a crap ton of trouble if they're discovered and Brandon's story turns out to be true?"

"Even if Harris's ramblings are accurate, there could still be another explanation for the threats against you, and we need to explore that. So think, please."

"Besides Brandon? Completely separate from this…?" She blinked fast. "I hadn't considered that."

Liam frowned, stepping alongside the general to follow more closely. As much as he wanted to be in there with Rachel, wrapping himself around her like an armored tank if need be, Sylvia was making headway here.

"Okay," Sylvia said, "assuming it's not, what about the other people you've helped?"

Rachel's lips went tight and thin with barely constrained anger. "Why does everyone assume that just because a military service member is suffering from PTSD, he or she is automatically going to start killing random people?"

"There's no need to get defensive. I'm only exploring every possibility, so truly, you can calm down."

"I will… when you stop patronizing me."

Sylvia's eyebrows shot upward, only a brief break in her cool before she smoothed her features again. "My apologies."

"Apology accepted." Her fingers resumed stroking her dog's head, something he was fast realizing she did to calm herself. "It just freaks me out to think of how they would react to this kind of inquisition. They've already been through so much without having you hassle them."

"Understood." Sylvia thumbed a smudge on the side of her iPad absently. Or so it seemed. Nothing about this woman appeared anything but calculated. "Let's change gears and go back to my earlier question about possible suspects. How are you supporting yourself? I don't imagine there's much money in therapy dogs for disabled vets."

Liam angled closer to the window, wondering why Sylvia had backed off questioning Rachel about Harris when it was obvious she knew more than she was sharing. Had the general picked up on that as well?

"I teach dog obedience classes and I'm training service dogs. It brings in enough to let me do what I want with my life." Rachel shook her loose curls back over her shoulders with a dry smile. "You may have noticed I'm not exactly into haute couture."

Grinning back, Sylvia twisted one pearl earring. "And how do you afford the dogs?"

"My animals are all rescues from shelters." She frowned, her eyes darting from side to side as her mind appeared to race. "Except…"

"What?" Sylvia pressed, her hand falling to her lap.

"Not all of the dogs are owner surrenders or strays. Some have been seized due to neglect or abuse by so-called humans—scum of the earth, actually. Charges were pressed and sometimes evidence of further crimes was found in the homes."

"Ahhh..." Sylvia nodded. "And those people could have a grudge."

"Do you want me to make a list? Sadly, it could well be a long one."

"Eventually, yes, but right now, keep talking. Follow where your mind was headed. You'd be surprised what comes up when we don't overanalyze." No question, the interrogator had a knack for putting people at ease, which made them spill more.

Rachel leaned forward, her fingers gliding down Disco's spine as the dog stayed immovable by her side. "Some of the dogs are what you would call pit bulls."

"What I would *call*?"

"*Pit bull* is a catchall phrase for a number of different breeds—bull terriers, Staffordshire terriers, American bulldogs. People use the phrase *pit bull* pejoratively. But bulldogs make great therapy dogs because they bond so strongly with people. There are owners out there who will abuse that bond and turn them into fighters."

"These people wouldn't be happy about your taking their livelihood. Dog fighting is often tied to gang activity. Could one of them be out for revenge or trying to get an animal back?"

"That's certainly possible... but I'm not able to give you anything helpful there. I know the history of the dogs I take in, but I don't know names of their original owners."

Sylvia shifted her attention from her iPad to her briefcase, beside the chair. "Relay what you can of the adoptions and I'll track the rest. I have… resources." She passed over a notepad. "Now you can make that list of the names and details you do know." She smiled dryly. "Unless you have an issue with my hassling any of them with uncomfortable questions?"

"Hassle away." Rachel scooped up the pen and paper, not in the least ruffled. Damn, she was amazing. "I'm not going to object to any heat you want to bring to an animal abuser."

"But you don't think it's one of them."

"I wouldn't presume to do your job."

"My job is to gather impressions."

Rachel pressed the notepad to her knees. "Then my impression would be that this doesn't fit the kind of retaliation I would expect. They would retrieve their dogs and put them back to work, not poison them. And the anonymous calls—"

"What exactly was said during the threatening phone calls?"

"Things like 'back off' and 'you don't know who you're taking on'…" Her voice trailed away. "All threats that could have been said by anyone. The timing just seemed too coincidental."

"I'm not discounting your fears. But we'll still need to speak to the airman—once we can locate him."

"He's actually a first lieutenant."

"Right, of course," Sylvia conceded with a professional smile. "I can promise you the interview will be handled compassionately."

"Thank you." Her face didn't broadcast confidence.

"Meanwhile, you need protection because someone, somewhere, for whatever reason, truly is gunning for you." Sylvia pushed to her feet and stepped closer to the one-way mirror, staring straight through. She tapped her ear where her tiny earbud radio was hidden in case someone needed to feed her information during the process. Nothing had been left to chance.

"If you'll excuse me, Rachel, I need to step out and have a word with General Sullivan."

—⁓—

"Cat, are you ready to go back home?" Brandon asked, leaning against his truck.

The acrid stench of smoke still blanketed the air, even though the fire department had long ago doused the blaze on Rachel's block. He'd read an article once that said smells evoked the strongest memories. Damn straight. With each smoldering inhale, images of bomb sites mushroomed inside his skull.

The burned-out hulls of town houses stared back at him with vacant black eyes for windows. Hollow. Charred insides weakened and vulnerable from a sucker punch they couldn't possibly have seen coming.

He understood the feeling. His stomach rolled, acid eating away at the fast-food double cheeseburger he'd bolted down earlier.

And then on his next breath, a hint of honeysuckle mingled good with the bad. Settled his stomach. Chased away a couple of those crappy memories.

"Brandon?" she said softly. "Whenever you're ready, I'm ready."

It was nearly midnight now, and the neighborhood

was winding down from the mayhem of fire trucks and
newscasters. But still, Cat's serenity wouldn't have
faded if a parade flooded the whole city block.

He appreciated her peacefulness. They'd just hung
out together for most of the ride. She hadn't pushed him
to talk, talk, talk as everybody else did. Yeah, he knew
his silences could be long. Creepy even, according to
the therapist who had gently pointed them out. But he
was working his way back. He needed time. Cat seemed
to get that.

Right now he needed time to get over his frustration
at not finding Rachel here. Most people would have
called the cops, but that hadn't gone so well for him
lately. He didn't know what to do next. She wasn't here.
And she wasn't answering her phone. He shouldn't have
told her everything. Well, not everything, but all that he
had. He'd been selfish. All caught up in the talk therapy
bull crap his therapist pushed for. He'd been a jumbled
mess, huddled up at home with his dog. Then Rachel
had shown up to check in on Harley…

The next thing he'd known, he was spilling his guts.

Better from now on to keep his mouth shut. He pivoted toward the truck and reached for her door just as—

Pop. A gunshot split the air. The noise sliced through
his brain and sent his body on autopilot.

He tackled Catriona, tucking to the side to catch the
brunt of the fall with his body before rolling on top of
her. His arms convulsed around her, his heart ramping up until he could feel it slam against her soft back.
Concrete bit into his knees and his cheek as he stared
under the row of vehicles and realized…

He wasn't in Afghanistan anymore.

That noise hadn't been gunfire. Just someone shutting a car door. God, he was a mess.

Rolling off her, Brandon lay on his back and stared up at the stars. Time passed and he wasn't sure how much. But since he already looked like an idiot, why not go all out? Besides, he wasn't sure his legs would hold him yet anyway. At least they were between cars and apparently not attracting any attention.

Eventually his heart stopped jackhammering in his ears so loud and he could hear the world around him. He could hear Catriona. Her even breaths, not the least bit disturbed. And then the scent of honeysuckle filled him, engulfed him, until he wanted to curl up and sleep for a decade.

He felt the cold muzzle of his dog against his hand. His palm curved over Harley's head, stroking, bringing him the rest of the way back into the moment.

Jacking one knee up, he turned his head sideways to look at Catriona for the first time. She sat cross-legged on the concrete beside him, not showing any other signs that she'd been body-slammed by someone nearly double her weight just minutes before. Only her shirt was askew and showing her bra strap—

His eyes hitched on the pale pink strip of satin, and hell if he didn't get an erection. Right then. Right there. At the most unexpected and worst time, he got his first case of wood since he'd returned from the Middle East.

Shit. Shit. *Shit.*

He sat up sharply, dropping his arm in his lap to hide the evidence. "Are you okay? Did I break anything when I wigged out?"

"I'm fine," she said simply.

"Aren't you going to ask if I'm all right?"

"Obviously, you're not."

"And you're okay with that? You aren't worried I'm going to go postal on you?"

"Should I worry?"

He shook his head. "I'm okay now."

"Good." She shoved to her feet and straightened her shirt. "How about I drive us back and you sleep on my sofa? You may think you're okay, but you look tapped out to me. Why risk driving?"

Pushing to his feet, he drew in deep honeysuckle-scented breaths and didn't even bother arguing.

Who the hell was General Sullivan, and why was he here?

Rachel was officially freaked out to have warranted a general's attention. Except then, he hadn't bothered to come in and interview her. He'd been called away on some emergency. She'd merely heard his gravelly voice speaking with Special Agent Cramer just beyond the opening doors, issuing orders before he was called away.

And then she'd been shuttled off to what Liam had called "some place safe."

For now.

She hadn't felt this claustrophobic since she'd been trapped in a mine after she and Disco once located a lost hiker. They'd waited for three hours underground, trapped by a rotten beam that had given way. Those three hours had seemed shorter than the three minutes she'd spent inside this "safe" location.

After her interview with Special Agent Sylvia Cramer

had concluded, two official-looking cars had escorted them to base housing packed with rows of tan stucco homes. On the outer edges of the community, they'd actually pulled into the driveway of one of those homes.

She'd been surprised, expecting they would be sent to one of the temporary lodging facilities, more like a hotel or condo. Or housed in some vault in Sylvia Cramer's top-secret bat cave. But this was a no-kidding three-bedroom house.

Not that it appeared anyone actually lived here.

It carried more of a model-home look and smell, with lots of cherrywood furniture that still sported a highly polished new sheen. The matchy-matchy blue and green striped sofa and wingbacks completed the decor. No personal photos. Stock framed images of beach sunsets and airplanes hung on the walls. Disco sniffed the dried moss around a potted silk palm tree.

Apparently General Sullivan had made special arrangements for them to use temporary lodgings on base with security guards outside, offering her protection until Brandon Harris could be located and his story looked into more deeply. As far as she was concerned, here was as good as anywhere else.

And Liam was here. They were linked in this now, and while she was still as afraid on base as off, she did trust Liam.

Which was strange, considering she'd known him for all of three weeks, six months ago.

She turned slowly in the living room. "So these are distinguished visitors' quarters."

"All the basics you could need are here—food, sodas," he announced, pulling open a drawer on a sideboard.

Except rather than place mats, he revealed, "They've even got shoulder boards and rank paraphernalia for any general in any branch of the services. Pick a star."

Sure enough, one-star up to four-star ranks lined the inside of the drawer. "This is so surreal. I feel like I actually am in some TV show, with our protective detail outside. Except in the movies, room service always turns out to be a bad guy, or the villains kill the guards."

"No one's getting through to you." His hands fell to her shoulders. "I won't let them."

He stood so close she could smell the coffee on his breath, and wow, but she was suddenly jonesing for a taste. She should step away. *Should.* But didn't.

Rachel soaked up the warm comfort, the strong sensuality of his hands. The heat of him seared through her simple cotton shirt. "I appreciate what you've done for me today. I sprung this on you without warning and hauled you into a nightmare… I'm sorry."

"I'm glad you came to me."

Her heart sped up. Was he going to kiss her again, and to hell with the consequences? She could see the memory of that earlier kiss scrolling through his eyes.

"Rachel?"

"Yeah." Was that breathy voice hers?

"Can I get you something to eat or drink?"

She exhaled hard. "I'm good. Thanks. Agent Cramer gave me enough Cokes to keep me awake all night."

Backing away, he resumed his scoping out of the place. "You held up well in there. I know that had to be tough, getting grilled." He played with lamp shades and peered out windows. "But she was only covering all her bases."

Looking in lamps? Did he think the place might be bugged? That seemed extreme, but then she couldn't have predicted anything that had happened to her recently.

She trailed behind him. "It's tough knowing who to trust. I can't blame her for doing her job." She leaned closer to whisper. "Doesn't it bother you that someone took my car from base? Brandon insists there's a mole in his chain of command, and yet we're here, on base?"

He shrugged. "Well, since the FBI and CIA aren't listening to anything either of you has to say, this is as good as it gets, unless we strike out on our own. Regardless, I intend to keep you in sight at all times."

On their own. Alone. Together. The notion sent a shiver of possibility through her. But it also brought a reminder that they had guards a simple shout away. While the briefest stroke of his gaze turned her inside out, sparking barely banked fires from their kiss earlier, there wasn't a chance of testing out one of those beds together. One wayward noisy moan and they could have guns whipping out left and right. This place might be large, but it was far from private.

"You're right. Of course." She stepped away self-consciously until the backs of her legs bumped the sofa. She dropped to sit on the edge, crossing her arms over her tingling tight breasts.

He searched her eyes and she forced herself not to fidget at the heat that gathered between her legs. An answering flame glinted in his green eyes a second before he pivoted away fast and walked to the flat-screen television mounted on the wall over a hutch. He picked up the remote control from the cabinet and flipped through channels until settling on an old John Wayne war movie.

He wanted to watch TV? Now? Really? She wanted to pull her hair and shout in frustration.

Turning back to her, he tossed the remote on the coffee table and crouched in front of her, one hand on the arm-rest, so close without touching her. "Maybe we should talk about what happened earlier, on the roadside."

Ah, now she understood about the television. He was making it easier for them to talk. Giving at least a sense of privacy, in case there were listening devices.

Although she wasn't so sure she particularly wanted to discuss the kiss. Like that was going to make her feel better? Let's dissect the kiss. Talk about the kiss. Think about the kiss until she died from frustration. That would end all their troubles.

Her chin tipped. "Why would that be? Unless it was important. Which it wasn't. It was…"

"Adrenaline."

"Of course." Which pissed her off, because she could have sworn the kiss meant more than that. Who cared if someone was listening? "Do you go around kissing women every time you get revved up from a mission? Because now that I think about it, last time we were together, adrenaline got pumping and you kissed me, so you're right, it must mean nothing."

He grinned. Actually grinned, damn it, as he shifted onto the sofa to sit close beside her, his leg pressed against hers. "And you don't get a rush after a mission?"

Her mouth went dry. "This isn't funny."

His smile faded. "You're right. I just need to know one thing. Are you having a relationship with Brandon Harris?"

Had that been what Liam's kiss was about? Some

he-man, jealous need to stake his claim on her? Not very enlightened, but God, it made her want to grab a fistful of his shirt and haul him in to put her stamp on him. "Brandon's not my type."

"And what would be your type?" He didn't angle closer, but he might as well as have. His presence reached out to her all the same.

Distance would be nice. Now. She reached for her old safety net for putting space between herself and disquieting feelings cropping up at a totally inappropriate time.

So she threw a dead body between them. Or at least the memory of one.

"Are you asking about my high school boyfriend?" She'd told Liam about Caden back in the Bahamas in hopes of scaring him off, and she was doing the same now. Liam had a way of getting too close, making her want to risk too much.

"Rachel, if I had wanted to know that I would have asked. We were talking about the kiss in the car. Whether it was important or adrenaline. Seems a logical conversational leap to me. Unless you have something else we can do to pass the time, other than talk."

Her skin flamed to life, her lips ached... and her mind shouted there were guards outside the door. "Are you serious?"

He tugged a strand of her hair. "You brought up the guy in your past for a reason, so you must have something you need to say."

She curled her feet up under her, the Scotchgarded fabric itchy against her skin. "I met him while he was volunteering at the animal shelter where my mom worked."

"Sounds like an altruistic sort of fella." He slid his arm around her shoulder, bringing her closer to him.

So they could talk softer and more freely? Maybe. And that provided all the excuse she needed to do exactly what she wanted.

She laid her head on Liam's shoulder, the past wrapping around her with a squeeze to her heart that made her wonder if she'd brought this up as much to give herself distance as to push away Liam. Except here he was, even closer to her than before.

"Caden—that was his name—was doing community service to work off some major speeding tickets."

"Not what I expected to hear about him." His voice heated the top of her head.

"You didn't expect me to go for the bad-boy type?"

His knuckles stroked along her arm. "I'm not sure what to say here without pissing you off."

"How about be honest."

The air hung heavy between them as he seemed to mull over the best way to dole out that honesty. There was only the sound of bullfrogs and a low mumble beyond the front door as their guards conversed. Disco finished his sniffing ritual and settled on the floor in front of the sofa with a doggy huff.

"Let's just say that every time you mentioned him in the past, there was such… hell, I don't know… *adoration* in your voice, I assumed he was a saint."

Adoration? She would have said it was love he heard. And yet somehow she shied away from searching deeper into what he said, as if flinching away from a finger poking a bruise.

"Caden was the epitome of high school bad boy who

wanted to turn his life around. He joined the military hoping it would give him some structure, help him get his life together."

"How 'not together' was his life?"

"Drinking, some drugs." She'd broken up with him once when she found a bag of pot under his seat during one of their dates. That he would risk getting her arrested… God, she'd been mad and heartbroken. "His parents were well-off, his dad drank, so he did too. Not that I'm making excuses for him. He wouldn't have wanted that. Caden did a quiet stint in rehab and he'd really turned things around for himself. For us."

"You loved him."

She'd told Liam that before, but finally she heard an understanding in his voice. He got that it wasn't just adoration, or some frivolous high school crush. She'd found and lost her soul mate and that still left a void in her today.

Finally, Liam seemed to believe and accept that about her. While there was victory in that, there was also a loss. Because now he would really understand she was unattainable. Or her heart was, anyway…

But her body?

"I just wish…" She scrubbed her wrist over her dry eyes, which had long ago been cried out of tears, but as she sat here curled up in Liam's arms, her emotions felt closer to the surface somehow. "Everything just feels fresh right now. He'd been in the service for a year when he went overseas."

The image of Caden in his uniform stayed just as clear in her mind as if she'd pulled his framed photo from under the album of high school prom memories. He'd said he joined up for her, to show her how committed he was to making a future with her, one he'd built and not one his parents bought for him.

She swallowed down the pride along with tears and regrets. "He got captured at a checkpoint. Recon teams searched for him and finally located him. By the time they could launch an offensive to rescue him, he'd been beheaded."

"God, Rachel," he said softly, tucking her closer, his other hand linking fingers with hers. "I am so sorry, for him and for you."

She let the silence stretch through half a commercial on TV for some deodorant until her brain cleared of the lingering grief enough to put words together again.

"Thank you, but I'm past needing sympathy." Although the warm firm grip of his thumb massaging the palm of her hand felt so very good right now. "I've done my best to channel what happened into something positive. That's part of what got me into search and rescue. A sense of how vital minutes, even seconds, can be in saving a life. Now I feel like a huge cop-out for backing away from the mission. But since the Bahamas, I'm just… hollow."

"That earthquake cleanup, the rescues, it was an especially rough gig."

Her eyes stayed dry but her throat was clogging fast. "Maybe I'm the one who needs a therapy dog."

"Search and rescue can take a lot out of a person."

"You're still working." She traced a finger around his name tag stitched to his uniform.

"I'm a robot."

She snorted on a laugh. God, she'd forgotten how he knew just when to roll out his sense of humor. "Hardly."

"And neither are you."

Humor and wisdom wrapped up in one hot guy. Not fair. "I let my brain get muddied when I met Brandon. So much of him reminded me of Caden." She glanced at Liam, close enough to notice a hint of a cowlick in his dark blond hair that seemed endearing somehow. "I don't have romantic feelings for Brandon. But there was still this sense that if I could help him, I was helping Caden. Does that make sense?"

"Completely. My buddy Hugh Franco always took on the riskiest assignments. He had this frenzy, like if he could save enough people, somehow his wife and kid would come back to life."

"Yeah, that pretty much sums it up. And I really thought the therapy and the dog was all working for Brandon. He seemed clearer. Not exactly happy, but focused. He started making plans for the future. He was building an agility course in his backyard to exercise his dog." She settled back into his arms more at ease now, as if they were genuinely curled together to talk and watch John Wayne save the day on TV. "I just can't reconcile in my head that he's anything but honest—and while he may not be one hundred percent steady, my gut tells me he's legit, in spite of all the PTSD jamming the wires. The same gut that led me through SAR missions… You understand what I mean, right?"

"I do. Absolutely."

They had so much in common, something that had really thrown her six months ago. She'd been drawn to Liam—beyond just wanting to boink his brains out. But all that in-common stuff had muddied the waters and scared her to death. Still did. Not many men understood about her work. Or rather what she used to do for a living.

Although he totally got what she did now too, and why she'd gone this new route with her life. He was scary good. "Why did you want to know so much about Brandon anyway? Do you still suspect him too?"

"I was jealous."

So she'd been right about the kiss earlier. "There's nothing going on between Brandon and me. There's no reason for you to be jealous of him."

"Of Brandon. Caden. Any guy in your past." He flipped her ponytail over her shoulder and cupped her neck, his touch sending tingling currents to the tips of her toes. "When have I not made it clear I think you're sexy as hell and intriguing to boot? I want you. No news flash there. I made it clear the moment when we pulled off the road, hell, when I just held on to you in my kitchen. My feelings haven't dimmed in the past six months."

The intensity of his words, of his voice, his eyes, everything about him, couldn't be denied. To be wanted this much was a heady thing. "I'm starting to understand how you talked three women into marrying you."

Chapter 7

LIAM TOOK IN RACHEL'S SMOKY BROWN EYES AND knew he could easily kiss her right now. He wanted to kiss her, feel the soft and familiar texture of her mouth fitting to his. Even if it turned out someone might be listening, no one was watching inside. He'd been promised that much at least.

So that kiss would probably go further, leading them into one of those bedrooms together. If they even made it that far, before ripping each other's clothes off.

He'd burned to have her since he first saw her lowered from a helicopter in the Bahamas. But he wanted more than one night. If he leaped on this opportunity—leaped on her—she could very well roll out a list of regrets in the morning. He wouldn't toss away this second chance to be with her.

Although his need to keep her at arm's length and in constant sight made for a serious pain in the libido. He needed help to rein himself in tonight for his sake, for her sake—and for the sake of any listening devices that may have been planted around this place. The television would muffle their voices, but it wasn't as foolproof a trick as they made it out to be in the movies.

Talking about his ex-wives should be as libido dousing as jumping straight into icy Alaska waters. "Three wives, but not at the same time."

She rolled her rich brown eyes. "Minor technicality."

He rested his chin on her head, breathing in the scent of his soap on her body. "I had my burnout time too, a while back. During my Army Ranger days. In those days, though, it wasn't acceptable to talk about it. PTSD was a career-ender. So most guys drank, quit, or one way or another self-destructed."

Easing back, she forced him to meet her gaze. "Since you haven't quit or self-destructed, is this your way of telling me you're an alcoholic?"

"Not hardly." He glanced sideways at her, although it would sure be easy to lose himself in the intoxication of raw sex with Rachel. "I managed to get a career change that helped ease up my stress level."

She snorted, so magnificently natural and without pretense. "You call working search and rescue a stress reducer?" Rachel leaned back against his chest, his arms sliding naturally around until his hands rested on her stomach. "You *are* seriously screwed up."

"No argument there." The echoes of old explosions, images of friends he'd lost, flashed through his mind, setting him more on edge than ever. "Saving on occasion felt good. Although it still didn't keep me from sabotaging myself in three marriages. So I didn't get off scot-free. Or as you so eloquently said, I am seriously screwed up. Not very technical, but apt."

"Liam," she said softly, but firmly. "You can't blame yourself for everything. Back in the Bahamas you told me that wife number two was unfaithful."

Cheated with everything in pants, anytime he was deployed or on base. Or hell, she could sneak in a quickie cheat when he stepped out to pick up pizza.

Disco yawned, stretching and inching forward until

he head-butted Liam's leg. He patted the spot next to them on the sofa and the dog jumped up. He scratched the Labrador's sleek nose. "I was no picnic to live with."

"That doesn't excuse her cheating on you—" Her voice rose sharply, then she touched her lips as if realizing she'd spoken too loud. She continued, softer this time, "If she wanted out, she should have done so honorably."

"You're right." He leaned back to give himself space from the tempting scent of her. "Hey, let's give this a rest. The day's sucked enough already. And all the dating websites say it's bad form to ramble on about the ex. Or in my case, exes."

"We're past the initial dating stage… not that we've actually had a date." She touched his hand lightly and she might as well have stroked up his leg for how hot and hard that one simple contact made him. "But we've kissed each other and even faced a gunman together. So talking about your ex-wives doesn't qualify as bad first-date etiquette. And honestly, I want to know."

Her eyes brimmed with curiosity and something else he couldn't place but made him certain he needed more of that distance. Fast.

"My first wife—Whitney—and I met in high school." The words came easier than he'd expected. "We mistook puppy love for the real thing. When I enlisted, we didn't want to be apart, so we eloped. Of course then I went to basic and ranger training and deployed, so we spent no time together anyway."

He reached for Disco again before he registered the thought, and sure enough the dog rested his chin on Liam's knee. "Once I got home, I was a mess from combat and she'd been left alone in a strange city with no support system. Even with counseling from our pastor... we'd grown in different directions."

"I'm sorry, Liam." She rubbed his hand in much the same way as he'd stroked Disco's head in comforting circles. "First love is special."

"At least Whitney's second marriage has gone a helluva lot better than mine. She married a cop." And he was happy for her. She deserved better than she'd gotten first go-round. "Whitney was already well versed in the stress after being married to me, but she says at least her new husband's home at night to have supper with her and their three kids."

"You keep in touch with each other?" She blinked in surprise.

"Christmas and birthdays, she sends cards and photos. That therapy at least helped us part amicably."

"And her husband's cool with that?"

"I'm no threat to what they've got."

"Oh." Her eyes went even wider. "Okay, then. You don't love your *first* wife anymore. And what about the next one... the bitch... um, I mean the cheater."

Her scowl made him grin.

"My second wife—Priscilla—I married on the rebound." He stretched an arm along the back of the sofa, just to prove to himself he could be close to her now, almost touch her, and still restrain himself. "Huge mistake, by the way."

"So I've heard."

"We met in a bar. She came home with me that night and stayed." Not his finest or smartest move, and he wouldn't make excuses. "We ended up in front of a justice of the peace a month later, and partied our asses off when I was in town. Problem was, for her, the party kept right on going when I left. And it wasn't like she fell for someone else. Any guy would do. She told me the affairs were just about sex, scratching an itch, that her heart belonged to me." Priscilla still left him drunken messages to this day, no matter how many times his phone number changed with moves.

"That had to hurt," she whispered.

"It pissed me off," he hissed back automatically. "Talk about a double standard. Can you imagine if a guy said that? Tried to write off multiple affairs as scratching an itch?" He shook his head. "Bullshit."

"So you really never cheated? Not on any of your wives?"

"Never." He chuckled lowly. "I just married all my women."

Shifting, she cupped his face in her hands. "Hello? I'm not laughing."

Her cool, soft skin felt so damn good against him, too good. He wrapped his fingers around her wrists and eased her arms down slowly. Restraint. He could—he would—hold back tonight even though the more he talked about his past screwups, the more he wanted to forget.

"So, on to wife number three. I was determined to get it right that time." But he wasn't known for his relationship savvy. Like now, when he still held on to Rachel's hands, thumbing the speeding pulse along her wrists. "I mean, hell, two divorces behind me? I had to accept my share of the blame."

"How did you meet…?"

"Dawn? Her name's Dawn." He pinched the bridge of his nose, right over the building headache. "I figured since I'd met my last wife in a bar and it hadn't gone well at all, I should try something completely different."

"And that would be?"

"We met in church."

She laughed. Clapped a hand over her mouth and leaned into him. Then laughed again between her fingers, an all-out sexy and uninhibited sound that filled the room with musicality. "You went to church to pick up chicks?"

The way she said it made him sound calculating, but he couldn't argue with her point. So he shrugged it off the way he always did with things that made him uncomfortable. Jokes. Sarcasm. Anything to avoid something that dug too deep. "Hey, I'm baring my soul here and you're making fun of me. That's harsh."

She swatted his chest. "But seriously, you went to church to get laid."

"To find a wife. In those days—"

"In those days?" She crinkled her nose. "You make yourself sound ancient, when I know full well you're not. You're all of what…?"

"Thirty-eight."

"To my thirty-two, and I prefer to think of myself as young, thank you very much."

He hated talking about his age. Age was different in the military, when a man's useful years evaporated as fast as a pro athlete's—and the stakes were life and death rather than a touchdown.

"Fine. My point is, for me, it was always about getting married then." He folded his arms over his chest.

"Why is that so surprising? There are men out there who want to get married and have kids."

"Do you have children?"

"Nope. Never worked out for me." His biggest regret after each divorce, because he'd wanted kids. And his biggest relief, because he wouldn't be upsetting tiny lives through his own failures. "The first two times, we weren't married all that long. The third, it seemed like I was always deployed or out on maneuver right during her, uh, peak fertility time." His ex had even busted the bank on Victoria's Secret lingerie and froufrou heels… although best to leave that part out of the discussion. "We were even talking about going the artificial-insemination route—using some of my frozen swimmers. But the marriage fell apart before we got around to thawing them."

"And what happened to break the two of you up—if you don't mind my asking something so personal?"

That she would ask meant a lot to him, that she didn't just assume he was a screwup. By the third divorce, he'd decided it had to be him. Pretty much the consensus. That third hit him the hardest because he'd realized that was it—he wasn't going to have the gold ring, picket fence, and two-point-two-kids future. "Nothing hugely earth-shattering. She was a nice person. I like to think I'm a decent guy. We just had nothing in common. Zip. Other than both wanting to settle down and have children. I went in with my eyes open. I knew it was a long shot…"

"The breakup still left its mark on you."

He stayed silent, his eyes locked on John Wayne on the flat-screen TV, kicking ass and taking names—while still winning Maureen O'Hara at the end. Thinking about how hard that last breakup hit him was one thing. Saying it out loud? He swallowed hard.

"You loved her?"

"Yes, I loved her."

"And now?" she pressed, keeping her voice so low it was barely even a whisper.

"I wasn't the right guy to make her happy."

"Or she wasn't the right person to make you happy."

He looked over at her sharply. Again, she hadn't just assumed it was his fault, a three-time loser at happily ever after.

Christ, this woman was drawing him right in, making him want everything all over again even when he knew losing her would leave him gutted in the end. And for him, it always ended. Damn it, he'd gone into this conversation looking for a libido killer, and even after trotting it all out, he still wanted Rachel.

He untangled himself from her and shoved to his feet, away from her and the urge to peel her clothes off, stretch her out on the sofa, and likely propose before the orgasms faded. "You should get some sleep. Take the first bedroom on the right. There's a guard outside the window. I'll be out here asleep on the couch."

Rachel wished she could sleep.

She was exhausted all the way to the roots of her hair. But sometime after she'd changed into generic exercise shorts and a T-shirt with an air force logo, she'd found her second wind. All the same, she forced her body to rest, stretching out on the four-poster bed and hugging an itchy, fat pillow sham.

The ringing in her ears grew louder by the second, so loud it almost drowned out Disco's light snores from across the room, where he sprawled asleep in front of the door. She stared out the half-open miniblinds at the shifting shadows outside. A squat palm tree shook like a pom-pom in the wind. A welcome flag flapped from a porch rail.

And a reed-thin figure sat in the A-frame swing in the front yard. The guard, pretending to be hanging around outside for a smoke. A tiny red light moved from side to side with each puff. Not a bad cover, so those passing by wouldn't notice anything out of the way. Did the neighborhood realize exactly what this house was used for? Of course the same question could be asked of any safe house in any community—military or civilian.

Liam had come through for her. She was safe and Brandon's concerns were being investigated. Brandon would be looked after.

And who would look after *Liam*?

Her eyes slid closed as she thought back to their kiss in the Jeep, so much better to think about than what they'd been through that led them to the kiss. The way he had of distracting her from everything was scary and tantalizing. Always had been, even back when she'd first known him during those frenetic weeks in the Bahamas…

An aftershock rattled the ground clear up through her toes until it rattled her teeth and her nerves after an endless day on the pile, searching for survivors in the rubble. She tossed down her toiletries, tossing aside all hopes of a bath as well. She snagged up Disco's leash and he trotted into step alongside her as she ran for the door, bursting out onto the beach cabin porch, down the steps.

The narrow street filled with rescue workers and locals, pouring from the houses left standing—or half standing. The structure next door tilted at an angle toward the seaside cliff. And big buff guys pushed through the door, angling sideways to get out ASAP.

Big buff guys wearing nothing but towels, shower time apparently interrupted.

Her eyes locked on one guy in particular. The major she'd met earlier, when she'd first arrived. The ground settled under her feet and she breathed easy enough to allow herself a more leisurely look. She didn't date or even hook up very often, but this guy had been a serious temptation from the get-go, even fully clothed in grimy camo.

And now, seeing him in nothing more than an insubstantial bit of white terry cloth? Ho-ly cow, he was hot, hot, hot at a time when she could seriously use a distraction. His dark blond hair was even browner, glistening wet from a shower. His chest was like carved bronze muscle. He seemed totally unself-conscious that he stood in the middle of the road wearing nothing more than leather flip-flops and a towel.

She couldn't resist teasing him, since she didn't dare touch him. Not out here, and not before she figured out if he was affair material.

"Lose your clothes, Major?" She stood beside her black Lab, leash in hand. Her grimy cargo pants and body-hugging T-shirt stuck to her after a long day working.

Her dog started sniffing the edge of Liam's towel suspiciously, all seventy pounds of pooch tensed, hackles rising along the canine's spine.

"It's not my clothes I'm worried about right now, ma'am. Think you can get your dog to let go of my towel?"

"Disco?" She thumbed the clicker in her hand and her dog dropped to his haunches. "Good boy."

"Thanks."

"And Major?"

"Yeah?"

"You may want to invest in a larger towel." She clapped him on his bare shoulder matter-of-factly before striding past, toward the cabana next door.

His eyes lingered on her the whole way. She could feel his stare, feel how still he stood rooted to the spot for a solid five seconds, watching her walk away. Her ponytail, gathered high and haphazardly on top of her head, swished with each step, teasing her shoulders like a phantom touch. The way she imagined Liam's touch would be if she indulged...

Groaning, Rachel hugged the pillow tighter against an ache that had started growing six months ago. She'd convinced herself he was the kind of guy she could have an affair with, some uncomplicated, easy sex. Except then he'd shocked the hell out of her by saying he was falling in love with her.

As if she believed that. His track record with women didn't bode well for longevity. Which should have been a plus, but there was something so... intense and real in his eyes, in spite of his jokes and grins. The things he'd shared with her tonight, the intensity and hurt in his voice, had made her question her preconceived notions about how he charmed his way through chicks. Even now, she could feel the tension rippling through him as she sat pressed to his side. He confused her and aroused her and tugged at her heart all at once.

She knew one thing for sure. Nothing with Liam would ever be uncomplicated or easy.

—⁓—

Scanning the street, Liam approached Sylvia on the swing with a low whistle to alert her he was approaching. Wouldn't want her to shoot him, even though she was the one who'd texted him to come outside.

Leaving Rachel made him nervous, but he had her bedroom window in sight. And honestly, he needed a breather from the way Rachel had of prying out the deep-down crap from his past. He'd had enough spilling his guts for one night. Right now, he welcomed the fresh air and the chance to talk to Sylvia without a legion of agents crawling around the office. It was all about work now, and in that realm, he felt comfortable, in control.

"Just me," he announced. "Mind if I join you?"

An innocuous enough statement for anyone who might be listening.

Sylvia waved to the seat beside her, cigarette tip swirling a red glow. "Please."

The swing creaked as he sat. "Thought you were going to quit smoking."

"I have. Used the patch for six months. Have kept to it for four months since. For the most part. I only indulge myself on *special* missions like this." She drew in on the cigarette and exhaled a thin stream of smoke. "Stress reliever."

"How often do those sorts of occasion roll around, to snatch a smoke?"

"Not as often as my nicotine craving would like." She turned to him with a smile, cigarette between two manicured fingers. "But let's not talk about that. You're ruining a perfectly good and unhealthy nicotine moment."

She drew in hard again on the filter, the red tip glowing brighter. Exhaling slowly, she tipped her head back, blowing smoke skyward—and politely away from him. She flicked the extra ash into an ashtray in her lap next to her service pistol.

"Aren't you a little overqualified for this kind of guard duty?"

She laughed softly. "Are you insinuating I've gone soft from too long out of the field?"

"Doubtful. You could probably kill me five different ways just using your pinkies."

"Only four."

He laughed along with her this time. "Why did we never hook up long term?"

"I'm against marriage. You're against one-night stands. We reached an impasse by dessert on our first date. And then there was that lack of zing between us."

"You're a sexy woman. You know that, right?"

"So I've been told. And you're a hot man. But you're also a dim one when it comes to picking women. So I'll stick with handling my own relationships, thank you very much."

Great. He leaned back, elbows hooked on the back of the swing. "Appreciate the news flash about my skills in the love life department. But I gotta tell ya, it doesn't take a rocket scientist—or professional profiler—to figure that out."

"Then quit hitting on me to self-destruct what you're

feeling for Rachel Flores." She pulled a last drag off the cigarette before stubbing it out in her ashtray.

"Now I remember why I never date anyone with a psychology degree."

Again, he fell into easy laughter with her—and stopped short as a car started two doors down. He tensed in sync with Sylvia. His hand went to his Desert Eagle strapped to his waist as her hand covered her 9 mm.

Setting aside the ashtray, she stood abruptly. "Walk with me."

"What?"

Her eyes pinned him. "Please, walk with me. Just to the end of the driveway."

He eased to his feet, looking from Rachel's window to Sylvia, then back again.

"Keep smiling and simply listen," she said quietly, her head dipped as she walked toward the end of the driveway, her high heels clicking along the concrete. "I have thirty-eight seconds to talk before the replacement guard pulls in two doors down and wonders why I've taken you out of range of the microphones."

What the hell? "I'm listening."

She stopped at the curb and hooked her hands on his shoulders as if the two of them were hanging out romantically in the moonlight. As if she believed they might actually be watched. "Get Rachel Flores and get the hell out of here. Trust no one," she hissed. "Not even the people working with me. If you can get to Brandon Harris, bonus points for you. Hide him. Use all the evasion training you've ever picked up along the way in this crazy-ass life we lead and disappear. *And for God's sake don't tell anyone, not even me, where you are.*"

Careful to maintain her cover of acting like a couple, he palmed her waist, finding her muscles as tensed as his own. "How long am I supposed to drop out of sight and how do I know to trust you?"

"Stay out of the way until the international summit is complete. I'll take care of filing leave papers on your behalf. Your team will bring in a replacement leader for your little dog and pony show. No one will suspect a thing. And as for trusting me, you already know. Because if I wanted you dead"—she waggled her pinky against his jugular—"well, you'd already be cold."

And he believed her, absolutely. He'd looked in her eyes, using his own training to search for lies and tells. She was telling the truth about his need to leave this house, to hide Rachel and find Brandon Harris. She'd been honest about her intention to set up a cover for him when he left.

As for the rest of it... Was it the right thing to stay gone until the summit? That, he didn't know, and he sure as hell wasn't leaving his team hanging out here alone, twisting in the wind.

He slid his hands up her sides and into her hair, playing right along with her scenario of a couple stealing time alone. "Just one more thing."

"You have ten seconds." She nodded curtly. "So talk fast."

"Sylvia, I'm sorry." Because he had two fingers poised and ready for a good old-fashioned nerve pinch to the neck to knock her out cold for at least ten or fifteen minutes. He hoped. With luck, she would play it out longer before calling it in, since she wanted them off base ASAP.

Sylvia collapsed unconscious into his arms without the least hint of trouble.

Scooping her up, he stayed right on track with the whole romantic-couple gig. But moving fast, which also worked if a guy was really intent on getting the woman inside and he needed to do that before the replacement guard showed.

If she was completely legit, it was best she didn't know the details of how he would clear out with Rachel. And if Sylvia was following her own agenda? Then he intended to make sure she knew as little as possible about how he left this place.

Honest or not? He would figure that part out later.

Either way, right now, he had to wake up Rachel and disappear.

Chapter 8

THE EARTHQUAKE RUMBLED AGAIN, RATTLING RACHEL'S bed.

She pushed through the layers of fog, desperate to wake up and make her way to safety before the roof caved in on top of her. She needed to get underneath the furniture or to a doorway.

Except none of that made sense, because she wasn't in the Bahamas anymore. She was in Florida now, rebuilding her life and her nerves.

But she could swear Liam was with her, the scent of him, the intense energy he brought into a room. Something that hadn't changed in six months apart, something that haunted her dreams.

And oh God, how her dream felt so erotically real right now. She was in bed. With Liam. His whipcord-lean body over hers. She could feel the heat of his breath on her neck, anticipate the feel of his mouth on her skin.

Her legs thrashed at the covers, tangling in the sheets, her long T-shirt riding up until the canvas texture of his uniform abraded sensually against her bare legs. Want rippled through her until she arched her back to press more firmly against him. What harm was there in indulging herself in a dream?

"Rachel." His raspy voice stoked her fantasies.

The man could talk her to an orgasm with the husky suggestiveness in the way his tongue caressed her name.

"Liam," she moaned, and oh God, she really had spoken out in her sleep. The veil between sleep and reality became translucent, the two worlds blending. Fear gripped her that if she woke up, she could lose this chance to have Liam, even if only in a dream realm.

She twisted her fingers in the sheets to hold on to the nighttime delusion a while longer, long enough to assuage the ache between her thighs. Completion hovered so close, until the need to finish clawed through her painfully. It had been so long since she'd wanted someone this much.

Since losing Caden, infrequent sex had merely been about release. This craving for Liam went so much deeper... and just the word *deeper* made her want more. Now. Fantasies were private and unlimited...

She threaded her fingers through his hair, testing the texture. Damp? From rain? Details intruded on her dream state until—

"Rachel," he hissed in her ear, his hand clamping over her mouth. "Shhh. Wake up and stay quiet. And for God's sake, quit moving like that."

Okay, domination was *not* her idea of sexy.

Her eyes snapped open. He loomed over her, tall and lean, his tensed body covering her. His leg pressed between her legs, and it was all she could do in her half-awake state not to wriggle against the sweet pressure that should have faded in light of whatever was going on.

A low moan of pleasure slipped from her lips anyway.

His hand stayed clamped over her mouth, gently, but unmistakable in its message. His chest pumped against her with ragged breaths. His head dipped toward her. She swallowed hard, and God help her, if he kissed her right now, she wouldn't stop him, and to hell with anything else. Her body arched into him before she could think, much less stop herself.

His voice caressed her ear. "Rachel, honey, you're killing me here."

The hard length of him pressed into her hip, letting her know he hurt every bit as much as she did from this unconsummated attraction. As much as she wanted to lose herself in the moment, in the answering heat radiating off him, reason began to filter through.

"Liam?" she whispered. "What's going on? Why are you here?"

"You have to trust me and stay really quiet," he answered softly. "We need to leave without alerting anyone. Now. Get dressed fast and follow me out."

Passion turned to a frightening burn. Something was wrong. Very wrong.

She nodded under his hand and he rolled off her fluidly, sitting on the edge of the bed with his broad back to her.

A big black gun was strapped to his waist alongside a knife.

Oh God.

She slipped from under the covers and padded to her small bag quickly in the shadowy room. There was no time for modesty. Still, she turned away from Liam. She whipped the overlong T-shirt over her head and yanked a T-shirt and jeans from her backpack. He stepped up alongside her so quietly she almost yelped—then remembered the no-talking edict.

Silently, he passed her gym shoes and socks. She dropped to the bed and yanked them on. Tying the laces, she realized Disco had never made a sound during this whole encounter. He always, always alerted her to strangers approaching. Her heart lurched until she saw her dog standing just behind Liam. The Lab's black coat had blended into the darkness.

Now the two of them stood like sentinels between her and whatever waited outside that had stirred Liam to such extreme action. Her stomach tumbled over itself with nerves. It was one thing to lead a search for bodies in the aftermath of disaster. Another to be on the run as her world crumbled around her feet.

Her life was spiraling out of control rather than settling. But she'd brought Liam into this, because for some unknown reason, she trusted him more than anyone. That meant following him now.

Swallowing hard, fully dressed, she turned toward him and nodded.

Liam jerked his head toward the hall without a word, and as she walked through the house, she realized that all the blinds had been drawn. No one could see out—or in. Disco's nose swiveled left hard and fast, causing Rachel to stop short. She eyed the line of his attention to the living room—and gasped.

Sylvia Cramer lay stretched out on the sofa. With her hands folded over her chest and her upswept auburn hair only a bit mussed, she appeared to be—dead? Liam glanced back at her, his eyebrows pinched together, but he didn't show the least surprise or interest in Sylvia. Rachel grabbed her dog's collar, hair rising on her arms. Then she realized—thank God—Sylvia's chest rose and fell evenly in deep sleep.

Now that was almost strangest of all. The OSI agent

just taking a nap? In the middle of an assignment? She checked the clock hanging on the wall over the television armoire and saw it was only three o'clock in the morning. She'd slept only two and a half hours. Bullfrogs sang a full nighttime chorus outside.

Liam held up a hand, motioning for her to stay still. He crossed to Sylvia with steps so silent it unsettled her more than a little. Scooping up the sleeping agent, he carried her through the safe house and back to Rachel's room. Through the open door, she saw him place Special Agent Cramer on the bed and pull the covers over her. If anyone came in, they would assume it was Rachel.

Okay, he mouthed to Rachel a second before he wrapped his fingers around her arm, strong, gentle... *insistent.* His eyes spoke louder than any words. *We need to go.*

Tugging her attention from the oddly sleeping agent, she padded softly through the house until Liam reached the garage. Opening the door, he revealed two vehicles, both facing nose out, as if preset for a speedy exit. The closest, a nondescript blue sedan, was parked beside a dark blue Suburban with tinted windows. He motioned her toward the latter, on the far side.

Because of the windows? Or the sturdiness? Certainly not because of fuel efficiency, she thought with a hysterical bubble working its way up her throat.

Again, he held a finger over his mouth, reminding her to stay silent. He opened one door, the driver's side, and gestured her and Disco inside.

Were there listening devices in the house? Were agents at the OSI actually listening for how many doors closed? Although that made sense, since if Sylvia left, she would be alone, so only one door would shut.

Of course Sylvia was asleep inside, so there must not be cameras watching, or someone would already be after them.

What about any other guards outside? Were they all "napping" too?

She climbed inside and across the seat, her knee sliding in her haste. Liam's steadying hand cupped her butt, and holy crap, the heat seared clear through her jeans. And it was crazy that in the middle of a crisis she wanted to spin around and fling herself against his chest, wrap her arms and her legs around him while she finished the kiss they'd barely gotten to start earlier.

Actually not so crazy, considering she'd been having erotic dreams about him, when she should be too scared to breathe, much less lust. Although even in the middle of this hell, apparently Liam had the same feelings, which made her feel less like a freak of nature for being turned on when she should be worried about the people gunning for her.

Sitting upright, she yanked on the seat belt while Disco hopped into the back. Liam settled behind the wheel and opened the automatic garage door before her belt clicked.

Again, she was sneaking off base and she had no idea why. She reached across and touched Liam's shoulder lightly, asking silently if it was okay to speak.

He shook his head.

God, how much longer would this silence contest last? Her heart beat so loudly, surely anybody listening in would hear her.

Hours later—or more likely about ten minutes later—Liam pulled into a cluster of palm trees by a vacant outdoor mall. He moved so smoothly, competently. She'd forgotten about his efficiency of movement, nothing wasted, nothing out of sync. Using the illumination of outdoor streetlamps and a flashlight from the glove compartment, he searched the interior and exterior of the SUV, disconnecting wires inside, then sliding underneath the vehicle.

Minutes later he slipped out again, arced back his arm, and threw a fistful of tiny silver disks into a canal flowing between the dead mall and a pathetic used-car lot. Liam leaped the channel and moved among the cars. A temporary plate? Made sense. But what about the etched white letters on the side? He peeled a Maid Service magnet off the defunct service's Dumpster out front and slapped it on the side of the Suburban over the wording painted on the door—some kind of military designation?

He was frighteningly good at this.

Back in the vehicle, he slammed the car into reverse and back onto the road. "*Now* we can talk."

She wanted to ask a million different things, but she settled for, "Um, where are we going?"

"I don't know yet." His jaw was hard, his muscles bulging with tension.

"That's not very comforting."

"I'm winging it here." His eyes darted, checking the mirrors, sides, front, alert and ready for God only knew what. "Trust me. We needed to leave the base. And I'll have a plan before anyone even knows we're gone."

"What about going to the police? If not here, then how about I place calls to some people I know from when I worked in the D.C. and Virginia area? I probably should have called them in the first place, but I cut so many ties when I left the search and rescue field…" She shook her head, frustrated with herself that she hadn't thought of the cops and FBI agents she'd met during some of the more high-profile rescues. "Must have been subliminal, that I didn't think of them. But if you let me use the cell, I can try."

"Not now, Rachel."

"Back to the OSI?" In all her multiteam collabora- tive efforts, she'd never worked directly with the OSI, but their reputation was top-notch. She scrambled for something, anything, her brain still half asleep, her body caught somewhere between that erotic dream and the harsh edge of her dangerous reality.

"Definitely not."

They couldn't even trust the OSI anymore? Okay, *now* she was really freaking out.

He drove through the dark and deserted streets. Fog rolled in off the water in a greedy vapor, sucking up the road from sight. It felt as if they were truly alone in the world. Cut off from any source of help.

"What happened back there at the house to tip you off? Why did we have to leave?"

"I would tell you if I could, but you just have to trust me. That's why you chose to come to me for help, be- cause you trust me."

True enough. She knew that he would do anything… Anything at all? "Were you given permission to leave?"

He didn't answer, which was an answer in itself. Their departure wasn't officially sanctioned and Liam was pro- tecting her by keeping her in the dark on the details.

How would this play out for him at work? Was he risking his career for her? She hadn't even considered that possibility when coming to him for help. Bile burned her throat along with a hefty dose of self-loathing.

"Let's call this whole thing off now." She braced her palms on the dashboard. "I know nothing. You know nothing. Let Disco and me off at the next police station. You go back home and say I snuck away from the house."

"Not gonna happen," he said without missing a beat as he drove farther from base and the unconscious agent.

She hadn't really expected him to go for it. Time for plan B, which probably wouldn't work either, but she had to try.

At the next stoplight, Rachel reached for the door anyhow and yanked. No luck. He'd locked the doors. Of course he had.

"Damn it, Liam. This is crazy." She pounded the door with a fist in frustration. "You can't actually be kidnapping me."

"I could. But I won't need to." He glanced over at her, his eyes intense. He slid a hand under her hair and caressed the back of her neck. "You're a reasonable woman. You brought me into this because you were out of options. Now either you really trust me or you don't. Which is it?"

She stared into his eyes long after the red light had gone green. But there wasn't anyone on the road to honk or protest as they idled in the middle of the road. The strength in his gaze and gentleness of his touch worked together to remind her why she'd gone this route in the first place. As much as she hated to bring him into this mess, *her* mess, they were in it together now.

"I'm with you."

He smiled. God, how he smiled in a way that creased the corners of his eyes and made her ache to kiss those crinkles. "Good. Because I would hate to have to knock you out, too."

His words sunk in, icing the warmth in her belly. "Too?"

He looked away and accelerated through the intersection. "You don't need to know."

Frustration stirred. She'd lived independently for all her adult life, and this kind of full-scale control did not sit well, even if he was trying to protect her. "If we're in this together, how about we talk, rather than me asking questions that go unanswered. Tell me what I *can* know of your plan in progress."

Steering off the highway, he drove over a narrow bridge. The moon reflected off the marshy water along the barrier island. "We're going to see one of my team members before anyone sounds an alarm. We should have about an hour's lead."

Okay, that was something. Which team member would Liam choose to ask for help? She thought back to the other pararescuemen she'd met during their time in the Bahamas. The team member named Franco had been injured in the Bahamas and transferred out of the unit. So she moved on to… Cuervo, a charmer who wore marathon shirts and a smile. The guy they called Brick, because he was hardheaded but steady. Then there was Data, who'd managed to scrounge up electricity and an Internet connection before most of the specialists sent in. And an eerily quiet guy they'd simply called Bubbles…

They all seemed to have different strengths and she

didn't know any of them well enough to guess. She didn't know any of them as well as she did Liam... a man she trusted more than anyone. She needed to keep that in mind.

"What can your team member do for us that you and the OSI couldn't?"

"We have good toys. Sometimes we keep an extra stash of each other's toys for cases like now when it's more... expedient that I not return to my own house."

"Toys?"

"Guns. IDs."

"IDs? Plural?" She knew he was military, but different forms of identification? A little spooky.

"The kind of search and rescue extractions we're called to do aren't always straight-up, in-and-out kinds of deals," he explained as if detailing an uneventful, everyday kind of career. "Sometimes we need to go deep into hostile country. It can be... well, let's just say helpful to have a different identity."

There it was again, in her face, how badass elite his training was and how that placed him in dangerous positions beyond what even she could imagine—and she had a pretty good idea of the risks out there, given her prior work. He could die in a mission next week and she would never know.

Stop. She forced herself to take it down a notch. Breathe. Focus on the crisis at hand.

"Okay, this may sound like a nitnoid concern, but I'm just me. So if we're sticking together, your new identity plan has a flaw." Could he be planning to leave her with his friends while he went off Rambo-style to find Brandon?

"I feel confident I can rustle up something that will get us by until we locate your buddy and find some answers." He turned onto a sand and gravel roadway leading into a tropical thicket. "We won't have to fly under the radar for long."

"Thank goodness. I'd like to pick up my dogs by tomorrow."

"Um, I'm thinking more like a week." Tires crunched along the rocky road.

"A week? I work. I have a job. I have… well, I don't have plants or a house anymore." She slumped in her seat. "My job doesn't mean jack if I'm dead."

"Smart woman."

"What about Brandon?" Did he have any clue what kind of nightmare had been unleashed from their attempts to find help? Had she made things even more dangerous for him? "The same authorities you say we have to run from are already looking for Brandon. How are we going to get to him first?"

The headlights swept across a clearing in the palm trees, revealing a tiny, secluded beach bungalow. The one-story green stucco structure was raised up on stilts and had white hurricane shutters over the windows, shielding it from the elements as well as from prying eyes.

Liam killed the headlights. "Do you seriously expect me to believe you told them the truth on where to find him?"

Goose bumps prickled up her arms. "You think I lied to the authorities?"

"I know you did."

She didn't bother denying the truth. She had

deliberately misled the OSI regarding Brandon's where-abouts. "Are you angry with me?"

"I will be if you lie to me from here on out."

"Fair enough." She owed him the truth, given all he'd done for her. "After his therapy sessions, he works out for the rest of the afternoon. Sometimes he disappears for a day or two. So he leaves Harley at the same doggy day care I use."

"Harley is his therapy dog?"

"An Australian shepherd–beagle mix." Memories rolled over her of the day Brandon had been paired with Harley, the hope she'd felt then, how she'd allowed herself to buy into some rosy future where she fixed everyone's problems. Where there would be no more risk. No more pain of loss.

Could she really have been that naive?

Liam unlocked the doors. "We'll check in at the dog-sitter's once we finish up here."

Rachel gripped his arm, stopping him. "How would you know that I lied and they didn't?"

His muscles flexed and bunched under her fingers, his eyes a little sad. "I didn't know. I only suspected. Now I know."

Turning away, he stepped out of the SUV. She clambered out to join him around front, Disco leaping out and running to the nearest squat sago palm tree to mark it. At least he opted for a tree instead of the neatly fenced-in vegetable garden.

Satisfied her dog was safe, she tore her eyes off Disco and did a quick scan of the locale, orienting herself. Marsh grass leaned in the wind blowing a briny breeze across the lawn.

Old skills fired to life. They'd driven southeast, maybe fifteen miles from base. The drive had gone quickly in the night but would undoubtedly take much longer during daytime beach traffic.

Snapping for her dog, she caught up with Liam along the slate pathway. "I wasn't sure if they would toss Brandon in some military jail or lock him up for a psych eval. I just wanted a chance to get to him first."

"How can you be so certain he doesn't need to be in a hospital?" He pivoted hard to face her, bringing her up short.

She palmed his chest. Perspiration lightly dampened his T-shirt and dotted above his mouth. Her gaze sketched along the shape of his mouth as she ached to taste away the salty beads. His eyes locked with hers as he loomed a solid eight inches taller than her. Her body hummed with awareness, her pulse pounding in her ears as loudly as the waves beating against the shore.

Disco nosed her knee, reminding her where they were and what Liam had asked. "What I think about Brandon's mental state is irrelevant right now in light of the fact we need to find him first." She peeled her hand from his chest before she did something needy, like beg him to make this all go away. She was stronger than that and damned if she would be naive now. "After that, we can figure out the rest."

"We're on the same page then." He backed away, waving toward the front door. "You met my team buddy Wade in the Bahamas, and now you'll get to meet his wife, too. It's best if we say as little as possible about what's going on. I'll clue Wade in on the pertinent details, enough to make sure there's follow-through on solving this if something happens to us."

Preparing for the worst? She rubbed her arms, which didn't do a thing to ward off the goose bumps. "What should I say to them if they ask me about the situation?"

"They won't ask." He climbed the white wood steps leading up to the tiny landing in front of the door. "I just need to pick up my gear and we'll hit the road before anyone knows we've left the base. Once they do, they'll be looking for who we were. Not who we're going to become."

There it was again. That fuzzy area of gray he embraced so easily. Had she known this about him on some level even as she tried to think only of the civilian-rescue aspect, rather than the dangerous military missions? Intellectually, she understood that pararescuemen were trained in more than just saving people. She'd learned the basic history of the teams from meeting him, how they used to be called parajumpers—PJs—and that the name morphed officially to pararescuemen, even if the PJ nickname stayed in the culture.

They did far more than parachute in. They had to be prepared to fight back an assault that threatened their rescue target. She knew he was an elite warrior.

Knew that there were only about three hundred and fifty like him in the world.

Knew she should be grateful for all he was doing for her—and she was.

But oh God, what if they couldn't pull this off?

Liam cupped her face. "Trust me."

Trust? There was that word again. That word she hadn't allowed herself to consider when thinking of a man in so very long. His strong, callused hands felt familiar even after the months they'd spent apart. What a time to realize the tumultuous arousal she'd felt when they kissed and when he'd woken her, well, those feelings were easy.

The other feelings churning inside her, those were tough as hell. Because, God help her, she *had* learned to trust again after all.

———※———

Inside the entryway, Liam watched Rachel follow Sunny Rocha into the homey kitchen before he turned his attention to his teammate Wade. He hated to let Rachel out of sight. But she was safe here, and the two women were both already deep in conversation about their dogs. The Rochas' malamute-husky mix was sniffing Disco. Wade and Sunny Rocha hadn't even questioned their showing up an hour before sunrise. Sunny had waved them inside and offered to start a pot of coffee.

For now, Liam had a window of time to get his feet steady on the ground again, arm himself properly, and put together a solid plan. Wade angled his head toward the hall and led Liam past walls packed with framed photos of Alaskan landscapes and mountains. He pushed the door open to the spare room that doubled as a man cave in the two-bedroom bungalow. Uniforms showed in the open closet, his helmet and night vision goggles on top of a file cabinet.

Wade grabbed a T-shirt off the back of the desk chair and tugged it over his head to go with the low-slung sweatpants he must have stepped into on his way to the door. "You're cruising late tonight."

"I'm going out of town for a couple of days." He hated putting Rocha in this position, but as long as he guarded his words carefully, there would be nothing said that compromised any of his teammates. He was their leader, their CRO—combat rescue officer. He didn't want any of this coming off as an order. "If people come asking about me, tell them everything. Don't hold anything back, thinking that you're protecting me. I'll be fine."

"*If* someone comes asking for you?"

"I'm hoping things will be chill." If Sylvia had been straight up in saying she had his back covered. He hadn't discounted that she could be following some other agenda. Although he couldn't fathom what she had to gain in making herself look bad by losing the people she'd been assigned to watch.

Liam dropped onto the black leather sofa. "If all's well, then I've already been cleared off the schedule for the next couple of days and you won't need to answer jack."

"Does this have anything to do with the OSI interview earlier?" Wade sat in the office chair across from him.

Since Wade and Cuervo had been called in, giving them some of the lowdown wouldn't compromise them as long as he stuck with what they could have overheard while standing in the hall with him.

"There's a loose cannon out there, a lieutenant named Brandon Harris. He's wrestling with PTSD and making some wild accusations. He says he's got proof of a conspiracy set to play out at the satellite summit. His ramblings have stirred up a firestorm, and Rachel got sucked in when she tried to help."

Wade whistled lowly. "Damn, brother, that's serious stuff. No wonder the OSI is involved. And I assume you got pulled in helping her?"

"Turning away from Rachel is not an option."

"Which begs the question... What are you doing *here*?"

"Don't know who to trust on base. Until I do, I need Rachel tucked away safely."

"Okay." Wade nodded slowly. "I can buy into that. What do you need me to do?"

"Make sure the team stays on track with training for the security at the summit. I'm guessing they'll loan the team a captain from one of the reserve PJ units until I'm back, but I need you to keep the guys unified, solid. Stay under the radar. Do not call attention to yourselves. My leaving is going to cause enough unseen ripples. We don't need that coming to the surface."

"What do I tell people about why you're missing?"

"I've decided to take some time off with my new girlfriend."

"Girlfriend?" Wade's black eyebrow slashed upward. "Are we back in high school or what?"

"All right, all right... You can make the wording sound cooler."

"Shouldn't be too tough, since everyone's met her." Wade grinned. "She's a serious dime."

"Dime?"

"She's a ten. A dime, a ten piece. Like Gwyneth Paltrow and Kesha..." He leaned back in the office chair. "You *are* getting old."

"Thanks." Great. Just what he needed to remember right now.

"No disrespect meant, given your senior status."

Liam gave up and laughed, a rusty sort of sound. How long had it been since he slept?

"I mean it when I say to be completely open if authorities question you. I don't want to compromise you in any way. If Brandon Harris comes up at any time, feel free to say I'm as confused as the next fella about what's going on. Never even met the guy. But again, be straight up if asked. I arrived, picked up some gear I'd stored in at your place when I moved here."

"Like the gear I've got stored at your place?" There it was, the offer for more, for gear needed to fly under the radar for a while.

"Let's just say Rachel and I have reunited after the Bahamas and are heading out to commune with nature for a couple of days. Thus the need for firepower. There are wild animals out there."

"Fair enough." Wade shoved to his feet. He rolled back a rag rug and pulled a key from underneath the desk. He slipped the key into a nearly undetectable groove in the wood floor. A spring popped and a trapdoor eased open to expose a safe built under the floorboards. Gun cases, ammo boxes, survival gear. "Take whatever you need."

"Just my stuff stored here." Liam knelt beside him, knees popping. "Pass me that, and I'm good."

He lifted out a green duffel bag and hefted it over to the top of the desk. "You can take more from my personal stash. Might as well be better than good. No questions asked."

"Thanks. But I want to make sure you're armed as well." And he didn't want to cross a line. They would die for each other any day. That wasn't something he would ever take advantage of.

He unzipped the bag and sifted around inside, inventorying.

Remington 308, a sniper rifle.

AR-15, a smaller assault rifle, easier to conceal.

Body armor.

Three sets of IDs.

Two prepaid, disposable cell phones.

And lastly, a Baby Eagle 9 mm, a smaller version of his Desert Eagle semiautomatic handgun. He would be passing the 9 mm to Rachel along with lessons on how to shoot it.

"Be alert. I wish I had more than that to direct you… I swear the minute I have something concrete, I'll pass it along. You have to know I wouldn't leave you in the dark unless there was no other choice."

"Call me if you need anything." Wade clapped him on the back.

"I won't need you." He slung the duffel over his shoulder. "But thanks."

"Me? Hell no." He laughed. "I'm talking about Sunny. That woman's so resourceful, she can create a generator out of bubble gum and vegetable oil. She's like an eco-friendly MacGyver."

At least some guys got it right the first time. "She's a keeper."

"You don't have to tell me. Enough of the sweet flowery love stuff." He squatted down in front of the open safe again. "Let's talk extra ammo."

Chapter 9

RACHEL CRADLED A MUG OF COFFEE BETWEEN HER palms, killing time until Liam armed himself to the teeth. *Gulp. Ouch.* She blew into the coffee. "It's beyond nice of you to let us just walk into your home in the middle of the night."

The sun was just starting to tease the watery horizon visible through the open kitchen window. A fan kicked up a breeze, and while there were AC vents in the bungalow, apparently the Rochas preferred the morning breeze.

Sunny poured a cup of coffee for herself as well, looking surprisingly awake in running shorts and a tank top. Her brown hair swung loose, with a feather woven into the strands on one side. "It's nothing. Seriously. This is what we do for each other."

She placed a plate of pineapple-mango muffins on the table. Home baked. Clearly.

Even if she hadn't seen the muffin tin slotted in the dish dryer by the sink, she would have known. Everything about this place spoke of eco-friendly creativity, from the repurposed walnut table to the natural-fiber curtains. Rag rugs were scattered in front of the sink, by the door, in the hall.

Being here, bringing danger to their doorstep, felt so wrong. "I'm sorry."

"For what?" Sunny sat across from her and scooped up a muffin.

Rachel's mouth watered and she grabbed a muffin for herself, as good an excuse as any to give herself a moment to come up with a neutral answer. She thought of Liam's insistence that they wouldn't ask questions, which meant she should respect the need to keep them as uninvolved as possible. So what was she supposed to talk about?

The flippin' weather? "Your home is beautiful, like you've found Florida's little best kept secret nestled back here."

"It's a temporary place, just for their short stint." Sunny thumbed a crumb from the corner of her mouth. "Some folks think I'm crazy for not picking an inexpensive condo and a more flashy setting, but I value my privacy."

Short stint? Liam was moving soon? Suddenly sitting here was more than about killing time. Sitting here offered her an inside peek at what life would be like with Liam. Forget about denying she could ignore whatever it was she felt for him. She'd been trying that for six months and it hadn't worked. "What do you mean about a short stint?"

"The guys are filling a billet here because the reserve squadrons were undermanned. They've been working on some special project. It's all temporary, which isn't that unusual in the military, from what I understand so far. We'll be moving soon."

"Where to?" And why was she already considering options for expanding the therapy dog operation?

"Haven't heard yet." She sipped from the earthenware mug.

"That doesn't bother you? Not knowing where you'll

be living next?" Rachel had made a point of being in control of her life since Caden died.

"Would it do any good if I let it upset me?" She broke off another bite of pineapple-mango muffin. "There's nothing I can do to change the way things are. To live with the man, I have to live with the circumstances."

"Must be nice to have a marriage that solid. Um, I assume you're married. I thought Liam said you were. Sorry if I—" She stuffed a piece of muffin into her mouth, chewing extra long on the sweet bite of pineapple.

Sunny shoved to her feet. "Don't worry. We are married. I am officially Sunny Rocha. So my name is basically Sunny Rock." Grinning, she filled two dog bowls with water. "But Sunshine Rock would be even worse, and there you have it."

This woman was such a natural, at ease in her skin and so nonjudgmental. She was going above and beyond, and they'd never even met before. Rachel's hands gripped the mug until they numbed. The enormity of it overwhelmed her. "Thank you for helping us, no questions asked. Liam's lucky to have friends like you two."

"I believe the both of you will manage just fine on your own. You used to work search and rescue stuff, right?" She placed one of the water bowls on the floor for Disco, the other for her dog.

"With my dogs. Yes. How did you know?"

"I've heard about you."

"But I just got here yesterday..."

Sunny laughed softly as she reached into a cookie jar and passed the cookies to—the dogs? "The major got a little wasted at a beach picnic we threw right after they all got back from the Bahamas. He talked a lot about you before he passed out on the sofa."

Forget wondering about the dog treats. She wanted to ask what he'd said. Desperately. But that would sound... desperate? Exactly.

Sunny took her chair at the table again, sitting cross-legged. "You don't have to ask. I'm happy to spill all the deets. You made quite an impression on him in those three weeks you two spent together. He talked about how tough you were finding survivors. How tireless. He said if the air force ever let females into the pararescue field, you would make the cut."

Hearing how he'd thought of her every bit as much as she'd been unable to forget him was exciting and unsettling. Although was she even the same woman he'd been taken with back in the Bahamas? The loss of that identity hit her all over again, surprising her with the new ways it could hurt her. "Yet I burned out and stepped away from search and rescue. Guess he was wrong about me."

"I don't know if I agree with you on that, but hey, no matter." She leaned closer, her voice low. "He didn't just talk about work. He said how you didn't take crap off anyone, how you stood up to him. And he thought you were smart for giving him his walking papers, since he sucks at marriage."

An obstacle she still wasn't sure how to overcome. "That whole three divorce thing is tough to overlook."

"This is a rough career field for relationships, no question." Shadows chased through her eyes before she looked down into her coffee.

"If you don't mind my asking, doesn't that worry you?"

She looked up, eyes resolute. "Not being with Wade worries me more."

Her stomach clenched. She knew too well how much it hurt to lose a man she loved. This conversation was definitely veering too close to painful territory.

Rachel reached down to let the husky mix sniff her hand. "What's this handsome fella's name?"

Sunny eyed her for a second before smiling, seeming to accept the need to shift gears. "My dog's name is Chewie. We worked together as travel guides in Alaska when I, uh, lived off the grid."

"That explains why you chose to live in a more secluded spot here." And all of the natural touches to the bungalow. "If you were so remote, how did you two meet?"

"Wade thought I needed saving." She rolled her eyes. "He parachuted into an Alaskan blizzard only to have *me* show *him* the best place to camp and ride out the storm. And here we are."

"You're lucky to have found each other."

Masculine voices drifted down the hall. Too easily she could detect the difference between Liam's and Wade Rocha's. The six months they'd spent apart faded in an instant. Would that same hold true over multiple deployments, year after year?

And when had she started dreaming about the future? The present was so messed up and crazy, she shouldn't be wasting a brain cell thinking about anything else.

"The job's easier to take, knowing he's got such a tight team. And Liam McCabe? He's the glue." Sunny's voice trembled. "The team's freaking out over his leaving. Me too, for that matter."

"Leaving?" She sat up straighter, crumpling the napkin in her clenched hand.

"After some mission they've been working on finishes up at the end of the week, he says he's done, out. McCabe insists his body can't keep up anymore."

"Is he right?" She certainly hadn't seen any signs of him flagging—other than once in the Bahamas, watching him strap ice packs onto his knees. But good God, who wouldn't need ice after what they'd been through during the horrific, endless work in earthquake rubble?

"He may not be as fast as he was, but he still beats the hell out of most men ten years younger. Look at them now. After the workout they got yesterday, Wade's still aching, even if he won't admit it."

"What workout?"

"They do PT—physical training—pretty hard. But yesterday they finished off a day at work by swimming two miles, then hiking five miles back to base." She tipped back her chair to check down the hall before continuing, "I understand you're a strong woman, with the search and rescue training. We have that kind of background in common. But these guys have training beyond anything we've come close to seeing. If he says you need to run, then run. Don't think. Just act. For whatever you have going on right now, you need to trust what he says."

There was no denying the intensity or sincerity in Sunny's voice. But what she said scared the hell out of Rachel as much as it reassured her. It was one thing to participate in a rescue where she moved forward proactively, making decisions, leading. But giving over power completely? That was hard. Really hard.

Yet hadn't she turned over control already?

She pushed the empty coffee mug away. "I appreciate the advice."

"It's difficult to take a backseat when you're used to leading. I get that. Totally." She gripped Rachel's hand in a quick, firm squeeze. "But I learned something when we went through scary times in Alaska. If I'm following, I've got his back. And guys like these are so busy saving others, they don't take care of themselves. More than another leader, they need someone who's got their six."

"Their six?"

"Six o'clock. Like a position." She stood again and opened a cabinet, reaching to the top shelf and pulling down a canister labeled "Granola." She glanced over her shoulder, continuing, "Someone who has their back. That someone is you, and Liam's lucky to have you. Which is why I have something to give you."

Sunny plunked the canister on the table and pried open the top. She pulled out a leather pouch.

"What's that?"

"Something even Wade doesn't know about. And trust me, my junk-food-eating husband wouldn't go near the granola bin." She untied the pouch and opened the flap. "Papers. Identification. For you."

Leaning back, Rachel held up her hands. "Thank you, but no, I can't possibly take this. I can't let you become any more involved in this than you already are. Liam was very clear about making sure nothing happens here that puts you and your husband at risk if this goes badly."

"It's not mine, for heaven's sake." Sunny snorted. "That would only make things worse for all of them.

It's an extra I have lying around from when I lived in Alaska, one with a different name in case I needed to move fast. Nobody knows about this."

"Liam says he has more than one for himself."

"I didn't know, but I'm not surprised. It's just the nature of the business."

"So because he has his secrets, you have yours?" So much for her brief hopes of a perfect relationship in this stress-filled career field.

Sunny winced. "I wouldn't put it that way. It's certainly not meant as some payback on my part. More along the lines that being married to a man like that, well, you have to be incredibly independent." She toyed with the feather in her hair. "If you're not sure of yourself, you can lose yourself, lose your way, in this stressful lifestyle…"

She shook her head.

Rachel waited for her to gather her thoughts, not sure where this revelation was leading. She'd been looking for answers and direction here. But she hadn't expected anything like this.

"My husband understands that I used to live off the grid and how tough this transition has been for me. He knows I'm unaccustomed to rules and conventional structures of society. I'm happy with him. And even though he doesn't know about these, I'm not leaving myself an escape hatch. I've kept him in the dark to protect him." She caressed the leather pouch between her fingers. "I've been holding on to these in case my older brother ever needs my help."

"Your brother?"

"He's a conscientious objector. Or a deserter.

Whichever you prefer to call him. He was in the service and went AWOL. When we lived off the grid in Alaska, we kept extra identification for him and his wife in case they needed to move quickly. He disappeared into Canada about a year ago. His wife…" Sunny squeezed her eyes shut tight for three crashes of the waves against the shore before opening them again. "His wife is dead. And for some reason I never could get rid of these papers we kept around for them."

Her brother was a deserter? Rachel's grip tightened around the edge of the wood table, her mind filled with the soldiers she'd helped, their eyes ravaged with pain and trauma. They'd more than risked their lives holding the line in battle. They'd sacrificed their very mental well-being rather than turn away from their brothers in arms. Brandon was fighting for his life right now.

Reconciling herself to Sunny's brother's decision, taking his identity, even a false one, felt like a betrayal to each of those wounded veterans she'd helped.

But saying as much would be a slap in the face to the woman who was risking so much to help her. So Rachel settled for simply asking, "How does your husband feel about your brother?"

"Honestly? We don't talk about my brother… Phoenix." She glanced toward the hallway, the spare room where the men were making their plans. "Maybe avoidance isn't the healthiest decision. Married people should be open about everything, and someday we'll figure that one out."

"Sounds like a painful situation for anyone, forced to chose between a spouse and your family."

"I guess my time to choose has come." She passed the

whole leather pouch of papers across the walnut table. "For you and Liam. The ages even match up fairly well. There's a set with and without photos. You can stop by a drugstore that makes passport photos to replace the grainy pictures if you want."

"I still don't know if I can accept this." She searched for a diplomatic way to put it. "You've already done so much, more than I could ever thank you for."

"Actually, I should thank you." She crossed her arms over her stomach, hugging herself, her smile sad. "I'm finally letting go of my brother."

The woman's pain reached clear across the table. "I'm sorry."

Sunny shook her head. "This isn't your fault or even mine. Phoenix put our whole family at risk for years, then he ran when his family needed him. He even abandoned his child… It's time. Do this for Liam, okay? You may not even need the extra IDs. But just in case you need to watch his six."

For Liam.

To be his partner, rather than a helpless tagalong.

Tentatively, she placed her hand over the pouch, considering… Accepting. Liam had gone to so much risk for her, she could do something for him, be in control of something.

She hugged the pouch to her chest, smiling her thanks for more than the papers. She owed this woman for the insights and strength. "What if I turn out to be an awful person? What happens if I do something like steal a car while I'm using the ID you gave me?"

Sunny blinked with over wide eyes and exaggerated innocence. "IDs? I don't know what you're talking about and you can be sure those can never, ever be traced back to me. So tell me, are you going to do whatever it takes to watch Liam's back?"

Rachel tucked the pouch into her backpack. "I'm so glad I was able to buy these off that guy on a street corner."

"Exactly." Sunny nodded approvingly. "And hey, if you steal a car, make sure it's a really kick-ass convertible."

Chapter 10

LIAM TUCKED HIS DUFFEL INTO THE BACK OF THE Suburban as the sun cranked onto the horizon. He hefted a second, larger bag with borrowed camping gear. Hopefully things wouldn't get that desperate, but better to be prepared.

Wade loaded a box of MREs—meals ready to eat— alongside a flat of bottled water. "What else do you need from me?"

"I wish I knew exactly." He hoped he'd planned for every contingency, but he was shadowboxing with a faceless enemy. He glanced up at the kitchen window, curtains lifting in the muggy morning breeze. Rachel and Sunny sat at the kitchen table with their heads close as they gabbed. His mom would have liked Rachel's fighting spirit.

"Seriously," Wade said, shuffling the gear in the back of the Suburban so it wouldn't slide around, "talk around the subject if you have to, but give me something else I can do to help you out. You're a smart dude. Make use of all the resources."

Liam combed his fingers through his hair, his mind in three different places at once. Planning where to get a replacement vehicle. Here with this friend. Back at base, wondering what was going on. "I wish I had some big revelation to pass along, beyond Harris's suspicions. I gotta say that even if I did, I'm not sure I would tell you. Honest to God, I don't want you tangled up in this anymore than you have to be."

"How do I find you then"—Wade leaned back against the vehicle, arms over his chest—"if you're not going to tell me where you're going?"

Liam passed over a slip of paper with the phone number for the throwaway cell he'd bought even before he went to the safe house on base. From the start, he'd sensed he needed to keep his options open. "Memorize it."

Wade stared at the number intently, then reached into the camping gear and pulled out a small box of matches. One fast strike and a flame lit up. He burned the paper, holding a corner between two fingers until the ashes floated away in the wind. "Anything else?"

He weighed the options, hated like hell to drag anyone else in... but if what Harris said was right? If Sylvia was concerned enough to want him off base? For more than Rachel's sake, he needed to unravel this mess fast.

And like it or not, he needed help, and when it came to keeping Rachel safe, he would take all the help he could get.

Liam closed the back of the Suburban. "I need Cuervo to do some recon for me, see if he can find Brandon Harris before anyone else does."

"I could do that for you."

"You've got a wife and I've already put you two at risk enough. Besides, you're supposed make an appearance at work tomorrow, and Cuervo has the day off."

"And Cuervo needs to do what?"

"I've got an idea where Brandon Harris may be. If he's there, I need Cuervo to hide him." He slid another piece of paper from his pocket with the name of the dog-sitting service. "Start here looking for him. Once Cuervo locates Harris, use that info I gave you and contact me. I'll set up a meet."

"Call me dense, but why not find him yourself?"

"I need for Cuervo to figure out if Brandon's being watched first." Palm trees rustled overhead and seabirds called in the distance, but there were no other noises, no one approaching from the outside world. "I also need time to make sure I'm not being watched."

"The guy really does know something."

That much was certain. "I believe he does. Something big, and he's holding back. Somebody thinks Rachel knows more than she's telling. And I have to figure out what exactly they believe she knows before the wrong people try to pry it out of her." His hand gravitated to his chrome Desert Eagle strapped to his waist.

"What if she really is holding back? No offense, but your track record in reading women isn't the best."

"No offense taken. There's no denying my past." Muscles kinked along his back at memories of his second wife cheating, other wives walking because they couldn't take the crap that came with this job. He had plenty of reasons not to trust women, but damned if he could leave Rachel hanging out to dry. "My gut tells me she's innocent in all of this. There's nothing for her to gain and it's clear someone is seriously gunning for her. I can't walk away."

"For what it's worth, I really hope your gut is a hundred percent on the mark about her." Wade exhaled hard in the early morning heat, looking around the property, on guard. "Take care of yourself out there. If things go seriously to hell, contact Special Agent Sylvia Cramer."

"You're sure about her?"

"As sure as I possibly can be, and she's a better option than that suck-up Bernard. Watch your back regardless."

"Will do," Liam answered as the screen door squeaked open, drawing his eyes to the two women stepping out.

Drawing his eyes to Rachel.

She'd changed into fresh clothes borrowed from Sunny, shorts and a bright pink T-shirt with a recycle symbol in the middle. Radiating energy, she took the stairs at a sprint, each step determined, committed. Five feet, three inches of pure momentum, she took his breath away.

He blinked himself back to more practical thoughts. Rachel had pulled her wavy hair back into a high ponytail off her neck, to stay cooler, no doubt. Perfect for where they were headed next. The safest place he knew, and yet at the moment, nowhere felt safe enough where she was concerned.

He turned to Wade. "If something happens to me—"

"You don't even have to ask," Wade said, clapping him on the shoulder. "I'll look out for her."

Nothing else needed to be said.

It was time to roll.

―――――

Catriona wondered what Brandon would do if she just crawled right on top of him as he slept on her sofa. She would kiss him, feel the warm heat of his solid body against her. Maybe even slide her hand into his pants and stroke him awake.

Although on second thought, probably not wise to startle awake someone with PTSD.

So instead, as she stood in the archway between her dining room and living room, she allowed herself the luxury of staring at his big body sprawled on her mother's red velvet Victorian sofa. Harley kept guard over her owner from the floor. The shaggy Australian shepherd–beagle mix kept her head on her paws, but her eyes tracked back and forth, one blue, one brown.

Brandon twitched every so often, even jolted so hard sometimes, she thought he might bolt upright. Yet he stayed asleep.

His hand slid from the sofa and Harley nosed his palm. A sigh rattled through Brandon as his fingers slid into his dog's thick, tricolor coat.

What a restless way to make it through the night. He must be exhausted. What would it feel like to stretch out beside him, not for sex? Just to caress back the thick thatch of hair from his forehead until he settled into peaceful sleep.

They'd gotten back late after driving over to Rachel's. A fruitless trip, in that they didn't find her. On the bright side, at least he'd gotten a voice mail from her, one that had made him furrow his brow mighty deeply, considering he should have been relieved to hear her voice. He'd tried calling Rachel back, but no luck.

At least they knew she was okay. And Rachel's other two dogs were safe here.

Granted, all of the animals were agitated from so many drive-bys this morning. Usually, her little beach dead-end road was quiet, other than people dropping off their pets. There was a sign at the top of the corner that plainly said "Private" and "No Thru Traffic."

There had even been fresh tire tracks outside in the

driveway when they'd gotten back last night. Which could just mean someone had pulled in to turn around, then left. She'd actually forgotten about it until now. She'd been distracted from the tire marks when Brandon reached to take the pillow and blanket from her before crashing on her sofa.

And since he was still sleeping, she needed to keep the dogs quiet so they didn't wake Brandon. She pulled her eyes away from him and slipped through the kitchen to the back door to meet clients for the day. With luck, they would all drop off their pooches before he woke up, because she was really looking forward to sharing breakfast with him.

A year ago, she wouldn't have had the confidence to pursue him, but building her own business had given her a new sense of her own worth. She didn't need to "settle," the way her mother had always told her. And she didn't need to assume guys were only interested because of her parents' nonexistent money.

Yes, she'd dated a couple of losers in the past, but in those days, she'd been too swayed by her mother's influence. She hadn't trusted her own judgment enough.

But no longer. Others might have concerns about Brandon, but she saw deeper. She saw the man, and by God, she wanted him. She would find out what it was like to sleep beside him. To soothe him back to a peaceful rest when dreams made him twitchy.

Scratching Tabitha's head on her way past, she grabbed a bag of dog biscuits and headed for the fenced area. Just in time too, as another car cruised by slowly. Sheesh, was it her imagination, or was everyone driving silver sedans today?

Rachel grabbed the roll bar on the rusted piece of crap Jeep Liam had bought with cash at ten this morning. By eleven, they'd parked the Suburban at an airport and started driving south. She'd thought at first he planned to go find Brandon, but they'd passed that turnoff hours ago. Now it was late afternoon. The open expanse of ocean had long ago shifted to marshy everglades.

Trees stretched skyward, creating an intermittent leafy canopy. Disco was seriously loving the open-air ride, his muzzle tipped up into the wind, taking in the rush of scents.

With no roof, if it rained, they were screwed.

They hit a pothole and the nonexistent shock absorbers did little to keep her from lifting off the seat. Only the belt kept her inside. Disco jockeyed for balance in back with a skill earned from climbing over collapsed rubble during training and searches. The Lab tried to wedge himself between the seats, huffing as he rested his nose on her shoulder.

The Jeep ate up the miles to heaven only knew where. She wished she could just let the wind unravel the tension inside her the way it played with Liam's blond hair. But there wasn't enough wind to sweep away the stress of the past twenty-four hours. She'd been threatened. Almost run off the road. Questioned by the OSI. Running from the OSI.

And in the middle of it all, she'd reunited with the one man to break through her barriers since Caden had died.

For about the fiftieth time today, she wished she'd

come to see Liam when she first moved to Florida so they could have sorted through these feelings in a normal setting.

"I'm sorry for all you have to do for me. That sure was a lot of money to spend on a disposable car."

"Who says I intend to throw it away? I love Jeeps. And after seeing my pristine one get trashed, I may go for the beat-up look from now on." He draped his wrist over the steering wheel, wind ruffling his close-shorn hair. "When insurance pays on the other one, I'll make out like a bandit."

His weathered skin soaked up more of the sun high overhead, his five-o'clock shadow shifting more into a scruffy beard. He wore camo pants and a simple T-shirt now, looking more like a hunter than a clean-cut military man. The transformation was about more than the clothes. He'd somehow… changed.

And she found this side of him every bit as much of a turn-on as the other facets of Liam McCabe she'd seen so far. He was a formidable man.

Disco sighed again, letting loose a hefty dose of dog breath.

"Fine, Disco. Come on up here, boy." She hugged her knees, the back so crammed with gear, he might as well take up residence on the floorboards in front of her. Once her dog settled, she turned back to Liam. "You're nice to make this sound like it isn't a huge pain in the ass."

"We really don't have a choice, do we?"

"We? Me. I don't have a choice. You do. This isn't your mess."

"Well, it is now. And believe me, I wouldn't have left the base if I hadn't thought it was absolutely necessary.

If Special Agent Cramer hadn't thought it was necessary. Do you understand what I'm saying?"

Holy crap. She slumped back in her seat. It was worse than a matter of not trusting the OSI to believe her. If Agent Cramer actually wanted them away from the base, then something seriously bad was going on there.

"Can you tell me where we're heading now?" She tipped a bottle of water up. Then passed it to Liam. They needed to stay hydrated in this heat. Sure, it was a small way to take care of him, to have his back, but she would do what she could when she could.

He took the bottle from her and placed his mouth where hers had just been. Such a simple move. But so intimate all the same.

Liam passed the drink back to her. "I know a place in the Everglades where we should be able to hang out until I get a better handle on what's going down. I've got some feelers out to find Harris," he said vaguely, "and I want us to be available for a meet if that all works out."

"Why not try to find him ourselves?" The thought of how Brandon was going to freak out, to think she'd sold him out... She shivered in spite of the sweltering Florida heat. "He's not... stable."

"I understand that. And I also get that you're in danger." His jaw flexed. "I need to make sure he's not being watched before I put you in his path again."

"Oh God"—she pushed the heel of her hand against the throbbing headache starting to build—"I didn't even consider that, and I should have. I'm sorry."

"Nothing to apologize for. You were right to come to me. I have access to training and resources that were closed off to you—to Harris too, since people weren't listening to him." He inched up in his seat, pulled a slip of paper out of his back pocket, and passed it to her. "Contact information to reach members of my team. If things go to hell out there, you're not alone. You can turn to my team. I trust every one of them with my life. They'll take care of you."

She took the slip of paper from him, numbers scrawled in a list with the team members' nicknames beside each one. Brick, Cuervo, Data, Bubbles, Fang, and Slow Hand, the guy who'd transferred out of the team to teach. A lot of people to count on. A lot of support. He'd made some deep connections. "Liam, do you really think—?"

"Put the numbers somewhere safe. There are two prepaid cell phones in my duffel. If you use one, toss it away. Don't use it twice. I also have a weapon for you. Have you ever shot a gun like this before?"

"I've never even seen one like this. Honestly, all I know is what I learned in a basic handgun safety course I took for traveling to some sketchier places for rescues."

"Okay, I'll give you a shooting lesson with this one when we stop. Mostly you just need to get the feel for the kick so you don't jerk when you shoot."

She looked at the numbers, thought about the gun.

The possibility of having to call on any of these people—to reach for that gun—draped her with dread. "Liam, I can't face that something might happen to you because of me."

"Rachel, no. Don't think that way." He scooped up her hand and kissed her wrist. "None of this is your fault. The people who've threatened you and Harris, they're the ones to blame. And we will find them. They will be stopped, that much I can promise you."

He skimmed another kiss along her racing pulse before releasing her. She pressed her wrist to her stomach, holding on to the searing sensation of his kiss a while longer. If only she could hold on to *him* and keep him safe.

Safe from what? Someone who wasn't afraid to run people off the road or blow up buildings. She thought of her lonely town house. There was no one in her life other than her dogs, but still so much lost. All the photos of her SAR success stories. The diaries she'd kept. Sure, some of the photos could be recaptured from other sources, but not everything was replaceable. Like the thank-you note from parents whose two-year-old had wandered out during the night. Or the model clay black Labrador retriever made by the tiny hands of the seven-year-old girl who'd gotten separated from her parents on a camping trip.

That and so much else had been lost forever. And why? For what? She needed answers. "This is all insane, everything that's happened."

"No shit." He turned the steering wheel, veering off the rural highway into a small diner and gas station. "It's also been a long time since we've eaten, and I'm starved. Let's fuel up—Jeep and stomachs."

Guilt sideswiped her again. He hadn't slept last night either—dark circles under his eyes, the stubbly beard, which should have made him appear haggard.

But he just looked even more determined. Right now, he was the Liam McCabe she'd met in the Bahamas, the man who'd worked eighteen hours straight to save lives. He was pouring that determination into helping her, saving Brandon, even stopping whatever traitorous crap was going down on base.

He was all in.

For the first time in two weeks, in years actually, she was no longer alone. And there was something deeply empowering about that. Something she'd envied in Sunny Rocha. "Is there anything I can do to help?"

"You could go in and order food." He reached into his back pocket and pulled five twenties from his wallet. "Be sure to pay for the gas while you're inside. Cash for everything from now on. I'll hang out here with Disco, give him a walk around."

His thoughtfulness and the whole domesticity of the exchange tap-danced all over her already-exposed emotions. She hopped out of the Jeep and walked to him, stopping close enough to touch, to feel the heat of his strength, so much more tangible than even the steam coming off the asphalt.

"Thank you." She touched his chest lightly.

His words from the day before came rolling through her mind, about how they couldn't go back to pretending they weren't affected by each other. And he was right. This attraction between them only increased. His hand enfolded hers.

"Stop thanking me," he said gruffly. "What can you do? I need... food."

She laughed. He was such a man. "Anything in particular you want?"

"Want?" His eyes flamed for an instant, before he squeezed her hand once and let go. "You choose. Just be sure to keep a low profile."

He leaped from the Jeep by the gas pump.

Low profile. Okay. She could do that.

She plucked at her shirt, the heat of the day sticking

her clothes to her back. She'd gotten a fresh change from Sunny—a tee and jean shorts. Generous and definitely welcome, although the shirt was a little snugger than the looser clothes she wore for comfort when working—not to mention, it was hot pink. Not exactly a blend-in color.

Low profile, low key, she chanted mentally with each step. Easier said than done, when she was used to charging through life rather than fading into the walls. At least the place was pretty much deserted, other than an older couple parked in a corner booth and another guy outside walking his boxer.

Stopping in front of the cashier, she peeled off enough twenties so the guy with a Miami Dolphins shirt would turn on the pump. He flipped the switch, collected the cash, and passed her a laminated menu without pulling his attention off the game on television.

She eyed Liam, who was still filling the Jeep, Disco's leash securely in his other hand. Of course he could handle taking care of her dog. She was acting like a nervous mom, for Pete's sake.

Still, as she placed her order for three shrimp po' boys and two orders of fries, she studied the trees and marsh around the diner, wondering where he would choose to walk Disco. The parking lot only had a few cars—an old Cadillac, a Land Cruiser with surf boards on top, and a truck with fishing poles across the back window. Not many vehicles overall, but that area still might invite traffic—and attention.

The campground was deserted, other than a Porta-Potty. Lots of grass, but someone else had the same idea about using it for a dog walk.

Would Liam know to keep her Lab away from the

other dog, a boxer puppy—maybe seven or eight months old—walking over by the creek? The pup seemed more interested in pawing at a rotting log than taking a bathroom break, to the frustration of his owner, a young man who appeared to be around twenty or so. The dog was painfully thin. Probably looking for something to eat, poor pup.

Judging by the owner's loud board shorts and the cut-off sleeves of his shirt, he was probably on his way to the Florida Keys. And he was likely driving the Land Rover in the lot with surfboards strapped to the roof. Definitely on vacation.

Liam replaced the gas nozzle and she paid the rest of the tab to the indifferent cashier. She pivoted back to get her food…

Her eyes snagged on the picture window view of the guy with his boxer. Tugging his boxer, who very definitely didn't want to leave. Shouting at the dog until even the cashier glanced up briefly.

Her stomach lurched at the escalation. She could already predict where this was going even as she hoped otherwise.

Low profile. Low key. Low profile…

She paid the cashier, reached for her bag of food, and tucked it to her chest. Her lips pressed tight as she shouldered through the door.

Just as the shouting jerk kicked his dog right in the head.

―⁓―

Shit.

Keeping Disco on a short leash, Liam ran full out toward the jackass kicking his puppy. Rachel was nearer and closing in fast, with steam coming out of her ears. He was twice as far away.

Still, he pumped harder, faster, racing to close the gap and make it there before Rachel. He needed to stop the jackass, while defusing the situation before anyone got hurt—or drew undue attention to themselves. His pulse hammered in his ears. Hell, his heart was in his throat.

Yeah, he would have said something to the jerk even if Rachel hadn't been around. But he suspected if she got to the guy ahead of him, this wasn't going to shake down peacefully.

"Rachel!" Liam shouted, batting at a low-hanging pine branch, needles showering free. Disco raced alongside in step.

The college-aged guy looked over sharply, his eyes visibly bloodshot even from a distance. He stumbled drunkenly. Intoxicated and violent? It wasn't much of a leap to think the guy would turn that rage from an animal onto a woman.

Onto Rachel.

"Hey!" Rachel shouted. "Wanna lay off your dog there, dude? He's just a curious—hungry—puppy."

The guy pivoted, staggering in the sparse grass. Definitely drunk even this early in the day. His dog cowered closer to the ground, whimpering. "Wanna mind your own business, bitch?"

"That's no way to treat your pet. If you need help, I'll be happy to lend a hand—"

"Get the fuck out of my face." He jabbed a finger in the middle of her chest. Then hesitated. Eying her breasts in the tight pink shirt. Twisting his finger in the fabric.

She didn't back down even a step. Just held a hand up behind her, stopping Liam in his tracks. For now.

Disco crouched low to the ground, snarling. Liam echoed the sentiment. Completely.

Grasping the Lab's collar, Liam paused about five feet away. He held back the dog, respecting Rachel's request. But he stayed close enough to end this in a heartbeat. The guy was too wasted even to see Liam standing on the perimeter, ready to pound this dipshit loser into the ground if the bastard dared hurt Rachel.

Her eyes narrowed. "Move your hand. Now."

The bastard just sneered and poked her chest again. "How about *you* move your sweet little ass, lady."

Liam growled. Rachel smiled.

"I warned you." She moved in a flash, whipping her hand around his wrist. Her other hand bent back his pinky back until he dropped to his knees, shrieking.

"What the fuck? You're breaking my finger. Let go!"

"Does that hurt a little bit?" She pushed harder on his finger and leaned right into his face. "Lay off the dog, you psychopath."

She was frickin' magnificent.

Her confidence, her strength of will and passion, radiated off her in tangible waves. She didn't need to glam up or plaster on makeup. Pure, undiluted Rachel was absolute perfection.

Liam couldn't pull his eyes away.

A second lanky guy in board shorts shouted from the doorway of the Porta-Potty before he jogged toward them. "Hey, Chaz, dude, chill out. You're gonna make them call the cops and they'll find the weed in our—Just lay off."

Snapping into action, Liam put himself between Rachel and the second approaching guy—who appeared sober enough to grasp the wisdom of staying back from Liam and the tensed black Lab.

The sober guy raised his hands. "No harm, no foul, old man. We're outta here as soon as she lets go of my buddy."

Slowly, Rachel released his hand, but her guard was clearly still in place. The way she kept her arm extended protectively in front of the leggy puppy, she wasn't as ready to let this guy off the hook.

Shaking his hand, Chaz stumbled to his feet again. He dropped the leash and staggered away mumbling, "Worthless chickenshit dog... You want it? You take it."

His sober pal hauled him toward the Land Rover, mumbling warnings to shut the hell up as he stuffed him into the passenger side. Once they'd roared out of the parking lot, Rachel knelt in front of the puppy, extending her hand for the cowering pup to sniff.

"It's okay, little one. I won't hurt you." Carefully, she stroked her hands over the dog's sleek brown fur, checking the legs and paws for injury. "Want something to eat?"

She fished into the paper bag she'd dropped to the ground. She dug out... a po' boy. Their supper. Of course. She tore off pieces of *their* food and fed it to the puppy one bit at a time, making fast friends.

Watching the way she'd pulled the dog away from its abusive owner told him that while she might be taking a break from her profession, she would never be able to turn off that need to rescue. She might not know it yet, but she would be back one day, sifting through the rubble, willing the survivors to hang on until she could find them.

And he intended to make sure she lived a damn long time so she could take back her life.

"Uh, Rachel…" He glanced over his shoulder, more than a little uncomfortable with the way the older couple was openly staring at them on their way to their twenty-year-old Caddy. "Do you think we could feed the dog in the Jeep?"

Although how in the hell they were going to fit two dogs in with all the gear was a mystery to him. He needed a bigger car.

Or less baggage.

Rachel glanced up. "There's still plenty of food left in the paper sack. We have supper, like you asked."

"And I'm assuming we also have another dog." Crouching on one knee, he glanced at the collar. "No name. So, it's up to us to pick, and I choose to name him Fang." He stood, knees groaning. "Come on, Fang. Be nice to Disco if you want some of the dog chow in back."

Rachel pushed to her feet, the leash clutched in her fist. "Fang's a girl, you know."

"The name stays. Let's get out of here."

"Fair enough."

She placed the bag on the seat then shoved at least fifty pounds of puppy into the back of the Jeep. The pup whimpered as she watched her crappy prior owner drive away.

Rachel cursed softly. "Jackass took better care of his surfboard than he did his dog."

Liam watched her hand curve around the big puppy. Rachel was fierce. Protective. Strong and soft all at once.

To hell with less baggage.

She was everything he'd ever wanted in a woman. He may have fallen in love easily in the past, but damned if he could remember ever falling this hard.

———∿∿∿———

On the road again, Rachel opened the food bag on her lap and pulled out a po' boy for Liam. Disco curled up at her feet. The boxer—Fang—had wedged herself in the small floor space behind Liam, her wide brandy brown eyes never leaving Rachel.

She passed Liam the sandwich warily. "Aren't you going to chew me out for making a scene?"

"Nope." He took the paper-wrapped meal from her hand without looking over at her.

He'd gone strangely quiet right after they named the dog. Did he regret taking Fang? Was he pissed off at her? After all he'd done for her, she couldn't bear it that she'd upset him. Bad enough that she'd turned herself into more of a liability—and added another dog to their pack.

"Come on, Liam. You're obviously upset. I can see why you'd be mad at me. I was anything but low profile, except I couldn't just turn away—"

"Hey, stop. Really. I mean it when I say I'm not pissed, so don't go trying to read what I'm thinking. You needed to let off steam and he needed his ass kicked. A lot less conspicuous than if the guy at the register had called the cops."

The police. The fishy scents from the bag made her nauseous. "God, what if the cops had shown up anyway? What if the wrong people figured out where we are? What if somebody asks that older couple about us?"

"The cops didn't come and we're way off the radar."
He reached for his drink to wash down a bite.

She nibbled a French fry halfheartedly, her appetite fading. "I should have placed an anonymous call to animal services."

"With our untraceable phone? Maybe. But even if you had, the chances of them finding the guy, much less being able to pursue anything after the fact, are slim." He glanced over, his eyes... guarded, but not angry. "You should already know that. Didn't you tell me once that your mom worked for animal control?"

"That's right. I'm touched that you remember." She'd heard her married friends complain more than once about being tuned out by the men in their lives.

"Of course I remember. You told me how you mother died working that job. That had to have been awful for you and your father."

Rachel scratched at a rusty spot on the door. "My father and mother split when I was about eight. He moved to another state. I didn't see much of him. I still don't. My mom and I were... everything to each other."

Her mother had died investigating a dog-fighting ring. The owner hadn't taken well to seeing so many of his "assets" seized. He'd gone after her mom with a baseball bat to the head. She'd never regained consciousness. The loss, her mother's fierce bravery—it all welled up inside her until her throat closed.

Liam accelerated, the Jeep plowing deeper into the tunnel of Everglades foliage. "Seeing that guy go ballistic on his dog must have made you think of your mom and how she died."

"I wasn't thinking that at the time, but now that

you put it that way... Sure. I guess a lot of what I do is ingrained from watching her. She was an amazing woman, strong, passionate about her work being a voice for homeless and abused animals."

"She sounds a lot like you."

Chuckling, she shook her head. "I wish. I certainly wanted to be like her. I even got to go to work with her sometimes."

"To the shelter?"

"Sure. But sometimes I even got to ride along when she went out for a seizure. Not as often as I would have liked, though."

An eyebrow shot up toward his hairline, the tips of his hair bleached blond from time in the sun. She couldn't help but think how people paid serious bucks for a look like that, yet he was a hundred percent natural. She'd accepted that she wanted him, but the whole *how* of a relationship with him boggled her mind. Hell, what did they really even know about each other beyond sharing info about past relationships?

"Rachel?"

"Oh, right, my mom." She popped another fry in her mouth, suddenly ravenously hungry. "This one time, Mom got called in for an emergency seizure on a weekend. The shelter was understaffed—aren't they all?—so she couldn't say no. There wasn't a sitter to watch me, so Mom took me along. I was supposed to stay in the truck."

A smile dug a dimple into one cheek. "But you didn't."

"Of course not." She'd been so curious. So certain she would be just like her mother someday, a fearless defender of the helpless. And as much as thinking about the past hurt, she realized that Liam wanted to know more about her, which sent her digging around in that dark memory to share something of herself. "We drove to a crack house. There was a report of dog-fighting activity on the premises."

"God—please tell me you weren't there when your mother was attacked."

"No…" She rested a hand on top of his on the gearshift. "I wasn't. This was a different raid, much earlier than that horrible… I was twenty when she died."

"How old were you that time you rode along?"

"Nine. Old enough to understand what I was seeing was very, very wrong. The suspects were already in handcuffs, so I wasn't in any danger." But she could still remember the feel, the stench, of evil that permeated the place. "I snuck out of the animal shelter's van—it was getting dark by then. On my way over to the house, I saw all the standard dog-fighting paraphernalia—a rusted treadmill, blood-stained tarps."

The puppy scooched a paw between the seats and she stroked Fang lightly, gently building a bond. "Once I made it to the house, I watched from the bushes, through the window. There were nine dogs inside and not much else. Just some crates, a few bedrolls, and garbage from food wrappers. There wasn't even a television or refrigerator."

Tears and rage burned her throat. She set the bag aside. "But there were rats in cages. The people—and I use that term loosely—would entertain themselves by starving the dogs, then letting rats run free."

She tipped her head to the last rays of sun heating down on her, wishing she could fill herself, lose herself, in the lush nature scents around her, as Disco did.

"Out of the nine dogs confiscated that night, only one lived. Seven had been fought too aggressively to be rehabilitated, so their outcome was a forgone conclusion." The puppy pawed at her hand and she resumed petting. "The bait dog… God, he broke my heart, he was so chewed up. I rode all the way back to the clinic sitting by his crate, talking to him, begging him to hold on just a little longer. But he didn't make it."

Silence stretched while she stroked under the pup's neck rather than on top of the head, every touch chosen deliberately to help instill confidence in the cowed canine.

Liam cupped her neck, gently. To instill trust? "What about the one that lived?"

"The female breeder dog… Her name was Ruby." She could still see the reddish brown gleam of her shiny coat. "She was so terrified, she didn't even flinch from being touched. She just held herself completely still, and kept her eyes averted, locked on a faraway spot. The first time I looked into the eyes of a soldier suffering from PTSD, I saw Ruby's eyes. I saw the pain underneath the disconnect."

He looked across quickly, his eyes stunned, then shielded. "You and your mother kept Ruby."

"We did adopt her. She lived for four more happy years. I miss her every day." That sweet dog's unbroken spirit inspired her, helped forge her determination not to let life bend her.

What had happened to make her lose sight of that direction for her life from her mom and Ruby? Her spine stiffened, straightening with some of the old starch. She refused to cave. She had to fight to get her life back.

She had to be strong enough to be Liam's wingman.

"Rachel Flores..." He whistled softly. "You're an amazing woman."

The light in his eyes when he said those words had nothing to do with sex. But something deeper hummed across the air like a live wire snapping along the ground after it has been uprooted by a storm.

She was ready to acknowledge attraction, even some kind of kindred-spirit friendship. But what she saw in his eyes... she wasn't ready for that.

"Please don't tell me you're in love with me." She tried to make light of it. Rather than tell him outright she didn't think she could handle that much emotion right now, even when she knew his kind of love was the temporary sort.

Maybe *because* his love was temporary.

He looked back at her, not a smile in sight. "Is that supposed to make me laugh?"

The depth in his green eyes, packed with flint and spark and emotion, sent a longing popping through her veins. "I'm not sure."

Liam didn't answer, just drove deeper into the wilds of the Everglades until scents and sounds hummed all around them. His words hung there between them, all but floating on the humidity-laden air. And as she watched Liam feed every last bite of the po' boy to the puppy, her heart squeezed until *she* felt less and less like laughing too.

Chapter 11

BRANDON KNEW WHEN HE WAS BEING WATCHED.

He just hated that all the crap going on in his life made him question whether he was paranoid. But from the moment he'd woken up on Catriona's couch, he'd been certain. Someone was lurking around her place. The only question? Was that individual after him or her? Either way, he needed to stake out her place until he got the answer.

Parked deep in the driveway of an empty house for sale, he could see Cat's home, most of it anyway. Definitely the front access. His hand fell to rest on his Australian shepherd mutt, threading through the fur.

He kept the windows open on his truck so Harley stayed cool and he could listen for anything out of the ordinary at Cat's. Reaching behind him, he tugged a gallon jug of water over and leaned down to fill the bowl on the floorboards for Harley.

If he could just get in touch with Rachel. He'd heard her cell phone messages asking where he was, warning him to be careful, then nothing more. He pulled out his phone and thought about turning it back on. But that paranoia set in again. If someone was tracking his cell, he didn't want to draw attention to his locale. Especially this close to Cat's.

A fierce protectiveness filled him and he couldn't delude himself into thinking it was anything but personal.

He was getting involved with her at the worst possible time for a relationship.

So here he still sat. Alone with his dog. Staked out a couple of doors down from Catriona's house. At least he was good at his job—or had been at one time—and no one had noticed him watching her home.

Who was he supposed to tell, since Rachel had fallen off the map? He'd already tried reaching out to officials. If he ended up locked in a loony bin, he wouldn't be of any help to Cat.

He'd been all set to go home after breakfast, but while he was forking down French toast, he'd realized a silver sedan was casing her house. The vehicle had driven by at least three times before driving away. He'd warned her to be careful here alone, and she'd simply shrugged off his concern, insisting no one would mess with her because of all the dogs.

Her lack of concern fueled his determination to keep watch.

A movement caught his attention and he straightened in the seat, the weight of his gun in the holster familiar, comforting. A truck pulled onto the street, a black, crew cab Ford with a lone male in front.

Could just be someone dropping off or picking up a pet. Except the dude got out of the truck and—no dog. Catriona met him at the gate, no dog with her either.

Someone touring the place? Maybe. But still strange he hadn't brought his pet along.

He profiled the guy. Military haircut. Lean but fit. Wearing what looked like some kind of festival T-shirt and running shorts. The back of his truck had a huge Gatorade dispenser.

So maybe the guy was a boyfriend. Just because he'd gotten vibes from Catriona that she was attracted to him didn't mean squat. She could still have a boyfriend, or some guy who wanted to get to know her better.

Yeah, that fit better, because if she had a guy, there would have been signs.

Harley nudged him.

"Not now, girl."

She head-butted him harder.

"Really, in a minute. I'm busy."

She pawed him on the leg again and again.

"Okay, okay, you need to go out. All that water. Got it." He turned to get her leash from the back.

And saw a silver sedan cruising down the street. Straight toward Catriona's house. The guy riding shotgun *had* a shotgun. He pointed it through the open window, directly at Cat's home.

Brandon whipped the truck into drive and nailed the gas. Tires squealing, he peeled out of the driveway, the nose of his truck aimed at the sedan.

Catriona's breath whooshed from her lungs as she hit the ground. One quick gasp filled her mouth with sand.

Not all that surprising, since she'd been crushed to the ground by some guy she'd just met. A military guy named Jose James who'd said he was looking for Brandon a second before he'd body-slammed her to the gritty driveway.

Pops echoed. Like gunshots? Ohmigod, ohmigod, she gasped for breath, her chest going tighter.

A crash sounded, close, out on the road. Crunching metal and shattering glass. Then a bubble of silence.

Barking erupted in the aftermath. Dogs of all sizes charged and pawed at the fence, their frenzy deafening. Her senses went on overload trying to process so much at once.

Panic scratched at her nerves as tangibly as the sand and gravel under her cheek. Of course they were freaked out. So was she.

Desperate to see what was going on, she spit the sand out of her mouth. "What the hell are you doing? Get off me, please."

"Hold still," he warned against her ear.

"Really, I'm oka—"

Abruptly, he was off her as quickly as he'd flattened her.

She rolled to her back, then to her feet, and found not just the new guy but… Brandon running toward her?

Thank God he'd returned, because this stranger was seriously freaking her out. And oh God, Brandon's truck was buried in the side of the silver sedan. There were two men in front, both sitting up and alert. Apparently unharmed. Engine revving, the car squealed into reverse, then forward, spewing smoke as it roared away.

Brandon tugged her arm, the familiar feel and scent of him soothing her fear.

The gun in his hand, however, she did *not* recognize.

"Cat, get back!" Brandon hauled her to her feet, his body between her and the men in the car.

Where were her neighbors? She scanned the street for someone, anyone. But either her two elderly neighbors had their hearing aids turned down or they were already calling the cops. Hopefully the latter. The rest of the houses were empty, either for sale or foreclosed. She should call the police, except her cell phone wasn't clipped to her shorts anymore.

Brandon aimed the weapon at the departing silver sedan. He popped off shots, pocking the ground around the car, flattening one tire. The sedan didn't even slow. The tire rim shot sparks behind it as the car peeled out around the corner.

And what about her dogs? Oh God, what if one of them had been hit by a stray bullet from the guy with a shotgun? She yanked free of Brandon and raced for the backyard. She heard curses flying from both men but didn't stop to explain.

She shoved through the gate and into the backyard. The pack peeled away from the fence and circled around her. Frantically, she counted and inventoried, her heart pounding... Tabitha? Catriona dropped to her knees beside the massive Argentine Dogo to inspect the streak of red slashing across her white coat. Her training as a vet tech roared to the surface as she carefully examined what appeared to be a simple grazing. *Thank God.*

Brandon's hand clamped her shoulder. She looked back to see him standing guardedly by Jose James. Who also had a frickin' gun in his hand?

The two men scowled at each other, weapons gripped firmly.

Her heart hammered against her ribs and she wondered if she might need her old inhaler again. "Hey, fellas, can we all draw down now and maybe someone could tell me what's going on? Why were the guys in that car shooting at me?"

Brandon's big black gun didn't waver from Jose. "What are you doing here?"

Catriona gripped his shirt to restrain him—as if she really even could. "That's Jose James. He said he was from Patrick Air Force Base, and he was asking about *you*."

Muscles flexed with tension under her hands. "Is that so, James?"

Jose pointed the muzzle of his weapon skyward, his hands up, nonthreatening. "I'm here for Rachel Flores. She would have come herself, but we needed to know if you were being watched. Good thing we checked, isn't it? Now how about we step inside? While you're taking care of the dog's injury, we can talk."

Liam sent the dogs ahead of them into the seedy motel room.

As much as he hated calling it quits for the day, they weren't going to reach the cabin tonight. Traveling those Everglades waters in the dark would be dangerous enough on his own. But with Rachel along? Not wise. They could both use the sleep. With luck, he would hear something from Jose soon anyway.

Meanwhile, he needed to keep busy, recon the place, make contingency plans. Do anything other than think about the moment he'd seen her defend that puppy.

He had one mission tonight, keeping Rachel safe, and sadly, this place offered their best bet for flying under the radar.

"Sorry about the one-star rating on the accommodations." He gave the dogs the freedom to sniff at the two saggy beds and cheap laminate furniture with a serious seventies vibe.

"No need to apologize." She dropped her backpack

on the chair closest to the door. "I understand that find-ing a place that accepts cash without requiring you to show a credit card as well limited our choices. At least there aren't bugs."

Or were there? Best to keep a light on tonight for more than one reason.

He tossed her a bedroll he'd brought from the Jeep. "We can spread out the sleeping bags so you don't have to actually come into contact with the linens."

"It's not that bad, and it's certainly better than some places I've stayed. Remember those half-crumbling cot-tages we stayed at in the Bahamas after the earthquake? At least the floor's level here, we have hot water, and there won't be any aftershocks."

"True, true." He flicked on a second light under a cheesy dime-store painting of a palm tree on a beach. Music from the marsh-side bar thrummed through the night. He would have preferred somewhere more se-cluded, but as she'd pointed out, their choices were lim-ited. "I'm gonna get the rest of our gear out of the Jeep."

Before someone stole it.

He'd parked the vehicle right in front of their room. As he walked in and out again, he saw Rachel push back the curtains for better access to the AC. They could sure use some air moving in the muggy, musty room. How much more humid could it get without actually raining? Rachel twisted knobs until tepid gusts wafted from the groaning wall unit. He'd bunked in worse and so had she. That didn't mean he was happy with having her here.

Within five minutes, he'd stacked their stockpile in a corner. "Stay put, and I'll get the food this time."

She hitched a hand on her hip, her spunk increasing

exponentially since she'd first shown up in his life again. "Worried I'll make a scene by kicking someone else's ass?"

"Or that someone will *grab* yours. Have you looked around this place?" He paused in the doorway. Was it safer to leave her here, locked in the room, even though she would be alone? She had weapons—that she didn't know how to use. "Fine, then. Come with me, stick to my side, and we'll get supper together."

Laughing, she tugged his T-shirt. "You are such a man."

"I hope so." He eyed the dogs sprawled on the floor in front of the television, wrestling and rolling. "You two, behave while we're gone."

He closed the door behind him.

She hooked an arm through his.

Pulling his arm from hers, he hooked it around her shoulders, hugging her tighter to his side. Closer. Nowhere near close enough to keep her safe. With the handgun strapped to his waist he doubted anyone would mess with him. He had a permit to carry, but this also didn't look like the kind of place where people carded anyone.

He spotted at least seven trucks with gun racks full in clear sight. "Let's make this quick and seriously low-key this time."

"I've got your back."

Something in the way she said that made him glance over at her sharply. She simply smiled back and kept walking toward the one-story bar painted a gross, mucusy green.

Inside, the place smelled of smoke and unwashed bodies, sweaty from dancing their slicked selves against each other. He hauled her closer. Yeah, he was feeling primitively protective.

What of it?

He'd seen the same kind of dive bar in countless places around the world. Not that he'd hung out there, but rather hauled someone out before they landed in trouble. Or worse.

He stepped up to the bar and caught the bartender's attention, settling for the simplest order to speed things along.

"Three cheeseburgers, an order of nachos, and a jug of sweet tea." He glanced at Rachel quickly for confirmation, and when she nodded, he turned back to the guy wearing a beer-stained apron. "That order's to go. There's an extra twenty for you if you move the order to the front of the line."

He passed one bill over now, the other folded and ready. He didn't want to flash his wallet full of cash out in the open here.

"Done." The bartender snagged the twenty and shouted into the kitchen. "Three CBs, nachos, sweet tea—on skates."

While Liam waited, his eyes drifted over a trio clanking longnecks while they waited in line outside the bathrooms. He watched for any threat, the warm press of Rachel at his side a reminder of the stakes. Her body vibrated against his as she hummed along with the jukebox cranking out an old Roy Orbison classic.

Farther into a shadowy hallway, he saw a couple of other unobtrusive doors. Could have been offices. But he knew they weren't. As if on cue, a couple sidled toward one of those back rooms. A woman in fuck-me

heels, a shrink-wrapped miniskirt, and a tired perm led
a sunburned tourist by the hand. Liam scrubbed a hand
over his head and looked away, frustrated all over again
that he had to bring Rachel to a place like this. But then
the luxurious safe-house quarters on base ultimately
hadn't been any more secure.

He'd accepted the failures he'd made in his personal life. He refused to accept failure in his ability
to do his job. And right now, his job was keeping
Rachel alive and finding out why Brandon Harris's
accusations had set off such a hailstorm in the military community.

The crack and snap of a game of pool reverberated
from the back corner. A beer rested on the edge of the
table, serving as a paperweight for a couple of twenties. Angling over the velvet table, a middle-aged guy in
khaki cutoffs and a T-shirt lined up his shot.

A brawl could break out at any second in a place
like this.

Liam leaned on the bar to hurry things up just as the
bartender passed over a bag of food and jug of tea. He
passed the guy the extra twenty and made tracks back out
to the parking lot toward their first-floor room. How had
the air gotten even muggier in the span of—he checked
his watch—seventeen minutes? Could be something to
do with the woman tucked against his side, a woman
he would be spending the whole night with alone in a
motel room.

He rounded the corner and found… oh crap.

A local TV station, with bright lights and a camera
rolling, taping footage of God only knew what as they
interviewed a cop. Probably a knifing or robbery.

Their room was at least five doors down from the epi-center of the media frenzy, straight through the camera's line of shooting.

"Rachel," he hissed, turning her around. "We need to go back into the bar."

"Kiss me."

"Huh?"

"Turn away from the camera and kiss me." She grabbed his face and plastered her lips to his, dragging him until his back was to the crowd.

His brain went on stun for a second at just the feel of her mouth on his, her hands against his cheeks. Reason filtered through. But just barely.

He buried his nose in her neck. "Damn it, Rachel, I said not to draw attention to us."

"Hate to break it to you." She nuzzled his ear, cir-cling it with her tongue. "But people are already looking. We'll definitely blend into this place a lot more by acting like a couple of barflies on our way to a motel hookup."

She had a point.

Liam nipped her shoulder. "We can't just hang around here all night making out."

"Then kiss me the whole way to the room." She looped her arms around his neck, the half-gallon jug of tea thudding between his shoulder blades. "Do you have a problem with that?"

In theory? No. But the reality of tempting himself that much wreaked serious havoc with the rational part of his brain shouting at him to keep Rachel out of harm's way. The best way to do that? Stay objective.

And objectively speaking, she was actually right about the best way to blend in around here.

"Okay, I can see your point." He pressed a finger to her mouth. "Let's get to work and make the hookup look realistic."

"We need to do more than look realistic." She drew his finger into her mouth and circled her tongue around the tip.

The one simple stroke ramped the already steamy temperature close to meltdown.

Another car pulled up, headlights sweeping the lot.

Jug of tea in one hand, she pressed his palm to her breast. Before he could pick his jaw up off the cracked sidewalk, she tucked her fingers down into his jeans back pocket and dug her nails into his ass.

Shock held him still for only a second. She was right about making this look realistic. His hand filled with her sweet softness, he backed her toward their room. He drew her tongue into his mouth, massaging the soft curve of her breast, each step of the way careful to tuck them both behind the wall of onlookers eager to appear on television. He had to think, move, hide her away in their room as fast as possible.

Except how was he supposed to think with the taste of her flowing through his veins?

Her hitchy, surprised gasp of pleasure ignited the fire in his belly. She clawed his butt through his jeans pockets and plastered herself to him so convincingly, his hard-on throbbed against his button fly.

"Are we still acting?" He pressed his mouth to the pulse along her neck. "Because we're well out of range of the camera's lens."

"Hell no, I'm not acting. Get me inside," she gasped. "Now!"

Her demand unleashed molten lust. His feet tangled with hers as he guided her the final few steps to their room. He could barely process that she'd crossed this line along with him, that their act in the parking lot was as hot for her as it had been for him. He just hoped she didn't regret it tomorrow. He'd locked down his feelings for her for too long to fight off the hunger even one more time.

"Get the key," he said, his hands full with the food bag and her breast. He'd be damned if he intended to let go of either. "It's in my front left pocket."

She slid her fingers from his pants in a torturously slow glide of her nails that pulled his shirt free. The quick yank sent his wallet tumbling onto the sidewalk. The overstuffed billfold fanned cash along the concrete.

They both bent, heads nearly colliding. He snagged his wallet and she gathered up the bills and—holy crap—three condom packets. He snatched the condoms and she grabbed the cash, folding the money in half and tucking it down the front of her shirt.

"Enough foreplay, Liam." She plucked the carryout bag from his hands. "Open. The. Door."

"Yes, ma'am." He fished in his front pocket until he found the old-fashioned key. Metal. Not plastic. This place was so old and dingy, it didn't even have key cards. There had to be another way, another place...

"I can see where your mind's going." She skimmed her palm up his chest. "Quit thinking, and let's just get inside."

He pushed into the room, the need for her ramping up his already adrenaline-saturated body. The two dogs had claimed the double bed farthest from the door. Their ears perked up as he and Rachel stumbled inside, but once the pups seemed to realize they were going to be evicted back to the floor, both closed their eyes again, playing possum.

Good enough for him. He turned back to Rachel.

The door closed. He placed their late-night supper on the table. Food could wait.

Rachel sagged against the closed panel. The room key dropped to the floor. Finesse was gone. He didn't know the whys of her change of heart, and right now, he frankly didn't care. He just wanted her. Here. Naked. Then again in the shower. Anywhere he could have her. He hoped like crazy she agreed.

"Now? Really?" he asked.

"Absolutely *now*." She grabbed the hem of her T-shirt and tugged upward.

"Let me."

He swept away her hands and peeled her shirt over her head, easy enough, as she raised her arms to accommodate him. Which happened to put her breasts within easy reach for touching, licking, sucking until her head writhed against the door. And oh God, she had the all-over honey tone to her skin he'd wondered about. No tan lines. Just pure sweet Rachel, bared for his total and undivided attention.

Her nails scored down his back until her hand came around and grazed the front of his fly. His legs just about buckled underneath him.

Bracing one hand against the door, he stroked her hair away from her face with the other, enjoying the glide of dark strands between his fingers. "When did you decide on taking this step?"

"I thought about it the first time I saw you. And then

about a thousand times since then. As for when I decided to act on it? I'm not sure exactly. Maybe somewhere between when you fed the puppy and when you felt me up in the parking lot." She nibbled along his jaw, her tongue flicking his earlobe. "Some things in life just happen. *This* was meant to happen."

"That works for me."

She stroked the length of him. "Condom? Do you have one?"

"In my wallet, remember? Three of them, I think." He wished he had more.

"Yes…" She yanked the leather billfold out and open. More cash tumbled to the floor, but thank God, so did three plastic packets.

He grabbed one off the floor and tore it open while she unfastened the button fly of his jeans. The pressure of her hands, her touch even through denim, had him throbbing harder.

The floor vibrated under his feet. Or was it the door? His brain cleared enough to realize someone was pounding from outside.

His reflexes went on alert. He snatched Rachel's shirt off the back of the chair and passed it to her, pushing her behind him in one fluid movement.

"Police," a male voice shouted from outside. The fist pounded again. "Open up."

Biting back a curse, Liam buttoned his pants and reached for his .45 caliber on the table.

"Sir, ma'am?" the voice shouted again. "Open this door now or I'm going to be forced to kick it down."

Liam tucked his hand behind him, silver handgun in his fist, and opened the door. A burly dude in uniform blocked the doorjamb with his foot and flashed his badge. It looked legit.

Carefully, Liam tucked the gun into his waistband at the small of his back, hidden in the hem of his shirt Rachel had tugged loose seconds earlier. They really didn't need this kind of attention. But like it or not, this guy wasn't going to disappear.

The faster they settled this, the better. "Is there a problem, officer?"

Liam heard a clink, sort of like ice cubes, until he realized. Shit. The officer held up handcuffs.

"Sir, I'm going to have to ask you to put your hands behind your back. You're under arrest for soliciting a prostitute."

Chapter 12

RACHEL HELD THE SHIRT TO HER BARE CHEST, TWENTY-dollar bills on the floor around her feet. In a seedy motel room. This *so* didn't look good.

Neither did the gun in the back waistband of Liam's jeans. The cop really wasn't going to like that. Or the arsenal stowed away in the duffel bag. And oh God, was the television camera crew still filming? She peeked over the officer's shoulder and they didn't seem to be interested in the little drama unfolding in her life. Or maybe that was wishful thinking.

Liam nudged his loose T-shirt over the gun and brought his empty hands around for the policeman to view. "What do you mean, under arrest for soliciting a prostitute?"

The cop pushed the door open wider, his backup now visible a few steps behind. The partner—a fresh-faced kid straight out of the academy, most likely—had his hand on his gun and looked entirely too twitchy.

The senior officer hitched a thumb in his belt. "Don't bother denying it, sir. I saw your whole little exchange of cash outside the room—not wise, by the way. Especially in an establishment well-known for easy hooker traffic." The police officer shook his head wearily. "I have heard more bullshit stories than you can imagine, trying to crack down on this place. So don't even attempt to play on my sympathy by bringing in stories about your sick

wife or your kids or your mama. Look me in the eyes. I
do *not* care."

Once the cops found the weapons, they were screwed.
Road trip over. Right back in with the OSI and whatever
made Liam haul her out of there in the first place.

She had to fix this for him. Now.

Rachel forced a blush up her face. "But Officer"—
she glanced at his name tag—"Vogel, I'm not a hooker.
I *am* his wife."

Liam's head whipped around.

Officer Vogel didn't look impressed or convinced.
Apparently he *had* heard it all.

"Hold on there, sister, I'm about to get around to your
arrest. You may want to keep your mouth closed in the
meantime, because consider this your official notice of
you rights being read." His eyes narrowed. "I'm guessing you've had them read to you before."

Now that just wasn't very nice.

If only she could put this scene on pause and pull her
shirt back over her head, she would feel more comfortable telling him so.

"But I really *am* his wife." The lie rolled too easily off her tongue. She stepped up behind Liam, which
served the double duty of shielding that gun of his and
giving her the chance to pull on her T-shirt.

She spoke over Liam's shoulder. "We were playact-
ing here. Marital bed sex has been getting rather, well,
routine. We decided to spice things up, be spontaneous,
role-play…" She shook her head, willing another blush
up her cheeks. "God, this is embarrassing."

"But entertaining." Officer Vogel folded his arms
over his chest, bulletproof vest under his shirt giving

him extra bulk. "Whatever he paid you, sounds like he
got his money's worth."

"Now you're going to be sorry you said that when
you realize I really am his legal bride, till death do us
part." She leaned toward the chair for her backpack.

"Halt!" The cop leveled his gun at her in a move
so fast, Liam's hand shot behind his back toward
his weapon.

"Wait!" Rachel raised her hands fast.

God help them if Liam pulled his big-ass gun.

Damn it all, she knew better than to reach into her
backpack that way. She was just rattled. Her skin still
steamed from Liam's touch and now she was facing
down a cop. "Sorry, sir, I should have warned you first.
I apologize. May I please get my identification out of
my backpack?"

She could see the alarm in Liam's face, see how badly
he wanted to shout *no, no, and hell no*. He thought she
was about to make them completely traceable to here.
But she couldn't explain.

He might have a plan A, B, and C, but she actually
had a plan Z.

Holding her backpack, she thrust her hands out. "If
you would prefer, you can go through it yourself."

Please, please, she hoped he wouldn't accept her
bluff, since she had the chick gun Liam gave her after
they left the Rocha's home. With some luck, Officer
Vogel would prefer to keep his hands free for his
own weapon.

"Ma'am, you may get your ID, but go very slowly.
No sudden moves or we're finishing this at the station."

She set the bag back on the table and pulled out

the leather pouch. Only a flicker of surprise flashed through Liam's eyes before he shielded his expression again.

Rachel plucked free the fake identifications that Sunny had given her, ones for a husband and wife. She prayed the grainy photos would pass muster. The dim lighting was in their favor.

"Here's my driver's license from our home state of Oregon. And here's my husband's identification as well. Phil and Audrey Franklin. On the bed over there are our family pets, Disco and Fang."

Liam glanced at her, one eyebrow raised.

She babbled on nervously, while Officer Vogel flipped the IDs over. "Phil didn't have gray hairs yet in this photo, but he had the picture made back when he was using that Grecian Formula because he was worried about losing his masculinity."

Choking on a cough, Liam scratched the back of his neck.

She forged ahead. "And what do you know? All we really needed was a vacation in Florida and some naughty fantasies."

Frowning, Vogel passed the pair of IDs back to her. "These actually appear to be in order. You two should really be more careful. Places like this aren't the safest. People usually come here to find something bad or hide from something even worse. Understand, ma'am?"

"Completely."

"And Mr. Franklin, next time, just pretend to pick her up in a nice hotel bar and get a room, preferably one that sports clean sheets, okay? Protect your wife like a good husband."

"Will do, Officer," Liam answered, tight-lipped. He closed and locked the door. He flattened his hands on the frame.

His back expanded with a deep sigh before he turned around to face her again. "Wanna tell me what's going on with our IDs, Mrs. Franklin?"

—⁓—

Liam took in Rachel's tousled hair and plumped lips. She looked like a woman who'd been doing exactly what they had been doing five minutes ago.

Or rather, what they'd almost done before the cop interrupted.

Anger churned in his gut with an emotion he hadn't felt in so long he almost didn't recognize it. Fear. Fear for Rachel set his stomach burning with acid. "Well? Anything to say?"

"Should we leave now?"

He considered it. Then shook his head. "If we bolt, Officer Vogel might think we have something to hide, and the less he thinks about us, the better. Then there's that television crew. We're better off staying here for now."

"I can see that… Mr. Franklin." Her mouth twitched again.

"You've got a warped sense of humor, *Mrs. Franklin*."

Rachel stood toe-to-toe with him, sexy and seemingly unaffected by how close they'd been to deep, deep trouble. "Liam, you're not going to stare me down with that grim 'I'm in charge' face, so take it down a notch."

Grim? *Grim?* He wasn't grim. He was the fun guy, the team's cool CRO, the one who made people laugh and unified a group. Or rather he had been until about six months ago, when someone had kicked the props out from under his world.

"Then how about some answers, Rachel? What's up with the Franklin family fake IDs, and is there anything else in that bag I should know about?" Needing distance from the draw of her, the need to pull her close and safe, he placed his weapon on the table beside her backpack. "Keep in mind, I do not like being lied to."

Really didn't like it, especially after marriage number two.

"Sunny gave me the extra identification, just in case." She passed the pouch to him. "There was no need to tell you unless we needed it. Which we did."

He thumbed the well-worn leather. "And that's all?"

"That's it." She crossed her arms, which plumped her bra-less breasts against the snug T-shirt. "Come on, Liam, you have to admit what happened with Officer Vogel would be funny any other time."

"I'm not laughing."

"Maybe you need to." She flattened her hands to his chest. "This will make for a great bar story some day. Maybe you'll even get a new call sign out of it… like *John*, perhaps."

He bit back the urge to laugh, humor battling with anger.

Damn. Just damn. He was already on the edge, and seeing her like that? His body throbbed to life again with memories of how close they been to hooking up.

He took a step toward her, his boot crackling a twenty-dollar bill on the carpet. "You like to make up sex games, Mrs. Franklin?"

"My fantasies about you are the real kind, Liam." She

draped her arms over his shoulders, moving in close where there was no mistaking the honesty in her eyes. "I just want to be with you right now. In a bed or against the door. It doesn't matter as long as we let this happen, uncap the steam and tension that's building inside me until I'm going to scream if I don't get relief. For some reason I don't understand, and quite frankly am scared to analyze right now, you're the only man I want to ease this ache."

He knuckled back her hair and drew her to him until her breasts skimmed his chest. "What about the questionable sheets?"

One step at a time, she backed him toward the door. "We'll start here, and move to the shower next. Skip the bed altogether."

"Sounds like a plan." Arms around her waist, he lifted her off the floor until she was level with him.

Turning, he planted her against the locked door, already kissing before her back met the panel. Her fingers threaded through his hair, tugging him nearer. The ache to have her sliced him clean through again, the edge sharper, given how close they'd come to having everything blow up in their faces.

She unfastened one button at a time along the fly of his jeans. "No more finesse. No more waiting." She slipped her hands inside his boxers, right alongside his erection, without touching. "I hurt from wanting you."

Then her cool hands closed around him.

He fought down the need to finish now. He tore her shirt down the middle and latched onto her nipple. Her grip on him tightened in time with her groan. He completely agreed.

Reaching, he clapped a hand on the table and snagged

a condom. She picked it from his hand, tugging it open. He worked the zipper down on her shorts, sweeping the panties along with it. He stroked and lingered along her slick warmth. She rocked against his touch, breathy sighs encouraging him. She kicked her clothes aside as she sheathed him.

Pressing his forehead into her hair, he struggled to keep himself in check.

"Liam, no more waiting. We'll go fast now, and slow later in the shower. Then slow again wherever you choose. Stop thinking, analyzing, protecting, and just take me…" She hitched a leg around his hips. "Take me now, because I'm so close to the edge and I don't want to go there without you."

Her words snapped the last of his restraint. She tucked her hands into his jeans and urged him… inside. Her damp heat clamped around him. Her breasts beaded tighter against his chest. He thrust into her again and again. Thoughts of threats outside scattered from his brain and everything faded except for the feel of her. The whisper of her voice as she gasped in pleasure, telling him she was close, so very close…

She came apart and he had to watch every second. Take in this moment that had haunted his frustrated dreams for six months.

They'd been through so much in the past couple of days—six months ago as well. There hadn't been anyone since he'd seen her for the first time. He'd told himself he was too busy for a relationship, but he knew now he'd been burning for her. He'd been grieving over losing her in a way he'd never done for any woman before, not even a wife.

—*w*—

Rachel splayed her hands on the wet tiles, the aftermath
of her third release still rippling through her. Pleasure
tingled like the beads of water from the shower washing
over her again and again.

Her hands fell to rest on Liam's head, holding on to
his saturated hair as he knelt between her legs. His unshaven face rasped against the tender flesh of her thighs.
He eased his tongue along the tight bundle of nerves,
drawing out the last flashes of pleasure until her knees
gave way.

He caught her, his hands big and strong, triggering
another reverberation through her. She leaned into him
as he reclined in the tub, taking her weight as she blanketed his body with hers. A sigh of contentment vibrated
inside her. Silently, he toed the shower off, switching to
the faucet and closing the drain.

Earlier, coming together had been impulsive.
Reactive. Riding the wave of adrenaline from so many
close calls. And yes, even fueled by all the talk of being
a couple playing out fantasies to spark up their sex life.

Right now, being naked and vulnerable with Liam?
Things got complicated. This was about emotions. About
unresolved issues between them from six months ago.

She'd deluded herself since leaving the Bahamas that
she could avoid these feelings if she avoided the man.
Clearly, that wasn't true.

Her legs pressed against his hips, one leg against
his right buttock, where she'd found a green footprint
tattoo. He'd told her it was standard for PJs, in honor
of the earlier days when helicopters called Jolly Green

Giants flew them around. There were so many things left to learn about him, so many things she wanted to know. Sure, she'd heard about his ex-wives and met the members of his team on the job.

But what about his childhood? What had shaped him into the adult he'd become? She knew none of those private details about the man she'd already let have such access to her own life, her body, and maybe her heart.

She sipped beads of water from his chest, kissing her way along his collarbone. "I told you about my mom. Tell me about your family."

"I don't have family."

"Everyone has family, even if they're not blood related." She traced along his chest down to his six pack. How could one man be so lean and muscled at the same time? Every ounce of him was poured into sculpted strength—strength she'd enjoyed the hell out of since they closed that door behind Officer Vogel.

"Okay, then, the fire department of Dalton, Texas, is my family."

"Fire department?"

"I volunteered there when I was seventeen. I couldn't go into burning buildings, but I could ride with them. I got to play with the Jaws of Life. I ate good meals and had male role models to give me advice."

"Your father was dead?"

"No, but my mother died of cancer when I was eleven, and after that, honestly, my father didn't care what I did." He held up a hand and she linked fingers with him. "No need to make it a sob story. He wasn't brokenhearted over my mother's death. He didn't abuse me. I had a roof over my head. According to all of the different marriage counselors, he was a self-absorbed narcissist. And since my mother died when I was young, I was constantly seeking to re-create the perfect home life for myself through my many failed marriages." He rattled off the information dispassionately, as if reciting from a textbook. "And yet I kept re-creating the past by getting into relationships doomed from the start."

"Um, wow. That's… sad?" Tragic actually. Every woman in his life had left him, even his mother, who couldn't help what happened to her.

He kicked the faucet off. "Funny how knowing doesn't help stop the cycle."

"I think maybe you chose those women because you knew they weren't a threat to your military calling. Maybe they weren't a threat to your heart either. I know how much it hurts, losing your mother young."

His smile went tight. "Are you planning on hanging up a shingle and charging for the therapy too?"

"Not therapy. Just observations." She feathered her fingers over his eyebrows. "Just caring about you."

He captured her wrist. "You've got to know history shows caring doesn't usually end well, where I'm concerned."

Had so few people cared for him after his mother died that he was uncomfortable accepting affection? Had that been what his therapists meant? Liam, the protector, knew how to give and be in charge, but he didn't know how to receive. And he was right, in that one-sided relationships didn't stand a chance.

Damn it, she didn't know what the future held for them. But she couldn't turn away from Liam now without making sure she gave him something of herself and that he let her. Even if only on a physical level.

Sitting up, she straddled him, running her fingers over his broad chest.

He started to stand. "I'll grab some towels—"

She shook her head and pressed against his chest. "I'm not ready to get out yet, and neither are you."

His eyebrows shot up. "Is that so?"

"Mm-hmmm." She splayed her fingers along his pecs, fully aware he could hoist her out of the way with little effort.

But she willed him with her eyes to lean back. Give over control to her and let her give something to him.

Slowly, he reclined in the tub again, raising the water again to half full. Moisture clung to the sprinkling of golden hair on his chest. Still astride him, she rubbed against him. His erection pressed between her legs, his thick shaft applying tantalizing pressure as she rocked along the length of him.

They'd showered together, soaping each other thoroughly—so very thoroughly—then filled the tub. The motel might be low budget on style and housekeeping, but it had an unending hot-water tank.

Warmth lapped around them. Her soaked hair clung to her body. Her cheek sealed to his chest with the moisture, his heartbeat steady in her ear. "I can't believe we finally had sex."

One hand cupped her bottom, the other skimmed up and down her spine. "It was inevitable, once you showed up in my life again. Don't you think?"

She tipped her face up to look at him. "You knew I wanted you even when we were in the Bahamas?"

"Yes," he confirmed simply, without arrogance, just a calm assurance. "The connection was there, undeniable. But you also made it clear then you didn't want to act on it. I had to respect your wishes even if I didn't understand."

"I was scared."

"And were you right to be afraid?" He stroked her hair away from her face with an impossibly gentle hand. "Because the last thing I want is to frighten you."

"It's not you. It's me." There was no holding back anymore, not after what they'd shared. She had to tell him what was in her heart. "I'm afraid of what you make me feel. All those feelings are so amazing, but I can't escape the fear of being hurt, the fear of loss."

"Then yeah, I totally understand." His green eyes turned hazel with emotion. "What's going on here between us is scary as hell."

His answer stunned her.

"I've never heard a man admit to being afraid."

Liam pressed a lingering kiss onto her shoulder. "Then you've never heard a man be honest."

His words sent sparks showering through her body as tangible as his mouth on her skin. The grazing touch reignited the liquid fire in her veins, arousing. And yes, it unsettled her to the roots of her hair how totally it spread to every niche of her being. She was totally encompassed by the sensation, by him.

As his lips continued up her shoulder to her jaw, her ear, she wriggled against him. His body stirred against her, thickening against her stomach with rigid promise. Without thinking—just feeling—she rocked her hips, the solid length of him rubbing delicious friction against the oversensitive nub between her legs.

Spreading her legs wider, she wriggled closer, taking her pleasure higher. He cupped her bottom with both hands, guiding her, moving her faster, more precisely, until she gasped from the need clawing to be set free.

"Liam, I want—I *need* you inside me."

A slow smile spread across his face. "Then take me." He repeated her words from earlier. "Take me now."

Yes, yes, yes. She'd won this victory for both of them.

Arching up, she shivered as the air gusted over her damp body. Liam rubbed up her arms and along her back until she forgot about anything but the feel of him touching her. She gripped his wrists and brought his palms around to cup her aching breasts. She pressed more fully, her eyes drifting closed as she moved and guided his hands in just the way she wanted. His obvious approval throbbed against her.

Then his hands left her and she opened her eyes quickly, only to sigh with relief. He reached over the edge of the tub and pulled a condom from where it rested on top of a folded towel. She took the protection from his hand and covered him smoothly, taking her time to cover him, cradle him, and work him with both hands until his fingers dug into her hips.

Rising up on her knees, she positioned the thick head between her legs and lowered herself, slowly, carefully, taking all of him deep inside her.

The glide of him in and out as they moved in tandem felt too good, even more than before against the door or the tile wall. She molded her hands along the hard planes of his chest, his muscles and tendons bulging. She'd already come three times in the past couple of hours, so she just let herself enjoy the luscious sensation of his powerful strokes and soaked in the sight of him.

She was totally aroused by his wit, his honor, his assurance. But God, she would be lying to herself if she didn't admit his body totally turned her inside out with desire, passion, ragged-edged lust.

Then surprisingly, she started the climb to completion again. She quivered with the sweet build. Her head fell back. She rolled her hips faster. He thrust deeper while caressing her breasts. Steam wafted between them as if their heat ramped the temperature in the tub. Water sloshed over the edge of the tub onto the tile, but she couldn't bring herself to care or to slow.

The waves inside increased until finally, God yes, finally, release crashed over her. Again. And again. Her cries of bliss carried along the humid air with his growl of fulfillment. He pulled her to him and locked them tighter as the waves crested... and receded.

A sigh of total satisfaction racked her body until she wilted on top of him. He hugged her tighter and they simply lay panting in the cooling water.

At some point—she lost track of time—he lifted her from the tub and she was almost too exhausted to notice the drift of air across her naked flesh. He walked into the motel room, set her feet on the ground. Anchoring her to him with one arm, he unrolled their bed linens across the mattress. He scooped her up again and rested her on the clean sleeping bag before settling alongside her.

He was snoring before his head hit the pillow. Such a man. Her man. She curled against his side, the tepid air drying the water on them both. By all rights, she should have been ready to pass out after the past couple of days and the amazing sex they'd just shared. Instead, her body went on high alert.

Was she staying awake to keep watch so he could sleep?

She didn't know. But she couldn't stop cataloging details. The distant thrum of music carried from the bar. Cars revved and roared out of the parking lot, the sound of spitting gravel echoing. Disco and Fang leaped from the spare bed and padded together into the bathroom. Disco always preferred cool tile on a hot day.

And through it all, she held on to the hard-bodied bulk of Liam, wondering why her teeth were still chattering. Why was she more afraid now than at any other point during this crazy roller-coaster ride the past couple days? Because Liam was right. She had been lying. Just not about anything to do with Brandon's situation. She'd been lying to herself for years about why she avoided relationships.

She'd been fooled by Caden when he promised to turn his life around, then had pot in his car. He'd vowed he was clean and joined the service. Would he have stayed truthful over time? She would never know. She'd tried to tell herself she'd held back from love because she'd already lost her soul mate fiancé. But she'd deluded herself.

Because believing a possible lie was easier than admitting she was afraid of being betrayed again.

Chapter 13

LIAM WALKED IN THE LAND BETWEEN DREAMS AND REALITY, NOT sure where he stood or which side he wanted to land on.

But then the ground beneath his feet was shaky in the aftermath of the earthquake that had rocked this Bahamas island. He walked with Rachel in a strange kind of companionable silence, given the world around them. The landscape had changed somewhat.

Less dust. More volunteers erected temporary housing, hammers and saws echoing while dump trucks hauled away debris from fallen structures. Engineers worked on better water and sewage removal. Red Cross workers were everywhere.

The only thing that remained the same? The appalling scent of decaying bodies, still drifting out of the remaining rubble.

What a strange feeling to hang out with a woman who actually understood his job, who had experienced a good bit of the same kinds of hell he'd seen. So she would probably understand his need to leave it behind for a few minutes before they had to plunge themselves back into the thick of it all over again.

"So, ready for our hot date?"

"Date? Is that what we're doing here? I think not."

"Didn't anyone tell you that you want to sleep with me? I thought you already knew."

She choked on a laugh. "Wow, that was corny. Really corny."

"I thought you could use a smile."

"You're right, and thanks."

"Happy to oblige, again and again." He slid an arm around her shoulders. "So stop, drop, and roll, baby, because you're so hot you're on fire."

The scent of her freshly washed hair as she walked beside him chased away the rest of the world.

She groaned, but still kept on chuckling. "You're bad."

"No way. I'm entering the priesthood tomorrow. Wanna join me for one last sin?"

Her laughter turned to giggles until she hiccupped. "Okay, okay, enough already."

"I figure if I make you smile enough, you'll sleep with me."

She swatted his stomach. "You're so sensitive it's a wonder all those women divorced you."

Ouch. That one stung a little. But he liked the way she didn't pull punches. And no, he wasn't known for his sensitivity. But he was known for his ability to make a person smile in the middle of a crisis.

He stopped at the Red Cross supply station, holding up two fingers for the worker dispensing boxed lunches, complete with the little half-pint cartons of orange juice. Liam took the two stacked meals and looked at the crumbled street around them. The chaos of a few days ago had shifted into a steady grind of tackling a cleanup that would easily take years.

There weren't exactly a lot of places to hang out by the beach and eat, so he steered her back toward their

*cottages. One of the porches would be as good a place
as any to park it for now.*

*"Rachel, to be honest, I don't get the vibe from you
that you're looking for sensitive."*

*"Hmmm... True enough, I guess. Comes from the
way I was brought up. Around my house there was
lots of love but no coddling. My mother was an ACO—
animal control officer. Like those shows you see on the
animal channel."*

*"Was? What does she do now?" He fell into the ease
of their conversation much as they fell into sync walking
side by side.*

*"Nothing. She's dead now." She looked at him
quickly, then away. "She was breaking up a dog-fighting
ring. The owner didn't take kindly to having thousands
of dollars' worth of assets seized."*

Holy crap. "He didn't turn his dogs on—"

*"No! Heavens, no." She sighed heavily, rubbing
her bare arms. "The man was the killer animal—not
the canines. The bastard came after my mother with an
aluminum baseball bat and cracked her skull. She never
regained consciousness."*

*She went silent with the kind of thick quiet that
couldn't be broken with a smart-ass comment, the kind
of pause that was best to wait out while she put her
thoughts together on what she wanted to say next.*

*"I got my love of animals from my mom, but I can't
do what she did." Rachel kicked a chunk of concrete
ahead with the toe of her boot. "All of those people
who hurt animals? I would go after them with a baseball bat myself."*

The fire in her voice made it clear she would have

done just that, for the dogs and for her mother. Rachel Torres was the kind of woman who brought everything to the table in life. No wonder he'd missed the fact she was a foot shorter than him. Her personality, her force of will, was off the charts.

"God, woman, I think I love you."

She snorted, rolled her eyes, and pretty much did everything to punt him in the ego except laugh at the size of his Johnson. "Okay, that line was your funniest one yet."

"You don't think I'm serious." He looked forward to proving it.

"Not for a minute." She shook her head and the top-knot went a little loose and lopsided. "You can't really be trying that high school move to get in my pants? 'I love you, baby, really, I do.'"

"Who says I was trying to get into your pants? Okay, wait. I did say that. Getting you to sleep with me is way high up on my list of personal goals, but I can wait. Something tells me you'll be more than worth the extra time and effort."

She clapped a hand to her chest with the melodrama of a seasoned soap star. "You're willing to wait to have sex with me? I'm devastated. I may never recover from the crushing disappointment that I won't get to have you as my naked love slave tonight after work. Because heaven knows, there's nothing more romantic than an earthquake zone."

He stopped in front of the cottage where her search and rescue team was bunking. "You know you're only making me love you more when you get all feisty like that. Oh, and in case you were wondering, when I fall in love, I most definitely want to have sex. Love? Big-time aphrodisiac in my book."

Love.

Just the word rocked the ground under his feet. This woman rocked the ground until his vision fogged. Or was that dust from the earthquake? Except he wasn't coughing.

He struggled to rationalize the memory morphing in his dream fog. He reached to hold her, pulling her closer until her naked body merged with his.

Naked?

She was clothed in her SAR gear. He clung to the dream as tightly as he clung to her. Knowing he needed to stay with her. Keep her with him. Love her and protect her against a looming threat he couldn't identify.

A shadow stretched from behind her, over her, encompassing her. Then the shadow split in two, moving closer until he could see his mother standing beside a man swinging a metal baseball bat straight at Rachel's head—

Gasping, Liam shot up straight in bed. His heart jackhammered in his ears.

"Liam?" Rachel called out groggily.

She was right next to him in bed.

His hand shook as he cupped the gentle curve of her hip. "Sorry, everything's okay. No need to get up."

Rolling to her back, she flung her arm over her eyes. "Hmmm… can't remember when I was this tired."

"Huh?" he grunted.

"Are you okay?" She sat up, her hand rubbing the middle of his back.

"Fine, just dreaming." Dreaming bizarre shit Freud

would have a field day dissecting. Of course with Freud, it was always about the mama. "Thought I heard something. It's nothing."

"Are you sure? Should we get dressed and check?"

He shook his head. "I'm certain. Go back to sleep. We need to get up in about an hour."

She rested her cheek on his shoulder blade. "I'm already awake. We could hit the road early."

"Yeah, I guess." He scrubbed his hands over his close-shorn hair, wishing they could hang out here all day and make love. Being with Rachel in a rat trap motel beat having anyone else in five-star accommodations.

"You can have the shower first." She swung her feet to the ground. "I should probably get dressed and take the dogs out anyway. Poor puppy is probably ready to explode—if she hasn't already. If nothing else, she's gotta be going stir-crazy."

She padded across the room naked, and God help him, he went hard in a way that had nothing to do with morning wood. The swish of her hair along the sleek line of her spine hypnotized him. And the curve of her bottom... Damn. Just damn. She grabbed his T-shirt off the top of the television and tugged it over her head. The sight of her in his clothes was almost as hot as seeing her naked. Almost.

At the bathroom door, she stopped sharp, clapped a hand over her mouth. Then sank to her knees. "No Fang. No!"

What now? He rolled out of bed and lumbered over to the bathroom door. "What's wrong?"

She rocked back onto her butt, playing tug-of-war with the puppy and the prepaid cell phone. Liam sank to one knee, met the puppy's large brown eyes, and snapped, "Drop it."

Fang's mouth snapped open on command. The cell clanked onto the tile floor.

Rachel rolled her eyes. "Figures the dog would recognize the biggest alpha in the room."

He cradled the phone in his hand, wiping off the dog spit with a dry washcloth. "She doesn't appear to have done any permanent damage." He polished the slobbery LED screen, and damn it, the missed call light was flashing. When had that happened? "Did you hear the phone ring?"

She placed a finger on the light. "Of course not. I would have told you. And we've been with the phone the whole time."

His eyes slid closed as the realization crept over him. "Except for when we went to get supper in the bar."

After that, they'd been too distracted to think straight. He had been too distracted and he should have known better. He thumbed quickly through the commands to find the phone number that had tried to contact them, and there couldn't be many, since he hadn't been passing the number out on any street corners.

The screen scrolled a number he recognized all too well. He looked from the cell to Rachel. "It was Cuervo. He must have found Brandon Harris."

General Sullivan strode down the corridor, taking in the update from Captain Bernard and Agent Cramer. Sullivan focused on steady breaths, projecting calm. For now, they'd been able to keep the base commander,

Colonel Zogby, out of the loop on this. More importantly, the center commander—the only person to outrank him here—was still clueless.

Although how in the hell had Brandon Harris figured out what was going on?

Ted locked down his anger. He needed to keep this situation as contained and low profile as possible until the satellite summit. Just a few more days to hold back the tide.

A few more days until he leaked top-secret military information on U.S. satellite positioning and taskings to Internet news outlets. The world would label it a cyberattack. They would pin it on some foreign agency. A faceless crime. Damaging to the United States in the short term, but of great personal advantage to him.

But the center commander would take the fall for such a critical security breach happening on his watch. The man would lose his job, retire quietly—opening up a primo promotion for General Ted Sullivan. His career path straight to the top of the U.S. space community would be secured.

Yes, those leaked secrets would cost a few lives in the military communities. Having a foreign country learn the locations and taskings for intelligence-gathering satellites would be costly. But they were casualties in a bigger war.

He had plans for this command and could save so many more lives once he eliminated his competition. The space community needed him more than the guy currently in charge. The *country* needed him at the helm, guiding national policy on satellite-defense programs. Any fallout from the leaked data would be minor in comparison to what only he could offer.

If he could find Brandon Harris and shut him up. Sullivan had been lucky to get wind of the lieutenant's attempts to contact the OSI, thanks to an inside connection. But he couldn't count on that kind of luck again before someone actually took the unstable lieutenant seriously.

Cramer kept pace, her BlackBerry in hand as she walked past framed photos of missiles, spacecraft, and airplanes throughout history, each image a part of something larger than the gofers who scurried around giving updates. "McCabe's leave paperwork is all in place. No one will question him being gone. No one will be searching for him except our people."

"Excellent." Sullivan nodded, his mind already churning through the ways he could tank McCabe's career once that bastard resurfaced again. Going rogue on Cramer's watch? On *his* watch? Unacceptable. "I don't want any backlash staining us because you allowed him to get away."

He was walking a tightrope here with Cramer and Bernard, both unaware of his plans. They appeared loyal to him, but he couldn't afford to test that. The problem with butt-kissers is that they shifted loyalties when a higher-rank butt presented itself.

For now, he could play this out by making them think he was helping cover their mistake. He was saving their careers. They would owe him.

Captain Bernard pushed open the door into Sullivan's temporary office for use during his short-term duty assignment here to oversee the summit. A large wooden desk, flags, two chairs, and a couple of stock framed airplane prints on the wall rounded out the decor. Not much, considering his stature, but he was biding his time. He would have his walls of awards and personal memorabilia shipped here when he became a permanent fixture. For now, he made do with a space like this, adding only his brass nameplate and a framed family photo on the desk.

Bernard stopped in front of a utilitarian chair. "We really had no reason to hold him. He and the woman were well within their rights to walk out."

Sullivan took his seat behind his desk, a position of power. "In an official military vehicle? I don't think so, Captain."

Sylvia waved away the comment. "A minor infraction, easily explained away. We have the Suburban back in our possession."

"Picked up at the airport," Bernard said through tight teeth, not a smile in sight, with his job on the line. "Even though there are no signs they left the country. I'm not so much concerned with the fact they're gone as I am with *why* they felt the need to leave. What made them run, sir?"

"We'll have those answers when we find them, and we will. But Harris has to be our first priority. Your office does not need him going to the press and firing up conspiracy theorists, especially not this week."

Bernard nodded. "Understood, sir."

The plan was too deeply in motion to pull back now. Too many under him had already assisted in gathering the information, setting up the shielded leak. They expected their payback. He couldn't afford for even one of them to doubt his ability to lead.

"When you find Harris, I want him committed to a mental health facility." He trusted Sylvia to dispense with due process where necessary. "And do so immediately."

Harris would be discredited until a staged suicide could be arranged.

As for McCabe and his too-curious girlfriend, Rachel Flores? He would need to tread carefully in eradicating them, especially after the recent failed attempts on their lives.

But he had that covered. When he leaked the data about satellite data collection to the Chinese, it would be all too easy to ask for a little something extra in return. No one would question Liam McCabe's assassination, especially if the public believed he was a mole simply caught up in spy games gone wrong—his girlfriend an unlucky casualty by association.

He looked from Sylvia Cramer to Captain Bernard. "Is that all you have to report?"

Bernard nodded. "For now, sir. And thank you for your support in keeping this quiet. We're going to make this right. Sir."

Ted smiled, then looked to Cramer. "And you've got people watching the rest of McCabe's team to see if he contacts them?"

"Of course." Her hand gravitated to the leather portfolio tucked under her arm. Some might have thought she wanted her iPad. He knew she was craving a smoke. She always did when under stress.

But if she found his need for frequent updates stressful? Tough shit.

"Fair enough, then. Dismissed." He waved them out of his office.

He knew the underlings whispered behind his back, complaining, calling him a micromanager. They were too small-minded and inexperienced to understand the importance of being detail oriented. He even had an ace in the hole here at Patrick Air Force Base, someone he'd cultivated right away to be answerable first and only to him. A good leader always had troops on his side, loyal to the death. He left nothing to chance.

Details counted. He pulled his laptop closer and the cord hooked on the family photo on his desk. Which reminded him of another loose end to tie up, now that he had important business under control.

Dragging the phone toward him, he dialed his wife's cell. He could fit in a quick call. "Kelly, it's me, babe."

"Ted, thank goodness you called."

Her breathy panic had him settling back in the chair, ready for her list of idiotic problems. He could listen, *hmmm* appropriately while checking email.

"Ted, the tuition check for Teddy's fall semester drained the account. I thought we had enough in there. Credit card overdraft protection caught the overage, so our credit rating wasn't damaged, but what happened?"

Anger stirring, he creaked forward again in the chair. This went beyond her regular Chicken Little, sky-is-falling complaints. "The account is entirely empty? How did that happen?"

Kelly ran a tight ship. She was the perfect military wife. He'd been careful in choosing her twenty-two years ago. Even then he'd been certain of his future and the type of people he needed to bring along for the ride. She took care of the home front. Didn't ask any questions. And made few demands of his time.

The family picture he carted from desk to desk, even when he was deployed, gave him the image he needed to project. A beautiful family sitting in front of a fireplace.

Perfectly groomed wife, not too flashy, not so plain that people might wonder if he might be lacking. His son and daughter performed as expected, meeting standards in school with grades and sports.

He'd taught them well. They gave him the proper respect—his children had everything he'd craved growing up. A home they could be proud of. An old man to brag about. His kids could hold their heads high.

His family was safe, by God, and he would do everything in his power to make sure they stayed that way. He was in charge.

Like the medals on his chest, he'd won his family, and yes, he trotted them out when he needed the image boost. Small price to ask for all he'd given them. He would need them for just that during the summit starting this weekend. "Kelly, I'll just transfer funds from my travel account." He actually had a whole other account she knew nothing about. He'd been tapping it low of late, paying off help to deal with the Harris and Flores problems. "We've pulled finances tight this month outfitting everyone appropriately for the summit."

Money well spent. He needed his family shined up as perfectly as his medals.

"Well, then I'll take back the new formal I bought for the dinner. I have a couple of other old ones I can pick from. I never should have let you talk me into spending so—"

"Shhh. Babe, don't even consider it. You deserve something special for all the sacrifices you make. We'll be dining with dignitaries from around the world. Did you get your mother's pearls?"

"I did," she said promptly.

Of course she did. Kelly always came through. He could already envision her in the elegant, conservatively cut navy blue gown. Slim and attractive without being ostentatious or—God forbid—tawdry.

"And thanks, Ted, I really do adore the dress." Her smile reached through the phone. "I can't wait to thank you in person when I get there. Love you… bye-bye."

He gave her the appropriate response, like an obligatory box of Godivas on Valentine's Day. Easy enough to do.

After all, her thank-you was heartfelt and sweet. Even her little hint about showing her appreciation with reunion sex was perfectly understated.

He liked that about her, how proper and accommodating she was. He never had to worry about her fucking around on him while he was away.

And when *he* needed something more than missionary position in a marital bed? There were plenty of women out there who were more than happy to sit on a general's desk and spread their legs.

His hand fell to his crotch and he adjusted his stiffening dick off his zipper. He was so close to achieving his dream of pinning on a second star. Just a few more days and all the sacrifices, all the risks, would pay off.

If only Bernard and Cramer could get their heads out of their asses and locate Harris. The air force would mourn the loss of a brave—but emotionally wounded—lieutenant.

And General Ted Sullivan?

He would be assuming his new command. He would be the one advising the secretary of defense and even the president on intelligence-gathering satellites. He would influence missile defense treaties and the balance of world power.

No one would have the authority to smack him down to his knees ever again.

———————

Wind in her face, Rachel hooked her hands in both dogs' collars as Liam steered the airboat along the Everglades swamp. She did not need the dogs leaping out for an impromptu swim. The ripple of knobby alligator spines scored the water.

She'd barely had time to catch her breath since Liam found that missed call from his teammate Jose. At least Brandon had been found and was safe, and they would all be meeting soon. Beyond that, Liam hadn't told her much—just the basics. He'd relayed how someone in a silver sedan with heavy-ass weaponry had been stalking Brandon and Catriona. Jose had witnessed the whole thing go down. No one was imagining jack.

Liam had rushed to throw on clothes and hustled them out of the motel room, promising they could discuss in great detail along the way. The next thing she'd known, he was renting an airboat and they were driving deep into the Everglades. She hadn't had time to process the news about Brandon, much less analyze the shift in her relationship with Liam.

The mind-blowing sex.

Her fears of falling for him.

If she wanted a lifetime to sort out her feelings, she needed to focus on the present, where they were going, and what she could do to hold her own rather than be another responsibility for Liam to rescue. The speed of

the airboat eased the heat somewhat and kept the mos-
quitoes at bay. Ahead of them, snakes left a trail around
herons in the saw grass. She'd worked a search mission
in the Everglades once and was briefed to expect water
moccasins, coral snakes, rattlesnakes—all poisonous,
out in a place where medical help was a long way off.

She nudged Liam with her foot. "How much farther
to this 'safe place' to meet up with Brandon? With over
two million acres of wetland in the Everglades, this
could be one monster of a commute. Much longer and
I'm going to start wondering if you plan to dump my
body overboard in a plastic bag weighted with cement
blocks. You wouldn't go all *Dexter* on me, would you?"

"Five more minutes. Tops." He stroked her arm
briefly. "Trust me, it's worth the effort."

He'd said much the same in the Jeep as they'd driven
a mile to the boat rental. He'd sworn this place was
totally secure, no risk of listening devices. And it was
where he'd hoped to reach the day before, but they simply hadn't arrived before dark and he preferred not to
travel out here at night.

She just wanted to lay eyes on Brandon and be sure he
was okay. Someone had actually tried to shoot him and
Catriona in a drive-by. That would have been inconceiv-
able a mere month ago, but now anything seemed possible. Thank God, Brandon and Jose had been around to
protect Catriona—an unsuspecting, complete innocent
in all of this. Although for someone who'd been shot at,
Catriona had been surprisingly composed on the phone
as she'd shared the details of Tabitha's flesh wound
with Rachel. At least her dog was okay, treated quickly
thanks to Catriona's training as a vet tech.

Rachel drew in a humidity-laden breath, her shirt sticking to her back. A gator scrambled onto the shore and snapped up a wood duck. Or at least she thought it was a gator. This was a rare place in which alligators and crocodiles cohabited. Hopefully she would never be close enough to one to check the shape of the jaw to distinguish one reptile from another.

She secured her hold on the dogs. "And you're sure Brandon's meeting us out *here*?"

How was even he supposed to locate this place?

"With Cuervo. Don't worry. Cuervo can find his way." He steered the craft, the monstrous fan in back powering them over the murky surface. "They're also bringing the dog-sitter along to keep her safe."

"Catriona?" Her friend hadn't mentioned that, but they hadn't been able to talk long and the connection had been sketchy.

"Uh-huh. That's what Jose said." Liam whipped the craft around a narrow bend in the marsh. An osprey flapped away from its perch.

"What happened to all the dogs at her place? My dogs are there."

"What does she do if she has to leave home?"

"She rarely goes anywhere."

"She's a recluse?" Morning rays beat down on his sun-burnished face. His bristled jawline was taking on a look actors worked to cultivate. Tall and lean, Liam's raw masculinity came naturally.

Going dreamy over him at such a crazy time seemed strange and wonderful all at once. Didn't she deserve a moment to soak in what they'd shared last night?

She pulled her attention off her handsome lover

and back to their conversation. "Just shy. Not much of a social life. She's a truly nice person, devoted to the animals in her care… Although now that you mention it, she does have a backup for when she has to shop or if she's sick. She hires vet tech students looking to make extra money while they're in school."

"Then I'm guessing that's what she did now. All the more reason it was crucial to keep the plans from her at first. She isn't trained in this sort of crisis. She will be able to say with all honesty to the students that she would be staying at a hotel."

"You're right. Still…" She scraped her hair back from her face. "The thought of someone trying to hurt them, getting so close, scares me. Factor in that the gunmen were driving the same kind of car that followed me to base in the first place, and I'm really freaking out."

He pinned her with his glittering green gaze, as lush and virile as the Everglades. "This nightmare *is* going to end soon, Rachel. I promise you. We're going to put together a plan for reentering the base, depending on what Harris is able to tell us."

"Do you still think he's unbalanced?" Even though her instincts told her otherwise, she had to take Liam's concerns seriously.

"How am I supposed to know if I've never met the man?"

Valid point. "That's the real reason you have your friend along, isn't it? To make sure you outnumber him."

"Just playing it safe." He swooshed past a jutting cypress.

Safe? Where foxes and bears—not to mention the Florida panther—lived in this fragile wetland? Although the human beasts in the real world lately were every bit as lethal.

Liam navigated the airboat around another sharp bend with the skill of a race car driver, then cut the power back to idle. A shack came into view in the middle of a cypress swamp. A no-kidding *shack*. When he'd said a little out-of-the-way place and not to expect much, she'd expected to be pleasantly surprised, figuring he'd been downplaying so she wouldn't get her hopes up. Cedar red planks closed in what appeared to be a lean-to on stilts. The front porch doubled as a dock and it didn't appear there was much of a backyard.

At least the place had a roof.

Electricity, however, was doubtful.

"There's an impressive generator," he said, answering her unasked question. "And water from a well. The outside is deceptive. We'll be safe here while we regroup."

"If you say 'trust me' again, I think I'm going to scream."

His dry laugh mingled with the cacophony of frogs and crickets. Everything out here was bigger, louder. Even the dragonfly buzzed around her face at concert level volume.

"Do you own this place?"

"It belongs to the uncle of one of my exes." He worked the controls, slowing and revving the engine at just the right pace to ease up to the dock. "I have an open invitation to use it."

How open? "Dare I ask which ex-wife?"

"Jealous?"

Yes. "Curious."

"The second one."

"Priscilla." The cheater. The one Rachel actually wanted to kick for hurting Liam. Well, come to think of it, they had all hurt him.

"You remember."

"That was very important information you shared." And being jealous was churlish. She cupped his beard-stubbled cheek, full out touching him for the first time since they'd bolted out of bed. "I thought your parting with her was... acrimonious."

"It was," he said simply as he cut the engine. "But her uncle and I stay in touch even though I do my best to avoid her." He pressed a quick kiss into her palm before stepping back to tie off the boat.

The kiss was nice and she wanted another, one that lingered, rather than a brush in passing. Was he just taking care of business or retreating emotionally, destroying another relationship? She desperately wanted to know more, to help herself sort through the jumble of emotions stirred up by this man. But now wasn't the time. Maybe once they were settled inside.

The cabin windows were thick but surprisingly clean. Above the windows, there were metal roll-down shutters. And as she looked closer, she saw the generator he'd mentioned. It wasn't just large. It was huge.

Liam vaulted onto the dock and doubled up the tie-offs. The dogs leaped up and onto the planked walkway, sniffing. Intrigued, she climbed out. Even from the outside, she could see now that the cabin offered more than she'd expected, sprawling back with an unseen added space, enough for a couple of bedrooms.

Boat secured, Liam charged ahead of her. Sunlight glinted off his chrome weapon as he advanced toward the shack. He held up a hand for her to wait, reminding her again that while they both had rescue experience, he had a whole added level of combat training. But he blended the personal and professional parts of his life so much better than she did. One minute he was kissing her hand and the next he was ready for a shoot-out.

Watch his back. Sunny's advice filtered through her mind, sparking an idea she should already have considered if she'd been as good as Liam at staying clearheaded.

She touched his arm and whispered, "Wait."

He glanced back. "What? Is something wrong?"

"Send Disco in. He knows how to sweep a building. He's trained."

Liam blinked in surprise. "Uh, okay. Sure."

"Open the door. I'll send him in."

Liam lifted a small wooden plank beside the window and exposed a security system. He typed in a code, then leaned to twist the doorknob. The hinges creaked.

Kneeling, she looked Disco in the eyes as she'd done dozens of times for searches over the years, not so much lately. "Ready?"

Disco's ears twitched forward, his body rippling with tensed muscles. *Good boy.* She unclipped his leash.

"Go find," she ordered softly, intensely. "Go find."

The black Lab launched forward in a sleek bolt of determination, sniffing, zigging and zagging into the cabin. He thrived when working. She'd forgotten how much Disco put into his job. A job she'd denied him over the past six months. She blinked back tears.

God, why was he taking so long? Fang started to whine beside her. She petted the pup to calm her, to silence her. Fear burned as she thought of something happening to

Disco if he actually found someone. Had she sent him into a trap? Liam kept his gun leveled the whole time, his arsenal-filled duffel on the dock beside him.

Eventually—after what felt like forever—Disco trotted back through the door and stopped in front of her. She dropped to her knees in front of him.

"Good, boy, Disco." She ruffled his ears. "Good boy. Good work."

Liam caught Fang by the collar before she could bolt away into the house. "Are you sure?"

She looked up. "I trust him. If Disco says it's clear, then it's clear."

"Okay then."

Liam started toward the cabin, but she noticed he didn't put his weapon away. She followed, dogs at her side.

The place darn near sparkled, it was so clean—much like Liam's place. The kitchen included a two-burner propane stove with a huge white farm sink. The shelves over the stone counter were stocked full of jarred food, boxed milk, juice, and cans of mosquito repellent. A round rough-hewn oak table filled the middle of the room, with bar stools around it. Cane fishing poles were propped in a corner alongside high-tech reels.

And there were electrical outlets. Heavy-duty outlets for major equipment. She looked at the trunks behind the sofa with interest.

She started down the narrow hallway, finding a bedroom on either side and a bathroom at the end. The thought of a shower or a nap only made her throat close with memories of how close she and Liam had been a few hours ago.

How long did she and Liam have here before

everyone else showed up? Would they be setting up or shooting the breeze? Or just making love again so they didn't have to talk? They had so much emotional baggage between them, they needed a freakin' moving truck to hold everything.

The sound of an approaching boat snapped her back around. Liam was already at the door, weapon drawn. "Wait inside."

"Like hell," she whispered.

Heart in her throat, she pulled her Baby Eagle from her backpack and wished she'd had time for the shooting lessons.

Tucking behind him, she raced out onto the porch. She shaded her eyes against the high noon sun. A new airboat rounded the bend with five people on board. Five?

God, she hoped they were friends, because if not, she and Liam were seriously outnumbered.

Chapter 14

STORM CLOUDS GATHERED OVERHEAD AS LIAM LOOPED the line around the dock post. He secured the newly arrived airboat, jam-packed full of passengers—Jose James, the Rochas, and a couple he assumed to be Brandon Harris and Catriona Whittier.

And of course, there were two more dogs—the Rochas' husky-malamute, Chewie, and some Australian shepherd mix he didn't recognize.

Liam extended his hand to help the women disembark. Thunder rumbled in the distance. "Hey, Rocha, did someone mail out party invitations and forget to send one to me?"

Wade Rocha chuckled softly. "You didn't seriously think you could cut me out of this, and Sunny isn't the type to sit waiting in the wings, ya know?"

"I appreciate the backup." He should have known Rocha wouldn't be left behind. Liam would have done the same in his position.

But so many women to protect. Although better here than out in the open at home. And how much help would the new guy provide, especially if he was battling PTSD?

Liam thrust his hand out. "Lieutenant Harris? Nice to finally meet you."

Brandon hopped from the boat and clasped Liam's hand in a firm, steady shake. "Thank you, sir. I appreciate your help more than I can say."

The lieutenant's eyes appeared lucid. His hair was shaggier than regulation, but not unusual for someone on extended leave. He wore khaki shorts and a polo shirt with a college logo—The Citadel. Sure he was dusty and sweaty, just like the rest of the people stepping out of the boat, shoes thudding on the dock. No immediate red flags, but Liam withheld final judgment. Trusting this guy who'd put Rachel at risk would take time.

Rachel.

Even thinking her name right now made him want to hide her out here where he could keep her safe forever—and make love to her without worrying that all their new roommates would overhear.

Liam gestured everyone down the dock toward the cabin. "Let's get inside before those clouds open up."

He led the way down the dock, a fat raindrop landing on his nose just before he stepped under the porch on stilts. Swinging the door wide, he waved everyone inside without once taking his eyes off Harris. Gear piled up in the corner until it looked like a scouting camp out on steroids. Rain picked up speed, pinging the tin roof.

Murky light streamed through the windows. He would crank the generator soon, but for now, he needed to get a handle on Brandon Harris before anything else. Humid though it was, Liam simply opened windows for a cross breeze.

He dragged a chair from the table and started an unofficial circle. The women claimed the couch, creating a wall of estrogen, and his team buddies took seats. Harris chose the bar stool nearest the door, his Australian shepherd–beagle mutt firmly at his side as if they both might bolt.

Elbows on his knees, Liam leaned forward. "Okay, Harris, you have our complete and undivided attention."

The young security cop folded his hands over his stomach. "Open-minded attention?"

Cocky bastard.

"Are you in a position to be picky? We've gone to a lot of trouble for you."

"For Rachel. I know you're really here for her."

"Because you put her life in danger," Liam snapped before he could call the words back. Hell, he didn't even want to.

Wind picked up speed in the storm, the eaves creaking at the force, rain misting in through the open windows.

"I did. And I'm sorry for that." Brandon's eyes shuffled to Rachel's with unmistakable contrition. "Honest to God, Rachel, I wish I could go back and do things differently."

"How?" She reached out to him. "Believe me, I've thought about this a hundred different ways and I think we both acted in all the logical, legal ways to report suspicious activity."

Liam looked back and forth between them, searching for signs that they were more than just connected by the situation. And what do ya know? Catriona Whittier was watching their interaction with the same interest. The woman wasn't at all what he would have expected from a pet-sitter. She was so thin, damn near frail, she looked like the wind could carry her away. Even her red hair looked fragile, scraped back from her face. She appeared passive.

Except when she looked at Brandon Harris. Then her eyes went fierce.

All right then. Time to figure out exactly what Harris knew. "I guess that makes us your last hope, lieutenant. Convince us."

Harris's hand fell to rest on top of his shepherd mutt's head. "Back in the day before we were at war with everybody all the time, security cops were divided into two categories: law enforcement and base defense. Now we're all mostly focused on base defense here and overseas, and undermanned for the task."

Liam nodded. "That's a heavy load to carry, especially in a war zone."

Harris wouldn't be the first to crack from combat burnout. Who wasn't pulling double and triple duty these days?

"I asked for the deployment." Harris thumped himself on the chest. "I embraced it. I wanted to go over from the minute I finished training, to have my chance at defending my country."

Catriona gasped, her attention on Harris even as her hand gravitated into her hobo bag to pull out a chew toy and toss it to Fang. "Brandon, you *wanted* to go to the Middle East?"

Harris winced, looking down at the planked floor. "I thought I was a badass, that I could go over there and make a difference all by myself."

"Lieutenant," Liam said, to pull Harris back into the conversation, into the moment, rather than wherever he'd drifted off to. "What exactly was your tasking?"

The silence stretched out, filled only by the increasing storm outside. A crack of thunder vibrated through the cabin.

Harris looked up sharply, blinking. "I was a military

bodyguard for a high-profile civilian contractor in southern Afghanistan. I went everywhere with him… meetings, dinner, trips from base to base. Even his shopping trips to pick up touristy crap for his wife and kids back home."

"A regular family guy," Liam said, more to keep him talking than anything else.

"No," Harris's eyes hardened. "He wasn't. Those trips to different marketplaces were a cover. He was meeting with contractors from other countries."

"Not unheard of."

"That's what I thought at first." He swiped the perspiration off his forehead, taking his time, as if gathering his thoughts. Or preparing his story? As a military cop, he would have training in interrogation. Enough to fool the room? To fool a shrink?

"I'm just a lieutenant," Harris continued, "a lowly nobody, as far as they were concerned. Window dressing. So they talked more openly in front of me than they would around you, Major, or some other higher-ranking official. I know this sounds far-fetched, but as I pieced together those different meetings, I realized they were setting up the exchange of military information."

"Whoa." Jose held up a hand. "Contractors from different countries? That's treason."

"*If* I could prove it." Harris rolled his shoulders. "Which I couldn't. I spoke to my commanding officer, and he said they already had an eighteen-hour workday chasing down tangible threats with hard evidence. So I kept my mouth shut and ears open, waiting for something concrete I could take to the authorities, get some sense of who was pulling the strings. They talked a lot about their 'bosses' and reporting back to contacts in the military community, but I never got a name."

Liam smiled darkly. "That would be too easy."

"They were reckless, but not that reckless. It's obvious they worked with someone high up the military chain of command. At first I thought it was a money thing, but the more I listened, the more I got the feeling it was about affecting the balance of power."

"Whoa," Cuervo interrupted. "Balance of power?"

"Right," Harris continued. "It was about reshaping the face of the command structure, personal agendas for military armament programs that should excel versus which ones they would make sure failed."

Damn. It would have been so much easier to go after a greedy bastard. Money trails were simple. But power-hungry types with an ideological ax to grind? Liam focused back in on Harris.

"Maybe a month into the assignment, things shifted. It was about more than talk. They planned an actual exchange, something to do with the coordinates for when U.S. satellites would be conducting intelligence gathering. If another country knows when you're watching them…"

Shit. The implications were hellacious. U.S. intelligence operatives, military members on maneuvers… They would all be sitting ducks.

"Uh, yeah." Liam scratched the back of his head. "That would constitute treason."

Harris didn't smile. "I could hardly believe what I was seeing. An exchange. A simple little chip that they passed over by exchanging cell phones." He paused.

"The data chip was in the phone. All I had to do was report them to officials on base and…"

"And?" Rachel touched his arm softly.

"The marketplace was bombed." His voice went flat, his eyes hollow. "Bodies flew part. The two contractors died on impact. I heard sirens and screams. None of it fully registered. I just closed my hand around one of the cell phones and passed out. The next thing I remember, I woke up in a battlefield hospital ward."

Liam leaned back in his chair, churning over Harris's story in his mind. "That's it?"

"When I got out of the hospital, I was pretty rattled. Go ahead and laugh if you want. Lieutenant gung ho was totally freaked out after a few months of combat and one especially close call. They tell me I was catatonic." He shrugged. "When I came out of it enough to be moved to a rehab center, they gave me my stuff back. And there was that cell phone."

"From the marketplace?"

"Exactly. I tried to alert the authorities to what happened. They informed me I was suffering from battle stress and that my memories were faulty."

"Why didn't they at least check the chip in your phone? That wouldn't have taken long, to verify information."

"The first time I started to explain things, I wasn't as coherent or… calm. They gave me some kind of knock-out drug halfway through before I even got to the part about the cell phone. Next time I tried to tell, I was more cautious in holding back information, and before long I didn't know what to believe. Maybe I was a mix of rational and delusional. But I didn't know who to trust with that chip. I was afraid to let even my psychiatrist know. The paranoia paralyzed me. Until Rachel paired me up with the therapy dog, Harley."

Harley nudged his hand.

Harris stroked the dog's head in a way that appeared to soothe him. "Rachel said she would go with me to the authorities…" He shrugged. "It didn't pan out as we'd hoped."

"What about the chip in the cell phone?"

"I turned it over during my second interview with the OSI."

"And now there's no way to verify what you've told us." Damn it, this guy had been stringing them along for nothing. The threats could have all been set up by him, especially if he'd had a psychotic break.

Liam looked from Rocha to James and could see they feared the same thing. That they were stuck in the boonies with a seriously unhinged and dangerous individual.

Harris stuffed his hand behind his back.

"Gun!" Rocha shouted.

Liam and his PJ teammates piled on top of Harris, knocking him from the chair. Harley growled, and from the corner of his eye, Liam saw Rachel grab the dog's collar. Harris thrashed underneath them. Hard. Damned hard. With punches and kicks of a trained security force specialist. It took all three of them to pin his raging body.

Dimly, Liam heard Catriona scream, felt Rachel's hand on his arm. The red faded from his eyes and he calmed enough to assess the restrained lieutenant. Harris's chest heaved, his skin paling. His eyes darted from side to side. He appeared scared—but rational.

Liam leaned to catch Harris's attention. "Talk to me."

"No gun," he said through gritted teeth. "A cell phone. I made a copy of the chip and stored it in another phone."

Liam nodded to Cuervo to check it out. Cuervo reached into the guy's back pocket and pulled out…

An iPhone.

Liam rocked back on his heels. "My apologies, Lieutenant."

Harris sat up slowly, his muscles visibly twitching. "It's okay. I'd have done the same in your position."

Rachel knelt beside him with Harley. Harris hooked an arm around the dog's neck, but he wasn't meeting Catriona's gaze across the room. That sure answered a couple more of Liam's questions. Harris had a thing for the dog-sitter. Made sense that he would be embarrassed around someone he wanted to accept him as manly. Harris didn't appear to care what Rachel thought of his masculinity.

Harris rubbed the back of his neck. "Any chance you guys can decipher the information on the chip?"

"Good news, bad news. We're a team for a reason. We all have different skills. And our computer geek, Data—Marcus Dupre—is back home."

Rachel shoved to her feet. "Now would be a great time for the good news part."

"We have a generator and top-notch computers here. And thanks to the storm that's keeping us from leaving, it's also impossible for anyone to find us. So we have time."

Time to figure out if the cell phone contained world-shaking information—or if that phone was Brandon Harris's version of a crazy tinfoil hat.

Either way, he was keeping Harris the hell away from Rachel.

—⁓—

Rachel was going seriously stir-crazy.

The cabin that had seemed like such a safe haven initially had now become more of an overcrowded jail cell because of the storm. She sat cross-legged and pretty much useless on a bed with a sunburst quilt.

After Brandon's meltdown, they'd cranked the generator. Liam hadn't been exaggerating when he'd said it kicked ass. Air conditioners pumped cool air through the shack. Three computers had been set up on the dining table. The Internet was spotty, going in and out as they worked to reach Marcus Dupre. But Liam and the two members of his team were poring over the computer chip, with Brandon trying to break the code.

Catriona and Sunny were in the kitchenette and had quickly evicted Rachel, insisting she'd been on the road longer than they had, so she should rest.

Even the dogs had abandoned her. All four canines had piled pack-style on the porch, not a bad place, since they would serve as a first alert to anyone approaching. Their ears would be better tuned to nuances in the symphony of storm and marsh noises. She hugged her knees, resting her chin on them, drifting off…

She startled.

Looking around sharply, she found Cuervo standing in the doorway. The lanky PJ wore a marathon T-shirt and camouflage pants with combat boots. "Just checking on you for the major. Didn't mean to disturb you."

Liam sent the guy to check on her? Watch over her? Touching and frustrating at the same time. She didn't enjoy being pushed aside. She wanted to help. To do something. Anything.

She swung her feet off the edge of the double bed. "I'm not actually tired. Just bored to death after the frenzy of the past couple of weeks."

"We play word games to pass the time during a long swim or run."

"Seriously? You have the energy to talk in the middle of that kind of workout?"

A coal black eyebrow shot upward. "Do you think if we're in the middle of hiking our asses off an Afghan mountain with the Taliban breathing down our neck that we stop for a break every time we need to pass along a message to each other?"

Her stomach churned at the image he painted of Liam's life beyond civilian rescues and training exercises. Those scenarios were all too sharp edged, given what Brandon had shared tonight.

"Sorry," Cuervo said. "Sometimes I forget it's not everyday kinda stuff for the rest of the world. Part of why we play games to take the edge off, I guess."

She swallowed hard. "Like what kind of word games?"

Crossing his boots at the ankles, he settled more comfortably in the doorway. "We just started playing this new word game called marry one, screw one, kill one. *Some* people on the team think it's not PC enough."

"Hey," Wade Rocha shouted from the next room. "I heard that."

Cuervo continued. "But I think it's kinda like that 'people in a boat' game where you have to decide who gets tossed overboard and fed to the sharks."

Rachel grinned. "You're a bloodthirsty one."

"Our options are laugh or what? Become like Bubbles?"

Bubbles... back in the Bahamas... "The one who always cleans his gun and never speaks or smiles?"

"Right. As for me, I prefer laughing. So"—he spoke loud enough to be heard in the living area as well—"in the interest of equality and all, we'll give you ladies a shot at playing... with guys to pick from."

Sunny Rocha stepped up alongside Cuervo. "I assume you're not going to offer your own names."

Cuervo clutched his heart. "If only I could, without Wade kicking my ass. So, ladies, pick a subject, and I'll list three men. You too, Catriona. Come on in." The dog-sitter stepped into the room and sat on the edge of the bed. "For example... I'll choose three men from the *Ocean's Eleven* actors. Or three sports heroes. Or three guys from the cast of *Glee*."

"You're a Gleek?" Catriona gasped. "For real?"

"I own all the past seasons on DVD. Cross my heart." Cuervo drew an *X* over his chest.

Catriona shook her head. "I don't believe you. Prove it."

"Fine." He nodded officially. "Challenge accepted. Cast of *Glee* it is. Puck, Finn, Mr. Schuester." He named the characters with ease. "Marry one. Screw One. Kill one. And listen up in there, Major. You'll learn a lot about your lady friend here from her answer."

"Cuervo," Liam called from the other room. "We're working here. You should try it."

"I'm keeping your girlfriend safe, like you asked." Cuervo leaned out farther into the hall, speaking louder, "You're a psychology buff right, Major? On *Glee*, Puck is the bad boy. Finn is the football star. Mr. Schuester is the sensitive type. So who does your lady friend, Rachel, want to kill? And who will she—?"

"Okay. Enough games." Rachel shot to her feet and patted Cuervo on the cheek on her way into the hall. "I appreciate the laugh and protection. Truly. But no freebie peeks inside my brain."

Yet as she looked into the dark wise eyes of Liam's teammate, Rachel suspected she'd already given herself away. She hurried out down the hall and back into the living area.

Sunny stepped up behind her husband and rested her hands on his shoulders. "Wade, who did you pick to marry when you guys played?"

Wade didn't even look up from the computer at the long oak table. "I refused to participate. I'm permanently benched."

"Hey…" Sunny swatted his arm, then brushed a kiss over the top of his bent head. "I think that's a compliment."

"Totally." He snagged her hand and pulled her closer for a firmer lip-lock.

Their happiness just about glowed. Not even the current crisis could dim it. It was hard not to feel jealous right now. Her eyes skated to Liam, who was pinching the bridge of his nose. Of course he had bigger concerns. She needed to prioritize.

Cuervo slung an arm around Rachel's shoulders. "When we play the game, the major wants to marry all the women."

Liam glanced up, scowling. "Thanks, my friend, but I don't need your help watching over Rachel after all."

"Ah, so you care what she thinks." Cuervo winked at Rachel. "Got it. Officially backing off."

And why wouldn't he back off? He'd gone overboard in "protecting" her. He'd made his point by ensuring they both didn't forget the obstacles in front of them.

As if she already didn't know how much they both had working against them once they left this place and returned to the real world.

Liam stepped out onto the porch alongside Cuervo. With the moonless night and thick sheet of rain pouring off the roof, there wasn't much to see beyond the cabin. Wind howled through the trees, drowning out the bugs and bullfrogs for once.

He leaned against a post beside his teammate standing guard. "Are you through trying to make me lose my shit?"

Cuervo peeled spooned lo mein out of an MRE packet. "You shouldn't make your vulnerability so obvious." He looked at the closed cabin door. "Where's Rachel?"

"She ran screaming in the other direction," Liam snapped. "What did you expect, after your little mind game in there?"

"Quit trying to make me feel guilty for stating the obvious. Where is she? Seriously." He shoveled in another bite.

"She's gone back to the bedroom, trying to catch some sleep while it's raining." He wanted to make sure Rachel didn't overtax herself. She'd been open about her burnout. Seeing Harris offered up a harsh reminder of just how no one was immune from a breakdown. Would this mission help her return to her old drive, or was it too much, too soon?

"Smart to rest up while she can."

"First rule of a good warrior. Never stand when you can sit and never sit when you can sleep."

"You know it." Cuervo dropped the spoon into the brown plastic container, all humor fading from his lean face. "Are you really going to get out of the air force?"

Ah, so that's where the kid had been going with all the games and chitchat in there. He'd been attempting to get a handle on what Liam had in store for the future to see if Rachel had anything to do with recent decisions.

"It's not like I'm quitting. I'm retiring." Liam pulled out the crackers and packet of processed cheese spread from the MRE box. "The military lets you retire at twenty years for a reason. This job is hard on a body, as my creaky knees can attest. I've been in for twenty years. It's time."

"I forget sometimes that you enlisted at eighteen. That you even went to college while on active duty. The civilian world is going to seem—"

"Alien? Quiet?" He forced down a fear that rivaled anything he'd felt on the battlefield. "Yeah."

He squeezed the cheese out onto the cracker and stuffed it in his mouth. Tasted like crap but it was familiar. Safe to eat.

Safe.

The word tripped him up.

When had he started playing life safe?

Cuervo rolled up his empty food pouch. "We need the ones like you to stick around, the ones who put everything into the job. Too often it's the jackasses who only look after themselves that stay in. And how bad does that suck for those of us still left?"

"Is that what this is all about? Scaring Rachel off and convincing me to stay in the service so some jackass isn't in charge?"

"The two don't have to be mutually exclusive. You can have Rachel and the career."

Liam stared the kid down. "How old are you again? Twelve? Thirteen?" Anger roiled in his gut. As if the decision to leave the service had been made lightly.

"No disrespect meant." Cuervo stood taller, an invisible wall forming between them as surely as if the rain had started pouring through a crack in the porch roof.

Liam shook off his shitty mood. No good would come from taking it out on Cuervo. Wasn't his fault. "Hey, kid, seriously. I'm old. It's my time to step out of the field whether I stay in or not. Would you really be content to hang out in some war room watching the action go down live on a big screen?"

"Honestly, they'll have to bury me before I would quit." The darkness in the younger man's eyes made him look decades older.

Liam angled off the porch post and clapped the junior team member on the arm. "Don't joke around about crap like that."

"Without the missions"—Jose shook his head—"I don't have anything else. Don't want anything else."

"What makes you say that?"

"You've read my file." His throat moved in a hard swallow. "It's all in there."

And it was, the real reason no one ever saw Jose James with a drink in his hand, the sad irony behind his call sign, Cuervo. "You had a drinking problem, but you completed the rehab program. At our last feedback session, everything seemed cool. Or is there something you need to talk about?"

"I'm dry. Solid for today. One day at a time, you know?" Jose's hand slipped into his pocket and he stared at his five-year-sober coin, flipping it between his fingers. "This job keeps me level, gives me discipline and a reason to stay that way."

"And you're sure you're not having a problem I need to know about?"

"Seriously, I'm cool. If I'm ever having a rough patch, I just run another marathon." He laughed darkly. "I've never been healthier."

"In reading your file, I learned a lot more that you can be proud of. You broke a family cycle of alcoholism. It stops with you. That's huge, man." Liam dug up every ounce of insight he'd gained from all those marital-counseling sessions. It came in handy sometimes when leading his team. "Your nieces and nephews, your own kids someday, they can look to you as an example of how life can be."

"Thank you. Your opinion means a lot to me." More of that humidity-filled silence hung in the air before Cucrvo continued. "Although, I still think it's utter horseshit that you're retiring, dude."

Liam let the tension roll off and smiled. "That's still 'dude, sir' to you for now."

Laughing, they settled back into the routine of just hanging out. No need to talk. They'd spent hours on training ops and missions, silent, waiting, watching. He would miss this most of all, the team, mentoring.

But he couldn't dwell on that. Cuervo's words would have to roll right off like the rain sheeting from the roof.

For now, he had his final mission to complete before he could move forward with Rachel. *She* was his future. And God help him if he screwed up with Rachel in what was clearly the chance of a lifetime.

His last chance.

Chapter 15

HALF AWAKE, HALF ASLEEP, RACHEL FELT THE MAT-
tress dip as Liam slid into bed behind her. She didn't
even question how she knew it was him. The air just,
well, changed when he entered a room.

She rolled over in the split-rail bed and into his
arms. Her bare legs tangled with his, since he wore just
boxers and a T-shirt. The rain tapped hypnotically on
the roof. Trees swayed and twined in a shadow show
outside the window.

"I didn't mean to wake you." He tugged the sheet up
to their shoulders. The log cabin quilt was folded and
draped along a cane rocker. His jeans were draped on
top and she hadn't even heard him get undressed.

Sliding closer, she fit her body to his and toyed with
his dog tags. "Did you find out anything new?"

"There's definitely data on the chip that has nothing
to do with favorite phone numbers." He stroked her hair
back, then tucked his hand into the overlong T-shirt to
cup her bare shoulder. "But it's all in a code we're not
having any luck breaking."

Relief sparked through her so intensely she squeezed
her eyes closed. She hadn't realized until now just how
much she'd feared Brandon might be wrong. Although
how crazy was it to be happy there was a traitor out
there gunning for them? "So this nightmare is all
too real."

"I'm sure enough to be very careful that chip lands in the right hands."

"Thank you. Oh God, thank you." She rested her forehead on his chest, inhaling the familiar musky scent of him and letting it sweep away the fear she'd been carting around like an eighty-pound pack. Finally, she steadied her breathing enough to speak again. "Where's everyone else?"

"Cuervo's pulling a shift guarding out front. Sunny and Wade are sleeping on bedrolls in the living room. Brandon said he would watch over the dog-sitter in the spare room."

She scooted up to sit against the log headboard. "Were you able to call in? Did you speak with Agent Cramer or Captain Bernard?"

"The storm kept us from getting a steady signal."

So they were still on their own out here. But with more people aware of the situation, on board and believing, this wouldn't get shuffled under a rug. Whoever was trying to sell those secrets would be caught.

All those instincts she'd honed working search and rescue missions were coming back to life and shouting for her to be on the lookout for unfinished business in this crazy mess.

And her business with Liam? They'd taken a huge step in sleeping together, but where did they go from here? How would they fit into each other's everyday lives, when he'd screwed up commitment so often he was scared to go there again? And when she was starting to believe in the possibility of happily ever after for the first time since she'd lost Caden?

Liam shifted next to her again and then moved again. "Do you think we could fit any more dogs in this bed?"

Leaning forward, she shooed Disco and Fang to the floor. Their nails clicked against the hardwood until they settled on an oval braid rug at the foot of the bed.

She slumped back onto his chest. "Better?"

"Roomier."

"Do you have a thing against dogs on the bed?"

"A double bed? Yes. A queen- or king-size? No problem at all."

Wow, strange how important that one little question was to her. And even stranger to take hope from it, when they had such larger concerns waiting back in the real world.

"I can't imagine life without my dogs. Everything feels… simpler when they're with me. My PTSD patients tell their dog things they haven't been able to share. And once the wall comes down…" She wasn't sure how she would have made it through losing Caden without her own dog then. She'd been so alone, without her mother. "There are even therapy dogs in some schools to help children gain confidence in reading. Dogs don't judge. Their attention—their love—is unconditional, no matter how crummy a past they've come from themselves."

"Maybe I should have gotten a dog instead of getting married every other week." His voice was hoarse, groggy even, as he toyed with her hair. "I could have saved myself a boatload in legal fees and divorce settlements."

"Maybe you should have."

"I was joking."

"I'm not." She looked up to meet his eyes, the steady beat of the rain on the roof echoing the sound of her racing heart.

"Helluva way to tell me Fang is my new dog."

Again, he'd tried to deflect with humor, but she wasn't so easily sidetracked. "I would never push a dog on anyone. A pet deserves to be welcomed and wanted unconditionally. So do people, for that matter."

Dog nails clicked on the floor, tracking around to Liam's side of the bed. Fang rested her chin on the mattress next to him. His hand rested on top of the pup's head. "What'll happen to her now?"

"I'll find a good home for her," she answered vaguely, trying to push down how much she wanted that home to be with Liam.

For Fang. Not for her. That would be too rushed, of course.

"You could keep her and train her." His hand smoothed over the puppy's knobby brown head.

So he didn't want her to give the dog away, but he hadn't stepped up to claim Fang for himself. What was holding him back from doing that now? And why was she so certain committing to the dog would be a big cosmic sign he was ready to settle down for real?

"It's too soon to decide if she has the necessary traits for that kind of work." She burrowed closer to his side. "Have you ever had a pet?"

"My dad was allergic. Then I was traveling too much…"

The hesitation in his voice made her ask, "But?"

"There was this one time, back when I was an Army Ranger in Afghanistan. A stray dog hung out around our compound. He was a brown mutt type, like a German shepherd with no markings other than one white paw, his left front one. We unofficially adopted him."

All these years and he remembered exactly what the

dog looked like. Rachel's heart squeezed. "What was his name?"

"Rocky." Lightning sparked, filling the room with light as he stroked Fang's nose. "He was always there waiting for us on top of a rock pile, even warned us a couple of times of a land mine or approaching enemy. Until he didn't…"

"Didn't?"

"Animal control works differently over there… or rather not at all. The insurgents shot him."

Rachel didn't even respond. Words would be trite, and he wasn't really with her right now. His mind was clearly in another time and place.

"Things—missions—were tougher to cope with after he was gone. Rocky didn't have any formal training, but he sure helped a bunch of worn out rangers get through the day."

She'd heard about the horrors that soldiers faced, as they poured out their stories while holding on to any number of dogs. For some reason, rescued dogs seemed to have a special affinity for the job. Shared pain, perhaps? A wounded vet tapped into that belief in second chances.

And above all, dogs didn't judge.

Liam's hand slid from the puppy. "I probably could have used this little mutt back in the day, but I'm getting out now."

"How does the team feel about that?" How did *she* feel about that? She didn't know.

"It's not like we're guaranteed to work together forever anyway. Already one of our guys has transferred up to a training position in Panama City. Hugh Franco— you should remember him from the Bahamas."

"Hmmm…" She feathered her fingers over his furrowed forehead. "You're not happy about this decision."

He clasped her arm and kissed her wrist before setting it to rest on his chest. "The military has been my life, at the expense of my personal relationships. The time has come to make a change."

Nerves buzzed in her stomach. Could he be talking about the two of them? Except truth be told, she wasn't sure she could envision him hanging up his uniform. "I thought you were against relationships because of your ex-wives and childhood. But now you're saying it's because of your job too."

"Maybe it's all of the above. Or maybe now that I'm actually working through it, now that I'm ready to retire, I'm reconsidering my stance on relationships."

This was moving fast. Too fast? She was only getting used to the idea of sleeping together, maybe going out on a date where no cop showed up with handcuffs, and now he was talking about the future? "Don't you think we need to get through the present first? Conversations like this should be saved for times when we're not hyped on adrenaline."

"You think I'm just letting adrenaline do the thinking for me? After you've worked a particularly tough SAR mission, what was your first instinct? To propose to someone?"

Propose? Nerves turned to all-out panic. "Um, I usually took a hot bath and cried my eyes out." She kissed his nose, then stroked lower in hopes of distracting him. The sex part they could handle without messing up. "You don't look much like the bubble bath and cry type."

He covered her roving hand. "And I'm also not the type to jump into bed without thinking. I'm seasoned in my job, just as you are. I know the difference between adrenaline and reality."

She wasn't ready for deep conversations, especially not now. Would he press the issue though?

"Are you saying you object to having sex with me unless I agree right here and now to marry you?"

He held her eyes as steadily as he held her hand. Then his eyes slid lower, his palm guiding her hand downward as well. "I'm willing to table the discussion temporarily in the interest of not disturbing folks sleeping in the next room."

"Then we'll need to be very, very quiet." Angling her mouth over his, she kissed him, touched, and yes, God help her, even loved him.

Two hours later, Liam slid from bed, careful to keep the sheet draped over Rachel's naked body. He snagged his jeans off the cane rocker and tugged them on again. Stepping over Disco, asleep on the braid rug, Liam leaned against the window. Trees bent and twisted in the wind in a shadowy kung fu kind of display where arms and legs periodically snapped off.

A whimper drew his attention down to Fang. The puppy nosed his hand and probably needed to be let out. Hopefully the rain would let up soon. He scratched the dog's nose and looked outside again. He could feel himself zoning out with each snap of lightning and thunder that reminded him too much of past missions, until he settled in on the one that had changed his life forever.

The mission in the earthquake-ravaged Bahamas, when he'd met Rachel…

He lurched as the ground shook under his feet. He grabbed the tractor beside him for support. Debris shifted below his feet, rattling all the way to his teeth. Rescue workers scrambled down the piles, carrying the male victim he'd just stabilized and extricated—a businessman who'd been trapped in his office chair.

Frantic wails filled the air from family members who'd been digging with shovels, even hands, in search of loved ones. A German shepherd, Zorro, jockeyed for balance on top of a shifting concrete slab.

He had to get off this oscillating pyramid of debris. Now.

His pulse ramped with adrenaline. Splaying his arms for balance, he tested for firmer ground. The structural-triage report on this site had sucked, but Hugh had been ready to tunnel in once Zorro barked a live find.

He looked left fast to check on team member Wade Rocha. Combat boots planted, Rocha balanced with the feed line tight in his grip… the other end attached to Hugh Franco somewhere underneath the trembling hell.

Shit. Franco. Stuck below with his victim.

And just that fast, the earth steadied.

The demolished wasteland around him went eerily quiet. Sweat and filth plastered his uniform to his body, his heart hammering in his ears. Relief workers stood stock-still as if the world has stopped. But spirals of smoke affirmed the world hadn't ended, just paused to catch a breath.

He exhaled hard. Adrenaline stung his veins. The tremor hadn't been an earthquake, just another aftershock. Four so far today. Nerves were ragged, especially with the locals.

His headset blazed to life again with a frenzy of orders, questions, and curses from command center, along with check-ins from others on his team—Rocha, Cuervo, Data, Bubbles—spread out at other potential rescues in the sector. But the most important voice was conspicuously missing.

Hugh Franco.

Dread knotted his gut. Liam had lived through hell on earth before, but it was always worse when his men's lives were on the line. They were his family, no question. As his three ex-wives would attest, he was married to the job.

"Franco? Franco?" Liam shouted into the mic. "Report in, damn it."

His headset continued to sputter, some voices coming through piecemeal. None of them Hugh Franco.

Crappy headset… *Liam's hands fisted.*

"Shit." He punched the tractor. Knuckles throbbing, he resisted the urge to pitch the mic to the ground.

Rocha edged around the tractor. "I'm going in after him, boss. I'll follow the cable, dig through, and—"

Reason filtered through the rage. He needed to level out, stay in command.

"Hold steady. Not yet. I don't need two of the team missing." He refused to believe Franco was gone. Only his voice, only the radio connection, had faded. "Let's check in with the cleanup crew, maybe nab one of the search dogs again to confirm the exact location since things have shifted."

Scrubbing along his jaw, he scanned the crews returning to business as if nothing had happened. Training kicked into overdrive at times like these. The cold-sweat stage would set in later, once there wasn't anything to do but sit and think about how very wrong the day could have gone.

How badly it could still go, as they all hung out together in an active seismic zone...

All the same, Liam intended to bring as much help to the table as he could wrangle out of the already-overtasked people scurrying around the buckled piles of concrete and rebar. He scanned the construction crews—a mix from around the world—for a spare soul to help out.

And came up empty.

He scrubbed a gloved hand over his face. God, they were all maxed already, working alongside a rescue task force from Virginia for the past eighteen hours without sleep. He was running on the fumes left over from his catnap on the cargo plane ride over.

More C-17s dotted the sky, a trio landing one after the other in the distance with more supplies and personnel. Much-needed help. Except it would be hours before they were in place here.

But the helicopter hovering closer? The supplies and personnel that chopper contained would be available in minutes. His headset buzzed with news of a relief dog handler being sent from the Virginia USAR—Urban Search and Rescue.

He zeroed in on the cable lowering from the craft. A wiry figure dangled from the end, appeared to be a female in rescue gear with a dog strapped to her chest.

The helicopter was sending in a fresh search pair. A gold mine, when everyone else was running on fumes after over eighteen hours without sleep. They were also

closer than whatever troops or supplies might be loaded
in the C-17 still circling in the sky.

He clapped Rocha on the shoulder. "I'll be right
back. Keep talking to Franco."

Sure-footed, he jogged across the jagged debris to-
ward the chopper, eyes homed in on the duo spinning on
the end of the descending cable.

He was a scavenger from way back, and intended to
be first in line to claim her...

Liam turned from the rain-slicked window and back
to the bed. Rachel had been his from the start. In the
field or out. That hadn't changed.

So what was it that had him reaching for the mutt puppy
as if he needed a dose of therapy just because he'd hinted
at the *M* word? *Marriage.* Even thinking it now made him
break out in a cold sweat at the prospect of failure.

But the thought of losing her? Hell, that gave him the
shakes too. He was damned if he did and damned if he
didn't. The image of Rachel sleeping in his bed merged
with the vision of her descending from that helicopter
with her dog. Even in his memories, she damn near took
his breath away.

Realization filtered through him without the aid
of any therapy session—or hell, maybe the dog had a
magic all its own. Because he knew without a doubt,
just as he was reaching the point where he had to leave
his work in the field, the time had come for Rachel to
return to her calling.

And this time, he would be the one out in the cold in
a relationship with someone married to the job. It was
inevitable. God knew he'd lived through the scenario

often enough to see how it would play out. To know the hell that came from trying and failing. He wouldn't wish that pain on anyone, much less on Rachel.

Now he just had to figure out if he had the courage to back away from the only woman he'd ever truly loved.

—◆—

Catriona curled under the sheet on the bed, hugging a pillow and wishing she had Brandon to hold on to instead. But he was stretched out on the floor on a bedroll with his dog. Either he was being a gentleman or he wasn't interested.

Regardless, he was definitely restless. Every time thunder shook the ground, he thrashed, then settled again. Good God, how did he ever manage to feel rested, sleeping so sporadically? Sleep deprivation alone could send someone over the edge.

She didn't know what to do for him. Or if he would even want her help. She was in way over her head here with someone out of her league.

Lightning and thunder flashed and cracked in sync.

Brandon shot upright.

An encore of lightning slashed across his face, revealing a fear and horror that brought tears to her eyes. Before she could stop herself, she'd clambered off the bed and onto the floor beside him. Her arms wrapped around his shoulders and she held on tight. Rocking back and forth, she mumbled soothing words—she had no idea what, but kept on talking until the tension began to leave his body.

A long sigh racked through him. "You can ask."

"I'm not even sure where to start and I wouldn't want to say the wrong thing."

"How about asking what makes me lose my marbles every time a car backfires? What makes it so I can't sleep through the night?" His voice picked up speed and ferocity, even if he kept his volume under control. The tension crept up his back again. "What makes it so I can't even get a hard-on, much less make love to a woman?"

Whoa. Just whoa.

She'd asked herself some of those questions, but the last one had caught her by surprise. "Um, I was going to ask what makes you bite your nails? But since you mentioned the rest of that, I'm all ears if you want to talk."

He shrugged free of her arms—gently but deliberately. "I've talked and talked and talked some more to shrinks."

She leaned to grab her water bottle off the end table and passed it to him. "Sounds as if you think the talk was wasted."

"It didn't work, but I had to try if I wanted to end this purgatory of being on medical leave until I get my head on straight again—or don't. So far I've managed to convince them the therapy's making progress. We'll see."

"And your therapy dog?" She prodded carefully, afraid of doing more harm than good.

"I got a great trained free pet." His smile was dark and strained. "What's to argue about?"

"She doesn't help?"

"Of course she does." He slumped back against the footboard, his arm looped around Harley's neck. "In my opinion dogs are God's Prozac. And God's blood pressure medicine. They're pretty much the remedy to a lot of things."

She nudged his shoulder with hers. "Well, don't tell the drug companies about your theory. You'll crush them."

"I take it you agree with me then?" His eyes turned deeper blue, or maybe it was the dark. Or how close together they sat.

Her tongue stuck to the roof of her mouth. She wanted the water bottle.

She wanted *him*.

Brandon lowered his head... as if he was going... to kiss her. And ohmigod, he was really kissing her. His mouth brushed hers once, twice, then held with a firmness so there was no mistaking his intention. This wasn't an accidental connection. He palmed her head, his fingers in her hair. She held on to his arms, his thick muscled biceps.

Desire whooshed through her veins until she could have sworn her blood was sweet syrup. And she wanted more. To plaster herself to him until she went into a freakin' diabetic coma. She'd never been this attracted to a man, ached this much to have him touch her. She wanted him to lay her back on the quilt.

His mouth slid from hers and he angled back. She bit back a whimper of protest. She would not be that girl—needy or pathetic. She would not be the insecure little girl sitting on the sofa while her mother showed her literature on plastic surgery. What kind of parent offered a daughter a boob job and chin implant for her sixteenth birthday?

"Cat, I'm not sure if I'm supposed to apologize or not." He scooped up the water bottle again and rolled it between his hands as if wondering what to do with them next. "I only know that for the first time in months, I wanted to connect with a person. If I took advantage of our friendship, then I am sorry for that."

He was *apologizing* to her for the kiss? Apologizing for wanting to connect with her? The thought that he wanted a relationship with her absolutely rocked her socks—and scared the hell out of her. How could she trust him? Was he only reaching out to her because of his own vulnerable state right now?

"Brandon," she blurted before she even formed the thoughts, "would you have even seen me in high school?"

He looked genuinely stunned. "What are you talking about?"

"I'm not asking if you would have dated me." Of course he wouldn't have. "I'm asking if you would have noticed I existed. I'm the kind of person who fades into the woodwork of life. If someone had to describe me to a police sketch artist, they would be hard-pressed. There's nothing wrong with my features, but there's nothing unique. I just… am."

She held up a hand. "I'm not fishing for compliments here, simply stating facts. Essentially, I don't want to be any man's pity fuck."

He choked on a gulp of water.

"Surprised you, did I?" And she took more than a little pleasure in that. She tugged the water bottle from him. "I may look timid, but I can stand up for myself."

"Are you finished?"

"For now. But I reserve the right to climb up on my soapbox again without warning." She tipped back the water, thirsty and nervous.

"Fine." He took the bottle, set it aside and clasped

her hands. "First off, I resent the assumptions you made about my character."

"Your *high school* character, and was I wrong?" Why did she feel the need to push this?

"We're not in high school."

"Cop-out answer. I'll take that as a yes to your being a part of the popular crowd back then." The kind of people who'd walked past her as if she didn't exist. She tugged her hands but he didn't let go.

"If you want to know the God's honest truth"—his thumbs worked along the inside of her wrists—"I'm starting to think you're the one hung up on looks, because you sure do talk about appearances and popularity a lot."

She stopped tugging and just let herself soak up the sensation of his caressing touch. "I'm just trying to make a point."

"So am I. You want to talk about high school? All right then. Try this one on for size. Would you have been drooling over me because I was the football quarterback? Would you have been drawn to the uniform and the so-called status?" His blue eyes shone with clarity, honesty. "Sure sounds that way to me."

"You're muddying the waters." Along with making her feel uncomfortable and even every bit as shallow as her mother.

"Did it ever dawn on you to think I might have been the vice president of the chess club?"

"Were you?"

"No—"

"See!" She squeezed his hands, laughing.

"I was the president, actually." He smiled, the first shadow-free grin she'd seen from him. "And of the math club too. I'm a smart guy who wasn't born wearing a pocket protector." His smile faded. "That's a part of why I was privy to overhearing some of the confidential crap in the Middle East. They saw me as a bodyguard without ears or the sense to put together what I was hearing. Shame on them. And shame on you."

His words deflated the air and fight right out of her. She really was every bit as awful as her mother. She slid her hands free and bracketed his face. "You're right. I was wrong, and I apologize, truly."

Peace settled inside her as she saw him with new eyes, found depths in him she hadn't realized before. He was everything she could have hoped for—and more. Her insecurities had limited her perceptions, but not anymore. Not with Brandon.

"Apology accepted." His eyes shifted to violet blue again, the kind so deep a woman could climb right in for a swim. Did he know he was looking at her that way?

Her heart rate sped up. "I guess I should go back to sleep then."

"You could." He slipped his arms around her and settled her on his lap effortlessly. "Or you could find out what it's like to make out with the president of the chess club."

Chapter 16

BRANDON HAD BEEN TOLD AGAIN AND AGAIN BY HIS therapist that he could have a second chance at regaining his life. But until this moment with Cat, he hadn't really believed that could be possible.

He threaded his fingers through her loose red hair, the fine strands almost translucent in the intermittent flashes of lightning. And she was here with him now, which scared the hell out of him. She should have been at home with her dogs and friends, enjoying a normal day with people who didn't have screwed-up lives.

Definitely not on the run, in some remote cabin, hiding out from drive-by shootings and criminals who bombed homes and God only knew what else. Fear had gripped his gut and clouded his mind until all he could think about was making sure he didn't let her out of his sight.

She deserved so much better than what he had to offer, but for some reason she wanted him anyway. He reached past her to lock the door before angling back to slant his mouth over hers again. The soft plumpness was so much sweeter than he'd even imagined over the past months. And hell yes, he'd imagined kissing her more than once, only to hold back.

Her stroke was featherlight along his chest, just enough to arouse without veering into ticklish.

"You can touch me too, you know," she whispered

against his mouth, the scent of honeysuckle filling the space between them. "I'm not going to break."

"I don't want to scare you off. You're so… fragile." Which made her career choice all the more curious.

She'd forged an unconventional lifestyle from work that was fairly physical. She was running against the mainstream in two ways—by not following the customary expectations of her community and by working with her hands in a way that was fairly humanitarian.

"I'm going to just accept that as a compliment rather than get offended at the implication I'm some fragile helpless innocent."

Well, yes, he had been thinking that. Although these past days were making him rethink a lot of things about her. He should have looked deeper before now. She might be a quiet sort, but she was living a renegade lifestyle with her dogs on the beach. Plus, she was living alone, no one protecting her except her dogs.

"Honest to God, Cat, I'm not sure what to think right now."

"How about just listen while I dispel some more preconceived notions?" She sat back on her heels, her hazel eyes fierce in the dim night. "I'm tougher than I look. I've learned how to go after what I want from life, and from the minute I first saw you walk onto my property, I wanted you."

The determination in her words was unmistakable— and one hefty turn-on.

"O-*kay* then."

"Just to clear up another point, I'm not innocent, but I'm not particularly experienced either. Wait—" She held up a hand, then twirled it in a circle. "Back up. I have had relationships and they were sexual, but it wasn't great, so it wasn't like I learned much from the encounters."

Her words stunned him quiet. Not what she said, but that she was discussing this at all. He'd planned on kissing her and she was already fast-tracking to discussions of getting naked. Or maybe that was how those other guys had handled being with Catriona.

"You're saying the guys you dated were duds in bed."

A smile chased away some of the worry on her face. "That sounds better than saying I was the dud."

And right there, he saw it. What he'd been misunderstanding about her all along. She seemed so at peace and confident in her world. He'd put her on some kind of "serenity goddess" pedestal. While she had accepted him, flaws and all, he hadn't looked clear through to *her*, to see her insecurity—over what, he didn't know. But apparently somewhere along the line something or someone had done a number on her, making her lose sight of how perfect she was—an original.

She'd certainly pulled him out of the fog he'd been walking in.

And then there was the way she'd insisted on being here with him rather than being tucked away at a hotel with another PJ team member watching out for her. She'd packed her clothes, loaded up his truck while he flipped in and out of flashbacks and flights of panic. Her quiet determination yanked him through a time in his life when he could have easily lost it altogether. But she wanted to be here.

She'd refused to be anywhere else.

Brandon lifted her hands and kissed her knuckles. "If

he had an orgasm and you didn't, that makes him the dud for not doing his part of the work."

Her eyes went wide, then she coughed through a laugh. "I hadn't thought of it that way. While I'm not a hundred percent sure I agree, it's a lot more fun to think of those guys as duds than just jackasses."

Those *guys*. Plural? How many men had let her down? How many times had she opened her heart to an unworthy bastard who hadn't given a damn about her? He didn't want to know. He didn't need to know.

He did know that if he was ever lucky enough to sleep with her, he would make sure she came—more than once. Although the jury was still out on whether he could close the deal for himself. No matter how many times the shrink told him the cause was in his mind—or rather in the head above his waist rather than the one below—the end result was the same.

There was no end result for him…

A branch smacked the window and he realized he'd zoned out and Cat was staring at him patiently, waiting for him to return. He tucked her to him and put his all into kissing her, thoroughly, the way a man should kiss a woman. With his whole focus on her.

Tuning into when she tugged him closer.

Listening for those kittenish sighs that told him he'd touched her in just the right place.

For the first time in too long, he enjoyed the hell out of having a woman in his arms. There was no rush, because he wasn't going to take advantage of her trust. He wasn't going to screw her on the floor of a cabin with too many people a wall away.

So like a kid in high school again, he was just making

out on a quilt. Lying alongside her, hands roving, he kissed her, and hey wait, she was guiding his palm to her breast. He eased back to check her eyes, make sure she was in the moment and not just doing what she thought he expected. Although it was tough to see her eyes, with her lashes closed and her head thrown back in pleasure.

Yes.

A distant part of his brain told him this was going beyond just making out. This was heading toward something more—everything more. She'd meant what she said about knowing her mind, being strong and determined. Right now it was clear she wanted him every bit as much as he wanted her.

Damned if he had the strength to tell her no. He would gladly take this as far as she wanted.

Dipping his head, he nuzzled her neck, which stirred another of those purring sighs from her, so he kept right on. Tasting, listening, feeling her nipple harden.

And so did he.

The blood rushing south caught him unaware, then settled while his thoughts scattered. He bunched the hem of her T-shirt in his hands and inched it up, slowly, revealing inch by inch of creamy pale skin and freckles. Regardless of what she said about being tough, unbreakable, he couldn't remember ever seeing anyone so delicate. Actually, he couldn't think of anyone else period. She filled his eyes and hands and senses.

She raised her arms and he tugged the shirt the rest of the way over her head. She shook her hair free in a gingery cloud that settled around her bared shoulders. Wearing nothing but her shorts and a sports bra, she wasn't overly exposed, but there was something erotic about her natural beauty that didn't need glamming up.

As he stared, her nipples went harder, pushing against the gray cotton of her bra, letting him know just how much he turned her on. And wasn't that heady stuff?

She shimmied out of her shorts, revealing gray cotton bikinis with lace along the edges, the high rise making her slim legs stretch even longer. She started to pull the matching lace-trimmed sports bra upward, and he swept away her hands.

He traced the straps over her shoulders—lace and cotton, sexy and down-to-earth at the same time. "Call me greedy, but I want to do the unveiling."

"And if I want to go the striptease route?" Her plump lips went pouty and sultry.

"Next time." God, he hoped there could be a next time. So far, his body was still full on, hard throttle.

"Or I could undress *you*." She punctuated each word by kissing his chest, moving lower and lower still, all the way down to his navel. Her hand landed on his fly in an unmistakable message. In a moment of clarity, he realized she was operating off some old agenda from those jackass duds who took and never gave back.

He brought her face back up to his. "Next time. Right now, I want to see you. All of you."

Her hands stilled, her eyes searching his, so he let her see just how much he wanted her. Not too difficult a task at all.

"Okay, then." She spread her arms wide. "I'm all yours."

"Now that's what I wanted to hear." He eased the sports bra over her head and flung it across the room.

His mouth went dry—then watered. Perfect breasts, pert with dusky nipples tight and calling to his hands, to his mouth. All of the above, actually.

He cradled her in his palm and her husky sigh encouraged him to keep right on. He captured one taut tip in his mouth and she more than sighed. Her head lolled and a moan vibrated up her exposed throat.

She cupped the back of his head and drew him in closer, pressing for firmer contact. Damn straight, that was more like it—her letting him know what she wanted.

He was more than happy to provide.

Brandon worked one breast then the other with his mouth, tongue, and teeth until she writhed against him, moaning and whispering her pleasure until he wondered if she might finish right then and there. Which was okay by him. He was a big fan of orgasms. Lots of them. As many as she wanted.

Her fingers tugged tighter in his hair and he realized she was pulling him away, then kissing him. Her mouth was open and eager, her tongue touching his, her arms locking around his neck and holding on tight.

She scooted until she sat in his lap, her legs looping around his waist.

With her breasts pressed to his chest and the hot core of her pressed against his erection, he wondered if *he* might finish before he even got his clothes off.

No way was he letting that happen. He eased her back onto the blanket, licking and tasting his way down her body until he tugged her panties with his teeth. He looked up at her briefly to see her reaction. He found hesitation but acceptance.

He tugged at the waistband of her underwear and

discovered... two tiny tattooed pawprints along her hip bone. Now wasn't that a surprise?

"How many of these are there?" He kissed one, then the other.

"Why don't you count?"

Which meant there were more beneath her underwear. He yanked her panties off. "I still see just two."

She stroked his cheekbone. "I was trying to get you to take my clothes off faster."

"Smart woman." He smiled against her skin, then lower into the silky soft curls between her legs. "You'll need to make sure you're quiet."

She leaned on her elbows. "You're mighty confident that you can—"

His mouth closed over her and she gasped. He drew in the scent and taste of her, all the while still tuning in for cues of what she wanted. More of those breathy gasps and her slick readiness. Her elbows slid away and she gripped the quilt in her fists.

Just the sign he was looking for. He teased with his tongue and fingers, hitching her legs farther apart with his shoulders. She spread for him, welcomed him, and heat surged through him until his heart just about pounded out of his chest. The need to be inside her, deeper, seared him with an aching drive. But he held back.

Watching her. Working her. Waiting for her.

She bit her lip. Hard. Encouraging him with the way she wriggled her hips. The rapid rise and fall of her breasts. How her heels dug into his sides as her legs fell open.

He coaxed her the rest of the way over the edge. A

moan vibrated up her throat, and as much as he reveled in the sound, he didn't want her to be embarrassed. Just as he considered moving up to kiss her and finish her with his hand, she twisted her fingers in his hair, holding him in place. She stuffed her fist in her mouth fast. Her back arched and, hell yeah, he felt her come apart for him. Perfectly. Beautifully.

"Magnificent," he whispered against her with a light cooling puff that brought another moan from her.

He damn near ripped his clothes off, finesse fading fast. Until he remembered he didn't have a condom. Damn it. He was without protection when he had the first for-real, usable erection since a bomb exploded beside him in the Middle East.

Catriona's hand landed languidly on his shoulder. "Looking for one of these?"

Her other hand came out of her hobo sack—holding a condom packet.

He cupped the soft curve of her bottom, bringing her even closer. She suckled gently on his bottom lip before kissing and nibbling along his jaw. Nipped at his ear.

Her cool hands stroked his chest before he had time to think, much less warn her.

Gasping, she rocked back on her heels. "Brandon, oh my God."

Her fingertips hovered over the scars wrapped around his abdomen, striping upward. Healed burns and grafts mottled his flesh. Lightning streaked through the room, illuminating what she hadn't already felt. He should have told her before now, but he hadn't been thinking. Just feeling—feeling good—for the first time in so long.

Discussing what happened overseas sounded like a

massive mood killer for the first hard-on he'd experienced in months. He wanted to shove her hands aside and just push inside her. Except she clearly had questions, and as much as he ached to put those questions on hold, he owed her better. He needed to be sure she understood just what she was signing on for in sleeping with him.

He shuffled to sit beside her and turned on the small lamp beside the bed. She might as well see and hear it all.

"These came from the explosion in Afghanistan, a mix of chemical burns and fire." He relayed the information in a flat voice, the easiest way he'd found to get it out when asked. By rote. Just the facts. Don't think about the pain or the fear, and then the deeper pain that made thinking of anything else impossible. "There are more scars on my back and on the inside of a thigh, but those are from the skin grafts."

Scars gained from protecting a traitor. Except the guy died, was given a hero's funeral, and any chance at getting the truth from him was buried along with the man. Now all Brandon had were suspicions and an encrypted disk he wasn't even sure would be enough to stop this.

The heat of the attack, the betrayal, and the gut-twisting horror of having his life stolen from him flamed in his head until—

Gentle hands.

Catriona, touching his chest. Stoking the fire all over again.

He blinked through the haze and looked into her clear hazel eyes. His body reacted to the sight of her every bit as much as her touch.

She smiled softly, rolling the condom along the hard length of him. "Do you want to finish this or not?"

He laughed. For the first time in months, he laughed and meant it. Tucking her against him so every silky inch of her pressed to his overheated body, he rolled her under him. "Yes, ma'am, if you're still willing, we're most definitely going to finish this."

"Thank God, because I was starting to get worried there for a second."

Her little wriggle to settle beneath him sent a bolt of lust straight to his groin. A most welcome bolt that made him want to shout *yes, yes, yes about damn time*, to reclaim this part of himself.

He pushed inside her, drawn in by her moist heat, ready. Just one stroke and he had to fight back the urge to come, it had been so long. Which made him all the more determined to work harder for her—sliding a hand between them, kissing her and caressing her as he plunged again and again. The need to explode inside her almost tore him apart. He ached for it. For her.

Her slim legs wrapped around him with surprising strength. And thanks to the lamp, he could see her more clearly, be certain of when she was ready again so he wouldn't leave her behind… Male pride? Maybe. But he needed her there with him.

She gripped his hair again and brought his mouth to hers as she cried out her release, her body clenching and holding him tighter with wave after wave that pulled him under. Pleasure sliced through him like lightning cleaving him in half.

So much.

Almost too much, the good so good, it almost hurt

until he collapsed on top of her. He didn't even have the strength to lever off of her. He just buried his face in her neck, twitching in the aftermath.

For how long? He didn't know. Another zone-out? Or a micronap? Either way, not how he wanted to end this encounter. He rolled to the side and pulled her against him.

He knew sex wouldn't fix everything, and already the myriad complications ahead of them was weighing on his shoulders like an M1 main battle tank. Although for right now, he planned to savor this night, this moment in time with an amazing woman who'd just given him one incredible gift.

He hadn't solved all his problems. But he was going to give thanks that life could still surprise him with something so beautiful in this long trudge through hell to get back to normal.

—⁂—

Sunrise weakly pierced the drizzling rain.

Sitting on a plastic sheet on the porch, Rachel hugged her knees and stared out over the misty swamp. Her Baby Eagle rested beside her. The weather was clearing enough that she could actually see for target practice, but they didn't need to draw attention to themselves with gunshots. And they needed to prep as much as possible to leave.

The Internet signal was strengthening. Jose had uploaded whatever that chip stashed in Brandon's phone contained and sent a copy to their buddy Data and another to Special Agent Sylvia Cramer.

Now they just needed to wait for the okay to return

to base, where finally the right authorities would take Lieutenant Brandon Harris seriously and get to the bottom of this. She willed that call from Sylvia Cramer to come through, itchy to get moving. To make something happen. To expose the people responsible for trying to kill her and her friends—people who wanted to do a lot worse.

She wanted her life back. And she wanted to know why—after hinting around at marriage—Liam was suddenly so reserved this morning. Was he angry because she avoided the conversation? Was he regretting what he'd said? Good God, for a funny guy, he sure was moody underneath all those laughs, and her heart was getting a serious workout, being yanked around this way.

Watching him prep the airboat, she thought of how she'd woken to an empty bed, the dent in the pillow and tenderness between her thighs the only proof he'd even slept with her. Sure he'd smiled at her from across the room and touched her shoulder as he walked past, but there was no missing the shadows lurking in his expression.

She sipped lukewarm coffee, more for the caffeine and something to do with her hands than out of any need to drink. "What can I do to help?"

Liam checked the magazine on his gun, tucked it back in the holster. "There's not much to load up, but the more we get done now…"

"The faster we can leave later when the call comes."

"Roger that." He hitched his duffel over his shoulder and strode down the dock toward their airboat.

She scooped up her backpack. It felt like eons since

she'd loaded it up, rather than just three days prior. Might as well have been a lifetime ago.

Liam stood at the end of the dock and shouted, "Toss it to me. No need to get wet until you have to."

It was almost as if he didn't even want to be near her. What the hell? Could he possibly be the kind of jerk who stopped wanting a woman the minute he got her?

Although he had been divorced three times.

"Here!" She threw her backpack like a basketball, pushing away from her chest. Hard.

He caught it without budging. It figured. He turned to walk away.

"Liam?" she called out, frustration stirring. "Liam? What's going on?"

"I'm busy packing," he said without looking back. "We can talk later."

"Liam!" Aggravation tangled up with anger, not to mention all the fear piling up these past couple of weeks. "Liam! William McCabe! I'm not some quiet, laid-back person who's just going to sit back and pretend I don't notice you're in a mood. What's wrong with you today?"

He tossed her pack on the boat without a word and started back down the dock. His closed-off face didn't promise much conversation. His boots hit the muddy bank. He picked his way over the wandering tree roots poking out of the muddy incline.

"Damn it." She stomped her foot, not caring who heard. "Just talk."

He turned sharply to face her, smiling. Sort of. "Now isn't the time."

"Because I'm getting too close? Too real?"

Cursing, he looked away, but he didn't leave. He

seemed to be gathering his thoughts, and she wondered if maybe, just maybe, he might tell her what was bothering him. What had changed between last night and this morning?

She'd opened up to him after pushing men away ever since Caden's death. Her relationship with Liam was significant for so many reasons—not the least of which was because she was actually falling for the guy—and now she was scared of something she couldn't pinpoint.

"Well, Liam? Aren't you even going to answer me?"

His head went back as he stood tall and hard bodied in the rising sun. The only man who'd hadn't eventually backed off from her strong will—okay, she'd pushed most men away. But there was no pushing Liam.

He was all man.

So much so, he didn't even sway as the ground shifted under his feet. She frowned, trying to figure out what wasn't right about the picture in front of her...

"Liam?"

He looked back at her. "Okay, Rachel, you want to talk, then okay. Let's talk."

"Liam," she interrupted, stepping forward, "something's wrong with the bank." A mudslide? "See the ground—"

Move.

She screamed as an alligator emerged from the muck, racing straight for Liam.

Chapter 17

LIAM TURNED HARD AND FAST AT RACHEL'S WARNING. But not fast enough.

He stared straight into the cold eyes of an alligator. He didn't even have time to figure out how he'd been caught so off guard. He zigged and zagged, hard left, then right. Again. And again. It was his only defense against a gator that could definitely outrun him. The beast had to stop and adjust for each turn.

The mud made speedy moves tougher, but not impossible. *Shift right.* He reached for his gun, already calculating how to shoot the reptile in its one vulnerable spot—where the skull joined the neck.

He heard Rachel cry out to him again a half second before the gator's tail whipped his feet from under him. Liam slammed to the ground. His gun slid from his hand and into the water. He could see inside the alligator's open jaws as it prepped to grab him for a death roll.

Instincts kicked into overdrive. He sprang up and onto the alligator's back. There were a thousand places he would rather be, but the only way he could think to buy time and stay out of the beast's gullet.

"Rachel, get your gun," he shouted, arms and legs wrapped around the reptile.

Knobby bumps dug into his gut. His muscles screamed with the force of holding on to the thrashing creature sliding back into the shallow marsh. If they reached deeper water, he was screwed.

Dimly he heard the dogs going nuts in the cabin and Rachel screaming for help as the scaly rough skin scratched his face. But he also heard her feet running along the porch and down the steps. She'd called for backup but she wasn't waiting around.

Brackish water slid over him and into his mouth. "I can't let go," he said through gritted teeth. "You're going to have to shoot the gator."

"With you on it?" she asked, only a hint of panic leaking into her voice as she climbed up onto the dock.

"Don't think I can go anywhere unless you do." What a time for his humor to come back. "Shoot right where the skull joins the neck."

"That itty bitty spot right in front of your face?" Her voice cracked. She jockeyed for better positioning as the gator slipped into deeper and deeper waters.

"Anywhere else and it'll ricochet off and send bone shrapnel everywhere." All over him. "Aim. Shoot. Don't jerk back. Hold your arms steady after you pull the trigger."

Where the hell was his team?

"Right." She raised her Baby Eagle pistol that he'd never had the time to teach her to use.

Braced.

Shot.

Missed.

Shrapnel bit into his arms. The scrapes burned like a son of a bitch. But not half as bad as the razor-sharp teeth of the alligator would if the scaly bastard got hold of him.

"Oh, God. Oh, God. Oh, God, Liam, I'm so sorry."

"Shoot again, damn it. Shoot, Rachel!" He looked at her for what he hoped wasn't the last time.

God, she was incredible, standing down an alligator without question. Not backing off. Not even shaking. He couldn't have asked for better from anyone on his team.

She lined up the shot. Hands steady. Pulled the trigger.

The alligator went limp.

Rachel dropped to her knees on the dock.

The shrapnel scratches on his arm hurt, but he kept holding on anyway. "Rachel, hon, you did great. Now, I need you to pass me the tape out of the duffel so I can seal this guy's mouth closed. I'm not taking any chances that he's playing possum."

She bolted into action, leaping into the boat and racing back before he finished catching his breath. She passed the roll of industrial duct tape with hands shaking so hard she almost dropped it in the water. He wrapped it around and around the alligator's mouth until finally… he gave himself permission to haul himself up onto the planked dock with Rachel. She locked her arms around him and he realized she was sobbing, hard. From shock, no doubt.

He looped an arm around her and kissed the top of her head. "You did good, Rachel, damn good."

"I missed," she gasped.

"And then you didn't miss."

She was every bit as incredible as the first day he'd seen her. She was so much more woman than she even realized.

The world expanded, his vision widening beyond just Rachel and himself. His team and the other women stood on the porch and along the shore. Guns out. Dogs restrained.

Liam scanned them all, his ragtag team, with Rachel an unofficial but fully contributing member. The enormity of everything he would be losing soon kicked him in the gut as hard as any swipe from a gator tail. "I got us some fresh meat for breakfast."

Rachel had never felt less like eating in her life. Her stomach was stuck somewhere in her throat while she waited for Sylvia Cramer's call. Or for some other "divine blessing" from the string of computers set up on the rough-hewn table. Periodically, one pinged with a new message, which turned out not to be Sylvia as they'd hoped.

Nerves ragged, Rachel leaned against the counter with the others, chowing down chunks of cooked alligator tail. The same gator that had tried to eat Liam. The same reptile she'd shot. After missing once and sending shrapnel all over him.

Her stomach climbed up into her throat again. Her full plate stayed in front of her while everyone else replayed the whole event as if it were a particularly fun episode of *Swamp People*, for God's sake.

Cuervo repacked his first-aid kit, his dish of gator chunks waiting beside him. "Hey, McCabe, where did you learn to do that?"

"Do what?" Liam's shirtsleeves had been cut off, his shrapnel wounds cleaned and bandaged by his teammate.

"You're joking again, right?" Cuervo threw away empty packets of antiseptic ointment. "Where did you learn to wrestle gators?"

"Training." Liam speared the tip of his knife into a chunk of pan-fried meat. "Were you sick that day? That's too bad."

Cuervo threw a half-empty roll of gauze at his patient. Liam snagged it in midair without so much as a wince, as if both his arms weren't covered in bandages. Thank heavens there had been medical help on-site.

She forgot sometimes that the PJs were trained medics, so multifaceted… ready to do more than rescue anywhere, anytime, but provide medical aid when needed, fight back enemy forces, even. Do whatever was necessary to bring home the person in their care.

Her heart lurched up there into her throat with her stomach.

Catriona scrunched her nose. "Who trains to fight off alligators?"

Brandon stood beside her, shoulders touching in subtle intimacy. "People who do rescues in the Everglades."

Catriona forked up another bite. "Did the class include how to cut it up and prepare it, too?"

Wade diced more of their pan-fried brunch with his jagged-edged survival knife. "Sunny deserves all the credit. She's a whiz at cooking in rural situations. Besides, our gourmet cook was busy getting patched up."

Forcing a smile, Rachel speared a bite. "Really, it's great. Better than great, Sunny. Thanks." She stuffed it in her mouth, chewing it fast into teeny tiny bites so she could force it down her tight throat. "I'm just praying we don't get a ticket for hunting out of season."

Jose lifted his plate for more just before a computer pinged.

Liam checked and shook his head.

Jose said, "Nothing could be as bad as that stringy goat we ate in Afghanistan when McCabe and I got stuck out in the desert for five days."

Liam uncapped a water bottle. "And you're all questioning why I'm ready to retire?" Tipping back his drink, he grinned with his mouth, if not his eyes. "Can't imagine why."

How could they all sit here so calmly and joke, after Liam had almost been hauled to the bottom of a swamp by an alligator? She wanted to scream. But of course that was impossible with her throat full of her stomach and heart.

She shoved away from the counter, unable to take even one more second of pretending everything was okay. She needed air. Quietly, she ducked out the front door and plopped onto a simple wooden bench. Nothing fancy, it didn't even have a back. But there was plenty of humid air to suck into her constricted lungs. Disco nudged her knee and she realized she was still holding her plate full of that alligator meat.

The evils of feeding a dog table scraps be damned.

She set the dish on the ground. "Have at it, pal."

As Disco ate the hell out of the godforsaken gator, Rachel's eyes zipped right back to the muddy bank, the swirls and patterns in the shoreline chronicling each detail of Liam's battle on the way into the water. She swallowed down bile.

The cabin door creaked open. Out of the corner of her eye she saw Liam's broad shoulders fill the void. Silently, he stepped over and sat on the bench next to her. The gauze on his arms snagged against her skin.

She blinked back tears.

He reached toward her and she instinctively leaned into him. He tapped a mosquito off her arm, then caught it in his fist.

Straightening again, she scratched her arm where the insect had been. "Thanks."

"No. Thank *you*."

"There's nothing to thank me for. I did what had to be done." She stared down at her feet beside Disco licking the plate clean. "Why were you pulling away from me back at the dock?"

"Before the gator tried to eat me?"

She looked sideways at him. "Not funny."

"Yeah it is." He grinned. Sort of.

She touched his arm lightly, beside one of the bandages covering a shrapnel wound. "You've been putting distance between us all morning, and I don't understand."

He covered her hand with his, his green eyes getting the pale hazel streaks that came when he was emotional. Those streaks offered the only clue in a man who held himself so tightly in check, always in command. "I'm letting you go, Rachel, if that's what you really want."

She snapped upright, stunned, hurt, angry, overflowing with emotions after the nightmare of seeing him nearly mauled to death by a fucking alligator. "You're *dumping* me?" Hysteria frothed inside her. After the morning she'd been through, she was due a meltdown. "I thought you married your women before you dumped them."

"Not funny and not fair."

"No damn kidding." She gasped for air. "What the hell is wrong with you?"

Undaunted, he calmly took her hands in his as they

sat side by side on the bench. "You're an incredible woman. The work you've done with the therapy dogs is amazing. You've helped spread that gift and it's clear the momentum will keep on rolling."

"I hope so." Except what did that have to do with breaking up with her?

"But you also have to know what you're really meant to do, you and Disco."

"Whoa! Stop right there." She yanked her hands out of his, recognizing his hand-holding now for what it was—a pacifying gesture, his way of being the man in control, doling out comfort. "I've already told you why I stepped out of the field. And if we're playing fair here, I've gotta call foul on your using that against me now. If you've suddenly decided you're in over your head with this relationship, then man up and say so. But don't you dare make excuses."

Frustration flecked his eyes. "You're not hearing me. You may have needed a break, but when you're work-ing a rescue mission—when you're shooting an alligator between the eyes—you are *magnificent*."

"I'm so magnificent that you're dumping me?" She wanted to kick his butt back into the water. Instead she continued to wade through the convoluted path of his reasoning, because she cared about him. She loved him, damn it, and now he was trying to leave her too. "And about me going back to search and rescue work. What does that have to do with the two of us as a couple?"

"I'm retiring."

"Yeah, that's what I hear," she said, gripped the edge of the bench until splinters dug into her palms. "What does that have to do with anything?"

"We're taking different paths now. I'm stepping off the adrenaline junkie treadmill."

His placating—bullshit—tender expression made her want to scream. She should have seen this coming. Six months ago, she'd predicted something just like this happening, so she'd stayed well away from Liam McCabe even when her body and heart screamed *go for it*.

"You know what, Liam? You *are* making up excuses to walk away." She shot to her feet, unable to sit there any longer while he played out this letting-her-down-easy farce. "You may be a badass out there on the job, but when it comes to falling in love you're scared to death. Maybe it goes back to losing your mom or the divorces or combat stress. But it's time for you to let yourself be happy."

"Rachel, listen to me." He stood, clasping her shoulders, slipping back into his protector mode as surely as if he'd put on his uniform. "I just want to be fair to you. I want *you* to be happy—"

"No. You want to play this safe, which is a long way from anyone being happy. No risk, no glory, pal." She jabbed his chest, hard. "You love me, Liam McCabe. You really love me, not the halfway measures of picking the wrong woman. I am the best thing to happen to you, and you are making the biggest mistake of your life in being too afraid to admit it."

Her rant left her breathless. Even more so the longer he just stood there staring back at her, saying nothing. His eyes were distant. Already he was putting up walls, just as he'd told her he always did. Even knowing he was protecting himself from the hurt of losing his mother, of history repeating itself with his self-destructive relationships, here he went all over again.

He'd already decided, damn him.

Every gasp was a trial. She'd lost one man she loved... *Ah shit. Shit. Shit. Shit!*

She wasn't falling in love with Liam. She was already there. Yes, she loved him, so much that losing him could devastate her, wipe her out. She'd barely survived Caden's death. Oh God, it had been so much easier believing she'd lost her one soul mate, and that therefore her heart would never be at risk again.

She'd been dead wrong.

The screen door creaked open again, fast, banging against the cabin wall. Cuervo burst through and onto the porch.

"Agent Cramer just gave the all clear. Meal's over. Time to report in."

"Agent Cramer, step into my office," General Ted Sullivan barked from his open door.

The day was going to hell fast, and he was running out of time to stop a plan two years in the making from unraveling because of one insignificant lieutenant who just wouldn't go the fuck away.

Which left him to deal with what he could. Grab control wherever possible. Line up his allies and eliminate the obstacles.

Special Agent Sylvia Cramer had been his staunchest ally when he first arrived here. Ideologically, they'd been on the same page about the proper realignment of the satellite missile defense program and how badly the program needed a regime change. They'd spent hours after work discussing, theorizing on the effectiveness of different strategies. Her input on the effect such changes would have on the intelligence-gathering community were inspired.

He'd found a kindred spirit. He hadn't doubted her loyalty, her willingness to do anything he asked—until Liam McCabe and Rachel Flores turned up missing.

Either Sylvia Cramer wasn't as good an agent as he thought or Liam McCabe was far better than he'd anticipated. The culmination of too much work depended on the exchange of information at this summit going off without a hitch. He needed confirmation that people were loyal to the death.

Special Agent Sylvia Cramer glided into his office on her mile-long legs in red high heels. Her hair a bit mussed, but not a wrinkle in her skirt and blouse. The perfect professional. Until she wasn't.

He closed the door behind her.

And locked it.

Time to find out if she'd betrayed him, too.

Sylvia pivoted on her heel, one perfectly plucked eyebrow arching slowly. "Correct me if I'm wrong, but it's common courtesy to ask a lady first."

He planted his hand on the door, his body grazing hers. "And since when do you want to be treated like a lady? Correct me if I'm wrong"—he tunneled his palm under her skirt and up her leg to the band of her silky thigh-high stockings—"but I was under the impression you wanted something entirely different from me."

Her leather purse slid from her shoulder to the floor.

He slipped his hand into her thong and thrust two fingers deep inside her. Her body clamped around him. Tight. But dry.

"Too fast for you?" He pulled her closer with just those two fingers until the tips pressed against just... the right... spot.

Her lashes fluttered and she stumbled back against the door before regaining her balance, her hands flat against his chest. The slick juices of her arousal began to cream his fingers.

Damn straight, he knew what to do. He wasn't taking advantage of anyone. He always pleasured the hell out of her before they finished any encounter. He might be her superior, but she wasn't in his chain of command. Not a thing wrong with what they'd been doing the past month, since a late night spent working together had led to a shift in their relationship, a mutually satisfying shift.

He kissed the side of her neck, never her mouth. He hated the taste of cigarettes and she'd been sneaking smoke breaks more and more often lately. Stress. Came with the job. They all had their methods for working it out. Some exercised. Some drank. Sylvia smoked.

And *this* was his way of releasing tension.

He moved his fingers inside her, nudged the collar of her blouse with his chin until he could grab the strap of her bra with his teeth and inch it aside. The scent of her filled the air and he lifted his head, tipping his face to catch a whiff of her, going harder, knowing how she couldn't resist him. He slipped his fingers in and out, faster, until her nails dug into his shirt.

Sylvia panted softly. "We haven't been together in a few days. I thought you were angry."

"Over what?" he asked, even though he knew.

He wanted to force her to spell out how she'd fucked up, to test her, to see if she could still be trusted. Just because she was screwing him didn't mean she wouldn't screw him over to get ahead. He flicked open the buttons down her blouse, exposing white lace.

"How McCabe"—she gasped as his knuckle caressed the inside curve of her breast—"and the Flores woman disappeared from the safe house."

"Nothing to worry about. We'll find them." He pushed under the demicup, lifting her breast until her dusky nipple slid into sight. A growl of appreciation crawled up his throat.

"That's good," she purred. About his tongue flicking over her nipple or that he would find the missing couple? "Although we really had no legal reason to hold them. We were doing them a favor by protecting our own asses with the cover story once they left."

He looked up. "That still doesn't excuse them getting away without your knowledge. You knew how important it was to contain the Flores woman, to keep her from racing to the nearest reporter with her wild"—too damn correct—"claims."

"Of course."

"You deserve to be reprimanded for your mistake."

"Is that so?" Her eyes narrowed as she rubbed her breasts against his chest. "What are you going to do? Write me up?"

He almost exploded in his pants like an untried teen instead of a forty-nine-year-old man, and she knew it. He could see the glint of power in her eyes.

But that was okay with him. Power plays were fun. He liked his mistresses strong and demanding. It made the rush even better when they came apart for him, because of him.

And for that reason, never once did he take his eyes off her. He slipped his fingers from her, sliding his hands around to cup her ass, cheeks bared by her thong.

"It's my job to dole out your punishment." He slapped one globe. "You're good, but mistakes have to be rectified."

He smacked her again.

Her pupils widened as she flicked her tongue along her lips, distracting him for a second.

"You like to play rough?" She slapped him across the face.

The sound echoed in the quiet room. He grabbed her wrists and held her arms akimbo, backing her up against the edge of his desk, already panting in anticipation over what she might do next.

"Ted, you either trust me or you don't," she said with a grit that made him throb all the more. "But don't think you can play mind games with me like you do with everyone else. I see you for exactly who you are."

"And you keep coming round for more."

He kissed her, hard, grinding against her, and yes, the taste of her was smoky from a recent cigarette, but he was past caring as she thrust her tongue in his mouth. His grip on her loosened and she clawed his back. He shoved his fingers inside her again, rougher this time. She sucked his tongue, drawing it into her mouth.

Her damp warmth clamped around his fingers and his thoughts scattered, his every ounce of concentration zeroed in on *her*. Her head lolled, giving up her neck. He could see the second her restraint snapped. Just a second before she tore at his belt and yanked open his trousers. Her cool hands cupped his hard-on, one hand stroking, the other cupping his balls, already tight against his body.

"Ted…" Her voice rasped free, husky and raw, and she worked him until his eyes nearly rolled back in his head. "Anything we do now will have to be hard and fast, which, don't get me wrong, is fabulous sometimes. But today, I want slow and explosive. If you're a good boy and wait until tonight, I'll let you pick the toys. So? What'll it be? Fast now. Or *everything* later…"

Toys? Not even a choice. "Later it is."

He was a patient man in all aspects of his life. Made the payoff all the sweeter.

"Wise decision." Nipping his earlobe, she pulled her hand away too damn slowly. "While you're behind your desk today, know that I'm behind mine, fantasizing about all the things I'm going to do to you once we're alone. Now, no cheating and coming to my office before then. I'll meet you at our regular place, eight o'clock tonight."

Stepping back, she adjusted her thong and brushed her skirt back down, swiping away any telltale wrinkles. She had admirable poise in the workplace, but almost too much so right now. As she calmly tucked her breasts back into her bra, he considered pulling her to him again, taking her over to the big leather sofa and going down on her until she screamed. But as he reached for her, she neatly sidestepped.

"No, no. We agreed." She patted his cheek right over the spot she'd slapped earlier. "And besides, I have a meeting with my boss in five minutes about security for the summit. Good thing you opted for later and we didn't take longer now, or I would have had a tough time explaining why I'm hanging out of my underwear."

She made fast work of her buttons, retrieved her shoe, and slicked back the lone strand of hair that had worked its way free. All before he'd finished zipping his pants.

"Wait," he ordered. He was in control. Not her. He buckled his belt. "Now, you may leave."

She arched an eyebrow at him again and he would have been pissed, except he noticed her hands shaking. She wasn't as unaffected as she wanted to pretend. Sylvia scooped her leather purse from the floor and before the door clicked closed behind her, he saw her dip her hand inside for her leather cigarette case.

Her sign of nerves.

Damn right, she wasn't unaffected. He'd gotten to her. As much as she tried to play it cool, she wanted him. Sure, he was sixteen years her senior. And even though he kept in shape, he didn't suffer any delusions that he looked like some thirty-year-old kid.

He had something far more valuable than youth. He had power, and that turned women on.

It had turned Sylvia on within a month of his setting foot on this base.

She was a good lay, more adventurous than most in the sack and didn't have a problem at all dropping to her knees for him, but he wasn't going to do something insane like leave his wife for her. Kelly was the perfect spouse for him, one who made no demands. And as long as he stayed married to her, he had an instant barrier against committing to another woman.

A knock on the door snapped him back into the moment. Maybe Sylvia had come back after all. He smiled at the thought of her begging for more.

He opened the door to. . Captain Bernard, Sylvia's

active-duty counterpart in the OSI. And serious suck-up, always trying to kiss ass to get ahead. As if everyone couldn't see what he was about.

"What?" Sullivan barked. "This isn't a good time."

"Sir, I'm here for the briefing on bringing in Lieutenant Harris. Agent Cramer's secretary said she'd been called to your office, and I know what a personal interest you've taken in lending your assistance with the investigation into Brandon Harris."

Ted blinked. What the hell was the captain talking about?

One thing was certain. He wouldn't find out standing here in the hall. "Yes, come in. Agent Cramer had to step out for a moment, but we can get started without her and catch her up when she returns."

Bernard stepped into the office, apparently all but pissing himself to have a private moment alone to speak with a general. "Lucky thing, Harris calling in on his own and sending the data he'd collected. Once it's decoded… holy crap, sir. The air force owes Major McCabe a huge debt of thanks for pulling this one off."

Ted placed his hand on the edge of his desk, right over the spot where Sylvia had leaned minutes ago, writhing against him and panting about plans for tonight, all the while knowing she was about to betray him. Of course she hadn't been able to turn him down when he called her. That would have stirred suspicion.

So Special Agent Cramer knew Harris had been found and she hadn't said a word. If she had Harris and hadn't told him, then she must have accessed the information he'd worked like a madman to bury—the data on the exchange with the Chinese coming up this weekend. And as much as she'd claimed to agree with him ideologically, she'd apparently gone squeamish when confronted with how far he was willing to go.

Then she'd used her body and talk of sex games to distract him from learning the truth. Rage boiled so deep in his belly he wanted to storm out the door and put his hands around her neck.

The bitch had played him.

But she'd also overestimated herself and she'd underestimated him. Sure, his career here was finished once the incriminating data was decoded. He'd accepted that possibility from the start and made contingency plans. He was smarter than them in the end. He would survive and come out on top.

Sylvia Cramer was the one who'd lost this game. It may have been years since he'd seen combat, but he hadn't forgotten how to coolly, effectively eliminate his enemies.

And then make a clean escape.

Chapter 18

Sylvia had certainly delivered a top-notch ride. Liam adjusted his headset attached to the main feed in the CV-22 that had been sent to escort them from the Everglades back to Patrick Air Force Base. He was losing himself in routine, doing his damndest not to think about how his fight with Rachel had split him wide open inside. Damn it, he couldn't even look at her sitting across from him, but he felt her eyes on him, her hurt and her anger radiating.

He focused on work the way he'd done in the past to get through the pain of a breakup. Gauging by the ache in his chest, that plan wasn't going as well for him this time.

He just prayed clearing up the mess in his professional life would go better than how he'd handled his personal life. He and his guys hadn't been able to decode enough of the chip to decipher more than that it dealt with satellite coordinates.

Leaking data on where U.S. satellites were focusing intelligence gathering could compromise entire undercover ops years in the works. Lives were at risk. As for who was responsible? Sylvia must have figured that out or she never would have called them back in. He'd requested that as few as possible know about them coming in, and she'd agreed. Only her immediate staff. She'd been clear she didn't even intend to risk telling the senior ranking officers. Which he'd been relieved to hear. The last thing they needed was General Sullivan micromanaging the hell out of every move. If so, it could be months before they made it back in. She'd simply *hmmm*ed in response.

And beyond that, she wouldn't talk, not over phone lines.

Would he ever be privy to those answers she'd uncovered? After all he, Rachel, and the rest of them had been through, he sure as hell hoped he would get some closure, rather than being given one of those stares that said this was a need-to-know-only deal—meaning he didn't get to hear squat.

Either way, they would be landing within minutes.

He stared across at Brandon Harris, pale and strapped into the red webbed seat between Rachel and the doggy-sitter. The young lieutenant held himself stock-still in the belly of the cargo hold, his hand gripping the collar of his dog.

Would the already-fragile Harris be able to hold up under the stress of the ensuing investigation? At least Sylvia had assured them she knew who was responsible and would make sure the responsible parties were taken into custody.

And if they were too late to keep the top-secret intelligence out of enemy hands? At least the powers that be would know what information had been compromised and could work at protecting those exposed.

Liam let his head fall back as he lost himself in the familiarity of the moment, the steel cavern with cables and wires like fiber-optic veins feeding the beast.

The CV-22 engines vibrated the craft, powering them closer to Patrick Air Force Base. The tilt-rotor aircraft had been waiting for them the minute their airboats docked. Waiting in the parking lot, no less. The CV-22 could take off and land like a helicopter. Then once in flight, the rotors shifted forward so the special-ops craft flew like a plane, far exceeding the speed of any chopper.

Voices from the pilots up front and the passengers in back mingled together over the airwaves. All but his and Rachel's. He didn't feel her eyes on him now, but he didn't expect she'd given up. He would have to hold strong.

The way she'd stood him down had been a surprise. He'd expected... hell, he didn't know what. But she'd charged into him just like she had the alligator.

She'd been incredible both times. He was so proud of how she'd taken the shot, saved his ass. And he was pissed at himself for putting her in that position. Just as he should have known better than to start a relationship with her in the first place.

Damn it, whether she believed him or not, he was doing this for her.

He just wanted to get this flight, this mission, this week with the security gig for the summit over with. Move on rather than hanging out in limbo, tormented every freaking second of the day with closing the book on this chapter of his life.

At least everyone else seemed pumped. Excited about the success so far. And the dog-sitter chick—Catriona— was having a blast learning how the headset worked.

"So," she said, testing the speak button, "why do you guys have so many nicknames? Like why do you some-times call Wade 'Brick'?"

Rocha raised his hand. "I got this one. I'm called

Brick because I'm thickheaded. And my last name, Rocha, means rock in Portuguese, so it all kinda fits. Cuervo over there got his because it just fits with his name Jose, and it just so happens, in his early days in the air force, he had a particularly memorable evening thanks to a bottle of tequila."

And wasn't there a sad irony in that? An alcoholic forever being stuck with a booze name.

Rocha continued. "Data, back at base, is a computer and math genius. He's one of our younger team members and used to be called Fang, which is what we name every fresh-faced kid who joins us. It means, uh, 'frick, another new guy.' But not actually 'frick.'"

Laughter rumbled over the airwaves. Rachel's eyebrows went up as she rested her hand on the boxer puppy's head.

Liam shrugged and looked away from the wide brown eyes—on the woman and the dog. "The name Fang goes to the next new guy, and the old Fang gets an official name. Our Fang while we were in Alaska became Data once the latest PJ joined the team."

Rachel snagged his eyes and held, giving no ground. "So you were once Fang."

"Back in the dark ages, yes." His knees ached almost as bad as his chest.

Rocha filled the stretch of silence. "Now we call him Walker, as in Walker, Texas Ranger. Because he used to be a ranger, but it was an Army Ranger. You should hear his Chuck Norris impression. Priceless."

"But so good"—Cuervo leaned forward as casually as somebody telling a frickin' fireside tale—"you might actually think he's really Chuck Norris in disguise.

Seriously, Major McCabe is so awesome he can make fire by rubbing two ice cubes together."

Rocha nodded. "When you open up a can of whup ass, Major McCabe jumps out."

Sunny held up her hands. "True story, I hear the bogeyman checks his closet at night for Liam McCabe."

Laughing, Catriona said, "Wait, wait, how about this one. Major McCabe can make onions cry—" She squeaked to a stop as the aircraft jerked slightly in flight.

The CV-22's engines slowed, the whine increasing to a roar as the rotors tilted upward. Humor faded like the air in rapid decompression as they landed.

The CV-22 settled without so much as a jolt, and the pilot called the all clear to begin unstrapping, which, thank God, brought an end to the Chuck Norris jokes.

Yeah, great. He was already a damn legend. Life as he knew it would be over after this final mission wrapped up.

His gaze shot back to Rachel and he wondered how it could have been for them if they'd met and connected ten years ago, back when he was at the top of his game. If they'd had time to build a foundation together.

If he even knew how to do that.

The back ramp lowered, the gaping hole revealing the runway. Familiar stretches of pale concrete and stark utilitarian outbuildings glowed with the orangey haze of the setting sun. Only the sea air and an occasional palm tree differentiated it from other landing strips.

A small greeting party waited in a roped-off area, led by General Ted Sullivan along with Captain Bernard from the OSI. Wind rippled the captain's uniform as he stood flanked by a half dozen security cops toting M16s. As if that weren't enough firepower, four Humvees were parked behind them, each equipped with a turret with a SAW—squad automatic weapon—mounted on top. Given Sylvia's assurance things were being kept low-key, Liam did *not* have a good feeling about this.

His battle-honed instincts went on alert. They were either being highly protected—or were about to be taken into custody.

"Divide and conquer," Rachel said, bracing a hand on the dash of the Humvee as General Sullivan sped down the flight line, dusk closing in like a fading camera shot.

The second they all stepped off the back ramp of the cargo aircraft, they'd been split up for questioning. Although she didn't understand why she and Brandon were placed with the general. She would have thought they would be separated in order to compare their stories. But no one had second-guessed the senior ranking officer when he'd issued the order for loading up. At least someone had had enough sense to send the dogs with Catriona.

"I'm not sure what you mean, Ms. Flores."

"Dividing us into smaller groups for questioning, divide and conquer… Okay, it's a cliché, but I'm a little nervous here, sir." All this time, had Liam been cracking jokes to cover nerves or help others over theirs? She wished he was with her now so she could ask. Hell, she just wished he was here with her. Period.

In spite of the assurance via email from Special Agent Cramer, Rachel had a seriously creeped-out feeling, much the same as when she'd driven onto base a few days ago. She scanned the lines of parked aircraft, checking the rearview mirror. Brandon sat in the back alone. In the distance, the other Humvees drove in the opposite direction, Liam tucked away inside one of them. "Why aren't we following them?"

"Because we're going somewhere else. Information will be relayed to you on a need-to-know basis, and right now, you don't need to know shit."

His final word snapped her upright in her seat. Her instincts shouted something was wrong here. Way wrong.

She glanced up at the rearview mirror again at Brandon in the back. He looked as confused as she felt. And then his body tensed. His eyes narrowed. And she realized he was about to act.

The general's left arm whipped around in a flash so fast Rachel barely had time to register the black gun in his hand. He reached over his right shoulder and—

Pop. Pop.

General Sullivan shot Brandon.

Rachel screamed. Panic and shock crackled through her body, threatening to immobilize her. She shook off the fear and scrambled over the backseat. She had to get to Brandon.

One look at him and it was all she could do not to scream again. Blood bloomed across the front of his shirt. He lay slumped in the backseat, already pale. Panting, he clutched his stomach. She reached out—

The general grabbed her by her waistband and slammed her back in place. Her head banged against the door. Stars snapped in front of her eyes and nausea welled at the acrid scent of gunfire and blood.

She sucked in deep breaths, willing the world to steady again. "What in God's name are you doing?"

General Sullivan jabbed a gun into her side and snarled, "Don't even think about running. This is a restricted area where deadly force is authorized. The guards will shoot you on sight."

"I just want to get back there to help him."

"Not gonna happen, ma'am."

Ma'am? His show of manners in the face of such horror jarred her. She slumped back in the passenger seat and watched as the general rolled down the window and waved at a security vehicle heading toward them. The cops must have recognized him, because they pulled a U-turn and headed back up the parking ramp.

That easy? He was driving wherever he wanted? Shooting people?

But why? Panic popped through her like those bullets that had torn through Brandon's flesh. Gut-wrenching guilt piled on top of her fear. He was bleeding to death, and it was all her fault for encouraging him to spill his story. And now she was grateful deep inside her that Liam wasn't here, because if more of those bullets had torn through him... She bit her trembling lip until she tasted blood.

The general steered through the entry control point and turned in the opposite direction of the security patrol. He headed toward some dark airplanes with large propellers. He swerved the Humvee sharply and Brandon groaned from the back.

Sullivan popped another shot over the seat into Brandon.

Her ears rang, but the vehicle was silent. Dead silent.

As much as she wanted to squeeze her eyes shut and cry, she forced herself to look in the rearview mirror, to assess whatever she could about Brandon in case she was given even a split second's chance to help.

The latest shot had torn into his shoulder. His left shoulder. Near his heart. His eyes were closed and, dear Lord, she couldn't tell if he was still breathing or not.

The general slid the Humvee into park between two large generators. Her whole body trembled with rage and injustice and grief over Brandon's murder until it exploded from her.

She launched herself at General Sullivan, nothing left to lose. "You bastard! You godforsaken piece of shit traitor!"

Screaming, she kicked and clawed, hoping someone would hear her before it was too late. And if not, at least she would leave some scars on Sullivan for the world to see.

The butt of his gun slammed into her jaw. Pain blasted through her. So much. She hadn't even known it was possible to hurt this bad.

He pinned her to her seat and his evil eyes bored straight into her. "Keep it up, bitch, and we can really celebrate." His gun dug into her neck, his erection pressing into her stomach. "I like my women with fight in them."

She went very, very still.

Sullivan smiled, blood dripping from one of the four welts she'd clawed down his cheek. "That's what I thought."

He grabbed her arm and hauled her out of the Humvee. She dragged her heels and started to struggle until he pushed the cold steel of the gun against her forehead. He was clearly taking this to the death, so she might as well fight.

And in that moment she realized how right Liam had been earlier. She was a fighter. She hadn't stepped off, just taken a breather. But Liam was wrong about their not having what it took to build a future together, and she intended to do everything in her power to stay alive and grasp that future with both hands.

Her fists clenched at her side.

The general yanked her arm with brutal strength. "Don't give me a reason to kill you now. You wouldn't be the first bitch that got in my way and paid the price."

Timing. Timing was everything. She needed to wait for the right opportunity. She forced herself to relax in his steely, repugnant grasp. "Where are we going? What are you going to do with me?"

"Shut up. Be a good little girl and you won't get hurt. I don't have time for this. Now walk!" He shoved her forward past the open back ramp of some kind of cargo plane and toward the rear wheels.

He kicked the wooden chocks out from the rear tires and dragged her under the aircraft to the other side, where he kicked out the chocks in front of those wheels.

"You're stealing a plane?"

"It's on alert for possible rescue missions, so it's all fueled and cocked on. I'm a general. Nobody questions me." He started up the ramp, yanking her until her feet tangled. "Come on."

That was his plan? Bravado, and pull a Steve McQueen with a military aircraft? If so, there should be help on the way soon. She could seriously use some of that Chuck Norris whup ass right about now.

She searched the late-day horizon for the security vehicle's taillights, just barely visible in the distance.

General Sullivan laughed. "No help there, little lady. We will be out of here before they even know it."

He dragged her to the entry door on the side of the airplane and pushed her ahead of him roughly. "Turn left and head up to the cockpit."

She moved forward in the dark toward the murky light-illuminated windows ahead, hearing the aircraft door closing behind her.

"Get in the right seat. Now! That's an order, understand?"

"Okay, I'm listening, behaving." She crawled into the copilot's seat and sat down.

He kept his eyes on her while he climbed into the pilot's seat on the left. "Put on your seat belt and the shoulder harness."

Strapping herself in, she willed her hands not to shake, to show no weakness. "There's not a chance in hell you can get away with this."

"Your opinion is duly noted. Not that I care."

He leaned over and pushed the gun into her face. While staring at the gun touching her nose she heard a click. She flinched, and oh God, the squeak of fear had come from her.

General Sullivan smiled, the scent of breath mints and overpriced aftershave thick and cloying. "That was your harness locking into the seat so you won't be moving around."

He turned back toward the panel in front of him and started touching different controls. He seemed to be searching for something.

Does he even know how to fly one of these? "What are you looking for?"

"Why do you keep talking?" He resumed his scan of the cockpit.

"You don't actually know how to fly one of these, do you?" Hysteria bubbled through the horror. She had a deep understanding right now of how Liam must have used humor in the past.

"Listen, bitch, I am not only a general. I am a fighter pilot." His voice rose with increased agitation. "I can certainly fly one of these trash-hauling sorry excuses for an airplane."

"Okay, okay"—she patted the air—"calm down."

If he did get this thing off the ground, she certainly didn't want him crashing the plane. Although if it took him long enough to figure this out, surely someone would come and stop this insanity.

He seemed to find what he was looking for and started flipping switches. The instrument lights came on, bathing the cockpit in a red glow.

The general looked out the windows and said, "Nobody around. Time to roll."

He moved levers until an engine coughed to life. The cargo plane jerked into motion, moving forward toward the dimly lit runway ahead even as the general wildly manipulated controls, starting the rest of the engines. By the time they reached the runway they had a head of steam. He was figuring this out too fast. She needed more time. Where was help?

The general overshot the center of the runway and ended up almost on the grass.

"Piece of crap airplane," he mumbled. "Steering's screwed up."

Felt like operator error to her. But best to keep

that to herself. The last thing she wanted was more of Sullivan's attention.

As she held herself still and quiet, she wondered what had happened to Liam and the others. If the corruption went this high up the chain, there was no telling how deep it went.

Sullivan veered back in the center and pushed up the throttles. Lights flashed ahead. Her stomach lurched. A security vehicle drove toward them about halfway up the runway.

Someone had figured out this was wrong. Someone knew. She wasn't completely isolated with this maniac.

Except the airplane and the security vehicle were on a collision course, playing chicken in a game where no one seemed ready to give up. She threw her arms up in front of her face…

Swoop.

The nose lifted off the ground.

The plane bucked as they climbed. Up and down. Side to side. As the general turned the yoke back and forth quickly.

Good God, was an aircraft able to do this and stay airborne? Never, never, never again would she complain about turbulence during a flight. That was nothing. This guy was going to crash at any minute.

She'd put herself in dangerous situations her entire adult life. But not until this moment had she realized she'd done so hoping to join Caden. What a helluva time to realize how very much she wanted to live so she could fight to win back the man she loved—Liam McCabe.

Brandon's body was on fire with pain.

His mind fogged with images of the bombing in the Afghan marketplace. Was he back in that nightmare, in some cosmic do-over loop where he screwed up again and again? He coughed, tasting blood. Clamping a hand to his chest, he felt the pulsing stickiness. If he just closed his eyes, he could sleep. As he'd done last time. Surrender to the pain.

Wake up in the hospital. Marked. Discredited.

Groaning, he rolled to his side, seat belt jabbing into his side. Seat belt? Not the marketplace.

He opened his eyes and the past half hour came rushing back with mind-blowing clarity. He was in the back of General Sullivan's Humvee. He'd been shot by General Sullivan, who could have only one reason for resorting to such extremes. Sullivan was the one dealing intelligence secrets. And the bastard had left with Rachel Flores.

Rachel Flores, who'd put her life on the line for him. The only person to believe in him. He couldn't leave her out there alone.

He lifted his hand. Or rather, he tried to. God, it hurt, really hurt like nothing he'd ever felt, and he'd been messed up mighty bad in that marketplace explosion. He clamped hold of the seat and hauled himself upward. If he could get out of the vehicle and shout for help... He pulled a handle. Locked. He fought down devastating frustration, the kind that could make him surrender now.

Of course the doors were locked so he couldn't run while they were driving. Pressing his palm to the worst of his wounds, he leaned over the back to look for something. Anything. Maybe a way out the rear hatch.

Runway light illuminated a tarp draped over gear. Inching his fingers to grip, he tugged aside the canvas and uncovered—

Oh God, a body. He'd exposed a face—a woman's face. Her features were masked by her red hair. Her shell of an ear peeked out, a simple pearl earring on the lobe. He stared at the red hair, his chest gripped in a panic tighter, more painful than the gunshots. It couldn't possibly be Catriona. He'd seen her get in another Humvee with Sunny Rocha.

He wanted to sink into his seat and howl out his grief. To surrender completely. This time, no waking up in a hospital. Just. Quit.

Silence echoed.

In that silence, he thought of her. Catriona. The way she waited patiently while he got his head together rather than telling him what he should be feeling or thinking. With her, he wasn't a PTSD patient or a wounded mess. He was a man, a cop, a guy who could take a regular walk on the beach and make love to a woman.

And the cop within him was shouting, loudly, not to let blood loss and shock cloud his judgment. Catriona got in a different Humvee.

He edged up on the seat again and looked closer at the auburn-haired woman. *Auburn* hair. Darker and coarser than Catriona's whispery ginger hair. His arm slid over the seat and he brushed the strands clear until he could see more clearly.

It wasn't Catriona. He didn't recognize her, but some other poor woman lay lifeless from a broken neck.

He collapsed back into his seat. Sullivan was a traitor and a murderer. And he had Rachel.

Each breath rattling harder than the last, Brandon searched the Humvee. He didn't know if he would make it out alive or not, but he refused to let Rachel die because of him. He scoured the inside of the vehicle that was fast becoming his coffin, hunting until his eyes landed on the radio on the front dash.

One inch at a time, he crawled forward.

—◦◦◦—

"He did what?" Liam asked, stunned.

Less than ten minutes into his interview with the OSI, questioning had been interrupted. He was told the base commander wanted to see him at the command post.

Pronto.

No sooner did Liam arrive than he was pulled into a small room with the base commander—a young colonel—who said General Ted Sullivan had stolen an airplane. And damn it, that made him want to pound a wall. He'd known something was wrong back on the flight line when they'd all been separated, and there hadn't been a thing he could do about it. Refusing to go with their escort hadn't been an option. Drawing his weapon… also not a good idea then. Demanding that Rachel stay with him would have netted zero results, given that he was outranked.

Their plan to come in had turned into a cluster fuck and he had no idea how. Most important of all, where was Rachel? Last he'd seen of her, she was with the OSI captain.

Colonel Mary Zogby stood with her hands behind her back, a pulse ticking in her forehead along her dark hair-line. "General Sullivan stole an airplane off the flight line. The only logical conclusion I can draw is that he has something to do with Lieutenant Harris's data that's being processed by our decoders."

He didn't need her to spell out the obvious. Protocol dictated the plane would be shot down without delay. "And I've been brought in, ma'am, because...?"

"Just as we became aware of the plane taking off, we received an emergency call over the radio in General Sullivan's Humvee—from Lieutenant Harris. There's no easy way to say this. The general shot Lieutenant Harris and then abducted your friend Rachel Flores."

Liam reeled back a step, the air whooshing from his body as if he'd been kicked in the gut. Rachel was going to die. Either at General Sullivan's hand or when that plane was shot down. And Liam had brought her here. To what he thought was safety. He couldn't speak. He could barely stay on his feet.

Thank God, the colonel seemed to understand and continued talking while he got his shit together.

"We're not sure how exactly, but the HC-130 on alert fired its engines and was rolling down the runway before security could get to it. Once we received the call from Lieutenant Harris, General Sullivan's Humvee was recovered near the airplane, hidden between some aerospace ground equipment—generators, to be exact."

"Lieutenant Harris?" he choked out.

"On his way to the hospital. Critical condition. He passed out before we could learn anything more from him." She drew in a bracing breath. "In the back of the Humvee, a body was discovered. Special Agent Sylvia Cramer. Preliminary signs indicate she was strangled to death, and since she was in the vehicle Sullivan was driving, we can assume he's the one who killed her. Right now, General Sullivan has nothing to lose."

Liam closed his eyes briefly as he absorbed the news of Sylvia's death and how her plans to bring them in had led to it. He would mourn the loss of his friend later. Right now, he had to focus on Rachel. They couldn't have called him in to watch her die too. "And I was brought here because...?"

"NORTHCOM has a track on the craft and is launching fighters from Homestead." Silence hung in the room for a few seconds.

Finally McCabe spoke. "They're going to shoot it down."

Colonel Zogby nodded. "General Sullivan is over the water, heading south, so he isn't an immediate threat to homeland security. But once he turns toward land, we'll have no other options."

Options? She was talking options?

Hope stirred and took root tenaciously. "Ma'am, are you telling me we have a window of time to come up with a better plan before NORTHCOM launches that shot?"

"That is exactly why you were called in and exactly how I expect my elite force to react. My battle staff is already convening, awaiting you and your team." She walked through the door, talking as he kept stride with her. "We want General Sullivan taken alive. And of course we want to prevent the loss of an innocent life."

His creaky old knees didn't give out on him, but it was a close call, with relief threatening to down him. He would hold strong, focus, and work with this colonel who'd offered an unexpected second chance for him.

For Rachel.

"Yes ma'am. I assume you are already getting a new alert aircraft fired up." Determination powered his steps.

"We are."

"Do you have a track on the aircraft?"

The colonel opened the door into the "war room." A wall-size screen lit up. Rows of manned computers packed the room. She gestured toward the screen. "Our stolen aircraft headed away from the coast and is now turning south. Fighters have launched from Homestead, but they really can't reach out to them until a tanker from MacDill gets to the area. Any idea where the general's headed?"

"No, ma'am." McCabe cleared his brain of distracting thoughts of Rachel playing with her dog. Or her standing down an alligator. Of her face just before he kissed her.

He focused everything he was and everything he'd learned on this moment. He studied the electronic map showing the stolen aircraft and the F-16s waiting farther south.

"Looks like we could cut them off if we took an angle and stayed near the coast." The logical plan of action took shape in his mind, the one a team leader should propose. He was zeroed in for Rachel. "What do you think about getting my team on the alert plane? Have the F-16s force the airplane down in the water instead. Then we can parachute in with rafts and secure survivors until the chopper arrives."

"Roll it," the colonel said without hesitation.

She'd accepted his long-shot plan, one that stood such a miniscule chance at succeeding, even he couldn't believe he'd suggested it. Yet what other choice did he have, to save Rachel?

Less than ten minutes later, Liam and his team piled out of a bus up the back ramp of an HC-130. Propellers were already turning. The loadmaster pointed the team to the troop seats lining the walls in the rear of the aircraft, the same red nylon and metal tubing, uncomfortable seats they had spent countless hours strapped to. Before they were even settled in, the ramp was coming up and the plane was taxiing toward the runway.

He took in the faces around him, the gritty resolution in their eyes, the readiness to give their all for the para-rescueman's motto, "These Things We Do, That Others May Live." That today, Rachel would live.

These were his men. His team. There wasn't anyone on earth he'd rather have with him. And yet something about his plan didn't sit right with him. His team would follow him. He didn't doubt that for a second. However, something tugged at the back of his brain, a sense that there had to be another way, one that didn't involve Rachel stuck inside a plane crash-landing into the ocean.

McCabe unstrapped from his seat and moved up to the cockpit and the communication station. Studying the radar screen, he watched the *blip, blip, blip* of light pulsing like a heartbeat. That light was his only connection to Rachel.

He tapped the staff sergeant manning the position on the shoulder. "What is the status of the target?"

The sergeant moved one of the cups of his headset off his ear. "The F-16s have just left the tanker and will intercept in ten minutes."

"What are their orders?"

"They are going to intercept and attempt to turn them back toward the United States, forcing them down into water. Air traffic controllers tell us he's having a helluva time flying the plane. He's all over the place."

"And if they don't turn back?" he asked, even though he already knew. Hope was a crazy bastard that ignored reason.

"They were told to be prepared to shoot them down, but they are weapons tight right now."

Weapons tight, not allowed to shoot yet. He didn't like the notion "yet." And he wasn't feeling as good about the plan of an erratic pilot's ability to crash-land in the ocean.

McCabe patted the sergeant on the back and headed aft to the team waiting in the cargo bay.

Barely contained fury welled inside him for coming back to the base. Anger at himself. Had he been so eager to push her away with both hands—so cry-ass scared of taking a chance with her—that he'd missed a warning sign that they were walking into a trap? He would not accept, *could not* accept, that anything would happen to her on his watch.

He paced the metal deck, then stopped and stared at a winch fixed to the aircraft. An alternate plan formed in his mind. An even crazier plan than the one he'd proposed first, and a plan he would never assign to anyone on his team.

But then he wasn't asking them to carry it out.

This was his mission. His woman. No room for failure, because a world without Rachel...

Facing his team, Liam cleared his throat and his thoughts. Lining up his plan. Becoming one with the uniform as he'd intended since he was eleven years old, patting his mother's hand while they watched old war movies. He would win this battle or die trying.

"Hey, did you ever see that movie where a special-ops guy is lowered from one airplane to another to save the president?"

Rocha stared at the winch and shook his head. "Yeah, and I thought it was bullshit Hollywood glitz. Besides, that was a different kind of plane than this. I don't think that would have a chance of working unless the back ramp was down. You can't just open the doors from the outside, and the props are way too close anyway."

"Valid points"—which was why he had a team, to think through all angles—"but if the ramp is still down… If Sullivan didn't close it after takeoff because he's a fighter pilot, unfamiliar with the cargo plane… If we flew at just the right altitude above him so he can't get a visual on us…"

Cuervo asked, "What makes you think that he just won't crash the plane once the PJ boards?"

That part was easy. He'd had a wealth of training on getting inside a person's head after all his time in therapy. And from the start, he'd had the general's number—an intense narcissist. Once he was face-to-face with the guy, he knew just how to play the bastard. "I don't believe that anything is more important to General Sullivan than General Sullivan. He won't risk a crash landing. If he was on a suicide mission, he would have shot himself back in his office."

Decision made, Liam charged up the deck to the communications sergeant. "Get me a patch to NORTHCOM. I need to get clearance for a change of plans."

Chapter 19

FOR THE MILLIONTH TIME, RACHEL LOOKED AROUND the cockpit and toward the back of the plane for a way out. Although that seemed an unlikely occurrence.

Even if she knocked the general unconscious, grabbed his gun, or clawed his face until he bled to death, she was stuck in an airplane she couldn't land. The back ramp was still open, but it was a long, long way down into the darkening sky. Panic had shifted into a dull numbness.

Bump. The cargo plane bounced, then settled.

Hell, the general could barely even fly this aircraft. Every few minutes he pulled his attention from the early-night sky to the instrument panel. The plane would lurch, drawing him back to the yoke. The general would curse the airplane again.

Bump.

Right on time.

"This airplane blows," he shouted over the roar of wind through the back. "I don't think they rigged it right."

Sullivan looked down again, searching for something. The airplane jolted.

Bump.

He gripped the yoke tighter. "Autopilot? How's the damn autopilot work?"

Like she would actually answer? Shivering, Rachel turned her head and looked out the window at the dim shadow of a fighter jet that had been trailing them just off the wing for the last thirty minutes. It stayed on her side of the plane, where the general couldn't see. She wasn't ready to surrender. She was willing to fight. But she feared the decision might be out of her hands.

How much longer until the fighter shot them down? The jet *was* there to shoot them down. She accepted that and wondered why Sullivan hadn't considered it. Granted, he didn't seem to be thinking all that clearly.

Bump. "Fuck!"

Hysterical laughter bubbled inside her. She clapped a hand over her mouth, but she couldn't hold it back. It just flowed and flowed out of her until tears ran down her face, blurring the stars winking to life outside the windscreen. *Starlight, star bright, first star I see tonight...* She gasped for air. Okay, she was on her way to a major panic attack.

But what did that matter? She was about to die anyway. All her great intentions to fight her way out of this were just that. Intentions. She needed something with a lot more firepower.

It wasn't as though Liam would come swooping in to save her. She couldn't even leave him a message about how much she loved him and how deeply sorry she was for fighting with him earlier. How she wished she could go back and treasure up every minute they'd had together. How she wished she hadn't wasted the past six months they could have spent together. He wouldn't know any of that even if she could write it down, since paper and the rest of this plane would be at the bottom of the ocean very shortly.

Bump.

She considered just jumping out of her seat and making a mad dash toward the back after all. Maybe she could grab a parachute. She knew how to jump from a plane. Well, not with a parachute, but she'd been lowered on a cable with her dog countless times on search and rescue missions.

God, she'd had an amazing life, but she could have had more. She *wanted* more. The waste, the futility, clanked inside her again and again until the sound became an almost tangible part of the roaring wind.

Was her subconscious trying to tell her to go for the parachute anyway? Even if she wasn't sure she could put it on right? If the general couldn't find autopilot, he couldn't chase her down in back. He might try to shoot her, but at least she would go down fighting.

Maybe *he* planned to parachute out before they shot him down? If there was any justice in the world, he would suck at parachuting as much as he sucked at flying planes.

And if he planned that escape route, she needed to beat him to the punch before she was left in a plane she most definitely couldn't fly. She glanced over her shoulder to assess the possibility of—

In the gaping back hatch of the cargo plane, another plane flew higher and just behind. Not a fighter jet, either. It was larger, much like the one she was in, so she didn't think a final shot was pointed their way. Images shifted in the shadowy haze between day and night. The other plane coasted so close, she couldn't fathom how the pilot maneuvered. Or why. She squinted at something off kilter, something strange about the whole vision.

Oh my God. She jerked back reflexively.

A man dangled from a cable harnessed to his body. She inched to look again, careful not to draw attention from the swearing general. The cable swung closer to the back ramp. The helmeted man came closer.

Toward the open back ramp.

A man was—no kidding—being lowered into the plane. And not just any man. Somehow she knew it could only be Liam.

Bump.

The ramp slammed into Liam and sent him spinning away into the evening sky. She bit back a scream of horror. Heaven forbid that Sullivan figure out what was happening and jerk the plane around even more.

Then impossibly, incredibly, Liam swung closer again, arms extended, reaching for a cable that supported the ramp. He missed, swinging out to the side.

But he hooked his leg.

Then a hand.

And suddenly he was standing on the metal ramp. He released the cable attached to his vest, sending the line snapping away into the night.

A movement from the general yanked her attention forward. The last thing she needed was him noticing anything in back. Not now. Not when Liam had pulled off this unbelievable Hail Mary pass beyond even Chuck Norris legend.

Liam McCabe was an original and he was hers, by God.

Sullivan leveled his gun at her again. "Don't even think about running for a parachute. I'll shoot your kneecap before you can clear the cockpit. Just because you're my hostage doesn't mean I can't hurt you, maim you, torture you. Are you with me on that?"

"Right… Of course…" Rachel faced front, working to keep his attention forward, to give Liam as much of an edge as possible, although right now it seemed as if he was capable of anything. Still, she would have his back any way she could. "I shouldn't have even considered a parachute. I'm so sorry. The last thing I want to do is distract you from flying."

"Be more careful from now on." The general smacked her with the muzzle of his gun.

Pain exploded through her head. Sullivan arced his hand to hit her again. She fought the urge to cower, not to mention the urge to puke.

Liam launched into the cockpit.

Sullivan jerked with surprise, lurching the airplane sideways. Rachel slapped her hands against the window, bracing herself. Liam stood sure-footed and grabbed Sullivan's gun.

He jammed the man's own weapon right against the general's temple. "That's enough. Now fly the airplane. Just fly the plane. Nothing else. Rachel," he said without looking away from the stunned general, "are you all right?"

Liam may not have glanced her way, but she heard the tense fear, the concern, and yes, even the love in his voice.

"I'm fine. Do what you need to do. I'm okay"— seeing stars and stifling the urge to vomit, but she was alive. Thank God, she was alive because Liam had pulled off the unimaginable.

The general put his hands on the yoke and leveled the airplane. "I could just kill us all. All I need to do is drive this plane straight down into the ocean."

"Yes, General, you could try that," Liam said with an unshakable calm she'd seen before, in the Bahamas, when he ran missions. "But I'll shoot you before you descend even a hundred feet. And while I might do a crappy job flying a plane, I'm willing to give that a try rather than risk a guaranteed crash."

Rachel watched the general's eyes dart nervously. Sweat beaded his upper lip while Liam stood steady, a man in charge, a true leader.

"Okay then," Sullivan said quickly. "You two can take parachutes and jump into the ocean. Your PJ buddies can rescue you out of the ocean. That's what you guys do, right?"

"We could. And thanks for the generous offer," Liam said with icy sarcasm, "but I don't think you'll want us to do that. See, there's an F-16 that's been following you for quite a while now. If we're gone, you'll be shot down minutes later."

The general tensed like a cornered rabbit.

Liam leaned closer. "That would be a damn shame too, because I can tell you—inside scoop?—they want you alive, if possible."

They did? Although on second thought, of course they did. The military would want to interrogate him, find out how deep his espionage went. And listening to Liam manipulate the general with words as skillfully as he wielded any weapon, Rachel was humbled. A little awed.

And a lot grateful to have him on her side.

"General, being shot down or crashing isn't any way for a hero like you to go out. Your life and career will be defined by people who aren't fans of yours. You will never get a chance to have others understand your motives for doing what you did. History is written by the victors, and it's rare to find a victor at the bottom of the ocean."

"I'll get to explain," Sullivan echoed as if grasping a lifeline. His chest puffed with a sick, twisted bravado.

"Yes, sir," Liam answered, giving the superior officer a subtle ego stroke with the *sir*. "You can be certain there are plenty of people on the ground eager to talk to you."

General Sullivan's throat moved with a long swallow before he keyed up the radio, calling in to the tower with his landing plan as if this were any normal flight. The egomaniac. Liam had played him perfectly.

The plane banked left, turning toward home in his smoothest move since they'd started this nightmare flight. Liam's hand cupped Rachel's shoulder. He never took his eyes or the gun off Sullivan. But his warm steady grip on her shoulder never left her. She covered his hand with hers and squeezed tight in a connection that went deeper than just comfort. Liam held on to her.

And she knew now, he always would.

———

Catriona begged, pleaded, and finally bullied her way in to see Brandon.

After an hour of searching, she'd learned he'd been sent to a larger medical facility off base. Then she'd paced for more torturous hours in the waiting area before being told he'd come out of surgery, but only family was allowed in to see him.

Once upon a time, she would have backed quietly into the shadows. But not any longer. She wasn't blood related, but the only way hospital staff could keep her from him was to call in security, phone the cops.

And for their information, Lieutenant Brandon Harris was an air force security cop himself, and she was his girlfriend. Finally, *finally*, a sympathetic night shift nurse ushered her back if she promised to keep things quiet, and if the guard outside his door gave the okay.

"Of course," Catriona said primly. "I'm always quiet."

She ignored the chuckle from the wiry, older nurse and the guard as she pushed the door open into Brandon's ICU room.

One look at him and tears clogged her nose. There were oxygen tubes. IVs dripped meds and what looked like a transfusion. His face was pale and puffy. Gauze was wrapped around his chest, his whole chest. How many times had he been shot? How many new scars on top of old ones would he have to bear for his country?

The nurse patted her shoulder. "He made it through surgery. That's a good thing. You can sit with him and hold his hand. I'll be right outside if you need anything."

"Thank you…" Catriona choked out the words, trying to smile.

Her mom had been emphatic about manners, a good thing really. All the past frustrations at her parents felt so very small right now.

She pulled the chair closer to Brandon's bed and took his hand, the one without IVs taped on top. "I'm so sorry this had to happen to you. But I'm here. I tried to bring Harley, but they wouldn't let me, since she's a therapy dog and not a service dog. Hopefully soon, though, we'll work something out. For now, all the dogs are with Sunny. So don't worry."

Her voice faltered and she pressed her forehead to his arm, just letting the tears fall. She wasn't sure how long she sobbed her heart and fears out, but the sheet was getting pretty wet and she needed tissues for her nose. Still, she didn't want to let go. Touching him was reassuring, and they could toss her out at any minute. She would just stay like this a while longer, enjoying the way he stroked her hair—

He stroked her hair?

She looked up. "Brandon?"

"Yeah, Cat," he answered, his voice a hoarse whisper, his touch heavy and a little clumsy. "It's me. The others? Rachel?"

Clasping his hand, she pressed it to her cheek. "She's okay. Everyone is all right. You did it. You called base security and alerted them. You relayed details it would have taken critical time to figure out otherwise. They got Rachel out alive and arrested General Sullivan."

"Good. Thas... good..." His words slurred.

His eyes drifted closed and she tried not to be sad over that. He needed his rest.

Angling over him, she kissed his forehead and whispered what she hadn't dared tell him when he was awake. "I love you."

His eyes fluttered open and she blushed.

"Hey, now, Brandon, you weren't supposed to hear that yet."

He touched her lips. "You deserve better than me... so much baggage..."

She cupped his face and stared straight into his surprisingly clear eyes. "Who makes up the rules about what's fair and not fair? Because last time I checked, life rarely keeps a perfectly tallied scoreboard." She smiled. "Like that football analogy? I threw it in there just for you."

He laughed, then coughed.

"Shhh…" She pressed her fingers to his mouth. "You don't have to talk. I just want you to know that I do love you. The man you are now and the part of yourself you'll reclaim over time. I understand about journeys to strength."

"God, Cat, I love you, too"—his chest pumped for air, from exertion and emotion—"but I won't ever be… the same man I was before."

"Brandon, I can't imagine how anyone could remain unchanged after what you've been through." She kissed his hand, sitting by his side where she intended to stay. "I accept you as you are. That's a great gift, you know. You gave the same to me."

She'd waited a lifetime for someone to accept her, see her, the real her. But then maybe a part of that journey was learning to accept herself first. Whatever the path, she was just so very glad it had led her to this man.

Liam stood outside the emergency room door, where Rachel was finishing up billing paperwork after her exam. She'd been smacked around pretty bad by General Sullivan, and Liam had been hard-pressed not to return the favor by beating the crap out of the bastard.

But this arrest was going one hundred percent by the book. No jeopardizing the conviction. When everything came out, after the military justice system finished with Sullivan, he would be lucky to get only a life sentence—treason, kidnapping, murder, attempted murder. There wasn't a punishment harsh enough.

Liam cracked his knuckles.

The automatic doors from outside swished open, bringing in a gust of humid Florida heat along with Jose James. The younger PJ had changed into jeans and a marathon shirt, his gym shoes squeaking on the tiles.

"Everything okay with Rachel, sir?" Cuervo pulled up alongside him.

"Right as rain." Thank God. "We're out of here any second now."

"Awesome. Awesome." Cuervo nodded, fishing in his pocket and bringing out keys. "Data and I thought you might need some wheels, since that rat trap Jeep you bought is still down in the Everglades. So we brought you a rental car over. Data's on the phone with a lady friend now or he would have come in with me. She's pissed because he missed their date last night. I guess saving the free world isn't a good enough excuse sometimes."

"Data had a date?"

"Yeah, I know. Guess some gals go for pocket protectors." He passed over the keys. "Here ya go. We even made sure it's gassed up."

"Hey, thanks." He clasped the cool metal in his fist, searching for the right words, but hell, there weren't ones big enough to thank a person for helping save *his* world—Rachel. "I appreciate this, and everything else you guys did for us these past few days."

"*De nada.* It's what we do for each other." Cuervo leaned back, crossing his feet at the ankles. "You gotta know what the takeaway is from this whole little debacle."

"Move to the Everglades permanently? My car's already there."

Cuervo looked at him, really looked, with a maturity gained from the job more than of years. "If all the good ones like you get out, we're stuck with leaders like General Dickhead."

A laugh punched up and out. God, he loved his guys. "I appreciate the sentiment."

They settled into silence, soaking up that side benefit of being a team, spending hours in the field or on the road together. They didn't have to fill every second with meaningless chitchat. When they spoke, it counted. It meant something. And it was clear Cuervo had something more on his mind.

Finally, Liam nudged. "Go ahead and spit it out, kid. Whatever it is you need to say."

Cuervo stared at the floor, scuffing the heel of a gym shoe while he gathered his thoughts just right. "Seriously, I get that it's tough to stay in this profession, to screw over the ones you love again and again because the mission calls. I see that grief with the other guys in the unit over busted relationships. At what point does a guy go from being an altruistic serviceman to becoming a cold bastard ignoring the needs of his family?" He frowned. "God knows, I don't have the answer."

Liam swallowed hard, thinking of his exes, the break-ups, the pain he'd caused.

Cuervo looked up, pinning Liam with clear trusting eyes that would follow him into hell if he asked. "But I do know whatever happened in the past is the past. And the man I see in front of me today is sitting firmly on the altruistic side."

Liam scratched his chest right over his heart, which was starting to pump hard. Back in the plane, he'd realized how damn foolish it was to let Rachel go. But if he got out of the air force, his life forked in a different direction from hers or so he'd thought during that stupid-ass fight back at the cabin.

And if he stayed in the air force, well, the odds didn't bode well for military marriages, especially ones around his career field. "I've got a chance here with Rachel and I don't want to wreck it by making the same mistakes all over again."

"Then don't make 'em. You aren't that guy from before. It's that simple."

Could it be that easy? Could the kid be right in teaching the old guy?

Jose James pushed away from the wall. "Look for a purple Jeep. Sorry about the color. It was the only Wrangler at the rental place. Enjoy your ride, sir."

Liam watched Cuervo all the way into the dark parking lot, where he climbed into a silver sports car with Data at the wheel.

As they drove off, Rachel stepped around a cubicle wall, wearing borrowed surgical scrubs and holding an ice pack to her jaw. Butterfly bandages held together a split in her lip and another along her temple. He wanted to reach for her, but wasn't sure where it would be safe to touch her.

"Are you okay?"

"Bill's paid. Doctor says I'll be fine. No broken bones. Just a whopper bruise. The general hits like a girl." She snorted on a laugh, then winced. "Okay, moratorium on jokes for a while."

He rethought his stance on kicking the crap out of the guy. He readjusted the ice pack over the Technicolor bruise climbing up from her jaw. "Maybe we should go back in to see the doc again."

"I'm all right, Liam, really." She tapped his temple. "Think like a medic and you'll be able to dial back the worry. But what about you? Are *you* okay? What you did to save me up there... that was nuts."

"I'm fine. Didn't have to hammer my old knees with a jump, so it's all good." He waved away discussion of their time in the air, for the most part still a blur to him because he'd been so in the zone, focused completely on the mission. Maybe later he could decompress it, pull it out to examine for others to use in future rescues.

For now, he only wanted to think about Rachel, alive. Thank God, alive.

Looping an arm around her shoulders, he tucked her against his side, carefully, watching for the least flinch from her. "Let's go home."

"Where would that be?" She glanced up at him, her brown eyes dark, serious.

"Home with me," he said as the electric doors swooshed open.

She didn't argue, which he hoped meant she agreed. She just walked alongside him quietly, step for step in sync, like when he was with his team. Somewhere along the way, she'd become his partner, and he'd almost stupidly thrown that away.

He angled his head so he could smell her hair as the wind tossed it around. "I was thinking you could recover at my place, since you're currently homeless. I keep a clean house—should hold up to chick standards. My mom taught me that too, along with cooking, to make sure I was independent, you know, for after she died."

Dredging up that little painful nugget from his childhood hadn't been easy, but he was trying to be Joe Sensitive here, opening up and sharing something of himself the way the counselors had always been digging at him to do. Would she recognize that he was trying?

"Your mom sounds like a wise and practical woman." She glanced up, her jaw purple, her eyes full of… him. "Do you have a picture of her at your house?"

"I do. A few of them in an album tucked away."

"Good, I would like to see them."

And just that easily, she'd agreed to go with him. As Cuervo said, sometimes life was just that simple.

"First thing tomorrow," he promised. "I'll find them."

She leaned her head against his shoulder. "Can we pick up the dogs at Sunny's on the way home tonight?"

He exhaled, hard, relief whooshing through him as they made plans, wove their lives together. "Of course."

"And can you pick out a new name for Fang, please? I really don't like it now that I know what it means."

"Okay, we'll call her Rocki." In honor of the Afghanistan dog, Rocky. Yeah, that fit. It felt right. The way Rachel against his side felt right. "Rocki's mine, you know."

She smiled up at him, then winced. "Ouch." She adjusted the ice pack. "Tomorrow, I'd like to drive down to Catriona's place and get the rest of my dogs too."

He frowned, weaving around an ambulance on his way to patient parking. "How many would that be exactly?"

"Don't make me laugh. And don't worry. Just a couple more, Tabitha and Ruby Two."

"Four dogs total." Sounded like a family to him. His chest clenched up a little more, but he wasn't going to surrender to that fear. He was through self-destructing. "Cool. No problem. I can swing that."

"Because you feel sorry for me?"

His arm twitched, pulling her tighter against him. Too tight. He forced himself to ease up. He ushered her deeper into the muggy parking lot, one foot in front of the other, his heart in his throat.

He stopped beside the rental Jeep—had to be theirs, because no way in hell were there two metallic purple Jeeps on the planet—and faced Rachel full on, frustration pushing the words out until they exploded into the night air. "Because I love you, damn it."

"Well, good," she shouted right back. "Because I love you too, damn it."

Her chest heaved and the echo of their voices faded like sparks showering from the bolt of lightning he'd once seen skip through an airplane. Tingling. Singing, even. A little dangerous. Definitely scary.

But exciting as hell. She deserved to hear just *how* exciting. No assuming she understood. No repeating mistakes of the past. Rachel was a gift. She was his future.

He took the ice pack from her and held it to her jaw gingerly, careful not to hurt her.

"Rachel Flores, from the moment I saw you in the Bahamas I knew I would claim you. That may not sound PC or romantic, but I felt it"—he thumped his chest over his heart—"here. Right where you've stayed, no matter how much time we spent apart or even when you wouldn't return my calls. I have loved you. I still love you. I want you in my life as my partner, my lover, and if you can bring yourself to trust me, I would be honored to be your husband."

She clasped his face and said simply, "I love you, and I trust you. Now, and always. Lover, friend, husband."

His forehead fell to rest on hers, relief and happiness threatening to send him to his knees. "Let's go home, Mrs. Franklin."

He felt her smile against the ice pack.

"That sounds like a lovely idea, Mr. Franklin. Do you have any new sex games in mind to keep your old-guy libido revved?"

Stepping back, he gave her the ice pack and opened the door for her. "I was thinking that given your current condition, the best option would be for you to just lie back and let me be your gigolo."

She swung up into the front seat. "Now that sounds like the perfect proposition to me."

Epilogue

Ten days later

WIND ROLLED OFF THE OCEAN AND TUGGED AT THE frothy scarf Rachel wore to cover the fading bruises as she stood on the bleachers with Sunny Rocha. The United States Air Force Band played the national anthems of each country represented during the closing ceremony for the weeklong summit.

A blessedly uneventful week that went off without so much as a hiccup.

Today's Florida summer weather was sweltering but breezy, without a cloud in sight. The lush lawn stretched out a natural carpet for the dais. Leaders from around the world who'd attended the confab on global missile and satellite technology were gathered. Behind them, an air force rocket launch facility loomed with a missile at least twenty stories high. What a backdrop.

Impressive.

But what impressed her most went unnoticed by others.

Liam and his team had been in the background the entire week, providing a tight inner circle of security for the high-profile guests. She'd seen firsthand how very qualified they were to protect as well as rescue.

The pararescuemen dotted the perimeter, around leaders of foreign nations and heads of state. Her eyes, as always, were drawn to Liam. And oh my, what a sight he was today. An M-16 on his shoulder, he wore his uniform with the maroon beret. As he dressed early that morning, he'd told her the color symbolized the blood sacrifice of the PJ brothers who had come before him, a sacrifice made "That Others May Live."

She was alive because of just how far they would push themselves to carry out that vow.

The band reached a piercing crescendo of trumpets before finishing so the final remarks could commence. A two-star general stepped up to the lectern—the center commander—with Colonel Zogby at his side. No mention was made of General Ted Sullivan today.

News reports thus far had stated only that General Sullivan been brought up on a number of charges, from sexual harassment to dereliction of duty. His family had gone into seclusion, no comments forthcoming from them. But rumor had it, Sullivan's wife was most definitely *not* standing by her man.

Rachel had expected to feel vindicated, but more than anything she was just sad over all the lives ruined. Who knew how many? Liam had only been allowed to tell her that the general had planned to sell the targeted locations of certain satellites that gathered intelligence. He'd intended to pin the leak on the two-star general at the lectern now, discrediting him so Sullivan could take his place.

According to OSI profilers, General Ted Sullivan was a sociopath with a narcissistic personality disorder. He truly believed the world was better off with him in charge, regardless of who got hurt in the process. But then, Liam had figured all that out without the psychology degree and he'd played the guy just right to save her life. Beyond amazing.

Sullivan also seemed to assume it was his right to sleep with any woman he wanted. Including Special Agent Sylvia Cramer. Something none of them had seen coming.

As best they could piece together, she'd been clueless about Sullivan's espionage when the affair began, and once she suspected, had tried her best to bring him down while saving her own career. By sleeping with him, she'd already made her job all the more difficult, since who would believe an ex-lover's accusations based primarily on suspicion?

She might actually have succeeded if Captain Bernard hadn't stepped into Sullivan's office and told him about Brandon being found. In one instant, her plan collapsed.

Sylvia had died for her mistakes, strangled by Sullivan and tossed into the back of his Humvee like a sack of gear.

Brandon Harris, on the other hand, was beating the odds and recovering well in the hospital. Catriona was a constant fixture at his side and had even managed to wrangle hospital approval for Harley to stay in his room. The doctors were impressed by how markedly Brandon's vital signs had improved once the dog arrived.

A breeze slipped over her, crisp with the scent of the ocean and possibility.

No question, the work she'd done in Florida was good. She'd changed lives for the better and she intended to help grow the program supplying therapy dogs for PTSD patients. But she also knew Liam was right. She was ready to return to the field. Disco was ready. They had a mission of their own, wherever they moved to next with the rest of her pack.

And the *where* depended on Liam.

Her eyes gravitated back to him—tall, focused—and while others might not notice, she knew he had the sexiest glint of humor in his eyes again. He'd decided to stay in the military for now. She'd told him that thanks to Sunny, she saw how well things could work in a military marriage. He wasn't a hundred percent sold on the idea of advancing to senior leadership now that he would no longer work PJ missions. But he was willing to give it a try.

Their next base?

They would find out soon enough.

Today, though, they were in sunny Florida, where all was right with the world.

And she was engaged to be married to Major William McCabe, the last wife that man would ever have.

No doubt about it, life was good.

Read on for more of the
Elite Force: That Others May Live series
by Catherine Mann
Now Available from Sourcebooks Casablanca

An excerpt from *Cover Me*

IT WAS A COLD DAY IN HELL FOR TECH SERGEANT Wade Rocha—standard ops for a mission in Alaska.

He slammed the side of the icy crevasse on Mount McKinley. A seemingly bottomless crevasse. That made it all the more pressing to anchor his ax again ASAP. Except both of his spikes clanked against his sides while the underworld waited in an alabaster swirl of nothingness as he pinwheeled on a lone cable.

Wade scratched and clawed with his gloved hands, kicked with his spiked shoes, reaching for anything. The tiniest of toeholds on the slick surface would be good right about now. Sure he was roped to his climbing partner. But they had the added load of an injured woman strapped to a stretcher beneath them. He needed to carry his own weight.

Chunks of ice and snow pelted his helmet. The unstable gorge walls vibrated under his gloved hands.

"Breathe and relax, buddy." His headset buzzed with reassurance from his climbing partner, Hugh "Slow Hand" Franco.

Right.

Hold tight.

Think.

Focus narrowed, Wade tightened his grip on his rope. He'd earned his nickname, Brick, by being the most hardheaded guy in their rescue squadron. Come hell or high water, he never gave up.

Each steady breath crackled with ice shards in his lungs, but his oxygen-starved body welcomed every atom of air. Lightning fast, he grabbed the line tying them together and worked the belay device.

Whirrr, whippp. The rope zinged through. Wade slipped closer, closer still, to Franco, ten feet below.

"Oof." He jerked to a halt.

"I got ya, Brick. I got ya," Franco chanted through the headset. Intense. Edgy. Nothing was out of bounds. Franco would die before he let him fall. "It's just physics that makes this thing work. Don't overthink it."

And it did work. Wade stabilized against the icy wall again. Relief trickled down his spine in frosty beads of sweat.

He keyed up his microphone. "All steady, Slow Hand."

"Good. Now do you wanna stop horsing around, pal?" Franco razzed, sarcastic as ever. "I'd like to get back before sundown. My toes are cold."

Wade let a laugh loosen the tension kinking up his gut. "Sorry I inconvenienced you by almost dying there. I'll try not to do it again. I'll even spring for a pedicure, if you're worried about your delicate feet chafing from frostbite."

"Appreciate that." Franco's labored breath and hoarse chuckle filled the headset.

"Hey, Franco? Thanks for saving my ass."

"Roger that, Brick. You've done the same for me."

And he had. Not that they kept score. Wade recognized the chitchat for what it really was—Franco checking to make sure he wasn't suffering from altitude sickness due to their fifteen thousand foot perch. They worked overtime to acclimate themselves, but the lurking beast could still strike even the most seasoned climber without warning. They'd already lost one of their team members last month to HACE—high altitude cerebral edema.

He shook his head to clear it. Damn it, his mind was wandering. Not good. He eyed the ledge a mere twenty feet up. Felt like a mile. He slammed an ice ax in with his left hand, pulled, hauled, strained, then slapped the right one in a few inches higher. Crampons—ice cleats—gained traction on the sleek side of the narrow ravine as he inched his way upward.

Slow. Steady. Patient. Mountain rescue couldn't be rushed. At least April gave them a few more daylight hours. Not that he could see much anyway, with eighty-mile-per-hour wind creating whiteout conditions. Below, his climbing partner was a barely discernible blur.

Hand over hand. Spike. Haul. Spike. Haul. He clipped his safety rope into a spike they had anchored in the rock on the way down. Scaled one step at a time. Forgot about the biting wind. The ball-numbing cold.

The ever-present risk of avalanche.

His arms bulged, the burden strapped to his harness growing heavier. *Remember the mission. Bring up an unconscious female climber. Strapped to a litter. Compound fracture in her leg.*

His job as a pararescueman in the United States Air Force included medic training. Land, sea, or mountain, military missions or civilian rescue. With his brothers in arms, he walked, talked, and breathed their motto, "That Others May Live."

That people like his mother might live.

Muscles burning, he focused upward into the growl

of the storm and the hovering military helicopter. A few more feet and he could hook the litter to the MH-60. Rotors *chop, chop, chopped* through the sheets of snow like a blender.

The crevasse was too narrow to risk lowering a swaying cable. Just one swipe against the narrow walls of ice could collapse the chasm into itself. On top of the injured climber and Franco.

On top of him.

So it was up to *him*—and his climbing partner—to pull the wounded woman out. Once clear, the helicopter would land if conditions permitted. And if not, they could use the cable then to raise her into the waiting chopper.

Wind slammed him again like a frozen Mack truck. He fought back the cold-induced mental fog. At least when Hermes went subterranean to rescue Persephone from the underworld, he had some flames to toast his toes.

Wade keyed his microphone again to talk to the helicopter orbiting overhead. "Fever"—he called the mission code name—"we're about five minutes from the top."

Five minutes when anything could happen.

"Copy, the wind is really howling. We will hold until you are away from the crevasse."

"Copy, Fever."

The rest of his team waited in the chopper. They'd spent most of the day getting a lock on the locale. The climber's personal locator beacon had malfunctioned off and on. Wade believed in his job, in the motto. He came from five generations of military.

But sometimes on days like this, saving some reckless thrill seeker didn't sit well when thoughts of people like his mother—wounded by a roadside bomb in Iraq, needing his help—hammered him harder than the ice-covered rocks pummeling his shoulder. How damned frustrating that there hadn't been a pararescue team near enough—he hadn't been near enough—to give her medical aid. Now because of her traumatic brain injury, she would live out the rest of her life in a rehab center, staring off into space.

He couldn't change the past, but by God, he would do everything he could to be there to help someone else's mother or father, sister or brother, in combat. That could only happen if he finished up his tour in this frozen corner of the world.

As they neared the top, a moan wafted from the litter suspended below him. Stabilizing the rescue basket was dicey. Even so, the groans still caught him by surprise.

The growling chopper overhead competed with the increasing howls of pain from their patient in the basket. God forbid their passenger should decide to give them a real workout by thrashing around.

"Franco, we better get her to the top soon before the echoes cause an avalanche."

"Picking up the pace."

Wade anchored the last... swing... of his ax... Ice crumbled away. The edge shaved away in larger and larger chunks. *Crap, move faster*. Pulse slugging, he dug deeper.

And cleared the edge.

Franco's exhale echoed in his ears. Or maybe it was his own. Resisting the urge to sprawl out and take five right here on the snow-packed ledge, he went on auto-pilot, working in tandem with Franco.

Climbing ropes whipped through their grip as they

hauled the litter away from the edge. Franco handled his end with the nimble guitarist fingers that had earned him the homage of the Clapton nickname, Slow Hand. The immobilized body writhed under the foil Mylar survival blanket, groaning louder. Franco leaned over to whisper something.

Wade huffed into his mic, "Fever, we are ready for pickup. One survivor in stable condition, but coming to, fast and vocal."

The wind-battered helicopter angled overhead, then righted, lowering, stirring up snow in an increasing storm as the MH-60 landed. Almost home free.

Wade hefted one end, trusting Franco would have the other in sync, and hustled toward the helicopter. His crampons gripped the icy ground with each pounding step. The door of the chopper filled with two familiar faces. From his team. Always there.

With a *whomp*, he slid the metal rescue basket into the waiting hands. He and Franco dove inside just as the MH-60 lifted off with a roar and a cyclone of snow. Rolling to his feet, he clamped hold of a metal hook bolted to the belly of the chopper.

The training exercise was over.

Their "rescue" sat upright fast on the litter, tugging at the restraints. Not in the least female, a hulking male pulled off the splint Wade had strapped on less than a half hour ago.

Wade collapsed against the helicopter wall, exhausted as hell now that he could allow his body to stop. "Major, have you ever considered an acting career? With all that groaning and thrashing about, I thought for sure I was carting around a wounded prima donna."

Major Liam McCabe, the only officer on their team and a former army ranger, swung his feet to the side of the litter and tossed away the Thinsulate blanket. "Just keeping the exercise real, adding a little color to the day."

The major tugged on a helmet and hooked into the radio while the rest of his team gaped at him—or rather, gaped at McCabe's getup. He wore civilian climbing gear—loud, electric yellow, with orange and red flames that contrasted all the more up next to their bland sage green military issue. Laughter rumbled through the helicopter. The garish snow gear had surprised the hell out of him and Franco when they'd reached the bottom of the chasm. They'd expected McCabe, but not an Olympic-worthy ski suit.

McCabe could outpunk Ashton Kutcher. For the most part they welcomed the distraction at the end of a long day. McCabe's humor was also a needed tension buster for the group when Franco went too far, pushing the envelope.

End game, today's exercise hadn't pulled out all the stops for a mountain rescue. Nobody had to parachute in.

Suddenly the major stood upright as he gestured for everyone's attention. "Helmets on so you can hear the radio."

Wade snapped into action, plugging in alongside his other five team members, some in seats, Franco kneeling. The major held an overhead handle, boots planted on the deck.

"Copilot," McCabe's voice piped through the helmet radio, "have the Rescue Coordination Center repeat that last message."

"Romeo Charlie Charlie, please repeat for Fever two zero."

"Fever two zero, this is Romeo Charlie Charlie with a real world tasking." The center radio controller's Boston accent filled the airwaves with broad vowels. "We have a request for rescue of a stranded climbing party on Mount Redoubt. Party is four souls stranded by an avalanche. Can you accept the tasking as primary?"

Mount Redoubt? In the Aleutian Islands. The part of Alaska the Russians once called "the place that God forgot."

The copilot's click echoed as he responded. "Stand by while we assess." He switched to interphone for just those onboard the helicopter. "How are you guys back there? You up for it?"

The major eyed the rest of the team, his gaze holding longest on him and Franco, since they'd just hauled his butt off a mountain. His pulse still slugged against his chest. Franco hadn't stopped panting yet.

But the question didn't even need to be asked.

Wade shot him a thumbs-up. His body was already shifting to auto again, digging for reserves. Each deep, healing breath sucked in the scent of hydraulic fluid and musty military gear, saturated from missions around the world. He drew in the smells, indulging in his own whacked-out aromatherapy, and found his center.

McCabe nodded silently before keying up his radio again. "We are a go back here, if there's enough gas on the refueler."

"Roger, that. We have an HC-130 on radar, orbiting nearby. They say they're game if we are. They have enough gas onboard to refuel us for about three hours of loiter, topping us off twice if needed." The copilot switched to open frequency. "Romeo Charlie Charlie, Fever and Crown will accept the tasking."

"Copy, Fever," answered their radio pal with a serious Boston accent. "Your new call sign is Lifeguard two zero."

"Lifeguard two zero wilco." *Will comply.* The copilot continued, "Romeo Charlie Charlie copies all."

The radio operator responded, "We are zapping the mission info to you via data link and you have priority handling, cleared on navigation direct to location."

"Roger." The helicopter copilot's voice echoed through Wade's headset, like guidance coming through that funky aromatherapy haze. "I have received the co-ordinates for the stranded climbers popped up on a data screen and am punching the location into the navigation system. Major, do you copy all back there?"

"Copy in full." McCabe was already reaching for his bag of gear to ditch the flame-print suit. "Almost exactly two hundred miles. We'll have an hour to prep and get suited up."

McCabe assumed command of the back of the chopper, spelling out the game plan for each team member. He stopped in front of Wade last. "Good news and bad news… and good news. Since you've worked the longest day, the rest of the team goes in first. Which means you can rest before the bad-news part." He passed a parachute pack. "Speaking of which, chute up. Because if we can't reach someone, you're jumping in to secure the location and help ride out the storm."

Apparently they might well have to pull out all the stops after all. "And that second round of good news, sir?"

McCabe smiled, his humor resurfacing for air. "The volcano on Mount Redoubt hasn't blown in a year, so we've got that going for us."

—␣␣—

A wolflike snarl cut the thickly howling air.

Kneeling in the snow, Sunny Foster stayed statue-still. Five feet away, fangs flashed, white as piercing icicles glinting through the dusky evening sunset.

Nerves prickled her skin, covered with four layers of clothes and snow gear, even though she knew large predators weren't supposed to live at this elevation. But still... She swept her hood back slowly, momentarily sacrificing warmth for better hearing. The wind growled as loudly as the beast crouching in front of her.

She was alone on Mount Redoubt with nothing but her dog and her survival knife for protection. Cut off by the blizzard, she was stuck on a narrow path, trying to take a shortcut after her snow machine died.

Careful not to move too fast, she slid the blade from the sheath strapped to her waist. While she had the survival skills to wait out the storm, she wasn't eager to share her icy digs with a wolf or a bear. And a foot race only a few feet away from a sheer cliff didn't sound all that enticing.

Bitter cold, at least ten below now, seeped into her bones until her limbs felt heavier. Even breathing the thin mountain air was a chore. These kinds of temps left you peeling dead skin from your frostbitten fingers and toes for weeks. Too easily she could listen to those insidious whispers in her brain encouraging her to sleep. But she knew better.

To stay alive, she would have to pull out every ounce of the survival training she taught to others. She couldn't afford to think about how worried her brother and sister would be when she didn't return in time for her shift at work.

Blade tucked against her side, she extended her other hand toward the flashing teeth.

"Easy, Chewie, easy." Sunny coaxed her seven-year-old malamute-husky mutt. The canine's ears twitched at a whistling sound merging with the wind. "What's the matter boy? Do you hear something?"

Like some wolf or a bear?

Chewie was more than a pet or a companion. Chewie was a working partner on her mountain treks. They'd been inseparable since her dad gave her the puppy. And right now, Sunny needed to listen to that partner, who had senses honed for danger.

Two months ago Chewie had body-blocked her two steps away from thin ice. A couple of years before that, he'd tugged her snow pants, whining, urging her to turn around just in time to avoid a small avalanche. If Chewie nudged and tugged and whined for life-threatening accidents, what kind of hell would bring on this uncharacteristic growling?

The whistling noise grew louder overhead. She looked up just as the swirl of snow parted. A bubbling dome appeared overhead, something in the middle slicing through...

Holy crap. She couldn't be seeing what she thought. She ripped off her snow goggles and peered upward. Icy pellets stung her exposed face, but she couldn't make herself look away from the last thing she expected to see.

A parachute.

Someone was, no kidding, parachuting down through the blizzard. Toward her. That didn't even make sense. She patted her face, her body, checking to see if she was even awake. This had to be a dream. Or a cold-induced hallucination. She smacked herself harder.

"Ouch!"

Her nose stung.

Her dog howled.

Okay. She was totally awake now and the parachute was coming closer. Nylon whipped and snapped, louder, nearer. Boots overhead took shape as a hulking body plummeted downward. She leaped out of the way.

Toward the mountain wall—not the cliff's edge.

Chewie's body tensed, ready to spring into action. Coarse black-and-white fur raised along his spine. Icicles dotted his coat.

The person—a man?—landed in a dead run along the slippery ice. The "landing strip" was nothing more than a ledge so narrow her gut clenched at how easily this hulking guy could have plummeted into the nothingness below.

The parachute danced and twisted behind him specter-like, as if Inuit spirits danced in and out of the storm. He planted his boots again. The chute reinflated.

A long jagged knife glinted in his hand. His survival knife was a helluva lot scarier looking than hers right now. Maybe it had something to do with the size of the man.

Instinctively, she pressed her spine closer to the mountain wall, blade tucked out of sight but ready. Chewie's fur rippled with bunching muscles. An image of her dog, her pet, her most loyal companion, impaled on the man's jagged knife exploded in her brain in crimson horror.

"No!" she shouted, lunging for his collar as the silver blade arced downward.

She curved her body around seventy-five pounds of loyal dog. She kept her eyes locked on the threat and braced for pain.

The man sliced the cords on his parachute.

Hysterical laughter bubbled and froze in her throat. Of course. He was saving himself. Nylon curled upward and away, the "spirits" leaving her alone with her own personal yeti who jumped onto mountain ledges in a blizzard.

And people called her reckless.

Her Airborne Abominable Snowman must be part of some kind of rescue team. Military perhaps? The camo gear suggested as much.

What was he doing here? He couldn't be looking for her. No one knew where she was, not even her brother and sister. She'd been taught since her early teens about the importance of protecting her privacy. For fifteen years she and her family had lived in an off-the-power-grid community on this middle-of-nowhere mountain in order to protect volatile secrets. Her world was tightly locked into a town of about a hundred and fifty people. She wrapped her arms tighter around Chewie's neck and shouted into the storm, "Are you crazy?"

An excerpt from *Hot Zone*

THE WORLD HAD CAVED IN ON AMELIA BAILEY.

Literally.

Aftershocks from the earthquake still rumbled the gritty earth under her cheek, jarring her out of her hazy micronap. Dust and rocks showered around her. Her skin, her eyes, everything itched and ached after hours—she'd lost track of how many—beneath the rubble.

The quake had to have hit at least seven on the Richter scale. Although when you ended up with a building on top of you, somehow a Richter scale didn't seem all that pertinent.

She squeezed her eyelids closed. Inhaling. Exhaling. Inhaling, she drew in slow, even breaths of the dank air filled with dirt. Was this what it was like to be buried alive? She pushed back the panic as forcefully as she'd clawed out a tiny cavern for herself.

This wasn't how she'd envisioned her trip to the Bahamas when she'd offered to help her brother and sister-in-law with the legalities of international adoption.

Muffled sounds penetrated, of jackhammers and tractors. Life scurried above her, not that anybody seemed to have heard her shouts. She'd screamed her throat raw until she could only manage a hoarse croak now.

Time fused in her pitch-black cubby, the air thick with sand. Or disintegrated concrete. She didn't want to think what else. She remembered the first tremor, the dawning realization that her third-floor hotel room in the seaside Bahamas resort was slowly giving way beneath her feet. But after that?

Her mind blanked.

How long had she been entombed? Forever, it seemed, but probably more along the lines of half a day while she drifted in and out of consciousness. She wriggled her fingers and toes to keep the circulation moving after being so long immobile. Every inch of her body screamed in agony from scrapes and bruises and probably worse, but she couldn't move enough to check. Still, she welcomed the pain that reassured her she was alive.

Her body was intact.

Forget trying to sit up. Her head throbbed from having tried that. The ceiling was maybe six inches above where she lay flat on her belly. Again, she willed back hysteria. The fog of claustrophobia hovered, waiting to swallow her whole.

More dust sifted around her. The sound of the jackhammers rattled her teeth. They seemed closer, louder, with even a hint of a voice. Was that a dog barking?

Hope hurt after so many disappointments. Even if her ears heard right, there had to be so many people in need of rescuing after the earthquake. All those efforts could easily be for someone else a few feet away. They might not find her for hours. Days.

Ever.

But she couldn't give up. She had to keep fighting. If not for herself, then for the little life beside her, her precious new nephew. She threaded her arm through the tiny hole between them to rub his back, even though he'd long ago given up crying, sinking into a frighteningly long nap. His shoulders rose and fell evenly, thank God, but for how much longer?

Her fingers wrapped tighter around a rock and she banged steadily against the oppressive wall overhead. Again and again. If only she knew Morse code. Her arm numbed. Needle-like pain prickled down her skin. She gritted her teeth and continued. Didn't the people up there have special listening gear?

Dim shouts echoed, like a celebration. Someone had been found. Someone else. Her eyes burned with tears that she was too dehydrated to form. Desperation clawed up her throat. What if the rescue party moved on now? Far from her deeply buried spot?

Time ticked away. Precious seconds. Her left hand gripped the rock tighter, her right hand around the tiny wrist of the child beside her. Joshua's pulse fluttered weakly against her thumb.

Desperation thundered in her ears. She pounded the rock harder overhead. God, she didn't want to die. There'd been times after her divorce when the betrayal hurt so much she'd thought her chance at finally having a family was over, but she'd never thrown in the towel. Damn him. She wasn't a quitter.

Except why wasn't her hand cooperating anymore? The opaque air grew thicker with despair. Her arm grew leaden. Her shoulder shrieked in agony, pushing a gasping moan from between her cracked lips. Pounding became taps… She frowned. Realizing…

Her hand wasn't moving anymore. It slid uselessly back onto the rubble-strewn floor. Even if her will to live was kicking ass, her body waved the white flag of surrender.

—〜〜—

Master Sergeant Hugh Franco had given up caring if he lived or died five years ago. These days, the air force pararescueman motto was the only thing that kept his soul planted on this side of mortality.

That others may live.

Since he didn't have anything to live for here on earth, he volunteered for the assignments no sane person would touch. And even if they would, his buds had people who would miss them. Why cause them pain?

Which was what brought him to his current snowball's-chance-in-hell mission.

Hugh commando-crawled through the narrow tunnel in the earthquake rubble. His helmet lamp sliced a thin blade through the dusty dark. His headset echoed with chatter from above—familiar voices looking after him and unfamiliar personnel working other missions scattered throughout the chaos. One of the search and rescue dogs aboveground had barked his head off the second he'd sniffed this fissure in the jumbled jigsaw of broken concrete.

Now, Hugh burrowed deeper on the say-so of a German shepherd named Zorro. Ground crew attempts at drilling a hole for a search camera had come up with zip. But that Zorro was one mighty insistent pup, so Hugh was all in.

He half listened to the talking in one ear, with the other tuned in for signs of life in the devastation. Years of training honed an internal filter that blocked out communication not meant for him.

"You okay down there, Franco?"

He tapped the talk button on his safety harness and replied, "Still moving. Seems stable enough."

"So says the guy who parachuted into a minefield on an Afghani mountainside."

"Yeah, yeah, whatever." Somebody had needed to go in and rescue that Green Beret who'd gotten his legs blown off. "I'm good for now and I'm sure I heard some tapping ahead of me. Tough to tell, but maybe another twenty feet or so."

He felt a slight tug, then a loosening, to the line attached to his safety harness as his team leader played out more cord.

"Roger that, Franco. Slow and steady man, slow and steady."

Just then he heard the tapping again. "Wait one, Major."

Hugh stopped and cocked his free ear. Tapping, for sure. He swept his light forward, pushing around a corner, and saw a widening cavern that held promise inside the whole hellish pancake collapse. He inched ahead, aiming the light on his helmet into the void.

The slim beam swept a trapped individual. Belly to the ground, the person sprawled with only a few inches free above. The lower half of the body was blocked. But the torso was visible, covered in so much dust and grime he couldn't tell at first if he saw a male or female. Wide eyes stared back at him with disbelief, followed by wary hope. Then the person dropped a rock and pointed toward him.

Definitely a woman's hand.

Trembling, she reached, her French manicure chipped, nails torn back and bloody. A gold band on her thumb had bent into an oval. He clasped her hand quickly to check the thumb for warmth and a pulse.

And found it. Circulation still intact.

Then he checked her wrist—heart rate elevated but strong.

She gripped his hand with surprising strength. "If I'm hallucinating," she said, her raspy voice barely more than a whisper, "please don't tell me."

"Ma'am, you're not imagining anything. I'm here to help you."

He let her keep holding on as it seemed to bring her comfort—and calm—while he swept the light over what he could see of her to assess medically. Tangled hair. A streak of blood across her head. But no gaping wounds.

He thumbed his mic. "Have found a live female. Trapped, but lucid. More data after I evaluate."

"Roger that," Major McCabe's voice crackled through.

Hugh inched closer, wedging the light into the crevice in hopes of seeing more of his patient. "Ma'am, crews are working hard to get you out of here, but they need to stabilize the structure before removing more debris. Do you understand me?"

"I hear you." She nodded, then winced as her cheek slid along the gritty ground. "My name is Amelia Bailey. I'm not alone."

More souls in danger. "How many?"

"One more. A baby."

His gut gripped. He forced words past his throat, clogging from more than particulates in the air. "McCabe, add a second soul to that. A baby with the female, Amelia Bailey. Am switching to hot mic so you can listen in."

He flipped the mic to constant feed, which would use more battery, but time was of the essence now. He didn't want to waste valuable seconds repeating info. "Ma'am, how old is the baby?"

"Thirteen months. A boy." She spoke faster and faster, her voice coming out in scratchy croaks. "I can't see him because it's so dark, but I can feel his pulse. He's still alive, but oh God, please get us out of here."

"Yes, ma'am. Now, I'm going to slip my hand over your back to see if I can reach him."

He had his doubts. There wasn't a sound from the child, no whimpering, none of those huffing little breaths children make when they sleep or have cried themselves out. Still, he had to go through the motions. Inching closer until he stretched alongside her, he tunneled his arm over her shoulders. Her back rose and fell shallowly, as if she tried to give him more space when millimeters counted. His fingers snagged on her torn shirt, something silky and too insubstantial a barrier between her and tons of concrete.

Pushing farther, he met resistance, stopped short. Damn it. He grappled past the jutting stone, lower down her back until he brushed the top of her—

She gasped.

He looked up fast, nearly nose to nose now. His hand stilled on her buttock. She stared back, the light from his helmet sweeping over her sooty face. Her eyes stared back, a splash of color in the middle of murky desperation.

Blue. Her eyes glistened pure blue, and what a strange thought to have in the middle of hell. But he couldn't help but notice they were the same color as cornflowers he'd seen carpeting a field once during a mission in the UK.

Hell, cornflowers were just weeds. He stretched deeper, along the curve of her butt, bringing his face nearer to hers. She bit her lip.

"Sorry," he clipped out.

Wincing, she shrugged. "It was a reflex. Modesty's pretty silly right now. Keep going."

Wriggling, he shifted for a better path beyond the maze of jagged edges, protruding glass, spikes…

"Damn it." He rolled away, stifling the urge to say a helluva lot worse. "I can't reach past you."

Her fingers crawled to grip his sleeve. "I'm just so glad you're here, that everyone knows we are here. Joshua's heart is still beating. He's with us, and we haven't been down here long enough for him to get de-hydrated, less than a day. There's hope, right?"

Less than a day? Nearly forty-eight hours had passed since the earthquake occurred, and while he'd partici-pated in against-all-odds rescues before, he had a sick sense that the child was already dead. But alerting the woman to her own confusion over the time wouldn't help and could actually freak her out.

"Sure, Amelia. There's always hope."

Or so the platitude went.

"I'm going to hang out here with you while they do their work upstairs." He unstrapped the pack around his waist and pointed his headlight toward the supplies. "Now I'm gonna pull out some tricks to make you more comfortable while we wait."

"Happen to have an ice-cold Diet Coke? Although I'll settle for water, no lemon necessary."

He laughed softly. Not many would be able to joke right now, much less stay calm. "I'm sorry, but until I know more about your physical status, I can't risk letting you eat or drink." He tugged out a bag of saline, the needle, antiseptic swabs, grunting as a rock bit into his side. "But I am going to start an IV, just some fluids to hydrate you."

"You said you're here to help me," she said, wincing at a fresh burst of noise from the jackhammers, "but who are you?"

"I'm with the U.S. Air Force." Dust and pebbles showered down. "I'm a pararescueman—you may have heard it called parajumper or PJ—but regardless, it includes a crap ton of medic training. I need to ask some questions so I know what else to put in your IV. Where exactly did the debris land on you?"

She puffed dust from her mouth, blinking fast. "There's a frickin' building on top of me."

"Let me be more specific. Are your legs pinned?" He tore the corner of a sealed alcohol pad with his teeth, spitting the foil edge free. "I couldn't reach that far to assess."

Her eyes narrowed. "I thought you were checking on Joshua."

"I'm a good multitasker."

"My foot is wedged, but I can still wriggle my toes."

He looked up sharply. If she was hemorrhaging internally, fluids could make her bleed out faster, but without hydration...

The balancing act often came down to going with his gut. "Just your foot?"

"Yes. Why? Do you think I'm delusional?" Her breath hitched with early signs of hysteria. "I'm not having phantom sensations. I can feel grit against my ankle.

There's some blood in my shoe, not a lot. It's sticky, but not fresh. I'm feeling things."

"I hear you. I believe you." Without question, her mind would do whatever was needed to survive. But he'd felt enough of her body to know she was blocked, rather than pressed into the space. "I'm going to put an IV in now."

"Why was it so important about my foot?"

He scrubbed the top of her hand with alcohol pads, sanitizing as best he could. "When parts of the body are crushed, we need to be… uh… *careful* in freeing you."

"Crush syndrome." Her throat moved with a long slow swallow. "I've heard of that. People die from it after they get free. I saw it on a rerun of that TV show about a crabby drug-addict doctor."

"We just need to be careful." In a crush situation, tissue died, breaking down, and when the pressure was released, toxins flooded the body, overloading the kidneys. And for just that remote possibility, he hadn't included potassium in her IV.

Panic flooded her glittering blue eyes. "Are you planning to cut off my foot?" Her arm twitched harder, faster, until she flailed. "Are you going to put something else in that IV? Something to knock me out?"

He covered her fingers with his before she dislodged the port in her hand. "There's nothing in there but fluid. I'm being honest with you now, but if you panic, I'm going to have to start feeding you a line of bullshit to calm you down. Now, you said you wanted the unvarnished truth—"

"I do. Okay. I'm breathing. Calming down. Give me the IV."

He patted her wrist a final time. "I already did."

Blinking fast, she looked at the tape along her hand. A smile pushed through the grime on her face. "You're good. I was so busy trying not to freak out I didn't even notice."

"Not bad for my first time."

"Your first time?"

"I'm kidding." And working to distract her again from the rattle overhead, the fear that at any second the whole damn place could collapse onto them.

She laughed weakly, then stronger. "Thank you."

"It's just an IV."

"For the laugh. I was afraid I would never get to do that again." Her fingers relaxed slowly, tension seeping from them as surely as fluid dripped out of the bag. "The second they uncover us, you'll make Joshua top priority. Forget about me until he's taken care of."

"We're going to get you both out of here. I swear it."

"Easy for you to claim that. If I die, it's not like I can call you a liar."

A dead woman and child. He resisted the urge to tear through the rocks with his bare hands and to hell with waiting on the crews above. He stowed his gear, twisting to avoid that damn stone stabbing his side.

"Hey," Amelia whispered. "That was supposed to be a joke from me this time."

"Right, got it." Admiration for her grit kicked through his own personal fog threatening to swallow him whole. "You're a tough one. I think you're going to be fine."

"I'm a county prosecutor. I chew up criminals for a living."

Acknowledgments

The rapid evolution of the cyberworld has been incredible to watch. (My very first laptop computer in college weighed as much as a sewing machine!) There are so many gifts that have come with technology—especially for military families, who spend far too much time apart from each other. Through this gift, we're able to stay connected better than ever from even a world away.

But there are always those who would manipulate those positive inventions for selfish purposes, shielding themselves behind the anonymity of a computer screen. These cowards participate in anything from cyberbullying to spreading viruses to ruining lives.

Over the years my husband and I have tried to impress on our children how character is often measured by what we do when no one is looking. That axiom provided the brainstorming springboard for all the characters in this book—from the cowardly villains to the unsung heroes.

As always, in bringing a book to fruition, I owe a huge thanks to the many people who helped along the way.

I'm eternally grateful to Sourcebooks for offering me the opportunity to showcase the unsung pararescue heroes. Thank you to Dominique Raccah (publisher), Deb Werksman (editor), Danielle Jackson (publicist), and the whole Sourcebooks dream team. What a pleasure it is to work with you all.

I'm blessed with the most patient, savvy (and

witty!) agent on the planet. Thank you Barbara Collins Rosenberg for sharing your wisdom and friendship with me for over a decade.

And speaking of amazing friendships, I am so grateful for the critiques and input from my author pals Joanne Rock and Stephanie Newton. I can't imagine traveling this writing journey without you both. I look forward to many, many years of shared brainstorming, Jelly Bellys, and Diet Cokes.

A special thanks to *New York Times* bestselling authors—and incomparable mentors—Sherrilyn Kenyon, Suzanne Brockmann, Lori Foster, and Dianna Love. You've taught me so much about keeping it real and staying grounded.

I openly confess to being an Internet junkie. I thoroughly enjoy using most of my "coffee breaks" to visit with readers via social media. Thank you to *Publishers Weekly* contributing editor and blogger Barbara Vey for persuading me to broaden my community by giving Twitter a try. I appreciate the invaluable advice and delightful chat over Moe's tacos in the Atlanta airport! Thank you also, Paula Robinson, for spreading your message of peace, love, and romance novel recommendations throughout the Internet. And Judy Flohr and Amelia Richard, thank you for your generous reviews online from the very beginning!

As for the technical details in my novels, I'm gifted with generous research help. To those who know me, it's no surprise that dogs wag their way into my stories. My life has been changed profoundly by my volunteer work at my local Humane Society. Thank you to my friends at the Panhandle Animal Welfare Society in Fort

Walton Beach, Florida. A special shout-out to Vickie Taylor, FEMA canine trainer and published novelist. Thank you for sharing your expertise in SAR. (And for power-driving to meet me in Louisiana so a Labrador retriever named Jafar, who'd grown up in a shelter run, would have the chance at a forever home.)

Regarding all things military, I owe endless thanks to Dr. Ronald Marshall, DC, former pararescueman, and to my air force flyboy husband, Rob. Thank you for sharing your stories, your lingo, and most of all, your deep patriotism.

Last, but definitely not least, all my love to my four children—Brice, Haley, Robbie, and Maggie—military brats extraordinaire!

About the Author

USA Today bestseller Catherine Mann has over two million books in print in more than twenty countries. A winner of the prestigious RITA Award, Catherine resides in Florida with her military-hero husband, their four children, and a menagerie of shelter rescue pets. For more information on her upcoming releases, check out her website at www.catherinemann.com. Visit with her on Facebook at Catherine Mann (author) or on Twitter at CatherineMann1.

The Night Is Mine

by M.L. Buchman

NAME: Emily Beale

RANK: Captain

MISSION: Fly undercover to prevent the assassination of the First Lady, posing as her executive pilot

NAME: Mark Henderson, code name Viper

RANK: Major

MISSION: Undercover role of wealthy, ex-mercenary boyfriend to Emily

Their jobs are high risk, high reward:

Protect the lives of the powerful and the elite at all cost. Neither expected that one kiss could distract them from their mission. But as the passion mounts between them, their lives and their hearts will both be risked... and the reward this time may well be worth it.

"An action-packed adventure. With a super-stud hero, a strong heroine, and a backdrop of 1600 Pennsylvania Avenue and the world of the Washington elite, it will grab readers from the first page."—*RT Book Reviews*

For more in The Night Stalkers series, visit:

www.sourcebooks.com